INTO THE MAINLAND

LOST COLONY SERIES, BOOK #3

JO GRAFFORD

Sign up for my New Release Email List at www.JoGrafford.com.

No part of this book may be reproduced in any form or by any electronic or mechanical means, including information storage and retrieval systems, without written permission from the author, except for the use of brief quotations in a book review.

To Shirley and Glenn with love
for making countless trips, including several overseas ones, to join
our family's adventures

ACKNOWLEDGMENTS

A huge, heartfelt thank you to Trudy Cordle for beta reading this story!

CONTENTS

INTRODUCTION

Agnes Wood is forced from her country parish to the social whirl of London when her aunt and uncle negotiate her betrothal to an older nobleman to satisfy a gambling debt. In the attempt to avoid an unhappy marriage, she agrees to serve as the apothecary on a colonial venture to the Chesapeake Bay area. During the trans-Atlantic crossing, she and her shipmates become embroiled in a terrifying conspiracy that throws them in the crosshairs of a ruthless pirate.

As the web of lies and danger unfold, two powerful men fight over her heart in the winner-take-all rugged wilderness of the New World.

The Lost Colony Series is an epic historical romance saga, based on the Lost Colonists of Roanoke Island.

LOST COLONY SERIES
Book #1 — Breaking Ties
Book #2 — Trail of Crosses
Book #3 — Into the Mainland
Book #4 — Higher Tides

MAP

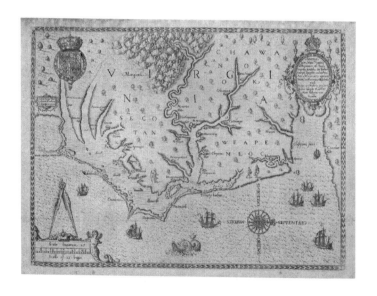

PREFACE

A crime can change a person's life forever, horribly and tragically, even if it's an accidental one — like mine was.

I've waited months for the opportunity to find redemption, and that day has finally come. I'll be facing one of the region's most terrifying enemies, unarmed and with only a single witness if I fail — a native who hates me due to the English blood running through my veins.

The only common ground we share is our plan to sacrifice ourselves so everyone we love can finally be free.

— *Agnes Wood*

CHAPTER 1: LEAVING
WORCESTERSHIRE

January 15, 1587

*A*gnes gazed out the window of her departing carriage, already homesick and not at all convinced a season in London was the best way to celebrate her eighteenth name day. Having been raised in the country, she knew nothing about the ways of the ton — not the latest fashions, dance steps, or gossip — but her mother refused to listen to her pleas to remain in Worcestershire. Where her life had purpose as Agnes Wood, apothecary in training to a fast growing parish congregation. Where she was needed.

Her mother's only sister was childless and begging for company, and she could think of no better solution than to deliver up a dose of Agnes's youthful companionship. *Her words. Not mine. Faith! Why couldn't Mother pay a visit to her own sister and be done with it?*

The esteemed Lady Hester Ravenspire was fetching Agnes in her private carriage to save her the discomfort of public transportation. As much as she appreciated her aunt's kindness, the gesture didn't generate the least bit of excitement about being tossed into the frivolity of city living on such short notice.

Mother positioned her tiny self atop the knoll beside the parsonage, no doubt for the better view, as Agnes rolled away. She waved to her daughter, the glossy strands in her white-blonde hair gleaming in the morning sun. Neither age nor her somber navy morning gown could mute her porcelain beauty. Her stance was regal enough to grace the Queen's Court, and her mannerisms were a dead giveaway of her highborn heritage.

And now she was sending her only child back to everything she'd willingly left behind. To the parties and the balls she claimed were wearisome and the politics she hated. She'd not smiled once since her decision a week earlier. Agnes's insides prickled with foreboding, though she could come up with no tangible reason for her concerns.

Mother was desperately in love with Father, and they'd been a happy family of three for as long as Agnes could remember. They'd endured their share of lean years, true, but this was not one of them. A new flood of churchgoers from around the countryside had begun flocking to Father's sermons. They adored the way Abbott Wood served the poor and nobility alike, trading in his priestly garments for more simple apparel when he visited the humbler sections of town. And they often lingered long enough to purchase the poultices and herbal potions she and Mother spent so many hours preparing during the weekdays.

Why send her away so abruptly when things were going so well? It made little sense.

She returned her mother's wave, never dreaming it would be the last time she would see her.

Agnes settled back against the seat cushions, already missing home. She clutched the smallest of her three travel bags to her chest. There was no telling how far back a six month visit to London would set her apothecary work. Mother was still training her, and she couldn't help feeling guilty at the thought of taking such a long break from her studies. As a precaution, the bag in her lap contained dozens of packages of her precious seeds. Mother had assured her there would be plenty of room to continue their planting and mixing experiments in the herb gardens of her sister's London mansion; but Agnes also knew that meant her mother would have to work twice as hard in her absence to tend the needs of their parishioners.

Again, why? Why was Mother sending her away, when she needed her daughter so much more than her bored sister did?

Endless minutes of fretting ticked into hours of even more fretting. It was difficult for Agnes to do much, even to read her medicinal journals. The interior of the carriage was too dim and the roads too bumpy, so she spent most of the journey staring out the window at the gray skies and barren landscapes. She huddled beneath her thickest winter cloak, grateful to be wearing an extra pair of woolen stockings in the damp, chilly January temperatures. Her driver, a heavily bearded man of few words, dropped her off for the night at a rustic roadside inn where the expenses were generously covered by a purse provided by her aunt. They set off again at daybreak.

By the end of the second day, the wide open moors carpeted by frost-bitten heather transitioned to city streets, tightly packed with hawkers, street performers, pedestrians, and more carriages — *lots* more carriages. Accustomed to the wide, open spaces of the country, Agnes immediately found it harder to breathe. The city was darker than the country, too, and not just because of the arrival of eventide. Despite the lights pouring from the taverns and shop windows, London was hidden from the sky by an extra layer of smoke and fog. A gentle rain started to patter down; and, with it, rose an unholy stench.

She was blessed with an acute sense of smell, which came in handy while working with herbs and chemicals. It was not such a blessing other times — like now. Gone were the familiar scents of heather, wild grasses, and good clean earth. In its place was a curious mixture of fish, horse dung, and unwashed bodies. The rain didn't help; it merely churned the streets into slimy muck. Agnes could only hope London would smell better when it dried out.

The carriage rolled deeper into the city, passing through gardens and parks, and arrived at last before the imposing stone walls and towers of Ravenspire Keep. Part of Agnes's apprehension dwindled at the sight of the magnificent structure. It was exactly as she remembered it from her last visit three years earlier. Much larger than most of the newer surrounding mansions, it resembled a small fortress. Its dark, weathered stone and arched windows lent it a gothic appeal. She could easily imagine ghosts roaming its shadowy halls at night.

She allowed herself a delicious shiver at the prospect of coming face to face with a ghost, but her reverie was cut short when a uniformed footman materialized to open the carriage door. Another footman with her travel bags in hand followed her up the damp stone stairs to the front entrance.

A woman gave a cry of excitement, and a blur of lavender silk swept in her direction across the wide, sweeping porch landing. Moments later, she was crushed against Lady Hester's ample lacy bosom.

"Why, Agnes! You turned out far lovelier than I imagined possible. Everything considered," she added with a sharp, "Harrumph!"

Her bluntness did not surprise Agnes. She remembered her aunt as an outspoken woman; nevertheless, her words gave her pause. Had she considered Agnes an ugly child? It was an oddly refreshing thought, following years of being ogled for her unusual white-gold hair and ultra-fair complexion. She was beyond weary of being compared to china dolls and fairy princesses. Her shortness of stature and petite frame did nothing to staunch the flow of rumors concerning said magical ancestry.

Lady Hester shoved her back an arm's length and peered over the top of her spectacles. "Aye, you are a real beauty, lass. Just like that sister of mine. To the end of my days, I'll never understand why she laid aside her good name and lineage to run off with such a rapscallion."

Agne tried to wrench away from her aunt's embrace, but her clasp on her arms tightened with surprising strength. *Ah, well. At least she left off the boil-brained part about dolls and pixies.* So she was prettier than her aunt expected, eh, tainted as she was with the blood of a lowly country vicar?

Agnes swallowed the sour taste in her mouth at the insult, having been taught by Mother that a true lady always controls her temper. *Faith!* What a lifelong task that skill was turning out to be! She compromised with her inner demons by staring boldly into Aunt Hester's piercing blue gaze, finding it harder and harder to believe she and Mother were actually sisters. Instead of Mother's blonde hair peppered with a few elegant strands of silver and frost, hers was a fuzzy all-white poof. A layer of lace draped the tallest peak and was fashionably secured with pearl-studded pins. She stood nearly a head taller than Mother in her high-heeled boots and thrice as wide, ensconced inside endless yards of lavender silk. However, the effect was not the least bit regal. In her simpler garments, Mother was a far more stunning woman. She just was, and gentler spoken and more ladylike.

"You possess plenty of spirit, too, gel, to round out such beauty." Her aunt unhanded Agnes and motioned for her to step inside. "Once we replace your deplorable wardrobe, it shouldn't be too hard to find you a match."

"A match!" Agnes nearly choked on her tongue. "Oh no, madam aunt. I am only here for a visit, to serve as your companion for a few months." *Because Mother insists you are lonely.* "That is all." There was nothing wrong with her serviceable gown — other than a few wrinkles, perhaps, from two days of traveling, but that was entirely Lady Hester's fault for fetching her to London in the first place. She shook out and smoothed her skirts. They were crafted of sturdy navy wool from the same cut of cloth as her mother's winter gown. The neckline boasted a newly crocheted ivory collar.

"Is that all my sister told you?" Aunt Hester clucked in distress as she assisted Agnes's cold, half-numb fingers in undoing the buttons of her cloak. Her aunt all but tossed the garment to her butler. Then she guided Agnes through an arched doorway. "Apparently her ability to dodge an unpleasant conversation hasn't changed."

Agnes had no idea what her aunt was talking about, but the woman's continual barbs about her parents were becoming irritating. No wonder Mother had not wished to visit her sister more often, the unpleasant old biddie!

Behind them, the footman clattered up the stairs to the second story with her bags, while she followed her aunt into the parlor. Her thoughts spun as she sought a polite, yet firm, way to convince her aunt that she was only here for a visit.

Knowing Lady Hester wouldn't approve of the man in question, there was no point in mentioning Agnes was already spoken for. In a manner of speaking. Her lifelong friend, Timothy, had yet to declare himself, but everyone more or less expected them to marry once he completed his carpentry apprenticeship. Not that she was in any terrible hurry to marry and settle down with her quiet, hardworking friend. She adored him to distraction, but part of her — way down deep — had always longed for something more from marriage than a sweet and abiding friendship like hers and Tim's. She'd always dreamt of finding what her parents had — true love.

Agnes bit her lip at the thought. She may as well wish for a fairy castle to go with that dream. She was a lady at heart, thanks to an upbringing from a cultured mother, but she was a working class girl by birth. She was fortunate to have a beau at all, considering the many hours her parish work required of her. When the time came, she would do her duty, marry a solid, dependable man, and that would be the end of it.

CHAPTER 2: RAVENSPIRE KEEP

Though the exterior of Ravenspire Keep hadn't lost a bit of its magic, the interior was a bit worn. Faded rosy velvet couches and chairs anchored one side of the room, while a sun-bleached spot on the floor in the shape of a pianoforte graced the other side. Agnes scanned the room for the missing musical instrument and shrugged, presuming it must be undergoing repairs elsewhere. Bookcases laden with dusty volumes framed the wide marble mantle overlooking the hearth.

She held two fingers beneath her nose to muffle a sneeze, while homesickness wrenched her insides. Their parsonage was snug but clean. Always clean and always in excellent repair, thanks to their help staff of two. Dear old Maude and her husband, Ben, made sure of it. Agnes tried not to stare at the cobwebs in every corner of Ravenspire Keep, but she couldn't help it. Where there were webs, there were usually an abundance of spiders. *Ick!*

"There, child. You must be weary from your travels." Lady Hester fluttered a hand in the general direction of the faded couches. "Have a seat, while I pour us some tea and explain the true reason for your visit."

Agnes did not care for the sound of that, not one bit. The foreboding she'd experienced earlier in the day spread its tail in full plume like a peacock.

Her aunt handed her a teacup steaming with a mix of spicy scents. She cradled the warm beverage in her hands and sniffed its contents in appreciation, detecting overtones of cinnamon and cloves.

Agnes's whole body was stiff from the cold and from sitting. She stood, still holding the teacup, and paced the rug to get her blood pumping better through her extremities.

Her aunt frowned and set a tray of sweetmeats and breads on a low table in the center of the gathering area. She settled her large frame on the sofa, rustling as she arranged her voluminous skirts around her. "Where to begin?" she mused. "With the frightening truth, I suppose, now that you are all grown up. Sit, love." She gestured impatiently at the chair across from her. "'Tis difficult on my aging neck to keep track of your whereabouts with all your gadding about."

Agnes reluctantly perched on the edge of the nearest chair, and her aunt nodded in satisfaction. "Where to begin?" she repeated. "Well, I never was one to mince words..."

Agnes grimaced into her cup. *No. You weren't.*

". . . so I shall jump right to the meat of things. 'Tis quite simple, really. Your mother figured sending you here to live with me was your safest option." At Agnes's puzzled expression, Lady Hester leaned forward in a conspiratorial manner and lowered her voice to a loud whisper. "Given the recent arrests of dissidents." She looked as if she expected some sort of reaction from her niece. When Agnes continued to stare, she gave a long-suffering sigh. "Oh, come, child. I speak of church dissidents."

When Agnes still didn't answer, she added sharply, "like your father."

Agnes jolted so violently she spilled cinnamon tea all over her lap. She stared at the spreading dampness in dismay, trying to collect her thoughts. "My father is no dissident! He may be p-poor," she sputtered, forcing herself to hold her aunt's gaze, "but he is greatly loved and admired by our congregation." Her aunt's expression of haughty disapproval was almost more than she could bear. "If you've not a kind word to spare for my family, perhaps I was mistaken in coming here." Agnes stood and set her teacup on a side table before she spilled it again in her agitation. She was sorely tempted to fling it across the room.

"Ah, lass," Lady Hester chided. There was empathy and genuine distress in her voice as she stood and stretched her arms out to her niece. "Pray forgive your old aunt her lack of finesse. 'Tis unsavory news, to be sure, but I had no idea you were so ill informed of your father's troubles. Did my sister truly tell you nothing about this?"

"What troubles?" Agnes's voice shook. She half-turned from her aunt, pressing a hand to her heart and willing the wild pounding there to cease. She no longer dared to keep looking at Lady Hester, not while she wanted nothing more than to fly at her, tear out one of her ornamental hairpins, and stab her with it. Lucky for her aunt, Agnes's good breeding took over once more. She waited in seething silence for the woman to elaborate on her claims.

Lady Hester sniffed. "Such a naive question! 'Tis a prime example of the dangers of rusticating away in the country, my precious niece. I speak, of course, of the Archbishop of Whitgift. He is on a mission backed by the Queen to clean up the books, so to speak." She glanced around the room, though no one else was present, and lowered her voice again. "It means they are in the process of arresting all pastors and laity members who do not uphold the tenants of the Church of England."

Agnes's mouth fell open. "My father is loyal to his calling and to the Crown," she assured stiffly.

"Is that why he lays aside his priestly garments and parades around the countryside in patched breeches like a common ragamuffin?"

She felt the rush of blood to her cheeks, as indignation laced with alarm gripped her. "He is a humble man. There is no crime in that!"

"On the contrary," her aunt corrected in gentler tones. "Refusing to wear the uniform of his office violates Church law. According to your mother, he harbors a good number of other radical beliefs and practices. She fears it is only a matter of time before the bishop's men collect him for interrogating. Indeed, his name was recently published on a most-wanted list of radicals."

My kindhearted father is an infamous radical? A man on the brink of arrest? Agnes's legs gave out. She sank into the depths of the nearest armchair, twitching in mental agony beneath the cannon fire her aunt had launched at her. None of her claims made any sense. If they were true, why would her beloved parents have hidden such things from her? She scrambled to recall anything out of the ordinary in their recent lives and could only come up with one thing — the odd collection of pastoral visitors who'd arrived at their parish a few weeks earlier. They'd resembled gypsies more than men of the cloth and had remained an entire week, eating the cupboards bare like starving men.

"A traveling band of pilgrims," Mother had called them with a tightening of her lips. "Trailblazers and champions of change." Nothing had seemed unusual about her comments at the time, but Agnes's blood chilled at the memory. Had Mother been trying, in her own way, to warn Agnes of things to come? Her tone had not sounded disapproving of the men, though. Rather it had been accepting, albeit a bit fearful. Then there was the sadness in which she'd informed Agnes that she was sending her to London. *Oh, Mother, dearest! What have you and Father gotten yourselves into?*

"What am I to do?" she whispered, intercepting her aunt's troubled look. She wanted nothing more than to rush home to help protect her parents from arrest, though she didn't have the first notion as to how to go about doing so in a way that would ensure their safety.

Lady Hester's expression relaxed somewhat. "I shall look after you, of course, just as your mother asked of me. The first step will be launching you into society like a proper young debutante." She nodded in satisfaction. "That should help you acquire a bit of town bronze and acquaint you with a few eligible bachelors." She waggled her bushy white brows suggestively.

"My mother said all *that*?" Agnes was aghast. She'd served the last two years as her mother's apothecary apprentice, and not once had her mother pressured her to curtail her training to make time to court a man. With no dowries or titles at stake, there was little need for Agnes to rush into marriage. On the other hand, there had been plenty of need for her to mix and dispense medicines to their parish congregation.

"In so many words." Her aunt gave a girlish giggle. "Other than eligible suitors, what else is a young woman supposed to attract, once you launch her into society? Tree frogs? Crickets?"

Agnes was in no mood to smile at her aunt's attempted frivolity. She was too busy trying to process the shocking revelation about her father's tarnished reputation. Fortunately, her aunt did not appear to expect any response from Agnes. She prattled on and on.

"Aye, London is full of handsome men in want of a good wife. One in particular is quite anxious to meet you."

Agnes warily digested her aunt's animated expression. The woman barely knew her, so she was hardly qualified to select a beau for her, much less a husband. Lady Hester knew nothing about her niece's likes and dislikes, her hopes and dreams.

"I cannot wait to introduce you to Lord Hilbert Brandbury, Viscount of Habbershire, though I call him Hill in private. He was widowed last year, but don't let that discourage you. With his wealth and dashing looks, he'll be the prime catch of the season. Mark my words."

Hill. It was a rather un-daunting nickname for a man bearing the most intimidating title of Viscount. Did her aunt truly believe a titled gentleman would pay more than a cursory glance in her niece's direction? Wasn't she forgetting Agnes's severe lack of wealth and station?

"I shall introduce you to him at a small dinner party tomorrow."

"So soon?" Agnes glanced down at her stained and crumpled gown.

"Faith, child. Have your maid wash your travel clothes or burn them. I care not. My sister sent your dimensions months ago, so you will find a collection of much more suitable gowns hanging in your wardrobe. For now, the only thing you need to worry your pretty head about is a bath and a nap." She rang the bell pull against the wall.

Months ago. Agnes could hardly believe her mother, the woman considered to be her dearest friend and closest confidante, had planned so meticulously for her departure without including her in the plans. Right down to the ordering of new gowns. Where had Mother come up with the funds? An overwhelming sense of betrayal flooded Agnes. She wanted to weep.

A young woman about her age appeared in the doorway. She was lightly tanned with dark mahogany hair twisted in a coil at her nape. She wore a simple gray uniform with a spotless white apron. Fingers twitching nervously at her sides, she surveyed Agnes beneath long dark lashes, head slightly lowered as if trying to hide the fact she was staring.

"Holly will see you to your room," Lady Hester stated imperiously, staring down her nose at the serving girl.

"Yes, my lady." Holly bobbed a curtsey. "Follow me, my lady." She ducked another curtsy, this one in Agnes's direction.

Unused to the luxury of a personal maid, Agnes was uncomfortable with the young woman's deference. Considering the endless months ahead, in which she would be serving as her aunt's companion, the good Lord knew she could use a friend more than a maid. For this reason, Agnes waited until they were out of Aunt Hester's earshot then hastened to reintroduce herself. "I am Agnes Wood, but I prefer to be called Agnes." She carefully sounded out the pronunciation of her name. *"Ann-ess with a silent G."*

"Pleased to meet you, Mistress Agnes," Holly intoned politely, leading her by candlelight down a dim hallway of closed doors. Agnes liked her disciplined movements, her crisp enunciation of her words, the graceful rhythm of her gait. The young serving woman might be poor, but she was proud. She carried herself with an impressive amount of dignity for a person of lower birth. *Much like myself.* Her mother's words rang in her head. *Good breeding comes more from within than from without.*

"What I am trying to say is I prefer to be called Agnes. Just Agnes."

"Oh, my!" Holly clapped a hand over her mouth. "Begging

your pardon, my lady." Her large, intelligent eyes bulged with distress.

"Oh, fiddle! Enough of that my lady-ing nonsense." The young servant's ridiculous fawning was giving Agnes the start of a headache. "I am the daughter of a country vicar. We have much in common, since we both work to earn a living."

Holly darted a suspicious glance at Agnes over her shoulder. "Is this some sort of test? If it is, pray be assured my only wish is to serve you, my lady."

"No test." Agnes smiled. "And I do not need anyone to serve me. I am quite self sufficient."

Holly regarded her with a curious mix of interest and alarm. "Regardless of where you were raised, you are Lady Hester's niece. It is my duty to keep you comfortable throughout the duration of your visit. Here you are." She threw open the door of an enormous room. It was bigger than the entire home Agnes had been raised in. And — wonder of wonders — it was immaculately clean. Her regard for Holly shot up several more degrees. In fact, she was liking the young woman better with each passing moment.

An enormous four-poster bed draped in a snowy white lace canopy was centered against the far wall, and Agnes's travel bags were waiting on the rug next to it. A fire leaped in a nearby hearth. "It is perfect." Despite her upsetting conversation with her Aunt Hester, she skipped into the room. "You darling. You absolute angel. Thank you for stirring up such a marvelous fire." She stretched her hands to the flames.

"Tis my job, my lady," Holly muttered uncertainly.

"Come." Agnes waved her forward impatiently. Sooner or later, she would get it through the young woman's delightfully thick skull that she would genuinely prefer her friendship over her subservience. "Let us enjoy it together, while you tell me all about yourself." Agnes rubbed her hands up

15

and down her arms. "Faith, but 'tis good to thaw out at last. An hour ago, I feared I might never get warm again."

When Holly hesitated in the doorway, Agnes shot her a playful scowl. "You are wasting the warmth. Come in, and shut the door. Please," she added when the woman's expression turned abashed.

Holly hastily shut the door and stood in front of it. "Shall I draw you a bath, my lady?"

Agnes closed her eyes at Holly's persistence in employing non-existent titles on her behalf, but it was impossible to stay irritated for long. Not while she was faced with the sheer decadence of enjoying a bath on such short notice. In the middle of winter, no less. "Yes, indeed. If you will but show me to the kitchens."

"The kitchens?" The young servant drew back in horror. "Oh, nay, my lady. *I* shall be the one to preside over your bath." She hurried to the far end of the room and pulled back a curtain. A copper tub rested atop a short platform. Next to it, a second fire blazed from another fireplace where a series of kettles steamed. "Allow me a few minutes to draw your bath. Then I shall assist you in undressing."

"Surely, you jest." Agnes cocked a brow at her. "I have been dressing and undressing myself since I was a child. And I really do wish you would call me Agnes."

She shook her head. "You are the most unusual highborn lady I've ever met."

"Lady*like*, yes," Agnes corrected firmly. "But highborn, no." She thought she'd already explained she was the daughter of a country vicar. "My mother laid aside her claim to any titles the day she married my father."

"Oh, dear!" her newly acquired maid muttered faintly as she poured water into the tub. "I wish to please you, my lady. I do, but I shall surely lose my position if your aunt catches me greeting you with such familiarity."

"Then you may call me Agnes in private and whatever you deem proper in public." There. She dusted her hands. It was the perfect solution to their uncommon situation.

Holly offered her a tremulous smile, and the delicate first threads of friendship were born. Agnes never dreamed how badly she would be needing the young woman's friendship, nor how soon.

CHAPTER 3: MEETING THE VISCOUNT

*A*gnes might have been dressing herself since she was a child, but her nimble fingers were no match the following evening for the endless rows of buttons on her new gown. She simply could not reach the ones running between her shoulder blades.

After a harried glance in the mirror, she tried not to blush at the plunging neckline of the pale green silk. Mother would have never allowed her to wear something so scandalous. Agnes tugged at the bodice and gave up when it did not budge. Instead, she pinned a bit of lace in the V and tried to be satisfied with the result, though it still left too much skin showing for her comfort.

"Er, Holly?" Agnes didn't quite succeed in masking the sheepishness in her voice.

"Do not tell me you require my help, madam," the serving girl mocked with an exaggerated expression of surprise. "Surely, you jest." She mimicked Agnes's voice to perfection, throwing her words from the previous evening back at her. A good-humored grin plastered itself across her slender, fine-boned features.

In the short time they'd known each other, Holly had unbent considerably in her presence. Agnes entertained real hopes they would soon become friends.

"La!" she returned with a teasing glare. "Are you always so tedious?"

"Only on odd numbered days," Holly shot back.

They dissolved into snickers while she proceeded to truss Agnes up like a dinner hen minus the orange sauce. By then, Agnes was too concerned with breathing to worry about the swell of her bosom showing.

She had to take short steps and move slowly down the stairs. Otherwise, she might have entirely run out of air within the strict confines of her new corset. *Mercy!* She could not fill her lungs no matter how hard she tried. She paused halfway down the stairs to practice taking shallower breaths. How on earth was she supposed to fit a single bite of food in her stomach when she was already so short of room to breathe?

Beneath the flickering candelabra of the main foyer, a man positioned himself at the base of the stairs and gazed up at her.

He was exceedingly handsome. Tall and tanned with wickedly arched brows and a mouth with a faint smile lurking at its corners. Thick dark hair curled over the collar of his jacket and his artfully arranged cravat.

Lord Hilbert Brandbury, she presumed.

He filled his braided doublet and black trousers nicely, too, with the repressed energy of a man accustomed to activity. She liked that. As she approached the bottom of the stairs, however, she discovered he was much older than she'd anticipated. Old enough to be her father, with a light sprinkling of silver in his sideburns. He assessed her with sharp eyes that seemed to miss little. His rigid jaw bespoke a man to be reckoned with.

Agnes worked to quell a shiver of apprehension. Her aunt actually wished her to court a man of such advanced years?

His gaze affixed itself on her person. His expression registered admiration tinged with disbelief. "Miss Wood, we meet at last." He bowed low and brushed his lips across the tops of her knuckles.

Her nerves tightened like the strings of a harp at his flirtatious gesture. Though it made her feel mature and worldly, a part of her shied away from such familiarities. Not knowing how to flirt back, she stood there feeling awkward.

He seemed in no hurry to release her hand. "Your aunt has spoken of little else besides your pending visit for weeks."

For weeks. It was a stark reminder of how long her life had not been her own, of how long others had been plotting behind her back to alter it.

She offered Lord Hilbert a curtsy, along with a smile she hoped was unstained by her depth of uncertainty. "I am pleased to meet you, my lord."

He tucked her hand in the crook of his arm, placing his other hand over it. She was again struck by his show of familiarity, as he led her from the foyer. "I trust you are rested from your travels?"

"Very, sir. Thank you." She could think of nothing else to say, having no inkling what topics would interest a man of his rank.

Her Uncle Harry — a short, stocky, and much redder-faced man than she remembered — accosted them in the long dining hall. It was only her uncle's second appearance during her current visit. From his uneven steps and slurred greeting, she deduced he was well into his cups.

"Welcome!" he shouted a good deal louder than necessary. "Please b-be seated." He plopped himself at the head of the table, with no further ceremony, and reached for his wine glass.

The viscount held out Agnes's chair for her.

"Well, then," Aunt Hester announce brightly, while bestowing an embarrassed glance on her spouse. She took her seat. "Let us begin." She clapped her hands to signal the wait staff to commence with their serving. "Lord Hilbert is running for Parliament, dear," she announced to Agnes. "Do give us an update, Hill," she coaxed.

Was the woman actually simpering at their dinner guest? Agnes shifted uncomfortably, finding it even harder to breathe once seated.

"As you wish, my dear Hester." He turned to Agnes. "In these uncertain times, England needs more men at the helm who are unafraid of pursuing reform." He paused, as if expecting some sort of response from her.

She nodded encouragingly. "What sort of reform, my lord?"

"A good many, starting with the Church of England."

"The church, sir?" A spurt of fear pulled her brows together like an accordion.

"Aye, with pockets of dissidents springing up right and left across the country," his expression grew hawk-like, and he stroked his short, pointed beard between a thumb and a forefinger, "it is a vast and growing problem. One that will not disappear on its own."

Her heart thudded like a drum. She watched the young male servant who stooped to fill her bowl with a meaty stew.

"They call themselves Separatists and claim they want nothing more than to worship freely, yet they manage to stir up trouble at every turn. In failing to accept the Queen as the Supreme Ruler of the Church and refusing to read from the Common Book of Prayers, they thumb their noses at centuries of longstanding traditions — the very traditions which have made our nation strong. Well, enough is enough!" Lord Hilbert pounded a fist into his hand so suddenly that everyone else at the table jumped. "Such behavior smacks of treason. They must be stopped! They *will* be stopped, I say, before the seeds of revolution can take root."

Agnes paused in the act of raising her spoon to her mouth. Sickness churned in her stomach. She longed to change the subject, but she was too desperate to learn more about the troubles facing men like her father. "How do you propose to stop them, my lord?"

"By throwing the full weight of Parliament behind the Church. By backing Archbishop Whitgift in his endeavors to arrest and interrogate the rebels. He is working his way from London to Shepherd's Moor, as we speak."

Agnes's hand shook so hard she almost dropped her spoon. The pastor who presided at Shepherd's Moor was one of her father's dearest friends. "How soon, sir?" she asked, striving to keep her voice normal. "How soon before the arresting party reaches Shepherd's Moor?"

"One week hence. No more than two, if the weather holds."

If the weather holds! She was wildly grateful she had been unable to take a bite of her soup, because she might have spewed it across the table. How dare the viscount discuss the pending arrest of her family and friends in such a nonchalant manner! As if rounding up dozens of church leaders like cattle was an every-day event. Anger curdled in her chest.

Lord Hilbert's features softened. "'Tis delightful of you to show such an interest in politics, Miss Wood. I feel as if I could converse with you for hours."

Heaven forbid! She fisted her hands in her lap beneath the table.

"My teenage daughter couldn't give two figs about what happens in our government. Or anywhere else in the world, for that matter."

Agnes coughed and raised a linen napkin to her lips. *Teenage daughter?* Her gaze flew to her Aunt Hester's for verification. Agnes was but eighteen herself.

"Pshaw!" Her aunt waved a hand. "You have lovely children with plenty of other interests besides politics beating in their lively, young chests."

Children, as in more than one? Lord, have mercy! Agnes clamped her lips shut. No wonder the man was so anxious to remarry. He needed help raising his brood. Not that there was anything wrong with needing a wife with a mother's touch, but finding out the man possessed children close to her own age smothered all prospect of any romance between them — or would have if his strong opinions on politics had not already done so.

With her appetite gone, Agnes itched to dismiss herself from the viscount and his odious opinions and return to her room. How long was this horrid dinner party expected to last, anyway? She desperately wanted to be alone to think.

If the raid on Shepherd's Moor parish was to take place a week from now, someone needed to warn its inhabitants. A plan blossomed and took shape in her mind — one that involved traveling to Shepherd's Moor, herself. It was probably best to travel at night, so she would not have to explain her whereabouts to her aunt. But how would she get there? A borrowed carriage and pair of horses from the Ravenspire Keep stables would surely arouse the very questions she was hoping to avoid.

The Viscount patted her arm as the meal progressed. "You grow quiet, Miss Wood. Methinks you are weary from your travels."

She blinked at him. "Your concerns are most kind, my lord." He had provided the perfect reason for her to excuse herself. She pretended to smother a yawn.

Aunt Hester eyed her with concern.

Agnes delicately cleared her throat. "Maybe I should retire before I ruin your impression of me altogether by falling asleep in my soup." Without giving anyone a chance to respond, she scooted back her chair. "Pray excuse me, my lord. My lady aunt. Uncle dearest."

Lord Hilbert rose and bowed over her hand before she could make her exit. "Rest assured my impression of you is all that is good, Miss Wood. Indeed, you are the loveliest woman I've the pleasure of meeting all season."

All season, eh? The wicked side of Agnes delighted in noting he was not paying her much of a compliment, considering it was still the beginning of the London season. In the meantime, she wished he would not caress her fingers the way he was doing. Such familiarity was hardly appropriate on one's first meeting, was it? Then again, what did she know about what was acceptable and what was not in London? Her knowledge of the city consisted mainly of her parents' disapproval of it. Father called it the City of Sin.

The Viscount let go of her hand with great reluctance. "'Til tomorrow, Miss Wood."

What? "Tomorrow, sir?"

"Yes, indeed. I will be escorting you to the opera."

A second outing in the space of two days? She shot another questioning glance at her aunt.

She beamed her approval.

"'Til tomorrow then, sir," Agnes murmured. It didn't appear she would be having any say in her personal schedule. The sense that she was fast losing control over her life was not a pleasant one, compounded by her growing concerns about her loved ones.

She made her exit with her thoughts in utter chaos. Did the Viscount of Habbershire truly intend to court her? It was an astonishing thought, considering they'd known each other hardly more than an hour.

CHAPTER 4: THE WARNING

"Why, Agnes!" Holly exclaimed when Agnes ran into her bedchamber, tearing at the buttons of her dress. "Are you well?"

Agnes nodded. "I am upset, is all."

Holly's features darkened. "The viscount has a bit of a reputation as a rake, I fear. Did he, er—"

"Aye, he is a despicable toad with a loud and heated opinion on entirely too many topics. 'Tis no wonder he is widowed. Probably talked his poor wife to death." After suppressing it the entire dinner, Agnes could no longer contain her venom.

At her maid's peal of laughter, she bit her lip. "Pray forgive me. I should thank the good Lord for not striking me down for speaking so irreverently of the deceased."

"I believe your statement was directed at the living," Holly pointed out with another loud and hearty chuckle. "From what I've heard about the man, your assessment is vastly accurate." With one last snicker, she sobered. "Glad I am he did nothing more than run away at the mouth. In the future, you may need to keep your eye on his hands, as well."

Indeed? A fresh wave of anger tightened Agnes's belly. She could mix a potion that would blister his wandering hands quite nicely, if need be, but she had more important things to worry about right now.

"Oh, Holly! If only the detestable viscount was the worst of my worries, but another matter has risen this evening. One that causes me even greater distress and requires my immediate attention." And departure.

"What can I do to help?" The serving woman moved to stand behind Agnes and undid the tiny buttons of her gown with ease.

"I received some terrible news." She stepped from the uncomfortable gown with relief. Yanking at the ties of her stays, she sighed when they loosened, allowing her to breathe freely once more. She indulged in several long and satisfy intakes of air before continuing.

"I can explain more tomorrow, if you wish. In the meantime, I need to travel to Shepherd's Moor. To deliver a message to my friends there. Tonight."

One quick scrutiny of Agnes's face had Holly racing for the door. "I shall inform Lady Hester at once. No doubt, she will be happy to lend you her carriage, and—"

"Nay, Holly!"

The urgency in Agnes's tone gave her maid pause. She turned to face her mistress, puzzled.

Most unfortunately, Agnes could not share the truth, so she opted for a carefully constructed half-truth. "I must beg your confidence. Most unfortunately, my aunt does not approve of my, er, association with this particular set of friends. They boast no titles, you see, or any wealth."

"Ah." She frowned and nodded slowly, as understanding dawned across her features. "I've nothing else to offer you but a hackney. My friend, Skip, runs a public carriage service." The color heightened in her cheeks, turning them rosy.

Agnes wondered if Skip was her beau. "How much would he charge to carry me to Shepherd's Moor?"

Holly named a price that amounted to nearly half the meager savings Agnes had traveled with. She swallowed hard before answering. "A hackney ride it is." Thank goodness, she could afford it. Barely. "How soon can you arrange for him to pick me up?"

"An hour, perhaps?" Holly's tone waxed soprano with concern. "Oh, dear! Must you travel so far in the dead of night?"

"Indeed, I must, and I've one last request. If it is not too much trouble, might I borrow one of your dresses and a work cap? Methinks it best for my aunt not to recognize me leaving the keep when I should be sleeping."

"A disguise, eh?" Holly rolled her eyes. "If you were not so nice, I would never allow you to embroil me in such a nefarious affair." She shook a finger in warning. "I better not lose my job over this, else I promise to hound you 'til the last of your days on this earth, then haunt you from the grave forever after."

"I thank you." Agnes crossed the room to squeeze her maid's shoulders in a brief hug. "I knew I could count on you."

Holly merely rolled her eyes again and took her leave.

True to her word, Holly handed Agnes into her friend's hackney within the hour. Not only did she lend Agnes an outfit complete with a cap, gown, and drab wool stockings, she managed to rustle up a tousled gray hairpiece and a pair of scratched spectacles. As a final touch, she smeared a few dashes of soot on her mistress's cheeks.

Agnes chuckled. "What is that for?"

"Doing my best to turn you into a frightful old hag, and do not bother putting up a fuss. You are far too pretty to be traveling alone."

What else could Agnes do but hug her? "I owe you dearly."

"Indeed you do," she muttered and hugged her back.

She shut the carriage door behind Agnes and signaled to Skip she was ready to depart. To Agnes's enormous relief, they rolled from Ravenspire Keep with nary a hitch. It took more than two hours to reach Shepherd's Moor parish. Two desperately cold hours, punctuated by scattered rain showers.

Beyond a pair of tall iron gates, the church loomed before her in shadowy patches of moonlight. It was a humble two-story stone structure with few adornments other than two cathedral style windows on the second floor and a steeple that listed to one side. A night watchman met their rig at the gates with a lantern held high in the misting rain. "Who goes there?" he called.

Agnes leaned out the carriage window to address the man. "I am a friend of your pastor."

He beheld her with suspicion. "We don' want no more trouble, ma'am."

More trouble? Faith! I am trying to help you avoid exactly that, good sir. "Tell him a friend of Abbott Wood, the vicar of Worcestershire, needs to see him," she urged, "concerning a matter of great importance."

Grumbling beneath his breath, the man trudged up the short and winding muddy path to pound on the door of the parsonage. Sprawling to the right of the church, it was a rambling structure of weathered wood and thatch that looked like it had been added on to multiple times. Several minutes dragged past before a light flickered on. The door cracked open, and the night watchman exchanged words with a shadowy figure.

Moments later, he ambled down the path and motioned for their carriage to proceed up the hill. Skip drove Agnes to the front door of the parsonage.

"I've an extra coin for you if you will wait for me," she pleaded softly as he handed her down from the carriage.

"Thirty minutes is all the time I can spare, miss."

"It is enough."

The shadowy figure turned out to be a woman in a nightcap. She waited for Agnes at the front door, tapping a leather slipper impatiently. "Who are you, madam, and how may I assist you?" She pinned her dark gaze on Agnes. A woman with plain, rounded features, she made up for it by the intricate stitching of her dark robes. They looked like real silk, which likely meant she was gently born.

Well, this is what I came for. Agnes drew a deep breath. "My apologies for calling at such a late hour. As I stated to your night watchman, I am a friend of Abbot Wood, the vicar of Worcestershire."

Her gaze kindled with warmth and interest. "Any friend of Abbott's is a friend of ours."

Agnes glanced over her shoulder to ensure Skip was still waiting in his hackney. Thankfully, he was. "I have an important message." She lowered her voice. "One important enough to necessitate traveling in the dead of night."

"Do come inside." Looking worried, Eleanor drew Agnes through the door and clicked it firmly shut behind them. "I am Eleanor Dare, by the way." She stuck out a hand.

Agnes grasped her hand. "Pleased to meet you, ma'am. Alas, I do not have much time to spare, so pray forgive my inability to exchange further pleasantries. I have come to beg an audience with your pastor."

Sadness clouded Eleanor's features. She scrutinized Agnes more closely. After a pause, she announced in a wary tone, "He is not taking visitors tonight."

"'Tis an urgent matter," Agnes pleaded. "I'd be greatly obliged if you would stir him."

"I fear that is impossible," she sighed. "You are too late." She gave an agitated wave of her hand as if to set aside something unwelcome. "He was arrested a fortnight ago by the Archbishop's men and charged of thieving from his own parish accounts."

Agnes gaped. The vicar of Shepherd's Moor was a devout and honorable man, making her immediately suspect the accusation was complete fabrication. What a witch-hunt the Church's decree was turning out to be!

"Falsely charged, mind you," Eleanor snapped, nodding in agreement at Agnes's indignant expression. "Never did I meet a more kindhearted or honest man. Fortunately, he has powerful friends in government. They will plead his case and bring him home soon, if it pleases the good Lord."

You are too late. Eleanor's words echoed in Agnes's ears like the clang of a death knell, making her wince as they played themselves again and again. *Too late. Too late.* "I reckon I was mistaken in coming here, then." She straightened her cap. The exhilaration of her earlier mission was fast turning to exhaustion. If the vicar of Shepherd's Moor had already been arrested, she was most definitely too late. "It is very possible I heard wrong, at any rate," she mumbled more to herself than to her host.

Eleanor's expression sharpened. "What did you hear, my good woman?"

With a shrug of uncertainty, Agnes spilled all that she knew. Maybe something she had to say would be helpful to others, even though it was too late to save the vicar. "I was at a dinner party this evening with the Viscount of Habbershire."

Eleanor's eyebrows shot up.

Realizing how close she'd come to revealing her true identity, Agnes hastened to amend the account of her conversation with the viscount. "What I mean to say is I overheard a conversation he was having with another noble-man. If I heard correctly, he indicated there was to be a raid at Shepherd's Moor one week from today, possibly two, for the purpose of rounding up more dissidents." But perhaps she'd misunderstood, since it appeared the raid had already taken place.

"Saints alive! More arrests?" Eleanor threw up her hands and began to stride the length of the sparsely furnished room. "You would think the bishop would have better things to do than continuously harass his church leaders. What with so many murderers and thieves running the streets these days?" She shivered in revulsion and spun around to face Agnes once more. "But nay! He would rather spend his time taking to task men of God over the state of their own consciences. 'Tis the real reason they took our pastor from us, mind you. It was to question his beliefs, his loyalty to the crown."

Eleanor grabbed the edge of a trestle table, leaning heavily on it for support as if being dealt a terrible blow. "You would think in a country so advanced in the arts and sciences, so free to think and create and explore, we would be more free to worship the way we please. According to our convictions, not according to the dictates of men." Her voice was wistful, her features fearful.

Our convictions? The phrase hung in Agnes's ears. Though Eleanor's words sounded reasonable on the surface, she knew most listeners would deem them to be outright heresy. Queen Elizabeth ultimately led the Church of England, and there were strict laws concerning how her constituents could practice their faith. Neither pastors nor laymen were free to merely worship however they pleased.

Agnes studied Eleanor's pale features, thinking it was odd how labored her breathing was. "Are you well, my lady?"

"Aye. That is, I will be in a moment. Trying to catch my breath, Miss, ah, I fear I did not catch your name." She rubbed her side, as if trying to dispel a cramp.

She had not caught Agnes's name, because Agnes had not given it to her. "My name is not important, only that I am a friend of Abbott Wood."

"Indeed." Eleanor sounded mildly affronted. "One begins to wonder what you have to hide, madam." She rounded on Agnes. "To begin with, I would delight in knowing how a friend of our country vicar happened to find herself in the presence of the Viscount of Habbershire." She assessed Agnes pointedly, from her spectacles to her boots. "You've not the look of one who would get invited to hobnob with genteel folk, not even as an upper servant. You look more like a scullery maid."

Agnes grimaced. "How I came to overhear his conversation is hardly important," she noted stiffly. Eleanor's words were disappointing. Agnes had expected gratitude for her efforts tonight, not an interrogation.

"I reckon you have a point." Eleanor still sounded suspicious.

Agnes straightened her cap and pulled it more firmly over her ears. "I must go before my driver abandons me. With a little luck, I shall be able to return to my, er, friends before I am missed."

The irritation rapidly evaporated from Eleanor's features. "Well, whoever you are, I thank you. Since you traveled in disguise and are as jumpy as an alley cat, I can only speculate the risk you took upon yourself to warn us. If ever you need anything, you may count us as friends here in Shepherd's Moor."

Agnes curtsied. Eleanor's gratitude might have been a little slow in coming, but it appeared genuine. That was more the reception she'd been hoping for. "I thank you in return, Madame Dare. One never knows when one might need a friend."

"How true." Eleanor's gaze turned speculative again. She took a step forward in the attempt to peer more closely at Agnes's face.

She ducked her head. It was probably best if Eleanor didn't remember her features. "I will pray for your safety during the coming raid." Assuming she'd heard correctly and there would, indeed, be another one.

"Be assured we will take the necessary precautions to protect our flock. Besides, we have the good Lord on our side." Eleanor sounded matter-of-fact.

Agnes turned to leave but a sudden thought had her whirling back in Eleanor Dare's direction. "What exactly will you do to protect yourselves?" She was burning to know how they could possibly hope to avoid arrest. How her own father and mother could avoid arrest.

Eleanor's gaze grew shuttered. "What we will do is our concern, not yours." She laid a hand on Agnes's shoulder and guided her to the front door with a strength that belied her small stature. Eleanor was only an inch or so taller, which Agnes found refreshing. It wasn't often she got to speak eye-to-eye with another adult instead of having to crane her neck up at them.

"Farewell, then." Agnes had stayed longer than she intended. She prayed her hackney would still be waiting on the other side of the door.

As Agnes stepped outside, she heard a male voice from the interior of the parsonage. "Who goes there?"

"A woman who refuses to give her name," Eleanor returned softly. The door shut behind Agnes before she could hear anything more.

She liked Eleanor Dare despite the radical views the woman espoused, enough that she would not have minded getting to know her better. Perhaps, under a different set of circumstances, they might have even become friends.

Little did she know how soon her wish would be granted.

CHAPTER 5: THE KISS

*H*olly's beau leaped down from the driver's seat to open the carriage door and assist Agnes inside. She toyed with her disguise, adjusting and readjusting her cap and wig as she settled in for the two-hour return trip to Ravenspire Keep. She would have to thank Holly for her assistance, because her mission had turned out to be a success. Though she had not arrived in time to warn the vicar, she had arrived in time to put the rest of his flock on alert for the next sign of trouble.

Throughout their encounter, Eleanor Dare had referred to Agnes as *my good woman* instead of *child* or *lass*, as she was more accustomed to being addressed. And the woman had not ogled her unusually fair hair and complexion, thanks to Holly's marvelously crafted disguise.

Agnes jolted in and out of sleep as the carriage rumbled along, hitting an occasional rut. At some point during the ride, the carriage picked up speed, jostling her fully awake.

Good heavens! Are we being chased? She slid to the edge of her seat, squinting anxiously out the window, but she could detect nothing more than shadowy darkness on the other side.

Skip maintained their elevated speed for a full ten minutes or more until they reached the outskirts of London's park district. They arrived a handful of blocks from Agnes's aunt and uncle's home all the sooner for their haste. As requested, he dropped her off at the nearest corner, within sight of the Ravenspire towers but not within sight of the front door.

His pair of horses were heaving from their exertions. Agnes pitied the poor creatures and wondered at the necessity of driving them so hard.

"Pray forgive the bumpy ride, miss." Skip glanced anxiously down the street from whence they'd come. "A man on horseback followed us the last few miles, but I don' see 'im now. Mayhap he was simply headed in the same direction as us."

To Agnes's surprise, he proceeded to return half the fee for the trip. "The Holly discount," he muttered, color darkening his wind-scalded cheeks.

Ah. Beau he must be. Agnes was secretly delighted that her speculations about her maid and Skip had turned out to be true. He seemed like a solid, dependable man.

One whose generosity moved her. No doubt he could have used the funds, himself, but she was in no position to refuse his kindness. "Bless you," she breathed, gratefully stuffing the coins in her cloak pocket. She spared a quick glance in either direction, hoping no would-be thieves were close enough to witness their exchange of money.

With a tip of his hat, Skip and his hackney continued on down the road.

Relieved to be so close to her aunt and uncle's home, Agnes set off at a brisk jog. Her booted feet made a soft thudding sound against the paving stones. *Almost there.*

The gates of Ravenspire Keep loomed as she neared the end of the block. Only a small copse of trees remained between her and home. Glee flooded her heart at the sight. She could hardly believe her good fortune in accomplishing such a tricky mission in the dead of night. She and Holly would celebrate on the morrow.

A man stepped from the shadowy copse of trees, and her premature rejoicing evaporated. She had no choice but to halt or run into him. He was tall. Then again, everyone was tall compared to her, but dear heavens! This man was very tall and very broad, as well as very good-looking. A gentleman according to his confident stance and I-own-the-world expression. He wore a long black cape that swirled around dark trousers in the night breezes and a pair of gleaming dark boots. Somewhere nearby, a horse whinnied.

Agnes plunged her hand in her pocket, fisting her coins. What could the man possibly want at this hour? She slowly backed away from him.

"Halt, madam," he commanded imperiously, holding up a gloved hand. He sounded moderately winded, as if he'd recently undergone some sort of heavy exertion. "I am the Sheriff of Huntington, and I have a few questions to ask you."

That stopped her. "Why? I have done nothing wrong." She frowned. "My lord," she added a wee belatedly, since he appeared to be a nobleman. There was no point in offending him.

"I shall be the one to decide if any wrongdoing has been committed here."

She resisted the urge to roll her eyes at his tone and stood before him, mute, waiting for his next move.

"State your name and business, madam."

"My b-business?" she sputtered. "I am merely returning from a visit with friends."

"What friends? Where?"

"They reside in Shepherd's Moor."

"What sort of *friends* would send you home from a country parish in the middle of the night?" He glared down at her from his impressive height.

"Ones that care about my welfare, my lord," she snapped. "I am at the mercy of a public carriage system and possess little control over their travel schedule. I am fortunate that I arrived as soon as I did, seeing as I must work on the morrow." *Surely attending the opera with a man I have no desire to spend time with qualifies as work.*

"What sort of work are you engaged in, madam?"

"I, ah...I serve as a companion to a noblewoman."

"Yet you do not wear a uniform."

"Nay, sir. As I have stated, I am off duty."

He moved closer and brushed at the dirt on her cheek with a gloved finger. "Did you fall into a puddle on your way home, Madam, er, I do not believe I caught your name."

His firm but gentle touch coupled with the probing of his dark gaze mesmerized Agnes into silence, which was probably for the best since she did not wish to reveal her true identity.

"Speak your name," he coaxed more firmly, brushing at her other cheek. "You are not nearly so old as I first imagined beneath all this grime."

"I, ah..." Agnes thought as quickly as she could in her tired state. Alas, it was not very quickly at all. Her voice stuttered into silence once more, while she floundered to form her next lie.

"You are quite the conundrum, are you not?" the sheriff mused, continuing to clean her cheek. "You dress like a scullery maid but speak like a lady of quality. And that's only the beginning of the puzzle you present. You possess the hair of an old crone but skin as soft as a newborn babe."

Her knees weakened beneath his probing curiosity. *Faith!*

The man was so blasted handsome it was downright distracting. She took a step back, hoping a bit of distance between them would help her think more clearly.

She stumbled on the uneven paving stones, and he lunged to break her fall. She tumbled against his chest, and an exquisite warmth engulfed her.

Her spectacles slid precariously down her nose. They were suddenly eye-to-eye, or as close as a woman of her stature could come to that. He was bent over her in concern while her head was tipped up to his. She was not certain who moved first. She would debate the details endlessly in the forthcoming days. Perhaps, it was a desperate bid on her part to distract the sheriff from his interrogating. All she knew was she ended up on her tiptoes with her lips pressed to his.

His arms tightened around her, and his lips moved restlessly over hers as he gently sought to deepen the kiss.

What am I doing? A blast of shock coursed through Agnes from the roots of her hair to the soles of her muddy boots. "My lord!" she gasped, wrenching herself from his arms.

In the flickering light of the street lanterns, his expression registered pure astonishment. She took advantage of his distraction and broke into a dead run, passing up the main Ravenspire Keep entrance and dashing through a narrow alley to the rear gates.

Though his reaction was delayed a few moments, the sheriff's footsteps soon pounded after her. Fortunately, the rear entrance to her aunt and uncle's home was not lit. She skidded to a halt and crouched in the shadowy wings of a pair of stately pines, fighting to control her panting.

"Hell and damnation," the sheriff muttered. "I've been outwitted by a woman no bigger than a tree sprite." He sped past her hiding place.

Agnes's shoulders slumped in relief. She quickly moved to

stand before the gate. With a shaky hand, she inserted the key Holly had given her and pushed it open.

———

*H*olly was waiting by the side entrance to the kitchen. She drew Agnes inside with a whispered oath. "I died a thousand deaths after you left." She produced a damp cloth and wiped furiously at her mistress's face in the candlelight. "The moment you disappeared from sight, I sorely regretted my part in this. I would have never forgiven myself if something bad had happened to you."

She was so distressed, Agnes dared not tell her about her brush with the law, though her toes curled in her boots as she recalled the exceedingly handsome Sheriff of Huntington.

"Your friend was most kind," Agnes whispered, trying to inject more calm in her voice than she felt. Her insides were a wild tangle of emotions. "He would not allow me to pay the full amount of my travel fare. He called it the Holly discount."

"Oh." Holly blushed, as in *really* blushed. "That was terribly sweet of ol' Skip."

Agnes waited for her to elaborate, but the maid held her tongue. Ah, well, the woman was entitled to her secrets. Agnes certainly harbored a few of her own.

Holly was too distracted afterwards to do much more than exchange Agnes's borrowed clothes for her night gown.

"Run along, my friend," Holly whispered. "If anyone accosts you, insist to them you could not sleep and decided to stroll through the library. You got lost along the way. No one will doubt your story in a home this size."

Agnes winked at her. "You are very good at this stuff, you know. If serving as a lady's maid does not suit you in the long run, perhaps you could take up a life of crime."

To her surprise, Holly stiffened. She studied Agnes for a moment, then relaxed. "Oh, get on with you." Humor infused her voice.

Despite her exhaustion, Agnes could not sleep. A few days ago, her biggest concern had been running out of supplies in her parish workroom to keep up with the endless demand for poultices and other remedies. Oh, to return to such simple days with such simple problems instead of the nightmarish ones now threatening to smother her!

If the Viscount of Habbershire was to be believed, the current efforts of the Archbishop and his men to quell the countryside of all dissidents, could easily turn into a full-blown Inquisition. How many of the people she knew and loved were on his wanted list? And how many of them would face arrest or worse when he caught up to them?

It did not help to find herself in the makings of an unwanted courtship with one of the biggest supporters of the arrests. Agnes considered, and quickly discarded, the idea that she might somehow manage to soften the viscount's views on the subject during their courtship. He was too stubborn to listen, and she was too opinionated and strong-minded to play the part of a sacrificial lamb. Nay, logic deemed it best to end his whole notion of courting her before things went any further. Tomorrow, she would beg an audience with her aunt to convince the woman she had no intention of making a match with her dear friend, Hill.

One problem solved, Agnes rolled to her side on the lumpy mattress, seeking a more comfortable position in which to tackle her next problem. *The sheriff's kiss.* She raised her fingertips to her lips in the darkness, still feeling the warm brand of his mouth against hers. *Mercy!* What had she been thinking to throw herself at the man like that? The whole point of a disguise was to make oneself as un-memorable as possible. Indulging in a kiss was risky and impulsive, wildly imprudent and — if she was being honest with herself — entirely wonderful.

Drat me, but I do not regret my actions half as much as I should! Nay, the man would likely not forget Agnes anytime soon. Nor would she ever forget him.

CHAPTER 6: TRAVEL WORN

*V*oices outside Agnes's bedchamber door awakened her. She rubbed her eyes and tried to sit up, but weakness pooled through her. With a groan, she flopped back atop the bedcovers. Her arms and legs might as well have been stuffed with lead.

"What do you mean my niece is still asleep?" a female voice harped shrilly. "Is she ill?"

Aunt Hester. Agnes tried again to sit up. No sooner had she mastered the position did her aunt burst through the door. Holly was right behind her, bearing bruising circles under her eyes and a breakfast tray in her arms.

Agnes straightened her spine and reached guiltily for the cup of tea her maid offered. She decided on the spot she would request a tour of the herb pantries of Ravenspire Keep today and mix Holly a poultice to soothe her swollen eyes. She did such a wonderful job taking care of her mistress. Agnes needed to start taking better care of her, in return.

"Oh, my darling. My precious niece! I had to see for myself your face was not riddled with the pox or some other awful malady." Aunt Hester waddled across the room in a

43

gown of pale gold silk. "You had me beside myself with concern at dinner last night. How do you feel this morning, love?"

"Better. I thank you." Agnes tried and failed to smother a yawn. Minus the entire deplorable situation surrounding the Viscount of Habbershire, she could see how a girl could grow accustomed to the life of a lady. *Good gracious!* You could sleep as long as you wanted, eat whatever you desired, bathe as often as you pleased, and make an occasional dash across the countryside in the middle of the night, apparently, if circumstances required it. Perhaps after she broke her fast, she would retire for a mid-morning nap. Under the guise of sending Holly on some errand or another, she would insist her maid do likewise.

"Good. I am relieved to hear it." Her aunt threw open the doors of her wardrobe and began to rummage through her new gowns. "My dearest Hill is likely already on his way. He and his daughter are paying us a visit this morning, but oh, dear dear dear dear dear!" She threw a despairing glance at Agnes over one plump shoulder. "Look at the time! We can hardly hope to get you in your gown in time, up-do that lovely hair of yours, and—" A squeal of frustration erupted from her as her gaze landed on Holly. "Well, do not stand there gawking, gel." She clapped her hands sharply. "'Tis your duty to assist my niece." She snatched a light blue silk from the depths of the wardrobe and shook it at the young woman.

"Aye, my lady. I shall have Mistress Agnes outfitted and downstairs in a wink."

"Indeed you shall, and I will deal with you later about allowing her to nearly miss her appointment with the viscount." Aunt Hester waved a finger under Holly's nose then sprang back with a sound of horror. "My lands! What is wrong with your eyes?"

"They appear a bit agitated this morning," Agnes cut in hastily. "Nothing one of my special-made poultices cannot soothe. I'll get straight to work on it after the viscount's visit."

"Huh!" Her aunt scowled. "I did not bring you to London to putter around the kitchens like a scullion. You must spend your time dancing and painting and such." She waved a hand in exasperation. "One does not become an accomplished lady overnight. Fortunately, we have Hill to advise us. He recommended the most wonderful dance instructor. You will begin lessons immediately."

Dance lessons? Agnes already knew how to dance. It was all she could do to hold on to her brimming temper. She had grown up in the country, not the bottom of a pond. Dear Mum, despite their meager income, had insisted she learn how to dance, paint, and play the pianoforte. If only Aunt Hester had bothered to ask, she would have gladly shared her litany of accomplishments.

"As for you," Aunt Hester continued in severe tones to Holly, "you must be more mindful of our social schedule in the future. Agnes is about to become a busy debutante. Do keep up."

"Aye, my lady." Holly sounded close to tears. She and Agnes watched as her aunt swept from the room.

Alarmed, Agnes swung her legs over the side of the bed. "What a muddle, Holly. It appears my aunt has descended to a new level of persnicketiness. I am sorry you took the brunt of it. Regardless of her poor temper, I *will* make you a poultice this afternoon." It was the least she could do for her assistance in last night's mission. She shook her head, trying to clear the last traces of befuddled sleepiness from it. "I truly had no idea the viscount was paying us a visit this morning. Did you?"

"Not at all," Holly stated grimly. "Sometimes I wonder if your aunt's wits have gone a-wandering. She says and does some of the strangest things, as of late. She and your uncle both. I worry about them."

At Agnes's startled silence, she struck a hand against her forehead. "Oh, pray forgive my loose tongue. I had no right to say such things. I must be more tired than I realized."

"We both know it is my fault you are tired," Agnes owned up softly, slipping from her night gown. "And I, too, am worried about my aunt and uncle. Tell me more about your concerns."

"If you don't mind, I'd much rather you forget I said anything at all," Holly muttered, as she helped her mistress don her new dress. It was constructed of so much gauze and lace, it was like stepping into a cloud. Agnes had never worn anything so lovely, but Holly did not give her much time to admire it in the mirror before spinning her around to fasten the buttons.

"Talk to me, my friend," Agnes commanded.

"I might as well," Holly sighed. "You'll only wheedle it out of me, otherwise." She gave a few light yanks at the fabric of the gown to smooth it into place. "Where to even begin?" she mused. "A few months ago, your aunt let the entire cleaning staff go. Insisted the whole lot of them were lazy and worthless. But she hasn't bothered to replace a one of them yet. Not a single one." She sniffed in derision.

"And?" Agnes prodded.

"Your uncle used to confer daily with his steward. He used to keep a real tight rein on his financial affairs, especially the crop yields. Now all he does is drink and gamble his days away at Almack's or White's. I am warning you, Agnes, Ravenspire Keep is in trouble. Your aunt and uncle are in debt to everyone from the butcher to the clothier. The steward says it's all he can do to still pay our wages, but for how much longer? I am beside myself with worry." She fluffed Agnes's skirts with a burst of ferocity. "Every day, I am at risk of losing my job."

The shabbiness of the keep's furnishings and endless strings of cobwebs dangling from the ceilings made sudden sense. Agnes's aunt and uncle were pressed for funds, which made little sense. Mother had always described them as wealthy. Old family money, she called it. Where had it gone? Had her uncle made some poor investments? Or worse, had he gambled away his fortune? It was a terrifying prospect for them all.

Holly's fingers flew as she braided the sides of Agnes's hair and looped it in an intricate twist atop her head. The result was lovely. "Pinch your cheeks a few times, dearie, and you'll be ready for the parlor games."

"You are a veritable wizard, Holly." Agnes pinched her cheeks a few times and dashed from the room, feeling as if she owed Holly far more than a simple poultice.

Despite her mad rush down the stairs, the viscount and his daughter were already seated when Agnes arrived. His daughter was no more than a year or two younger than Agnes but a good three inches taller, bless her. Then again, most people over the age of twelve tended to be taller than herself. The young woman was a female replica of her father with thick chestnut hair and dark, searching eyes. They settled on Agnes and turned sullen.

Agnes tried to catch her breath, a difficult feat with how tightly her corset was laced. Surely, a woman's waistline wasn't worth this much discomfort! "Pray forgive my tardiness, my lord. 'Tis good to see you again, sir." She desperately wished he'd saved himself the trouble.

Lord Hilbert stood. A look of irritation passed over his handsome features and was gone. "I trust you are recovered from your moment of weakness last night?"

My moment of weakness? Ha! She'd been forced to make an

all-night journey to warn her friends of the trouble *he* was bringing their way. "I am sufficiently recovered, yes. Nothing a few more days of rest will not cure, my lord. Traveling cross country can be so tedious at times."

"It is tedious *all* the time," the viscount's daughter announced in petulant tones. "I should know with the way Father persists on sending me away to boarding school instead of enrolling me in a finishing school closer to home."

"I do it for your own good, pet." Lord Hilbert smiled at her indulgently. "So you will grow into as lovely a lady as the one who stands before us. Julia, meet Miss Agnes Wood of Worcestershire. Miss Wood, my daughter, Julia."

Agnes tried to clasp Julia's hand, but the young woman merely pressed her fingertips and pulled away. "Worcestershire, you say?" Her lip curled. "What finishing school did you attend, Miss Wood?"

It was clearly an attack on Agnes's humbler upbringing. Her opinion of Julia dropped exponentially. What an ill-mannered chit she was turning out to be!

Lord Hilbert's expression turned so icy that Agnes experienced a moment of real fear on behalf of his daughter. To his credit, however, he kept his anger in check during the shocked silence that gripped their small group.

After a long, awkward moment, Aunt Hester gave a nervous titter. "Tea is served."

Conversation for the duration of the viscount and Julia's visit was miserably stilted. No sooner had they made their departure, than Aunt Hester began to rock in her chair, face flushed. She fluttered her fan with energy. "If only you'd not run so late, my love," she moaned. "Perhaps Julia would not have fallen into such a foul mood. The whole disaster could easily have been prevented."

Agnes stared. Her aunt couldn't be serious! The woman was blaming Julia's poor manners on her niece? She felt her cheeks turn red. "Or maybe," she countered, her ire rising, "the Viscount of Habbershire and I are simply not fated to be together."

"Fate?" Her aunt sat up straighter, fanning herself more vigorously than before. "Fate has nothing to do with it, love. Not with something as important as choosing the man you will marry. Not fate nor feelings nor romantic notions nor any other such fripperies the younger set likes to daydream about." Her movements stilled. "Nay, the most important thing in a good marriage is allying yourself with a powerful family name, one with a solid reputation." Her voice turned dreamy. "One with land, legacy, and the financial means to ensure it will continue for generations to come."

"On that, we disagree." Agnes clasped her hands tightly in her lap. "I was raised to believe something as important as marriage should be built on love and faith. Together, they form a much more sure foundation."

"Love," her aunt sneered. "Of course my wayward sister would fill your head with such nonsense. She has spent her entire adult life trying to convince herself of the same. Alas, she learned all too quickly how difficult it is to survive on something so frivolous. Love cannot put food in your mouth or a dress on your back, can it?"

Aunt Hester was obviously not in the mood to be reasoned with, and Agnes had no interest in debating her further on a topic on which they would probably never agree. She sat forward in her chair and tried a different tactic. "I appreciate all you are doing for me, Aunt Hester. Truly, I do. It was so kind of you to invite me here. So kind of you to take an interest in my affairs, but I'd rather you not spend the duration of our visit fretting about such things. You and I have already spent too many years apart." Agnes waited the space of several heartbeats to allow her words the time to sink in. "I wish to spend whatever time we have left together getting to know you better." Not courting a man she despised.

Her aunt was silent for several moments. She finally smiled. "You are a sweet-hearted lass. A bit on the naive side but as good as they come."

Despite her prickliness, Aunt Hester proceeded to take Agnes on a tour of her dim and dusty art gallery. Mostly pictures of their ancestors were displayed. Of the more recent family members, Agnes's mother's picture was the only one missing. Agnes imagined she had her portrait painted as a girl, since Aunt Hester, herself, graced the walls in painted form across the various stages of her life. Several places on the wall, however, were bare where paintings used to hang. Probably the paintings of Mother. It troubled Agnes deeply to see how her mother's family had so thoroughly erased her from their lives when she'd left home to marry.

"I would like to have you painted." Wistfulness crept into Aunt Hester's voice. "I would like to see your lovely face hanging here on these walls, along with that of your husband and children some day. If I could have one wish granted before I pass on, that would be it."

Her greatest wish? *Ha!* It was way too bad her aunt's heart's desires did not appear to include Agnes's happiness or peace of mind. Nay, the woman pictured her niece marrying a man of *her* choosing, a man of rank and consequence in society. Someone who could rescue Agnes's uncle from his poor financial judgment and despicable gaming debts. Well, her art gallery was destined to maintain its bare spots, then, because Agnes had no intention of complying with such odious plans!

She closed her eyes for a moment, mentally upbraiding herself for not seeing this coming. Her aunt was lonely and wished to be surrounded by family. Since the woman could not have children of her own and since her sister had left town for good, apparently her last hope in that direction resided with her niece.

Agnes opened her eyes, stood, and leaned over her aunt to hug her tightly.

"Oh, lass," Aunt Hester sighed, enclosing Agnes in her plump arms. "How long I have waited for this day! We will dwell happily together here. You will see."

Agnes rolled her eyes over her aunt's shoulder. Nay, she did not foresee much happiness, nor a future together, if her aunt continued to push her on the subject of courting. The prospect of spending any more time in the viscount's presence loomed over Agnes like a dark and dreadful cloud.

CHAPTER 7: THE OPERA

When Aunt Hester retired for her midday nap, Agnes was sorely tempted to do the same. Instead, she unpacked some of her medicinal supplies and made her way to the kitchen, getting lost and rerouted twice by passing servants.

"Why hello, miss. You must be the visiting niece." The cook scrubbed reddened hands against her stained apron. Her face was round and ruddy, her forehead beaded with sweat from working so close to the fire. She took a step closer to peer at Agnes through age-clouded eyes.

"Aye. My name is Agnes, and you are?"

"Everyone calls me Cook," the woman supplied dryly. "Do you be needing something?" She stooped to stoke the fire in the cooking hearth then straightened to stir something in a large iron pot. It smelled divine.

"Indeed, I do. I wish to make a poultice for Holly." Agnes held up her small tray of bottled herbs and mixtures plus a tidy pile of linen strips. "Alas, I find myself in need of a potato."

"Sure thing, miss." Cook bent her large frame to rummage through a basket of vegetables.

"The oldest one you can find," she added.

"If you be looking for old," the woman wheezed and shuffled over to the enormous walk-in pantry, "I've a few left from the earlier part of the digging season."

She produced a medium-sized potato that felt amazingly firm, not close to rotting or sprouting as Agnes feared it might be. "Perfect. I thank you, Cook. If my presence won't trouble you too much, I'll get to work right here in the kitchen."

Cook's expression was a mixture of surprise and consternation, but she pointed to the far end of her preparation area. "I don't see why you can't make use of that trestle table, miss. I'll help you pull out the leaves, if you need them."

"Please call me Agnes." She went to work grating the potato, peels and pulp alike, and placed the gooey substance between two squares of loosely woven white muslin. She sprinkled it with herbs and root dust. Then she whip stitched the ends together and created a second poultice identical in size and contents to the first. Since she'd used the entire potato, there was little to clean up. She dabbed up the small smudges of juice from the countertop and repacked her tray. "Cook, do you happen to know Holly's whereabouts?"

"Aye, I'll summon her, miss."

The guilty look on Cook's face told Agnes her maid was likely resting. "Nay, do not disturb her. I would much rather go to her, myself. She was not feeling well this morning. Hence, the poultices." Agnes held up her tray with a smile.

Cook's expression turned stony. She smoothed a hand over her tightly wound salt-and-pepper twist of hair at her nape. "The lady of the house would not approve of you visiting the servants quarters."

"She cannot possibly disapprove of what she does not know, can she?" Agnes inquired brightly. "Show me the way."

Cook sighed with no small amount of exasperation. She leaned out the kitchen door, called in a man from the gardens, and set him to stirring her stew. Then she beckoned to Agnes. "Follow me, miss." She led her to Holly, grumbling beneath her breath the entire way. "I'll lose me job, for sure, I will."

Holly was lying on a small cot in a basement room not much bigger than a broom closet. She cracked her swollen lids open and groaned at the candle Cook held to her face. "So soon? It feels as if I just laid down a few minutes ago."

Cook stepped aside and motioned Agnes silently into the room.

"See?" Agnes held up her tray. "I did not forget you, my friend." She set it down on a small trestle table next to the bed.

Holly tried to sit up, but Agnes pressed a hand to her shoulder. "I need you lying down for this to work. Close your eyes." She gently applied the potato poultices to each reddened lid. They were agitated by more than lack of sleep, as if Holly had accidentally rubbed pepper in them. Regardless of the cause, Agnes's treatment was the same. "The next part is even easier. You must lie still and rest for an entire hour. Only then may you discard the poultices and wash your face. I think you will like the results."

Cook's expression was much gentler than before when she led Agnes from Holly's chamber. They trudged back up the stairs. "Where did you learn such things, child?"

"From my mother." Agnes smiled at the compliment. "She is a skilled apothecary and herbalist. The best I have ever run across."

"You ain't too bad yerself." Cook sounded admiring.

"'Twas kind of you to help the lass. She's been singing your praises e'er since you arrived. Now I know why."

Agnes figured this was a good opportunity to press for another favor. "If it would not interfere too much with your work, I'd like to set up shop in a corner of the kitchen. I cannot afford to let my medicinal skills grow dull during my visit. If you know of any others in the household who could use my services, let me know. In confidence, of course," she hastened to add. "My aunt does not approve of my work. I fear she plans to fill my days, as much as possible, with dance lessons and such."

Cook's eyes rounded in her wide, ruddy face. "Why, sure thing, miss! Be no trouble at all to have you around. I could use a bit o' company, and I daresay the staff would welcome your services."

*V*iscount Hilbert arrived promptly after dinner to escort Agnes to the opera. Despite her concerns about spending the evening with him, she could not help but admire his carriage. It was a marvelously carved and gilded affair with his family crest emblazoned across the door. It was pulled by two saucy white mares who stamped the ground in their excitement to be off.

Aunt Hester accosted Agnes at the top of the porch stairs. "Do not worry about propriety," she instructed in undertones. "Molly will play chaperone; but if the viscount were to compromise you, why he'd simply have to make you his viscountess, would he not?" She did not sound as if she objected one bit to the prospect.

Agnes's trepidation increased tenfold. Sensing a trap, she descended the front stairs of the keep in yet another new gown. This one was a pale pink confection made from yards and yards of silk and lace. When Agnes had asked Holly earlier why all her gowns seemed to be in shades of pastel, her maid had explained they were virginal colors. Agnes would be permitted to wear darker colors only after she was married.

Agnes snorted at the thought. Faith, she'd been wearing darker colors her entire life — browns, blues, and grays in sturdy wools or linens. Such colors and fabrics were more affordable and generally considered more fitting for the working class.

Holly was buttoned up tight in her coat and muff and walked a half step behind Agnes as they approached the viscount's carriage. The skin around her eyes was back to its normal color, and she looked blissfully rested. A smile played across her features. Agnes suspected, from something her maid said earlier, she was excited about visiting the opera. Neither of them had ever attended one before.

Lord Brandbury exited his carriage and awaited Agnes at the base of the stairs.

She took her time descending, tempted at every step to plead a headache and flee to her room. She reached him all too soon.

"You look like a rose in springtime," he greeted, bowing and kissing her hand.

Despite Holly's warnings, he played the part of a model gentleman. He sat across from her in the carriage and maintained a much lighter conversation than the evening before. He pointed out the various parks and landmarks of the city as they rolled past each square.

Agnes studied his handsome profile, fighting a sudden bout of drowsiness and wondering if she'd feel differently about his attentions if she'd been raised at Ravenspire Keep. If she knew nothing about the plight of the Separatist dissidents. If one of them wasn't her own father. If she hadn't met and kissed the Sheriff of Huntington the night before.

The opera helped wake Agnes up. Despite her exhaustion, she thoroughly enjoyed it. She was completely mesmerized by the lights and sounds, the talented performers, and the lavishly dressed guests. Each private viewing box seemed to contain a more astonishingly decked out woman than the last. She'd never seen so many feathers, plumes, and gems.

Though Aunt Hester had warned her that Lord Brandbury would be the biggest catch of the season, Agnes was surprised by the number of patrons who trained their opera glasses on their box instead of the show. Was a man as old as the viscount really all the rage? Agnes squirmed in discomfort, unaccustomed to such ogling.

Fortunately, she had the opera to distract her. She turned, laughing, to her escort when it was over. "It was all so marvelous, my lord. I do not even know how to begin to describe my favorite parts. There were so many."

He was watching her with indulgent interest, as if she was far more interesting than anything happening below them on stage. "I do," he said and trailed his fingers down her arm. "I will begin by saying you are the loveliest woman in the room, Miss Wood."

So much for his model behavior earlier! Agnes twisted in alarm to ensure Holly was still safely ensconced in the seat behind her. She was conspicuously absent.

"You are most kind," Agnes murmured, edging away from her escort.

In response, he yanked on the red velvet cord of the heavy box curtain. It swung closed, blocking their view of the crowded arena. "There. Now, we can enjoy a little privacy." He drew an arm around the back of her chair and moved closer. "The attention of the ton can be rather intrusive, at times."

By now, Agnes was pressed against the wall of the box. There was no place else for her to go. Desperately wishing the crowd outside their box was still gawking at them through their opera glasses, she faced him tremulously. *This cannot be happening to me. Where on earth is Holly?*

"There are a great many other places besides the opera I would like to escort you." The viscount's baritone rumbled low in her ear. "'Tis my hope you will enjoy each of our outings as much as tonight."

Faith! He was busy ruining this one. How could she hope to enjoy anything with the way he seemed bent on smothering her?

"I know you are quite young and we've just met, but I hope you enjoyed my presence tonight, along with the opera?"

It was posed as a question, one Agnes hardly knew how to answer. If only she was not so tired from her middle-of-the-night outing, she would be able to think more clearly. "You are most kind to ask, my lord." She hated how her voice trembled. She sounded weak and uncertain. "I do look forward to seeing more of London, sir." *Preferably without you, though.*

"Good. That is good."

He bent his head and roughly captured her lips.

She froze. Unlike the sheriff's warm mouth, his was hard, cool, and far more demanding. She pushed against his chest. Hard. *Ugh!* His breath smelled fishy.

Not nearly soon enough, he raised his head with a regretful sigh.

"Why, s-sir!" Agnes wanted to demand an apology and ask if he'd lost his mind, but she was too shaken to say more.

"So young," he murmured. "I must remember to be patient with you."

His kiss left her feeling filthy and cheap. She wanted

nothing more than to scrub the imprint of his mouth from her lips and spend the rest of the night weeping.

"Come," he commanded briskly. "Let me escort you home."

Holly rejoined them in the carriage, casting a worried look at Agnes. Agnes stared out the window in distressed silence, mumbling polite niceties when it seemed the viscount expected an answer to his nonstop conversation.

He lifted her down from the carriage in front of Ravenspire Keep but did not immediately let her go. He bent his head over hers, and she feared he intended to kiss her again. Instead, he brushed his cool fingertips against her cheek, then gave the lobe of her ear a small, swift hank. "Dream of me," he urged huskily.

She gasped and clutched her ear. Red-hot rage infused her from the tips of her curled hair to her fashionably toed shoes. She so badly wanted to slap him, but her intuitions warned her it would be unwise. There was violence in the viscount, and cruelty. She did not wish to arouse such passions any further, at least not tonight.

He chuckled wickedly as if they'd just shared the most marvelous jest. He leaped back into his carriage. With a crack of the whip, his driver urged his horses forward.

CHAPTER 8: DIRTY LITTLE SECRETS

"Why did you leave me alone with him?" Agnes stormed as she and Holly mounted the entrance stairs. She knew it was unfair of her to lash out at her maid, but she was beside herself.

"I did not intend to. You must believe me." Regret infused Holly's voice. "The footman summoned me away. He swore it was an urgent matter." Her lips tightened. "Turned out all he wanted was a moment alone with me."

Agnes grimaced. It appeared they'd both had to endure a tickle and a squeeze. "I am sorry to hear it. It sounds as if your evening went as badly as mine."

"Not quite." Holly sniffed. "One mention of Skip's name and the footman let me go." But there was no humor in her voice. She eyed Agnes anxiously. "Tell me, my friend. How bad was it for you?"

Just thinking about the viscount's kiss again made Agnes gag and stumble.

"That bad, eh?" Holly clasped an arm around her mistress's waist and helped her the rest of the way up the stairs.

"I shall spend the next hour washing out my mouth. *After* I complain of his behavior to my aunt, of course."

To Agnes's utter disbelief, Aunt Hester crowed like a small child at the news the viscount had kissed her. "Oh, my child!" She grabbed Agnes's hands and pulled her into a giddy dance that left them both heaving for air. "I am so happy to hear how enamored he is of you. Not that I am surprised. Hill is a man of good tastes. Oh, my love! I cannot wait to hear the wedding bells chime." She tried to sigh dramatically, but it came out as more of a wheeze. "To see you walk down the aisle of the biggest cathedral in town. 'Tis all I could possibly have dreamt and more."

"Nay!" Agnes pushed away her hands. "Have you not heard a word I said, my dear aunt? I do not wish to encourage the attentions of Lord Brandbury. Not one bit."

Her aunt's wide face tightened at the outburst. "Why ever not? Trust me, love, 'tis perfectly normal to experience maidenly shyness. You need not let it scare you. Hill assured me he will court you with utmost patience."

"He pulled my ear!"

Aunt Hester's face reddened, but she chuckled. "Well, look at you, gel. As much as he may strive for patience, you can hardly blame him for losing his head now and then over your uncommon beauty."

Agnes decided Aunt Hester required plain speaking to snap her out of her fairy tale visions concerning her niece's future. "Nay, I do not wish to marry him," she stated coldly. "If you cannot accept my decision, then I shall return home first thing in the morning."

Her aunt's bulbous features turned a deep, angry shade of red. "You have no idea of what you speak, child."

"I am no child. I am eighteen, and I know my mind."

"I meant you do not know the ways of the world," her aunt snapped, "and I am fast losing patience with the foolishness my sister drilled into your head. She sent you here with a letter practically begging me to undo eighteen years of poor upbringing and turn you into a proper young lady."

"I highly doubt it. Show me the letter."

"Talking back to your elders is generally considered poor manners, niece."

"As I've already stated, I am prepared to remove my ill-mannered self from your home with haste." Agnes stalked towards the stairs.

"Where do you think you are going, niece? I did not dismiss you."

Agnes waved her hand in annoyance without turning around. "To pack."

"Very well. If you wish to behave like a spoiled child, then I shall treat you as such."

Agnes had no idea what her aunt was talking about, nor did she care, at this point. All that mattered was putting distance between her and Ravenspire Keep as soon as possible.

She flew up the stairs and ran to her guest room, slamming the door and locking it behind her. She yanked open her wardrobe, but her travel bags were missing. So were the garments she'd traveled in to London. *Where on earth are my things?* Thoroughly alarmed, she ran to the tiny cabinet beside her bed and pulled on the drawer. Tears of relief slid down her cheeks to find her rows of tiny seed packages intact. She could not bear the thought of losing them. They represented years of research. Some of the plants were quite rare.

She sat on the floor with her head tipped against the bed, clutching her precious seeds. After a while, the fire died inside the hearth, but she continued to stare up at the walls and ceiling. Just when she though her life could get no worse, it had taken an even darker turn.

"*A*gnes! Agnes?" The whispered voice jostled her into wakefulness. Agnes's joints were so stiff from cold, she could not move at first.

"What were you thinking, my friend?" Holly slid to her knees beside Agnes in the shadows. "Here, let me put those away for you."

"Nay!" Agnes snapped, clutching her seed packages tighter. "I will do it. *They are mine and mine alone.*

"At least let me help you get off the floor." Holly dragged her to her feet with a strength that belied her slender figure and eased Agnes onto the bed. "Merciful heavens! Your hands are like ice." She tossed a blanket around Agnes's shoulders and bundled it snuggly beneath her chin. "Stay here while I stir up a fire."

She blew on the embers and piled on a few new logs. In little time, a fresh fire crackled, taking the worst bite of coldness from the air.

"You should not have fought so sorely with your aunt, my dear. I tried to warn you something is wrong. I did not exaggerate when I told you she is not herself these days."

"It no longer matters," Agnes said dully. "I am leaving."

"On the contrary, you are going nowhere, my friend. Not until your aunt removes the guard from outside your door."

"A guard! What guard?"

"The groom she instructed to keep you confined to your room."

Blood rushed through Agnes's veins, warming her extremities. She sat forward, allowing the blanket to fall. "You mean to say, I am a prisoner here?"

"More or less," Holly confirmed sympathetically.

Good gracious! What a muddle! "To what end?"

"Oh, I think that much is clear. Your aunt fully intends for you to marry the viscount."

"Does she, now?" Agnes carefully set down her packages of seeds on the bed and pushed to her feet. She moved to stand in front of the fire. Turning and facing Holly, she deliberately grasped her neckline with both hands and yanked down on it as hard as she could. Fabric tore and buttons skidded down her back, clattering across the wooden planks of the floor.

"Oh, Agnes, nay!" Holly cried, hitting her knees to gather the buttons.

Agnes tore the fabric open wider, laughing hysterically. "She can hardly force me to marry if I've not a proper dress to cover my carcass, can she?" She twisted her body to reach around and untie the offending corset. Throwing it to the floor, she stomped on its bone-stiffened supports with all her might. After they were thoroughly mangled, she dashed across the room to open the sash and throw them out the window. Still laughing, she closed the window and pulled another dress from the wardrobe.

"Stop! I beg you!" Holly tried to grab the dress from her, which ensued in a wrestling match. "Destroying costly garments is not the answer to your troubles. Believe me, it will only make things worse for you."

"I no longer care!"

"Then think of whom your aunt will blame for this." Holly's voice changed from pleading to anger. "Not you, her precious niece. She'll find someone else to blame, mark my words." Her tone gentled. "So if you care one whit about *my* wellbeing, you will cease this madness." With one final yank, she removed the unspoiled dress from Agnes's grasp. Smoothing the wrinkles, she returned it to the wardrobe. "There now. We will think this through like reasonable creatures and come up with a plan to extricate yourself from your current situation."

"I will not be forced to a marry a man I do not love."

"Then we must find a way to convince your aunt you and he will not suit. I have an idea. However, it will require you to calm yourself and hold up your end of a reasonable conversation." She worriedly perused Agnes's tattered state.

Agnes doubted anything would convince her aunt to lay aside her hopes in the viscount's direction, but she agreed to try to speak to the woman.

An hour later, Holly led her aunt into the room and quietly shut the door, leaving them alone together.

"Oh, my lands!" Aunt Hester's hand fluttered to her throat at the sight of her niece sitting on the edge of the bed in her torn evening gown. "What is the meaning of this?"

"I destroyed my dress to prove a point."

"Oh, Agnes! You didn't." She slid into the chair Holly had conveniently stationed just inside the door. "You have no idea what it cost."

"I know it cost more than you can afford. I know you let your entire cleaning staff go to offset the expenses of launching your only niece into society. Regardless, you cannot make me marry against my will. If you think destroying my wardrobe is bad, consider this. I will turn myself into such a shrew that no man will wish to be seen with me in public."

"They will throw you in Bedlam," the older woman moaned.

"Better than being thrown into the bed of the lecher you have picked out for me."

At her words, her aunt dissolved in a fit of weeping. "We are ruined," she sobbed, "completely ruined if you refuse to marry Lord Brandbury. His generous allowance to launch you into society is all that is keeping your uncle's debtors at bay. Without him, your uncle would already be in prison or...or worse!"

Agnes gaped at her, hardly able to fathom the extent her aunt had gone to keep their sinking finances afloat. It was preposterous. Unconscionable! Agnes longed to wake up and find it was all a dream. Alas, she was very much awake, and there was nothing she could do but face the awful truth. Her aunt had gone and sold her like a package of market goods.

"So you decided I would be the one to save our family from financial ruin," Agnes concluded in a slow, deadly voice. It was a horrible turn of events. The only upside to their conversation was that she and her aunt were finally being honest with each other.

"You were our last hope. I remembered how lovely you were, just like my sister, and knew the viscount would be unable to resist you. The tough part was getting you to come to London. I knew my sister would never allow the courtship."

So Mother had not been a part of this nefarious mess after all. It was an enormous relief to have her wobbling faith in her dearest loved one restored.

Aunt Hester sniffed and wiped the tears on her cheeks with both hands. "When I received my sister's letter beseeching us to take you in, it was as if Providence had made the decision for us."

Or a most unfortunate coincidence. "Did you not once consider selling this old place, paying off your debts, and leaving London and your troubles behind?" Agnes inquired gently. "My parents would have gladly helped you. There is a small cottage on the parish grounds no one else is using. You could live there as long as you please." *So long as my father is not arrested and removed as vicar.*

"Oh, child! You know nothing," Aunt Hester ranted, standing and waving her hands. "Absolutely nothing!" She paced the room. "There is no house to sell. Not any more. After your uncle ran through our income, he gambled away everything else he could get his hands on — my jewelry, our paintings and tapestries, the pianoforte, our statuary, and finally the house. Fortunately, Lord Brandbury was present the night he gambled away our home. I am not entirely certain how he managed it, but at the end of the night, he was the one who left Almack's with the deed to Ravenspire Keep in his hands. And that is how the viscount came to own us, lass, right down to the last blade of dead winter grass in the courtyard out yonder."

She folded her arms on the mantle and dropped her head on them. Muffled sobs ensued.

Her words showered over Agnes like a pail of icy rainwater, effectively shattering the last of her youthful ideals. So much for being raised to think independently! To foolishly believe in things like love. Who was she trying to jest? The world was an ugly place, and she was standing at one of its terrible crossroads.

Agnes had two choices: She could either return home and face arrest alongside her parents or remain in London and try to save her aunt and uncle through a powerful, albeit distasteful, marriage alliance.

"You are right, Aunt Hester." Agnes hardly recognized her own voice. So empty of emotion it was. So lifeless. "I did not understand the state of things. Neither my parents' troubles nor how bad things were for you here in London." *I would have, though, if you'd but told me sooner. If my own mother and father had possessed the courage to confide their troubles in me.*

She stood and walked to her aunt, ripped gown and all, and wrapped her arms around her wide girth from behind. She rested her chin on the plump woman's shoulder.

"You have changed your mind, then?" Aunt Hester mumbled into her arms. "You will help us?"

"Aye, Aunt Hester, I will try. As you said, family looks after family."

"Bless you child!" She raised her head from the mantle, jostling Agnes's arms loose, and turned to face her. A fresh batch of tears coursed down her mottled face. "When you become Viscountess of Habbershire, I shall forever be in your debt."

"Nay, you will be my aunt. Just as you are now."

"Bah, my lovely little angel! Let me grovel a moment. Then I'll fetch Holly and see what she can do with your poor gowns. Perhaps, by some miracle, she can save at least one. Lord knows there are no funds to purchase more."

"I am sorry about the gown." And Agnes was — horribly. As far back as she could remember, she'd never done anything so rash or mean-spirited before. May the good Lord forgive her, because it would be a long time before she would forgive herself. "Holly has already salvaged the rest of them."

"What do you mean, love?"

Agnes walked across the room and swung open the door of the wardrobe. "She threw her body betwixt me and the rest of my gowns, refusing to let me near them. She begged me to speak with you, instead, in the hopes we might reconcile our differences."

"What a loyal little thing she's turned out to be." Aunt Hester ducked her head, shame-faced. "And to think how hard I've been on the gel."

CHAPTER 9: THE ENGAGEMENT

April, 1587 - London

*A*unt Hester removed the guard from Agnes's bedchamber door, and the two of them tried to fall into some semblance of a normal life, but it was difficult. Even the dancing lessons failed to bring any merriment back into the halls of Ravenspire Keep. If anything, the shadows in the corners of the unkempt fortress grew taller and the cobwebs thicker.

At the conclusion of Agnes's final dance lesson, Lord Brandbury went on one knee and declared his desire to marry her. As she'd promised her aunt, Agnes agreed to be his wife. He posted the banns, and their wedding date was set.

Aunt Hester was overjoyed and could speak of little else than returning Ravenspire Keep to its former glory. Agnes's unhappiness over the need to marry the viscount was long forgotten, as she prattled on and on about filling the castle halls with the voices of their offspring. Agnes spent every moment possible buried in the kitchen, trying not to think about her miserable future. She threw all her energy into treating the sick and injured. Her growing friendship with Cook and other members of the household staff provided the only slice of joy in her life, a slice that dwindled to smaller and smaller slivers with each passing day. Her forthcoming nuptials hovered over the keep like a death sentence.

Two weeks before their wedding ceremony, Lord Brandbury hosted a ball at Ravenspire Keep to celebrate their engagement. After many days of cleaning and preparation under the care of his personal staff, it looked like a new home. Crystal chandeliers, free of cobwebs, hung above freshly dusted paintings and cleverly arranged statuary. Brilliant tapestries graced the walls, and richly woven rugs covered the ancient floors.

Aunt Hester was beside herself with happiness, whereas Agnes's uncle pleaded an illness and refused to leave his rooms.

The ball opened with a flurry of greetings and curtsies. Lord Brandbury spun Agnes into the opening dance with a look of supreme satisfaction on his face. "Ravenspire Keep is one of the finest homes in London," he boasted. "The ton will be talking about our ball for weeks to come, for months, for years. I trust you are happy with the changes I've made to the place?"

"You have done a splendid job of redecorating, my lord." It hurt Agnes's heart to admit it, but it was true.

"I've only just begun," he scoffed. "Wait until the architects arrive. Never you fear, we will be updating the dining hall, our bedchamber, and the nursery to modern standards. Much more fit for a lovely viscountess and our growing family."

Agnes feared she might be sick. Throughout their brief courtship, the Viscount of Habbershire spoke often of building a family and a legacy that would last generations. He had not once spoken of love.

It did not keep him from attempting to be affectionate at every opportunity, however. Agnes endured his cold kisses and rough caresses in silence. There was no point in rebuffing him at this juncture.

In the middle of their dance, one of his manservants interrupted them. "Begging your pardon, sir. Madam. A member of Archbishop Whitgift's staff has arrived and requires your immediate audience."

The viscount's abrupt departure from the dance floor caused a flurry of murmured speculation and no small amount of sympathetic glances in Agnes's direction. There were a few spiteful glances, as well. She was convinced some of the hopeful mamas in the audience would never forgive her for whisking away the season's most eligible bachelor from beneath their noses. However, the dragons of the ton had given their blessing to their Cinderella story, so the pundits were forced to accept her. Or at least pretend to.

When Lord Brandbury returned, he led Agnes to a secluded alcove on the far side of the ballroom. "I must leave town at once, my love, but do not worry. I shall return in time for our wedding."

The prospect of enjoying two full weeks without his pawing was not exactly breaking her heart. She tried to keep the glee from her voice. "What urgent business takes you away from me, my lord?"

"Nothing terrible enough to trouble your lovely head about." His tone was light, but his expression was grim. "Pray continue with our wedding preparations, love." He cupped her face with both hands. "If you need to make any final purchases, my steward is ever at your service. I'll spare no expense for my lovely bride."

It was a generous offer, one that should have made her

happy. No doubt it would have thrilled most young debutantes in her shoes. However, Agnes wasn't a typical young woman of society. Nor was she a woman given to frivolous shopping sprees. A more perceptive man would have figured this out by now, which made her sad. Or maybe she wasn't giving her affianced enough credit. The viscount was a cunning man. Perhaps giving her such free rein with their wedding expenses was his way of diverting her attentions from his darker deeds, which he had somehow discerned that she found distasteful.

It took hours of polling the servants and no small help from Holly and Cook for Agnes to determine she was right. Her husband-to-be was accompanying the Archbishop's interrogation team on their latest round of arrests. He would be accompanied by several of his servants and a full detail of English soldiers. Among their intended stops were both Shepherd's Moor and Worcestershire. *My hometown!* They were scheduled to leave before dawn.

It looked as if her miserable luck was taking another plunge. No wonder the viscount had not wanted her to know the nature of his business. He was leading an arresting party to her hometown parish. More than likely, he intended to take her own father into custody.

Agnes was rabid with distress and scrambled to prepare herself for departure. There was no way to hide such a long absence from her aunt. Her goal was simply to leave the keep, undetected, and deal with her aunt's ire upon her return. It made sense to head straight for Shepherd's Moor, which was practically on the way to Worcestershire. Hopefully, Skip could assist her again with the first leg of her journey. From there, she would use some of the viscount's coin to hire a member of the Dare's parish to carry her the rest of the way home. She could only pray she would arrive in time to save her parents.

Holly worriedly confirmed her beau could carry Agnes once more to Shepherd's Moore. "This time I am coming with you, though," she declared.

She wouldn't listen when Agnes tried to dissuade her. In hindsight, Agnes wished she'd tried harder.

Like before, they waited until midnight to depart, so as to render the least amount of disturbance to her aunt and uncle's sleeping household. Holly continued to ignore her urgings to remain home, though Agnes wasn't entirely convinced she was coming along for any other reason than to spend a few extra hours with Skip. Indeed, she rode atop the coach with him a good part of the way, until it started to rain.

Agnes wore a similar disguise as before. This time, however, she packed a travel bag. Depending on the weather and availability of transportation, her absence from Ravenspire Keep could stretch on for days. To be safe, she packed a spare blanket in the bottom of her bag, tucked a couple changes of clothing atop it, and squeezed in a sizable array of toiletries and other personal belongings. When she stood back to view her work, guilt struck her at what a spoiled young woman she'd become in such a short time — the lover of fine things and creature comforts. Perhaps, she'd always harbored the bone of materialism. Perhaps, it had merely been lying dormant until recently. *Ah well, I have much bigger concerns at the moment.*

Unable to shake the feeling of pending doom, Agnes even brought along her precious packages of seeds. Just in case something prevented her return to Ravenspire Keep, altogether.

Skip loaded her travel bag into his carriage, and they took off at a brisk pace beneath the hazy glow of a white moon. It wasn't until they were away from London that the stars popped more clearly from the skies. It was a cold and rainy night, with an icy breeze that whistled through the cracks of the hackney. Holly and Agnes rubbed their hands up and down their arms and shivered the entire trip.

As they rolled within sight of Shepherd's Moor, Agnes made a terrible discovery. They had arrived too late. Soldiers already swarmed the grounds of the parish, lanterns swinging from their hands as they searched the property.

Holly pounded on the wall with both fists to warn Skip. "Turn around!" she cried. "Oh, please, turn around!" She made the sign of the cross over her bosom. Skip skidded the horses to a halt and began to turn the carriage.

Agnes wrenched open the carriage door and leaped out with her heavy travel bag in hand. "Do not wait for me, my friend. I shall secure my own passage home." She had plenty of coin to do so, thanks to the viscount's generous wedding allowance.

"What are you doing?" Fear thickened Holly's voice.

Agnes could barely make out her face in the shadows. "I must warn my family. You shall return to Ravenspire Keep and wait for me where it is safe." She shifted her heavy bag from one hand to the other. "Now, go!"

"Nay, I will not leave you here alone!" Holly seethed. "So help me—"

"Farewell, my friend." Agnes slapped the rump of the mare closest to her. In the same instant, a shot rang out. Skip's team of horses broke into a terrified gallop.

CHAPTER 10: NO TURNING BACK

*A*gnes crouched behind the low stone fence of the parish grounds, holding her breath and praying the Archbishop's men had not seen her exit the retreating hackney. When no further shots rang out, she started to breathe again — sharp, panicky little gasps of air. She crept along the perimeter of the grounds, keeping her head bent so the hood of her cape would hide her glossy mane of hair. Distant thunder muffled the sound of her squishy footfalls in the mud. Hopefully, the steady fall of rain would soon wash away any footprints she left behind. Above the fog, a full moon beat down, making the damp air glow and turning the surrounding trees into gnarled specters.

As she circled to the rear of the parish grounds, shouting broke out. It was punctuated by a sharp scream and the sound of a female weeping.

"Nay!" A woman cried, as a man was led from the side door of the church in chains. It was too rainy and dark to make out many details, but Agnes perceived an arrest was in progress.

She let herself in the back gate, surprised to find it

unlocked. She hitched her travel bag onto her shoulder and traversed a pebbled path to the back door of the parsonage. A tall hedge row bordered the path, providing a line of shadows to walk in.

Just as Agnes reached for the door handle, a loud explosion shook the ground. She gasped and dropped to a crouch, but all she could see was an orange glow beyond the parsonage. She pressed her short frame against the back wall and edged along it until she could peek around the corner.

A barn was on fire, and it was no small fire. Flames shot from every window and door. Smoke billowed through the missing roof. Pieces of burning thatch drifted in the wind, sizzling their way to the ground and extinguishing in the mud. The pitiful beasts housed in the barnyard mooed and bleated in fright as they scattered and fled the scene.

It was an odd sight to behold — a fire in the midst of a rainstorm. Had the barn been hit by lightning? Soldiers shouted back and forth as they converged on the burning structure.

With so many soldiers rushing in the direction of the fire, Agnes dared to creep around to the front of the parsonage. A lone man dressed in all-black wrestled with two lads on the muddy walkway.

"You were ordered to remain inside," he shouted impatiently.

"You took my pa," one of the boys accused, struggling fiercely. "I'll not let go of you, 'til you bring him back."

"Indeed you shall. I've a gun, you see, and I'll not hesitate to use it if you do not return to the parsonage, at once."

Dismay flooded Agnes as she recognized the voice of her affianced. The viscount sounded as if he meant business, too. When the lads continued to pummel him, he pulled a shiny revolver from his pocket.

The door swung open to the entrance of the parsonage.

"Mercy!" a woman shouted. "Have mercy, my lord! They are but children!"

Lord Brandbury pointed the pistol at the speaker. "Not another step."

The woman froze and raised shaking hands, while the boys bravely but foolishly continued to pummel him.

Agnes had no idea what the viscount would do when he recognized her, but she could not leave the boys to his machinations. She knew his opinion of dissidents, all too well. Maybe the shock of seeing her there would distract him long enough for her to extract the lads from his clutches. They were so young. She had to at least try.

"Please, my lord." Agnes pushed away from her hiding spot in the shadows and walked towards him. She stumbled as the black leather travel bag looped over her shoulder swung around to bang against her belly. She righted herself and stretched out her hands, palms up, so he could see she was unarmed. "Pray, let them go. They are hardly more than babes."

"As you can see, madam, I am trying." He cuffed one of the lads and sent him sobbing into the mud. "Alas, they listen as well as the rest of you rebels."

The viscount turned his pistol in Agnes's direction, while the other lad launched himself at his leg, blubbering threats and curses. In the effort to disengage the child's grasp, the viscount was forced to use both his hands, including the one holding the gun. Fearing it would go off any second, Agnes leaped into the fray, pushing upward with all her might against the viscount's firing arm. The gun shot in the air, missing them all, and the lad tumbled in fright to the ground.

The viscount whirled on Agnes. "By thunder, woman! I'll not stand for any more of your—" Astonishment made his jaw drop in mid-sentence. "Agnes? Is that you?" His surprise changed to dull resignation.

She was unsure how he recognized her through her disguise, but he did. They stared at each other, tense and poised for action.

"I should have known," he said bitterly. "All the interest you showed in my work. All the questions you asked. It was only to warn your rebel friends, was it not?"

It was true. Agnes had nothing to say in her defense.

"I was prepared to make you my viscountess. Indeed, I would have given you everything you dreamed of."

"Nay, you could not have." Her voice broke. "Not while arresting and imprisoning those I love. My parents and my friends."

"You were supposed to love *me*." Voice thick with betrayal, Lord Brandbury lunged for her. "I was supposed to be your family, along with your aunt and uncle."

Agnes wrestled with him for possession of the gun, and it went off again. This time, her affianced fell to the ground, clutching his chest.

She collapsed on her knees beside him, staring in horror at the darkness oozing beneath his gloved hands. "Forgive me, my lord! Oh, pray, forgive me! I never meant to hurt you. I only wished to save the boys." *From you.* Terrified the gun might go off again, Agnes swiftly removed it from his weakened grasp and tossed it aside in the mud.

Lord Brandbury reached for her with a choking sound. His fingers scrabbled weakly against her travel bag, which now rested between them. She shoved the bag aside and scooted closer to better examine the extent of his injuries.

"Stay with me, Hill." It was the first time she'd ever used his nickname. She pressed one palm atop the other and rose to her knees to put pressure on his wound, but her efforts proved futile.

His whole body seized, and his eyes rolled back in his head.

"Nay, do not die! I only meant to help. Do not make me a murderess." Agnes rocked on her knees beside him in the slippery mud, knowing she was completely and utterly doomed. She had fatally wounded the man she was supposed to marry — a nobleman, no less. She would hang for her crime.

Lord Brandbury shuddered into stillness beneath her bloody gloves.

Agnes heard screams.

Then hands covered her mouth, making it difficult to breath. Silence settled over the grisly scene. More hands pulled her to her feet. She twisted her head frantically, trying to catch a glimpse of her assailants. She dug in her heels as they dragged her from the corpse, but she could make out little more than their shadowy outlines.

They tugged her through the front door of the parsonage and firmly shut and bolted the door.

"I will remove my hand," a male voice counseled, "but only if you promise not to scream again." His tone was sharp but not unkind.

Scream again? Agnes was not some cowering nitwit who jumped at spiders. Nay, she was something far worse. A murderess!

An agonized wail tore from deep within her chest and was muffled by the man's hand. Only then did she realize she had been the one screaming over Lord Brandbury. *May the Lord have mercy!* If anyone in the parsonage had a hope of escaping arrest before Agnes's arrival, she had ruined it for them all.

Her knees refused to hold her any longer, and she sank to the cold, hard wooden floor. The man's hand came loose in the process. "I'll not scream," she assured in a sobbing whisper. "I've done enough harm already."

By the light of a single lantern, a room full of gray ghosts

79

shivered into movement and crept around her to form a semi-circle. Agnes recognized Eleanor Dare but none of the others. She perceived she was among two dozen or more parishioners instead of the Archbishop's arresting party as she originally feared.

The man who'd held her mouth bent his tall, rangy frame to a crouch before her. He was very good looking in a rustic, outdoorsman sort of way.

"Are you certain you are back in possession of your wits, madam? Our lives may very well depend on it."

Agnes nodded dazedly, quietly choking back a sob. Why had these people brought her into the parsonage instead of leaving her outside to face justice? In doing so, they'd put their own lives at risk. It made no sense.

The worried frown continued to wrinkle the man's brow as he rose and went to stand beside Eleanor Dare. He put his arm around her waist and bent his darkly tanned face over hers to confer in muted tones.

He must be her husband. Agnes burst into a fresh fount of tears at their grave expressions. Eleanor had claimed any friend of Abbott Wood's was a friend of hers. How she must be regretting those words now!

There was no easy way for Agnes to explain to those gathered what she'd done and why. It had all happened so quickly. She swallowed hard and fought to regain control of her composure. "As the Lord is my witness, I did not mean to kill the viscount." It was hard to speak past her chattering teeth. "Do with me what you must, for I have taken a life. But please believe me when I say I did not set out to h-hurt anyone." Her words ended on a sob.

"We believe you, lass. You saved the lives of two boys," one of the women assured softly. "One of them is my son. I will forever be in your debt."

"As will I," another woman chimed in. "The other lad is mine. Nay, we'll not be punishing you for saving our sons."

To Agnes's shock, a murmur of assent worked its way through the group. Though she was grateful they were not immediately turning her over to the soldiers outside, she harbored no hope of escaping punishment. She knew the consequences for killing a nobleman in England. It was a life for a life.

"The Archbishop's men will never believe me." Agnes's voice shook so much her words were nearly unintelligible. "I shall be arrested and hanged for my crime." Men like her deceased affianced held little regard for religious dissidents, and that is what her accusers would assume she was. She might not even be granted a formal trial. Faith, she might hang or lose her head this very night.

The icy dread filling her chest was far colder than the mud and rain soaking her garments. Her knees shook as the enormity of her circumstances sank deeper into her bones. All the way to her soul.

Eleanor Dare made a sharp gesture, and a pair of hands grasped Agnes's elbows from behind to raise her to her feet, once more. "If you remain here, yes. A swift and fatal punishment awaits you, but not if you join us. The first time we met, I told you any friend of Abbott Wood is a friend of ours, and that has not changed. I am not sure what brought you back to us tonight, my dear woman, but we are more in your debt than ever."

"J-join you in what?" Agnes stammered, unable to process anything beyond her pending doom.

Eleanor's husband stepped away from her and strode across the room to stand by a rear window.

"We are departing on a venture to the New World, where we will be planting a colony and building a new church. There we will be free to worship as we please, far from the dictates of the Archbishop. Think about it, friend of Abbott. No more persecution. No more arrests. No more interrogations."

A new church in a new country? What sort of church? To Agnes, it sounded like the talk of heretics and fanatics, yet what choice did she have but to listen?

"Our wagons are here," Master Dare announced, turning from the window.

"It is time to leave, my friend. Will you go with us?" Eleanor asked in a firm but pleading tone.

"I, er..." Agnes's mind was an impossible tangle of questions and uncertainties, but there was no time to sort them out. If she wanted to live, she was down to her final option — to leave her family and home tonight.

There would be no goodbyes and no coming back.

CHAPTER 11: THE DECISION

a shout sounded outside the parsonage. "Come quickly! The viscount has been shot!"

A few of the male parishioners leaped into motion, silently carting and stacking furniture to barricade the front entrance. "That should slow them down," one of the men noted in satisfaction, dusting his hands.

Moments later, fists pounded on the front door. "Open up!"

Eleanor cast an agonized look at her husband. "What is taking Anthony so long?"

A second explosion erupted in the front yard, followed by a third, making everyone jump.

"That is our signal." Master Dare stretched out his arms to beckon to everyone gathered. "Follow me, friends." Motioning for complete silence, he led them out the back door, noiselessly shutting it, and barred it closed with a length of wood. Agnes was amazed at all the precautions they were taking to slow down anyone who might try to follow them. Clearly, the Dares and their comrades had put a lot of planning into their escape strategy.

They crept single file through the rear gate of the parish grounds, where a half dozen canvas-topped wagons awaited.

To Agnes's surprise, their group was not immediately pounced on by the queen's men. A glance over her shoulder proved there were now multiple fires blazing in the barn and surrounding fields. It wasn't until they boarded the wagons and began to roll away from the parish that soldiers spilled like ants from the parsonage and swarmed the rear courtyard. The rain abruptly increased to a full pour, sheeting sideways and pounding the wagons so hard that Agnes could see nothing before or after the one she traveled in.

Lord willing, the carriages were equally indiscernible to their enemies.

In seconds, she and her companions were drenched from a thousand leaks in the canvas. However, they were blessedly free of chains and soon well away from the melee that remained at Shepherd's Moor.

Agnes lost track of time, huddled in the back of the wagon and clutching her travel bag, which — by some miracle — was still strapped to her shoulder. The strap was digging into the side of her neck like a noose. She reached up to remove it, and the relief was instant.

Her new companions scooted closer in the effort to stay warm. She counted thirteen people crammed in their wagon. Nay, make that fourteen. A young lad lay half-buried beneath his mama's large skirts. Though she didn't recall making any effort to join their huddle, Agnes somehow ended up in the dead center of their group. Minutes passed. Maybe hours. At least it felt like hours. Agnes was too numb to track the time.

Only when they neared the wharves did the rain abate. A distant horn sounded. A man shouted nearby. He was answered by the trill of sultry female laughter. The salty smell of the sea filled their noses.

The wagons halted outside a boarded-up warehouse. The

Dares hastily bustled them inside, where a fire burned in a giant hearth. Linen curtains hung from the ceiling to form makeshift walls.

Eleanor ushered the women behind one set of curtains. It was a long, narrow space punctuated with rows of bedrolls. They stood dripping and eyeing their new surroundings, while a pair of teen girls walked through their ranks, distributing an assortment of dry clothing. The women gratefully peeled off their sodden garments with numb fingers and put on the plain wool dresses they were handed. All the dresses were dark colors with few adornments, but they were clean and dry. At the moment, that was all that mattered. Agnes could have kissed the ground for the simple comfort of being warm again.

There was no point in remaining in disguise, so she tossed her foggy spectacles and rain-swollen wig on the growing pile of discarded items.

Eleanor breezed through a second time, issuing more instructions. "This is where the women will sleep tonight. You may take any bedroll that hasn't yet been claimed."

Agnes nodded and dropped her travel bag beside the nearest empty one.

Eleanor dabbed at her unbound damp hair with a towel. She caught Agnes's eye. "Have you made up your mind, lass?" she called.

Made up my mind about what? Agnes tried to focus on her words, but all she could think about were Lord Brandbury's accusing eyes.

"Faith, but you're the spitting image of your mother."

Agnes jolted at her words and stared as Eleanor claimed the bedroll across from her. "You know who I am?"

She made a sound of derision. "I do now that you've ditched your wig and spectacles. No one ever forgets a face like your mother's. What is your given name, my dear?"

"Agnes."

"Your parents will be very proud of what you did tonight when they learn of it."

Agnes wished with all her heart they would never have to hear about it. She'd just as soon they go to their graves without discovering they'd raised a murderess. "I am afraid for them." She coughed and tried to speak through the raspy, closed-up feeling in her throat. "Since your parish was closer, I thought to warn you first and go to them next." Alas, her mission had been cut short. Her parents were in God's hands now.

Eleanor cocked her head at Agnes. Beneath the dim light of a single candle, her dark eyes glowed with sympathy. "We will be forever grateful you decided to stop at Shepherd's Moor first. Methinks it was more than happenstance you arrived just in time to save the lives of two lads. If it gives you any comfort, we sent riders to all the surrounding counties, including Worcestershire, the moment we realized we were under attack. It was our pre-agreed-upon method of warning them they might be next."

A tiny strand of hope traveled up Agnes's spine. Maybe these men and women were more than simpleminded heretics, after all. They were far more organized than she'd been led to believe, and they certainly looked after one another. Being handed a sliver of a chance her parents and parishioners might survive was the best parting gift anyone could have given her before leaving her homeland.

"When do we leave?" Agnes was still coming to grips with the fact she would never be able to return to England if she joined their rebel cause.

"Tomorrow," Eleanor supplied. "We will dine and sleep here tonight and board our fleet of ships in the morning."

Agnes barely listened while Eleanor described how she would be sharing a cabin with five other unmarried women.

All she could think about was how she would never see her parents again or her scatterbrained aunt and friends at Ravenspire Keep. Worse yet, she had killed the man she was supposed to marry, may God rest his soul and pardon hers. Her life as she'd known it was over. In light of all that had happened the past several hours, the details surrounding the next day or week or month seemed of little importance.

"What sort of skills do you possess, my dear?"

"I, ah…" How could Eleanor ignore the monumental fact she was speaking to a murderess and move on to such a mundane topic?

The woman's innocent, piercing gaze, however, was confirmation she had, indeed, passed on to the topic of Agnes's skills.

What does it matter? "I am an apothecary, madam. At least one in training," she amended. "Mum taught me everything she knows." Memories of those happy hours flooded her mind, bringing with them the fresh sting of regret at the knowledge there had been no opportunity to say goodbye to her family. "I brought along some packages of seeds for planting and mixing into medicines." *If they survived the cold and sodden ride to the wharves.* "Oh, and I assisted our midwife during some of the deliveries at our parish."

"Praise be to God!" Eleanor breathed. "It will be like traveling with a second doctor."

A doctor of death, perhaps. My hands have blood on them. Any future she had tending patients would never blot out the enormity of her sin. How could Eleanor possibly overlook it?

"You are awfully quiet, my friend." Eleanor sounded bemused. "Do you have any questions about our trip? We are sailing to the other side of the world, you know."

Agnes blinked to realize Eleanor was still talking. "I, ah…no."

Eleanor looked surprised. "Well, then, my dear, perhaps

you might wish to write a letter to your parents? Look around and you will see a good many members of our congregation are doing the same for their loved ones. Pray do not hesitate to borrow a pen and ink from any of them. When you are finished, give it to me. I will ensure our delivery man receives it."

Agnes wanted to kiss her feet in gratitude. She drew a shuddering breath. "With all my heart, I thank you for the opportunity to write home, Madam Dare."

"Just Eleanor, please. Other than a few highborn folk, you will find our congregation doesn't stand much on ceremony."

"I see." Agnes did not particularly care what their group stood on, so long as it was something other than a scaffold with a noose swinging from it.

"You will eventually have questions. Come to me when you are ready to talk."

Agnes choked back a hysterical chuckle. "Indeed, I will." Everything that had happened back at the parish was still too fresh, too haunting, for her to ponder what came next. *Particularly the part about killing the Viscount of Habbershire.*

"You did the right thing, Agnes, in defending our lads," Eleanor offered gently, as if reading her thoughts. "Sometimes doing the right thing is not easy, but it is still the right thing."

"Even if you break the Lord's commandments in the process?" Agnes squeaked.

"The gun going off was an accident. Everyone who witnessed what happened says the same."

"Somehow, that does not make me feel any better." The dam holding Agnes's emotions at bay felt close to breaking. Tears of horror and remorse squeezed past her lids and scalded her cheeks.

"I would be more concerned for your soul if you showed no emotion at all over what happened. Cry if you must, my friend. 'Tis an entirely natural reaction to what you experienced tonight. But when you are finished, dry your tears and thank the good Lord you arrived in time to save the lives of two innocent boys."

"I will try, madam, and I thank you for your kind words." She knew Eleanor meant them as encouragement, and they helped a little. Not to ease the ache in Agnes's chest, but to lessen the sense of eternal damnation surrounding the ache. Perhaps, the future would offer some hope of redemption for her, but tonight she harbored no such hope.

"Eleanor. Not madam. Just Eleanor," her new friend reminded with a smile, "and you are most welcome, Agnes. I will leave you now to settle in, but I will check on you later." She started to walk away and paused. "I meant what I said about coming to me with questions. For that matter, come to me if you need anything at all. There are not many women on this trip, so we need to band together. The rest of the women won't follow us until we finish planting the colony."

Agnes nodded, too overcome with guilt and emotion to say more.

Eleanor's features were full of concern as she departed the women's curtained-off area. The moment the curtain fell into place behind her, a thin, spritely woman plopped down on the other side of Agnes's bedroll. She drew a comb through damp, graying hair. Kind, silvery eyes searched her face. "Greetings, young heroine! I could not wait to make your acquaintance, but I did not wish to interrupt our sweet Eleanor's tête-à-tête with you. My name is Helen Pierce." She spoke in normal tones, as if she were not addressing a person with tears ravaging her face and blood staining her heart.

"I am Agnes Wood." The intimacy of their surroundings made a handshake seem too formal, so Agnes did not offer one. She scrubbed her cheeks dry and removed the pins from her hair. Then she began the laborious process of finger coming her drenched hair. She worried if she did not keep her hands busy, she might scream or explode.

Helen continued in her low, soothing voice. "'Tis so good to have another woman join us. There are precious few of us on this trip and none so lovely as you. Bless you, child, I have never beheld such a beauty."

Agnes's disbelieving gaze flew to Helen's, because she knew she looked her absolute worse.

"There are even fewer of us unmarried women," Helen prattled on. "Only six of us in all, counting you."

Us? Agnes was surprised to hear a woman of Helen's advanced years lumping herself into the unmarried category as opposed to simply referring to herself as a spinster or widow. She looked old enough to be Agnes's mother, a thought that brought on a fresh wave of homesickness and regret.

"I am widowed. Twice, actually," Helen offered ruefully.

Aha. That made more sense.

"When I heard about this trip, I could not sign up fast enough. Figured it was my last chance to see the world before I die. I do not possess any special skills, but I can do enough of anything to get the job done, if you know what I mean. Cannot hurt, methinks, to have another set of hands on board to help with the cooking, sewing, weaving, planting, raising livestock, and such. What about you, child?"

Agnes dazedly ingested the woman's barrage of friendly prattle. Her brain was moving at a sluggish pace, so she had to ponder the question a moment before responding. "My skills, you say? I'm an apothecary in training and something of a herbalist. I know a little about midwifery, too. Like you, I'm willing to help out wherever I am needed, though I generally spend most of my time making poultices and mixing medicines." *And occasionally committing murder.*

"Is that so?" Helen's face lit. "What a fascinating mix of

talents! I know how to whip up a few basic remedies, but I would dearly love to learn more. Maybe you could teach me?" she asked hopefully.

Talking about work helped Agnes collect her shattered composure. She tried to focus on Helen's conversation and block out all other thoughts. "It would be my pleasure to share what I know. You are welcome to observe me at work or join in my experiments whenever you wish."

"I cannot wait to get started." The corners of Helen's eyes crinkled as she smiled. "You're a good lass. We are most fortunate you decided to join our venture."

Alas, Helen's kindly meant words merely served to underscore how desperate Agnes's situation had become. She was going to hell for murder. What would it hurt to join a clandestine group of religious dissidents and fanatics on her way down to the fiery pit?

CHAPTER 12: WAREHOUSE STOP

*A*gnes found herself missing her borrowed wig, which had been ruined by the rain. She'd rather enjoyed the rare anonymity provided by her disguise. Her spectacles, on the other hand, turned out to be salvageable, only needing a good polish after she retrieved them from the discard pile. She was already notorious for killing a man. She wasn't certain she was up to facing the added stares and commentary of her fellow colonists about her unusually fair hair and complexion. With her hair drying to its normal stark white-blonde shade, she was already starting to garner stares from the other women. It was enough to make her uncomfortable.

"Pretty," a plump young woman with dimples sighed wistfully. She tapped one of the ringlets at Agnes's temple to send it bouncing. Her own hair tumbled around her shoulders as dark as tea from the Orient and wildly disheveled. "Oh!" She drew back her hand as if burned. "Pray forgive me. I do not know what I was thinking. 'Tis just that you are uncommonly lovely, much like a—"

"Please don't say it," Agnes interrupted in a pleading voice.

"Aye." She tittered "I reckon you've been compared to a china doll before."

"Only a few thousand times."

At her mortified blush, Agnes's good manners resurfaced. Faith, the young woman was only trying to be nice. She held out a hand. "I am Agnes Wood, the new apothecary."

"Pleased to meet you." They shook hands. "I am Emme. Emme Merrimouth. I've no special training like yours, though I am more than willing to shoulder my part of the work. I'll admit I'm more than a little excited about the whole venture. I've never traveled beyond my hometown." Her eyelashes fluttered against her cheeks, and her blush deepened. She cleared her throat and met Agnes's gaze again. "We are to be cabin mates, I believe."

Ah. All her blushing was starting to make sense. The details clicked into place. She was single. No special skills. Volunteering to sail on a ship full of men. More than likely, she was hoping for marriage.

"So I've been told." Agnes smiled. "I just met Helen Pierce and look forward to meeting the rest of our cabin mates."

"There aren't many of us." Emme ticked off the names on her fingers, a friendly sparkle warming her eyes. "There is Jane Mannering. She is," Emme lowered her voice, "rather, er, manly, if you ask me. Always wearing men's clothing and toting a gun. Then there's Margaret Lawrence. As tart as vinegar but good of heart. And another new girl. I don't know anything about her other than Eleanor said she'll be joining us tomorrow. I hope she's nice," she sighed, "since we're going to be cooped up together for weeks."

A tinkling sound on the other side of the curtain interrupted their conversation. Emme's dimples reappeared. "That's the dinner bell." She hurriedly twisted up her thick mass of hair into a bun, tripping on her too-long skirts in the process. Then she managed to drop both the hairpin and bonnet she was holding.

Agnes bent to pick it up for her. She leaned forward at the same time, and they bumped heads. They rose, chuckling ruefully. She was clutching the pin, and her bonnet dangled from one of Agnes's fingers.

"Oh, just toss that shapeless monstrosity on my bedroll." She shook her head. "I'll probably be wanting the protection from the sun once we're at sea, but I can do without it tonight."

Agnes turned the wide, gray hat in her hands to better examine its two enormous side flaps. They reminded her of elephant ears. *Perfect!* She sent Emme a pleading look. "If you don't intend to wear it, might I borrow it for dinner?"

Her dark brows rose. "Why if I had hair like yours—"

"Thank you," Agnes cut in quickly and donned the unattractive cap. Emme's brows rose further when Agnes unearthed her spectacles from her pocket. She tucked them around her ears and pushed them higher on her nose. At last, she deemed herself ready to face the rest of their fellow colonists.

Shaking her head in puzzlement, Emme followed Agnes from the women's quarters to the main gathering room of the warehouse.

A mismatched assortment of wooden tables and benches sprawled before them, and a dinner line stretched along the far wall. The two women joined the line and received their allotted rations from a selection of dried meats, cheeses, and breads. A pair of teen lads offered a tankard of ale apiece at the end of the line to wash it down. They ate by candlelight and spoke in muted tones to avoid the attention of any passersby outside their walls.

Deploring any form of waste, Agnes tried, but failed, to choke down much of her meal. Despite Emme's animated chatter, all she could hear were the gurgling sounds Lord Brandbury made while he struggled to draw his last breath. And she could not rid herself of the shocked look on his face when he expired. He might have been an opinionated man on the wrong side of the issue when it came to religious freedom in England, but no one deserved to die the way he did — shot by his own fiancé a handful of days before his wedding.

Agnes suddenly and fervently wished she had been the one to die. A moan of anguish escaped her, and her tankard of ale slipped from her fingers, crashing to the floor.

"Mercy me!" A large woman sitting in the chair next to hers yanked away her skirts as the liquid spread along the floor. "Such a waste! You must be more careful, miss."

Mortified, Agnes rose from the table and fled for the rear exit of the building. Emme called after her, but she didn't stop or turn around. A scholarly looking man in spectacles was nodding off against the wall by the door. At her approach, he tipped his chair down on all four legs. "Nay, miss. You cannot leave the—"

Not waiting for him to finish his sentence, Agnes pushed her way out the door and stood in the darkness, unseeing and unhearing. Shoulders heaving, she sagged against the wall, feeling like she was going to shatter at any moment. *Is this what if feels like to lose one's mind?*

"Ah, we meet again." The familiar baritone voice resounded through her, bringing her back from the edge of madness.

Agnes wrenched her head up to meet the piercing gaze of the Sheriff of Huntington. She stared a moment before finding her voice. "You?" Her question was ineloquent and to the point.

"Me," he responded so cheerfully she wanted to slap him.

"Did you follow me here?" Of all the people in the world

she might have encountered this far from her aunt's residence, he was the last one she expected. In fact, there was no logical explanation for his presence. Until a few hours ago, she had not yet committed a crime worthy of his attention.

He answered with a question of his own. "Has no one ever told you how dangerous it is to wander off by yourself in dark and deserted alleyways? Alas, it seems to be a habit of yours."

"Perhaps it is not my safety you need to be worried about," she cried passionately.

"Why not?" he asked, far more gently than she expected.

The truth spilled from her before she could stop herself. "Because I killed a man today."

"So I've heard."

You did? She shot him a look of sheer irritation. "You are frightfully well informed. Should I save my breath on the details?"

"It is my business to stay informed and, yes, I know the whole story — right down to the fact that the man who died was a nobleman."

"You have come to arrest me, then." Her churning insides settled to calm acceptance. Her short-lived reprieve was over. In some ways, it was a relief to have the worst of her fears realized. Way down deep, she'd never believed Eleanor and her friends truly possessed the power to save her. There would be no distracting and outrunning the handsome sheriff this time. He would be prepared for her tricks.

"Generally, that would be the next course of action," he agreed slowly. "So far, however, every witness to your alleged crime swears it was an accident. They claim the gun misfired while you were defending two innocent lads."

He was willing to dismiss what she'd done as an accident? Agnes could only gape at him. Did he not understand she was ready to confess? To pay for her sins? Did he have any idea how much she needed to unburden herself, to come clean?

The words spewed from her. "He was a man I detested. A man I was being forced to marry to keep my aunt and uncle out of debtor's prison after he won their home in a game of cards. I was dreading our coming nuptials, praying for the good Lord to deliver me from such a disastrous union, and then I killed him." She sucked in a choking breath and lifted her chin. "Do you still believe it was an accident, my lord?"

The sheriff's brows rose at her tirade. "At what point during the encounter did you recognize the viscount was your betrothed?"

"While we were struggling for control of his gun."

"Why did you approach him in the first place?"

"Because he pulled his gun on a pair of lads scuffling with him and threatened to use it if they did not return to the parsonage at once."

"So you approached the gunman *before* you recognized his identity in the hopes of extracting two children from his clutches?"

"Aye." The sheriff made her actions sound so innocuous that she wondered at his game. He was there to arrest her, wasn't he? She'd already confessed to the crime. All that remained was for him to place her in chains.

"Then my answer to your question is yes. The incident has all the earmarks of an accident."

Agnes pressed a hand to her chest, hardly believing what she was hearing. "I recognized him before the gun went off. I knew who he was when the bullet was lodging itself in his chest. When he was falling to the ground. When he drew his final breath. It would feel more justified if—" She gulped for enough breath to finish.

"If what?"

"If we both had died," she choked. There. It was liberating

to finally get the words out. Like a judge administering her own sentence.

"On the contrary, you would feel nothing at all."

She blinked. The man saw fit to jest at a time like this? She could not be farther from smiling. Or closer to weeping. "I wish more than anything I did not feel anything. It hurts too much." She buried her face in her hands.

The sheriff's arms closed around her waist. He gently drew her against his chest.

She dropped her hands. "What are you doing?"

"My job." His gaze held sympathy and no small amount of male interest. "As a sheriff, I am honor bound to collect the facts when a crime has been committed. *All* the facts."

"B-but you said I was innocent!"

"I do, but you continue to claim you are guilty. Alas, that means I must continue my investigation." He bent his head over hers.

"What do you intend to do next?"

His voice turned caressing. "Circumstances necessitate I take measures to calm the accused in order to continue my interrogation." His mouth settled over hers, warm and steadying.

Her insides swirled with a new tangle of emotions, but she no longer felt like crying. She clung to him, tasting curiosity and desire. After her recent engagement, she was no stranger to courting. Instead of standing there and enduring his attentions as she had with the viscount, she found herself kissing him back, wanting to feel more of this sweet tenderness, wanting to lose herself in it to the point of no longer being able to feel anything else.

In the sheriff's arms, she felt less guilty, somehow, less marked for eternal damnation. It was a welcome feeling.

He broke off the kiss abruptly. "Are you going to keep

wearing that blasted hat and spectacles, or are you going to finally allow me to see what you really look like?"

She scowled, her churning senses returning to some semblance of sanity. And with her sanity, her logic returned. "I do not see the point. If you do not arrest me and cart me off to prison, I am leaving the country in the morning. We shall never see each other again."

To her surprise, he chuckled. "A pity. I would dearly enjoy getting to know you better."

"Alas, it is not meant to be."

"Where might you be headed, my delightful old crone who kisses so sweetly?"

She felt the heat rise to her cheeks at his colorful description. "To the other side of the world."

"One of those colonial ventures, eh?"

"I am told it is a risky one."

"Aren't they all?" he muttered and bent to kiss her again. "I knew you were not what you pretended to be when we first met." His breath warmed the corner of her mouth. "Are you certain you would not rather return to London? Since today's tragedy releases you from your engagement, perhaps it would be best to reunite with your family."

"Nay. There is nothing for me to return to," she cried. She could not face her aunt like this, or Holly or her parents. She no longer deserved a life of ease or comfort, not after what she'd done.

"An odd thing for a woman to say who was nearly a viscountess." He gave her shoulders a light shake. "You may have enjoyed wearing disguises up to this point, lovely lady. You might have reveled in the excitement of traveling at night to warn your friends. No doubt it has been a wonderful distraction from the tedium of a debutant's life, but serving as a colonist will be no such game. It will be every bit as difficult and dangerous as you were warned and then some. Are you truly ready to trade in the balls, parties, and revels of London for the hostile wilderness of the New World?"

She wrenched herself from his arms. How dare he treat her like some hair-brained chit who had nothing more to think about than her next party! "You know nothing about me!"

"Perhaps." She heard rather than saw the smile lighting his handsome face in the darkness. "But I have already admitted I would like to."

The admiration in his voice mollified her miffed feelings a fraction. Enough to foolishly wish he could see her in a better light, both literally and figuratively. "This is no high-born lady's game to me. I am made of sterner stuff. I can handle the path I have chosen for myself."

"I certainly hope so, for you appear to have one foot in the grave already," he teased, tugging on the ties of her bonnet.

Drat the man, but he'd managed to make her want to laugh in the middle of a murder investigation.

"Might I at least know your name?"

"Agnes."

"Is that your real name?"

"Does it matter?" she countered. "'Tis not as if we will ever meet again. Nor would you recognize me if you did."

"I would recognize your lovely voice." He tapped a gloved finger against the tip of her nose. "Your beautiful eyes. And I would most certainly recognize your kisses."

For a moment, she, too, wished they could have gotten to know each other better, but it wasn't meant to be. When she opened the door of the warehouse, the sheriff made no effort to stop her from returning inside to her comrades. A part of her was unaccountably disappointed at how easily he let her go.

CHAPTER 13: FOLLOWED

April, 1587 - Portsmouth

*O*nly a handful of colonists remained seated at the tables when Agnes reentered the warehouse. Few of them bothered to look up. She presumed the rest had disbursed back to the curtained-off areas. Eleanor and her husband huddled with a half dozen men around the table closest to the fireplace. They appeared to be engaged in some sort of meeting. Or argument. A short and slender man with a sharply chiseled Van Dyke beard was trying to speak, while a much larger and darker man continuously interrupted him.

For a group who'd been forced by the Archbishop's raiding party to be wrenched so heartlessly from their parish and homes, they were surprisingly at odds. On the other hand, the availability of food and supplies was truly impressive. The flurry of industrious activity indicated they'd been planning this trip for some time.

Eleanor glanced in Agnes's direction, caught her eye, and beckoned her to approach. Agnes patted her cap to ensure it was still in place and drew a deep breath. No doubt the woman wasn't happy about her abrupt exit during the dinner hour.

Agnes nodded a greeting and slowly approached her.

Eleanor merely smiled and beckoned her to step closer. Agnes found herself facing both Eleanor and a gentleman who could only be described as a man of consequence. In the candlelight, his hair waved darkly around a high forehead that was mildly wrinkled in consideration of her. He wore a simple white wool shirt and black overcoat, but they were of excellent quality and, on closer examination, were etched with fine embroidery at the lapels and cuffs. His gaze was frank and assessing like a man in charge.

"Agnes." Eleanor's hand fluttered in his direction. "I want you to meet my father, Governor John White."

Her father. The governor. The air leaked slowly from Agnes's lungs. She'd been right in her assessment of him as a man of consequence. He was *the man* in charge around here.

"Pleased to meet you, sir." She dipped a curtsy without directly meeting his gaze, desperately hoping he did not intend to detain her for long. Though she'd endured weeks of debutante training beneath her aunt's close tutelage, she was still far from comfortable in the presence of titled folks.

"Nay, the pleasure is all mine. Do come closer, my good woman." To her shock and further discomfort, the governor rose and took her hand with the grace of a ballroom dancer. A glint of genuine appreciation and admiration lit his kind gaze. "I wanted to tell you myself how grateful we are to have a woman of your medicinal skills on this journey." The appreciation in his tone was replaced with humor as he took in her floppy bonnet and spectacles. He lowered his voice, so only she could hear his next words. "My daughter has sung your praises at great length, Miss Wood."

Her lips quirked. Apparently, Eleanor had shared the

details of her charade with him. The breath she'd been holding eased from her lungs. These were safe topics.

"I would be remiss if I did not also declare you deserve a medal for your bravery on the battlefield today," he continued. "May the good Lord bless you again and again for what you did. We can neither thank you enough nor ever repay you in full."

Battlefield. His choice of words was a horrifying reminder that they were at odds with the Crown, itself. That Agnes's actions today — no matter how good her intentions had started out — were acts of treason and punishable by death. Her breathing hitched, and her heartbeat quickened with misery. Alas, she was no hardened soldier. Even if she managed to escape England with her head attached to her neck, Lord Brandbury's death would haunt her until the end of her days.

"Good gracious! You look exhausted," Eleanor exclaimed softly. "Do turn in and try to get some rest, dear. Tomorrow will be a big day for us all."

Agnes curtsied her farewell to Eleanor and her esteemed father, grateful for the woman's intuitive understanding of her raw feelings. She slipped noiselessly back to the women's sleeping area. A few were getting settled, but most were already bunked down for the night, eyes closed. Agnes counted fourteen other women besides her and Eleanor, who remained in the adjoining dining hall with her father. Plus, there was one more woman Emme had mentioned, who would be joining them on the morrow.

Agnes stretched out on her bedroll and pulled a thick wool blanket over her shoulders. With a soul as troubled as hers, she had little hope of finding rest tonight, but she could at least lie down. It was a good thing she did not expect to sleep, because the snores and mumbles of so many people in such close proximity continuously jarred her. She couldn't have slept even if her soul was as blameless as a newborn's.

In the wee hours of the morning, a babe whimpered. The mother shushed him. Soon after, the sounds of suckling joined the backdrop of muffled noises.

"A, baby?" Agnes said aloud, without thinking. She blinked rapidly and glanced around, trying to determine if she was awake or dreaming.

When Helen rolled to face her, Agnes jolted at the realization she was indeed awake, and this was no dream.

"Aye, it's a babe, and we've two more mothers in the family way," Helen declared. There was concern in her voice.

Another woman in our party besides Eleanor Dare is expecting? It looked as if Agnes's midwife skills were going to get some practice in the very near future.

***

*E*arly the next morning, their drivers returned to load them and their belongings back into the caravan of carriages. The colonists traveled with their mountainous piles of supplies farther down the coastline to a trio of awaiting ships.

Eleanor stood at the entrance of the gangway to the largest ship. "All women and children come this way," she called and ushered them aboard with much arm waving.

It was a galleon-style ship bearing *The Lyon* in large gold-gilded letters. It also turned out to be their flagship, which would lead their small fleet across the Atlantic. The Roebuck was anchored beside her, a smaller ship whose primary purpose was to bear cargo.

"That one contains our farming equipment." Eleanor pointed to the Roebuck, as she led the ladies up the ramp to The Lyon. "Plus our cannons and the largest pieces of furniture. Beds, wardrobes, trestle tables, and chairs. That way we will start with the basic necessities when we land."

Again, Agnes was amazed by the organization of this renegade group of would-be colonists.

Eleanor waved her hand at the smallest ship anchored just beyond the Roebuck. "'Tis only a pinnace, but do not discredit her size. We call her the Swallow, because she's like a tiny bird." She laughed merrily. "We'll be using her aplenty to sweep us in and out of the shallower waters when we reach our final destination."

Eleanor left Agnes at the rail with the other women while she joined her husband and father in the stern. It was located on the highest level in the rear of the ship. They remained at their post throughout the rest of the boarding activities, overseeing the hustling and bustling below them like a trio of royalty surveying their realm.

Like Agnes, many of the passengers appeared to be wearing disguises today. The only reason she recognized Emme was because she was wearing the grotesque elephant hat she'd borrowed the night before. Their precautions made sense, considering a good number of these colonists were on the Archbishop's most wanted list for arrest and interrogation. Best not to be recognized until they were far from England.

The governor was not among those in disguise. Neither was his daughter. Or the man hurrying up the gangway as the final call for boarding sounded.

It was the Sheriff of Huntington!

Agnes's hands gripped the railing. What cruel trick of fate was this? Had the sheriff changed his mind about her innocence? Was he coming to arrest her at the last possible minute? Riveted, she followed his progress with her gaze. But nay. He looked neither to the right nor to the left as he conferred with the man at the top of the gangway. He did not appear to be searching for anyone at all. Instead, he joined the leadership clustered in the stern, bending his head to confer with the governor.

Heat flooded Agnes's cheeks at his duplicity. All this time, he had known the Dares and their parishioners. No wonder it had been so easy for him to follow her. He was one of *them!*

Anger replaced her embarrassment. It had been a great lark to rendezvous with a mysterious stranger the first night they'd met, and it had been comforting for him to hold her last night and kiss away her hysteria. But she would not so willingly be caught in his web of machinations during their next encounter.

Anger turned to stubborn resolve. After all she'd endured the last twenty-four hours, the sheriff's duplicity was the last straw. Something inside Agnes snapped. She was weary of being used by the people in her life, people she should have been able to trust more. Weary of secret agendas and ulterior motives. Weary of games and subterfuge. From now on, she was going to be the woman she was born to be and none other. Agnes Wood, her mother's daughter. Lady on the inside and worker bee on the outside. Her own person. She was done hiding.

She had promised the Sheriff of Huntington he would not recognize her when they next met. Well, it was as good a time as any to make good on that promise. The thought filled her with unholy delight, which made her feel even more like her old self.

She stepped back from the rail as the horn blower signaled their departure. With a flick of her drab workaday skirts, Agnes ducked behind a crowd of fellow passengers. It was not a difficult task for a woman of her petite build to make herself scarce. The sound of the anchor raising grated in her ears, and the ship started to move beneath her feet.

She let herself through the nearest stairwell alcove and

descended a ladder-like set of stairs. According to Eleanor, the small sleeping chamber she would share with the other single women was located somewhere down here. Fortunately, it wasn't difficult to locate, and it was empty except for a row of bedrolls. *Magnificent!* She tossed her travel bag next to one. From the light of the small portholes dotting the outside wall, she began her transformation.

She shed her cap and spectacles and changed from her borrowed dress into one of the spare gowns she had packed in her travel bag. Since Aunt Hester had rid her of her normal wardrobe, she'd been forced to pack real lady's gowns. She selected a pale gold gown over a white muslin underdress. It had delightfully poofed sleeves bearing slits. A richly embroidered panel of lace covered her neck, and a fur cloak with a matching hood completed the ensemble.

She took down her hair and went to work on it. Thankfully, it was free of tangles due to borrowing Helen's comb the night before. It took nearly an hour to do her hair in a complicated set of braids and twists fit for a lady going calling. Tonight, she would tie the hair above her temples with bits of cloth, and tomorrow they would fall in pale white-gold ringlets around her face. For now, she settled with dampening the stray wisps and twisting them around her finger to give them a bit of a wave.

Not only would the sheriff fail to recognize her the next time they met, he would think twice before stealing another kiss. Make that thrice!

When Agnes finally ascended the stairs to return deck side, the shores of Portsmouth were long gone. They appeared to be hugging the coastline, not venturing more than a mile or so out, which made sense. They had no need to set out for deeper waters until they finished rounding the southern tip of England.

Agnes received a number of admiring and curious stares

from the male passengers and the sailing crew alike, no doubt wondering who she was and why none of them had noticed her presence before. She sought out Helen first, who stared at her for a moment, face wrinkled in concentration.

"'Tis me, Agnes." She twirled for Helen, so her skirts would fan out. "I figured it was safe now to shed my disguise."

"Land sakes!" Incredulity stretched the skin around the older woman's eyes into tiny wrinkles. "I hardly recognized you. Why, you look like an entirely different person!"

Mission accomplished.

Agnes caught the sheriff staring in her direction, but she pretended not to notice. Let him wonder as he had made her wonder. *It served him right.*

---

*T*he first night on the Lyon was far less comfortable than their night in the warehouse. Their narrow cabin settled into a damp, cold blackness after the last candle was blown out. The wind picked up, making the planks of the ship creak alarmingly as they rode the waves. Up and down they rocked until Agnes feared she would pitch from her bedroll straight into the arms of Helen who lay next to her.

A half muffled sob sounded from the far corner of the room. Agnes didn't recognize the voice. Probably the striking redhead who'd joined them at the last minute before they departed. She looked pale enough to swoon. Agnes wondered if she was ill. She would inquire about her well-being with Eleanor on the morrow and tend to her, if necessary.

"Bloody hell!" a female voice muttered in the darkness. This voice Agnes did recognize. It sounded like the one who'd introduced herself as Jane Mannering had finally arrived to their cabin. Like Emme had warned, Jane acted more like a man than a woman, toting a long rifle against her shoulder and stomping around the ship in a man's hat, topcoat, and boots. After months of mingling with the bored debutante's of London, Agnes was quite frankly fascinated with her. For one thing, the woman completely lacked guile, a trait Agnes found endearing. Not to mention, Jane seemed every bit as intelligent as she was interesting. She was to serve as the schoolmarm to their pack of lads on the ship. Agnes could not wait to get to know her better.

She also happened to agree with Jane's unladylike assessment of their circumstances. Normally an optimist, Agnes could not deny they were in hell right down to the bloody part. Faith, but she could not get the cold, dead eyes of Lord Brandbury to quit staring at her from every shadowy corner of their tight sleeping quarters.

Her last thought as she finally drifted into tenuous slumber was that hell wasn't nearly so hot as she'd been led to believe. Hell apparently drifted aimlessly beneath buffeting waves and coastal squalls. Hell was a floating coffin. Nothing, absolutely nothing, could be worse than this.

CHAPTER 14: NOTHING WORSE

October, 1587 - Virginia

*A*gnes clutched her wool blanket more tightly around her shoulders, but the coldness only settled deeper in her bones. She was never going to be warm again. Or safe. How wrong, wrong, wrong she had been to presume things could not get worse than they were back on the ship.

She finally gave up trying to sleep and sat up in the darkness. The makeshift tent she shared with Helen, Margaret, and Emme shook from the power of the frigid night breezes, a reminder of their need to journey inland as quickly as possible. Winter showed signs of arriving prematurely. Not good for their slow-moving caravan of pilgrims who still had more than forty miles to travel on foot in order to reach the place where they hoped to hunker down for the winter. They desperately needed the first snowfall to hold off long enough for them to construct a new fort and homes when they arrived. She didn't want to think about what would happen to them, otherwise.

Living through so many consecutive months of hell, it

was a miracle that those left standing had survived this long. The death of Lord Brandbury now seemed like eons ago. So many more deaths had occurred since then. Unimaginably brutal killings by hostile native tribes who did not want the English colonists, as it turned out, to move into and settle their land in the name of Queen Elizabeth. Agnes had nearly lost count of all the colonists who had died by cudgel, fire-tipped and poison-tipped arrows, and — by far their worst method, in her opinion — the horrific practice of scalping.

The ambush they'd suffered had brought their numbers down to a staggering scant third of the colonists who'd begun the ill-fated journey together. Not all of the missing colonists were dead, however. Nay, some were worse than dead, having been captured and sold as slaves to serve out their days a few miles inland in the dreaded copper mines.

They'd recently recovered five of their missing colonists when their only ally, Chief Manteo of the Croatoans, had sent his cousin Wanchese, the greatly feared Roanoke chief, to fetch Jane from the slave trading block. None other than the manly Jane Mannering who'd become one of Agnes's dearest friends on the ship ride over. He'd arranged her rescue as a wedding gift to Agnes's other dearest friend, Rose Payne, their ship clerk, whom he'd snatched up and married in short order after their arrival to the New World. Not to be outdone, Wanchese had done more than rescue Jane from the slave trading block. He'd returned with her as *his* bride.

Losing her two closest friends to marriage left Agnes feeling as abandoned as an orphan. She was happy for them, but their happiness had left her very much alone. There were only three other unmarried female colonists remaining in their dwindling group, but they could never replace her friendship with Rose and Jane. Helen was twice widowed, nearly old enough to be Agnes's mother, and content to be a spinster. Emme was wrapped up in future wedding plans with a beau of her own, and Margaret...well, nobody particularly wanted to spend much time with the bitter, spiteful Margaret.

What underscored Agnes's agonizingly single and unattached status were the colonists' growing expectations of the Sheriff of Huntington in her direction. The sheriff, better known to everyone as Lord Anthony Cage, and Agnes had settled their differences over the past several months. Actually, they'd more than settled their differences; they'd grown close. So much so that everyone in the colony expected them to marry, though he'd yet to officially declare his intentions towards her. The gossipers insisted it was merely a matter of time, but Agnes was not so sure. Her heart told her that if Anthony truly loved her, he would have already said so.

So unmarried and unattached she remained.

The scent of morning cooking fires invaded the air, signaling the start of a new day of travel. It was with stiff and cold hands that Agnes braided her hair and twisted it up into a simple knot that would easily fit beneath her hood. She no longer bothered tying it up in ringlets the night before. The wind would only buffet it to pieces.

Her comrades were too cold to exchange more than a few mumbled greetings of good morning, though their words lacked conviction. *And no wonder. What is good about today?*

Anthony nudged Agnes with his shoulder as she crowded closer to one of their campfires to eat her fast cooling ration of gruel. She tried not to dwell on the fact it was made from the last of their dwindling seed stores, which had originally been reserved for planting. Alas, they needed it to stay alive right now. They would be forced to forage for food in other ways if there was none of it left to plant come spring.

"A good morning to you, my lovely English lass." Anthony's voice rumbled across her bruised heart, scraping it afresh with his inexplicably cheery demeanor.

"If you say so," Agnes grumbled and took another bite of her gruel. There was no need to stand on pretense with him. He would see right through it if she tried. They knew each other too well.

"I do, indeed. Despite every obstacle in our path, we will soon arrive at our new home. Can't you picture it, Agnes?" His voice grew more animated. "A year from now, maybe two, we'll be walking down cobbled streets in front of our new church, school house, and places of business. We'll be plowing the land and sending a profit to our investors back in London, at long last. Then more English ships will bring more English people to these shores. Mark my words, the City of Raleigh is going to be every bit as glorious as we ever imagined it to be."

Glorious? Agnes blinked at him. They'd been driven from their colony and were down to one third of their original population. It would be a miracle if they survived the winter cold and an even bigger miracle if they didn't starve the following spring. Their plans for the City of Raleigh were dead, and each of them would be also if they did not lay aside such silly notions. They needed to focus on surviving and nothing more. If Anthony could not see that, then he was fast losing his grasp on his wits.

"I will believe it when it happens and not a moment before." She scowled at him and his foolish persistence in trying to bleed sunshine over their failed expedition. What a castle in the clouds the whole City of Raleigh venture had turned out to be! The English colonists had been cut off from their motherland, betrayed from within their investment company by another set of investors, and left to die at a hostile rendezvous point on Roanoke Island. Their governor had fled to England to gather much-needed resupply ships, but he would not return for months. By then, they would be tens of miles from where he left them, which meant it wasn't likely he would be reunited with them. Not in this lifetime, at least.

Why couldn't Anthony see this?

Agnes refused to spare another single moment imagining what could have been. She was too focused on what was — on their immediate survival.

"Come now. Why, still, the pouting face?" Anthony bent to brush his lips against her forehead. "Did you not hear a word I said?"

Mercy! He hadn't the slightest idea he was the main reason for her grumpiness. If only he would put half as much energy in the pursuit of her hand in marriage as he did in his pursuit of the phantom City of Raleigh. After all they'd endured together, all their near brushes with death, and all the victory celebrations that followed — both big and small — as well as their many stolen kisses in between, he had not once spoken to her of love.

"Do not mind me, my friend." Agnes brushed her fingertips over the imprint his lips had left on her forehead. "I have a lot on my mind. We all do."

He sighed and moved away to speak in hushed tones with Eleanor and Ananias Dare.

From beneath her lashes, she watched him go, inwardly noting how their courtship was becoming depressingly reminiscent of Lord Brandbury's courtship. Her aunt's choice of suitors had been willing to make her his viscountess, to lavish houses and gifts on her, but had put precious little effort in securing her affections. Agnes was well aware gentlemen usually married to ally their families and broaden their legacies. Since she possessed nothing to strengthen Anthony's social position or wealth, she was lucky he was courting her at all. Why, then, did she continue to secretly hope for more? Maybe she was guilty of harboring her own little castle in the clouds. Just as Anthony pined his heart away for the City of Raleigh, she pined for something equally elusive — love.

Jane sauntered in Agnes's direction, bumping into her so energetically she nearly huffed out her mouthful of gruel.

"I take it, from your expression, the dashing Anthony Cage has failed to come up to scratch." Her loud whisper blasted Agnes's ear with a mixture of heat and soothing sarcasm. "Again."

"Pshaw!" Agnes hurriedly swallowed her cereal. If anyone could shake her out of her funk, it was her beloved rapscallion Jane. "He is consumed with thoughts of getting us safely inland by winter. 'Tis all any of us has time to be worried about these days."

Jane snorted her derision. "Is that so? Well, I'd be willing to wager that a good number of our Native men spared the time last night to dream of bedding a certain porcelain princess."

"Oh, Jane! You are completely full of stuff and nonsense, and that is why I love you so much." Agnes waved her spoon at her friend and dissolved into laughter. *Drat the woman!* By being her normal crass self, Jane never failed to lighten her heart.

"You think I speak of stuff and nonsense, eh? Alas, that does not explain the many lusty sets of eyes trained in your direction this very moment."

Agnes stifled a giggle by catching her lower lip between her teeth. "You should not jest about such things."

"Who is jesting? Other than a certain young lord who fancies he will hold your interest forever without bothering to declare himself." Jane made a sound of disgust and spit on the frozen ground. "You really should send him on his way with a few choice words ringing between his cocky ears.

There are a good number of other deserving men on which to lay your affections."

A good number? Agnes poked her spoon in her cold gruel, not certain where Jane was getting her calculations from. There were precious few eligible men left in the dwindling English colony, and there lay the biggest problem for a woman like herself who foolishly dreamed of marriage. Most of the colonists were married, and most of the Natives did not speak a lick of English. It was a tough set of circumstances upon which to pursue a courtship.

She drew a bracing chest full of air. "Thank you, Jane. I appreciate your concern, more than I can say, but not everyone gets handed a fairy tale romance like you and Rose. Make no mistake. I am happy for the two of you. *Very* happy for you. I'm just not foolish enough to expect the same thing will ever happen to me, is all."

"Liar!" she snapped. "You try to be happy, but you are not. You are consumed with envy, my friend. And my husband, Wanchese, is *not* fairy tale material. Far from it. He is a dangerous man, one I would not wish to cross on the wrong side of a battlefield. Nonetheless, I love him to distraction. Aye, his bullheadedness and strength suit me just fine." She shot Agnes a sly grin. "Both in and out of bed."

Agnes flushed with embarrassment, which she suspected was Jane's intent. "Point taken," she grumbled. "Maybe Wanchese is no prince." Though he *was* a tribal chief. Wasn't that equally wonderful? "I only meant he loves you to pieces. 'Tis the stuff dreams are made of, and you are wildly wrong about my feelings on the matter. My happiness for you outweighs my envy." But she knew her reprimand fell on deaf ears. Jane would merely gloat over the fact she was partially right. Agnes hurriedly finished her last few spoonfuls of cereal before it turned icy.

"Fair enough." Jane's tone indicated she was far from

finished with the topic. Heavens, but the woman was doggedly determined at times! "I still say you could be happier. Correction. You *would* be happier if you would reach out and take what is yours for the taking like Rose and I did." She jutted her slender, tanned chin for emphasis. "Quit pining away for a man whose heart you will never possess. You might eventually convince him to marry you, but will he ever love you the way you long to be loved? Think about *that* before you settle."

The breath left Agnes in a rush. Jane actually thought marrying Lord Anthony Cage would be a mistake? It was the first time she'd bared her soul on the topic, and it threw Agnes mentally off balance. Rose had been against their union from the beginning, but Jane had seemed to support the idea until now. Her know-all attitude was beginning to chafe.

"Who are you so convinced is mine for the taking?" Agnes shot back, slapping her spoon into her empty bowl. "If you are going to make such harebrained statements, you might as well back them up with fact."

Jane shrugged, unmoved by her outburst. "Open your eyes, my friend. That is all I am asking. You've been blind to every man but Anthony for so long, it gives me indigestion. He is not the only man on this venture, and he is certainly not the only man interested in you, if you but half paid attention."

"I have no idea what you are talking about."

"The fact that I believe you is more the pity." Jane tossed her head in disgust. "Very well! I will spell it out for you. The newly appointed war counselor over both our tribes has not been able to tear his eyes from your lovely face and form throughout our entire trek inland. What would it hurt to ease the man's misery by tossing him a smile or a kind word now and then?"

A war counselor to both tribes? Agnes's gaze slid in disbelief to Chief Wanchese's elder brother, Riapoke. Technically, he was Chief Wanchese's half-brother, due to some mystery of marriages and alliances, and a cousin to Chief Manteo. It was hard to keep the Native's relationships straight sometimes. They had such odd methods of raising children, frequently fostering their offspring to other family members and occasionally to other tribes. Agnes did not understand it, though Rose and Jane had tried on more than one occasion to explain it. They claimed the tradition served as a means of building stronger tribes.

At any rate, Riapoke was staring openly at Agnes. It was no casual stare either, but one of intense regard. She shifted from one foot to the other, suddenly self-conscious. Staring was another habit of their Native allies. Back in England, it was considered rude or intrusive to stare. In the New World, however, it was common practice. Mainly, it was done of sheer curiosity about the foreign ways of the English, though Riapoke's stare impressed Agnes as something more than curious. As Jane claimed — *drat her for being right again!* — his was charged with unmistakable male interest.

CHAPTER 15: RIAPOKE

*R*iapoke's dark gaze was so arresting it was hard for Agnes to turn away from it. Something about his admiring stare soothed the deepest, darkest parts of her. The constant worries about where she stood in Anthony's regard. The fear that she was damaged somehow from past sins and therefore not truly worthy of any man's affections.

One shared glance with Riapoke made her feel eligible again, desirable, and very female. Agnes blushed, still unable to look away. Or, perhaps, she did not wish to look away?

Riapoke bore a triple streak of scars down the right side of his face. Jane claimed they were from a fight with a bear. They gave him a dangerous, formidable appearance. Agnes had noted how the English colonists tended to give him a wide berth when passing, though his scars didn't alarm her in the least. They were like badges of bravery. Something to be admired rather than feared.

She felt her blush deepen. Maybe it was unladylike of her to have such thoughts, but the thought of a man of his caliber showing interest in her was rather breathtaking. And thrilling.

Making a sound of resignation, Agnes did as Jane bid and raised a hand in greeting to him. *Faith, but the Natives grew their men big!* Most of the men in the Croatoan and Roanoke tribes stood several inches taller than the Englishmen they were traveling with. Riapoke was no exception, towering nearly a head over most of the male colonists.

He raised his large hand to acknowledge her wave with firm, precise movements, his arm held straight up. She did not fail to note how his muscular shoulders bunched beneath his deerskin tunic with his movements.

His visage was too dark, his features too stoic to be considered handsome in the traditional sense, yet there was something about his sharply chiseled expression she found utterly arresting. Maybe it was the depth of wisdom in his gaze or the hint of sadness...or both. She'd heard he was a widower — that his wife and unborn son had perished in battle, caught in the crossfire between the Natives and the first shipload of Englishmen who'd invaded their shores. It was a wonder he didn't hate her by association.

But there was no hate in Riapoke's gaze as he beheld her.

The wind picked up, whipping at his shoulder length hair. It was partially shaved on his shooting side and bound by a thick braid across the other shoulder. He did not bother to push back the lock that waved across his face, adding to the half-wild look of him.

Agnes stifled the urge to shiver. Despite his tragic past, Riapoke held an impeccable reputation with both the English and Natives, alike. Maybe Jane was right. Agnes could spare him a smile.

She mustered one and hoped it did not appear as anxious and uncertain as she felt.

Riapoke did not return her smile. As a whole, the Natives did not smile. Within their culture, it was considered a weak and silly practice, but they did not seem not to mind when the colonists bestowed an occasional smile on them. Maybe they were growing accustomed to their English ways after being stuck in their presence for so many months.

Riapoke's stoic expression softened, however, and a new level of male interest leaped into his gaze.

Agnes's heart thudded. *Mercy!* Jane was right. More than right. What had her friend been thinking to suggest Agnes encourage the man? Something told her the Native men were not well versed in parlor games and probably had no concept of what it meant to engage in a light flirtation. Too many smiles at Riapoke, and she might start something difficult to end.

It felt like the move of a coward, but Agnes lowered her gaze, unsure what else to do. However, she continued to feel Riapoke's scrutiny on her as his people and hers bestirred themselves for the long day's trek ahead.

Chief Manteo and Chief Wanchese gave the signal for their tribes to depart the clearing where they'd spent the night. Ananias Dare gestured for the colonists to follow suit. Eleanor's husband had taken charge of their small colony shortly after the departure of his father-in-law, the governor, to England.

The team of English wagons lurched into motion. In the absence of beasts of burden, the male colonists pulled the dozen wagons of furniture, small arms, and other supplies by hand. The wagons also carried those unable to walk the entire way — the smallest children and Eleanor while she nursed the orphaned babe, Harvye. His mother had perished in an ambush on their first attempt to reach the mainland. The Dare's infant daughter, Virginia, had been taken during the same ambush. According to Chief Wanchese, the babe had been sold on the slave trading block. *So tragic!* Agnes could not imagine living day to day, not knowing if her babe was still alive and not knowing if she would ever see her again. What a burden for poor Eleanor to bear!

Only one of the Natives rode on the wagons — Powaw, the elder Croatoan priest. He refused to admit he was ailing, but Agnes knew better. She wished he would let her examine and treat him, but none of the Natives had welcomed her English medicinal remedies. They preferred the strange practices of their own medicine men, who seemed to operate more on superstition than sound medical knowledge. Agnes hoped mightily to change that in the coming days, to gain the trust of the Natives and share what she knew about mixing healing herbs and potions.

She studied Powaw's stoic expression behind the ocean of coppery wrinkles rippling like waves across his face. His lips were pressed in a thin line and his dark eyes were edged with fatigue, yet his back was straight as an iron fire poker. How could a person not admire such strength of will, such delightful stubbornness? He seemed close to Riapoke. She observed them conversing daily.

Maybe Riapoke could convince him to let Agnes examine him. Her heartbeat sped at the thought that this might give her the perfect opportunity to approach Riapoke. The more she pondered the idea, the more she liked it.

Movement between the almost-bare tree branches caught her attention. The fleets of Croatoan and Roanoke canoes shoved into the water. Chief Manteo's wife, Rose, was in one of those boats at the insistence of her husband. She'd lost too much weight on her journey to the New World and had not yet gained enough back to suit him. Despite her protests that she was early in her pregnancy and perfectly fine walking, he flatly refused to risk her health further. The canoes were traveling on the river that ran parallel to the route of those traveling by land. They carried the Natives' supplies and the largest English items — a half dozen ploughs and four small canons.

The largest cannons were too heavy to transport and had been left behind on Roanoke Island. They hoped to return for them, at some point. They'd left behind a lot of furniture, as well. With their numbers so greatly reduced, it made little sense to carry three beds and four trestle tables per person. It was far more important to transport machinery and farm equipment, looms and construction tools.

Most of the Native women carried such enormous loads on their backs, Agnes did not see how they could keep up with the march. One of the most common items they carried were the rolls of birch bark mats which they would use to rebuild their homes. She was amazed at how quickly they could raise their domed structures and how delightfully snug they were after the installation of sleeping mats, furs, and painted skins that served as their wall art.

Having been raised in a far more genteel setting, Agnes was not in the kind of physical shape required to carry such heavy burdens. Her petite stature didn't help, either. People as small as her simply did not make good pack mules. Instead, she'd been given the task of discreetly keeping an eye on Eleanor while keeping charge of two scampering lads, Robert and Brose. They generally started each day like it was a big adventure and ended it by whining about how sore and heavy their feet were. *Poor young poppets!* It was an adventure most boys of eight and nine would turn down, given half a choice. Most adults would, too. Agnes certainly was not overjoyed at the necessity of marching ten to twenty miles per day in these biting November winds.

Fortunately, the lads had Blade to admire. He was one of their teens. He served as a runner between the fore and rear part of their caravan, proudly running up and down their ranks to deliver messages.

Robert's dark eyes lit against his pale, cherubim features each time Blade tipped his hat and grinned in his direction. "Someday," he told his younger friend in hushed tones. "I shall be a runner like Blade."

Ambrose nodded and pursed his lips. "I could prob'ly use a scout like you when I'm gov'nor."

Agnes hid a smile. *And so the dynasty of our yet unbuilt city continues.* Her smile slipped. For the sake of these young boys, they simply must make it to the river delta where the Chowan and Roanoke Rivers converged. They must survive the winter and carve out some sort of existence where the lads could grow up and live normal happy lives. If such a thing was even possible on this continent...

Most of the time, they traveled in silence so as to generate the least amount of disturbance to the various towns and tribal settlements they passed. They'd learned how quickly their environment could turn hostile. At the moment, they were traveling in complete stealth. A hunting party had been spotted by one of the scouts, so they were keeping as quiet as a group their size could despite the crunch of footsteps and wagon wheels over frozen clumps of underbrush.

The signal was given to halt midday. Agnes frowned as the caravan of wagons formed a circle, and their scouts positioned themselves in a protective perimeter. Ananias and Anthony motioned the women and children to step inside the circle of wagons.

A howl of a wolf sounded in the distance and then another.

"Those aren't wolves," Jane hissed as she stepped noiselessly in Agnes's direction in her deerskin moccasins. She lifted her bow and notched an arrow. Agnes knew from past experience that Jane had an entire arsenal of knives secreted on her person, as well.

Anthony dashed in Agnes's direction and slapped an icy

cold handgun against her palm. No matter how many times she protested she would never shoot another man, he refused to listen. "Protect the lads in your care," he ordered against her ear, "at all costs."

Blast you for pressing my biggest weakness! She rolled her eyes and dangled the dreaded gun at her side.

He kissed her cheek and disappeared.

Their newest attackers screamed their way into the midst of their gathering, arrows and hatchets flying. Agnes was fearfully familiar with their otherworldly screeches and howls peppering the air as they battered their way forward.

Alas, for the enemy warriors, their lithe copper bodies were no match for the belching English muskets. Matchlocks weren't terribly accurate over long distances, but they were deadly at close range.

Though the attackers sounded like a small army with all their whooping and carrying on, Agnes counted less than two dozen of them. Heart clenched in fear, she scanned the trees and boulders for more warriors. They had painted their faces red to signify their intent to fight. As if their war cries, bows, hatchets, and knives were not warning enough.

To Agnes's relief, no more enemy warriors joined the first wave of raiders, and the Croatoan and Roanoke braves, along with the Enlishmen, quickly beat them back. So intent was she on watching the battle, however, she did not immediately perceive the slow-moving underbrush creeping along the ground towards her feet. By the time she did notice, a mud-painted man was leaping up from the leaves and vines to tackle Jane.

Jane head-butted him and tossed her bow aside. A pair of knives appeared in her hands. When he attacked again, she was ready. They crashed to the ground, rolling and shouting along the hard-packed earth.

The men perceived the new threat and pushed through

the wagons to the aid of their women, but it was too late. A second warrior rose from the underbrush and launched himself at Agnes. It happened so fast, she did not have time to fire the pistol in her shaking hand. She closed her eyes, bracing for the fatal blow of his hatchet.

It never came.

All Agnes heard was the thud as something hit the ground near her feet. Snapping her eyelids open, she stared into Riapoke's concerned amber gaze. He stood between her and the corpse of her attacker, a bloody knife in one hand.

"Is Jane alright?" she quavered.

He moved aside, so she could see Jane as she rose from her scuffle, thoroughly drenched in red but triumphant.

Agnes glanced up at Riapoke, full of gratitude. For a moment, his harsh face wavered in the sunlight.

"I thank you," she breathed. He'd saved her life. Her knees shook as delayed shock set in. Men hurried forward to drag away the bodies.

Riapoke stepped closer, shielding her from the aftermath of the melee with his large frame, anchoring her chaotic emotions with his steady gaze.

The fierce concern in his features was her undoing. Agnes took the final step to close the distance between them and rested her head against his chest. For the space of several heartbeats, she soaked up the massive strength of him and felt safe.

His heartbeat picked up beneath her cheek. One sinewy arm hooked around her, pulling her closer. He muttered a few guttural words in his Native tongue against her temple. She could make no sense of what he said. She only knew she was drowning in the intoxicating knowledge she was wanted by this amazingly brave man.

Agnes breathed in the smoky, woodsy scent of him,

seeking more of the beautiful wash of feelings he inspired in her until guilt gave her pause.

Faith, what am I doing? She raised her head, mortified at her audacity, and took a step back.

Riapoke dropped his arm.

Lord, help me! As far as her countrymen were concerned, Agnes was all but officially spoken for as the future wife of Lord Anthony Cage. They would consider it unconscionable for her to encourage the attentions of another man.

It did not help that her heart was still racing beneath her cloak, or that Riapoke was gazing at her with a ridiculously satisfied male expression, or the way she longed to return to his arms and continue what she'd started.

But nay! What was she thinking? There could be no starting and no finishing with Riapoke. She was too close to being affianced to Anthony. *Burn me for listening to Jane's nonsense about claiming what is mine for the taking!* Agnes would throttle her the next time she saw her — after she squeezed the breathe out of her, of course, for the marvelous way she'd fought off her attacker.

The sheer joy of being alive welled in Agnes's throat, threatening to overcome her. She raised her head to meet Riapoke's dark, searching gaze again and trembled. *Dear heavens!* No man had ever looked at her that way before.

CHAPTER 16: THE COURTING

*R*iapoke returned to his place at the forefront of their group, presumably to reassemble the Roanoke and Croatoan scouts. An unaccountable emptiness settled over Agnes. It was wrong of her to want to spend more time with him, to want so badly to get to know him better, yet that is exactly what she wanted. *Drat my treacherous heart!* It was supposed to belong to Anthony.

She straightened her shoulders and hurried to Jane who was cleaning her knife against a fallen log. Strange how none of the braves had come to her aid as Riapoke had come to Agnes's. She laid a hand on Jane's shoulder. "Are you uninjured, my friend?"

Jane shook off her hand. "As you can see for yourself, I am fine." She sounded affronted by the question. "The man who attacked me is not."

Agnes crouched beside her for a closer examination of her stained garments. "But there's so much blood. Are you certain none of it is yours?"

"Quite sure. Ouch!" she snarled when Agnes's fingers clamped over a gash in her arm.

"Is that so?" Agnes taunted, relieved to be feeling useful again. If not treated properly, wounds like these could turn to infection.

Despite her friend's noisy protests, she dampened a cloth with her flask of water and dabbed at her wound. "Fuss all you wish, love, but it won't change the fact you need stitches."

"Such a tempest in a teapot," Jane huffed, but she remained where she stood while Agnes ran for her aid bag and returned with a needle and thread.

"Would you like me to dose you with wine before the next part?"

Jane shook her head. "Nay. Save it for someone who needs it worse than me."

"It will not take long. I promise." Agnes offered her a cylindrical post to bite down on before she began stitching.

Jane's lip curled in derision. "Unless you can light that thing for me to puff on, you can put it away. I've no need of it."

Agnes smiled at the reminder of her friend's love for smoking. She owned a pipe or two. Alas, they were fresh out of good English tobacco. "I could use a nip of something strong, myself, right now," Agnes sighed, willing her hands not to start shaking again at the memory of their most recent brush with death.

"So I noticed. Saw you bat your lashes at Riapoke earlier, and he came through for you rather nicely, I'd say. Pushed at least two other braves out of the way, so he could be the one to save the beautiful English damsel in distress."

Agnes felt heat stain her cheeks. "Stuff and nonsense!" She pinched together the two jagged folds of Jane's injured skin and pushed her needle home. "You are as full of it as ever."

Jane gritted her teeth but did not cry out. She forced another one of her sarcastic grins. "The way the two of you were plastered against each other a few minutes ago, I wondered if you were going to pitch a tent together right then and there."

Agnes was drowning in her own blushes by now. "The scandalous things you say sometimes."

"You felt something, did you not?" Jane insisted.

"I, er, we really should not be having this conversation." Agnes pushed her needle in again, falling into the natural rhythm of stitching. "Even though he has yet to formally declare himself, Anthony is the one who holds my affections. You know how much I care for him, Jane."

She slapped at the air as if to knock Agnes's words away. "Pshaw! We all care about him. He is a good and loyal friend. It's not the same as being in love, though, and you know it."

Agnes gasped at the accuracy in which Jane had managed to voice one of her deepest fears. Egad, but the woman was not one for mincing words. What was worse, she was right. Agnes wanted to wail out her pain to the heavens. Why did the truth have to hurt so much?

Jane waved her hunting knife. "Oh, come now. Catch your blasted breath and rail back at me. We've been through too much together not to speak what's on our minds."

When Agnes did not immediately respond, her voice gentled a fraction. "I know it's hard to accept, my friend, but don't you think more would have come of your relationship by now if the two of you were in love?"

Aye, it was something Agnes worried about all hours of the day and night, but only Jane had been bold enough to speak such fears aloud. *Is that the real problem? That I am not truly in love with Anthony Cage any more than he is with me?*

She set the final stitch to hold Jane's wound together, tied a knot, and cut the thread. Wrapping a fresh bandage around her arm, she pulled down the sleeve of Jane's deerskin tunic. "I shall check it again in a few hours and change the dressing."

Her friend let out a huff of air. "Nothing to say on the other topic, eh?"

"You told me to think about it, and I will." Agnes's voice caught on a knot of emotion. "I fear you are right, yet I have not the slightest notion how to undo what is already set in motion with Anthony." Even though he'd not formally declared himself, he certainly acted as if they were courting.

Jane gave a sage nod. "Sure you do." She shook a finger beneath Agnes's nose. "You've a good head and a good heart. Follow them."

Greatly troubled, Agnes made her rounds of the English colonists, stitching a few more wounds along the way. To her surprise, Ananias fetched her to examine one of the Natives who'd suffered a deep cut on his inner thigh. It was the first time any of the Natives had ever sought out her services.

It took quite some time and plenty of applied pressure to stop the worst of the bleeding. She dosed the warrior with a wee bit of wine she kept hidden for emergencies. His eyes widened in surprise at the taste and the burn of it, and he did not protest like Jane had. He obediently bit the cylindrical length of wood she offered him and gasped his way through the lengthy stitching process. After she applied a healing paste and bandaged the wound, she prayed her efforts would be enough to thwart any infection.

"Oh, nay you must not," she warned when he sat up woozily at the end of her tending. He'd lost too much blood. "You've earned yourself a wagon ride today." She pointed to the nearest manned wagon with what she hoped was a formidable glare.

When he stubbornly looked in the opposite direction, two more braves stepped forward. They lifted him between them and set him in the wagon.

"Thank you." Agnes climbed in beside him to elevate his leg on a crate. Best to limit the blood flow until the swelling went down and the stitches had more time to set. She wedged a blanket between his leg and the crate to make him comfortable.

When she hopped down from the wagon, she faced a hard wall of deerskin-clad chest. Riapoke was back.

He silently draped a copper chain around her neck. An eagle pendent was suspended from it.

Agnes fingered the heavy chain, awash with the awareness of how close they stood to each other. His gift both thrilled and terrified her. From the way Chief Manteo had courted Rose, she understood its significance. He was publicly claiming her as the woman of his choice and inviting her to court him. The next move was up to her.

She was greatly moved by Riapoke's gift. It was far more than a trinket. The eagle was symbolic of the strength and cunning of Chief Manteo's tribe. It represented sharp-eyed vigilance and the swooping, unexpected attacks their warriors were so famous for in battle. Most of the Roanoke scouts and warriors bore a set of spread eagle wings tattooed across their chests or upper arms. And now it dangled from a copper chain atop Agnes's winter cloak. Next to her heart.

She raised her gaze to his, trying to thank him with her eyes, since her voice didn't seem to want to work.

"For Ann…nes."

Unsure if she'd ever heard him speak before, Agnes shivered with pleasure to hear her name spoken in his broken English and guttural baritone. She wished she had a gift for him in return. He was the one who'd saved her and not the other way around. Then again, she wasn't so sure his gift had anything at all to do with saving her so much as declaring his intentions to court. Her heartbeat sped as her womanly instincts and reservations unfurled inside her chest. She knew her response to his gift could set their fledgling relationship on an entirely new and different direction.

But which direction would it be? Which one *should* it be? Jane had instructed her to follow what was in her head and heart.

Clasping his gift in a gloved hand that shook, she tipped her head up to meet his gaze more fully. An energy she'd never known before coursed through her frame, making her knees weak. Even her smile felt shaky. A skilled conversationalist, she'd never searched so hard for the right thing to say.

"I thank you, Riapoke." As soon as the words left her, she wished she could call them back and come up with something more gracious and flowery to say. Something more than a simple thank you.

Riapoke struck his right fist over his heart, dark eyes locked intently on hers. Then he spun on his heel and left her.

She stared after him, perplexed. Was he pleased with her response to his gift or disappointed? The Natives were so hard to read. The encounter earned her an afternoon of further emotional unraveling as she pondered all the possible implications of Riapoke's gift. Did it mean they were now courting? Or did she have to do something in return to start the courting process? Did she want to court him? If so, she should end her unofficial courtship with Anthony with haste. But was it even necessary to end anything with Anthony, since they weren't formally courting to begin with?

Riapoke continued to watch her from a distance, which kept the awareness zinging between them at a powerful and breathtaking level.

The distraction made her clumsier than usual. Several times during their trek, she stumbled over the uneven terrain like a toddler learning to walk. It earned her no small amount of teasing from her fellow colonists. She blushed with embarrassment each time, knowing Riapoke was also a witness to her state of befuddlement.

When they stopped to eat their dinner rations of dried venison, Agnes's emotions were in such a dither she thought she might explode. She rushed over to Jane to share the news of Riapoke's gift and relate to her their short conversation.

Jane looked uncommonly satisfied with herself. "I am happy you've met a man unafraid to declare his intentions towards you. You deserve nothing less."

The strange new energy Agnes had been plagued with all afternoon coursed through her again, invigorating and weakening her at the same time. "Court me!" She'd feared Jane would say something along those lines. "But we just met. Today was the first time we ever spoke."

Jane pointed to the gift hanging around Agnes's neck. "Apparently you made a good impression."

"So you think I did the right thing?"

She looked puzzled.

"By accepting his gift?" Especially if it meant they were now courting. *Lord help me! What am I going to say to Anthony?* Dread filled her mouth at the thought, but she was compelled by her honor to make it clear to Anthony that she no longer intended to wait for him. Only then would she feel free to pursue this new relationship with Riapoke.

Jane sniffed. "Well, do you like his gift, or is it too savage for your tastes, princess?"

Agnes ran her fingers over the sturdy chain around her neck. It was nothing like the English accessories to which she was accustomed — brooches, pins, and ornamental watch fobs. The eagle pendent felt like more, like Riapoke had given her a piece of himself.

"I love it," she confessed.

"There's your answer." Jane ate the last bite of her dried strip of venison and licked her fingers. She tipped up her

Native water pouch made of animal skin and drank deeply. Afterwards, she wiped her mouth with the back of her hand. "You might want to square things off with Anthony, so he doesn't interfere."

Agnes nodded. She'd already made the decision to do so and was sick to her stomach about their coming confrontation. Something told her, he would not make it easy.

To her surprise, Anthony did not check on her until nightfall when they stopped for a few hours of sleep. Even then, he did not mention the ambush or her brush with death. His casual chatter in light of such serious events was downright irritating.

The moment he paused in his cheery accounting of his own afternoon, she drew a deep breath and plunged in. "We had a close call earlier today."

"Aye, but we triumphed. Providence was on our side." He tipped up his mug of ale and drank. With a sigh of sheer satisfaction, he leaned against a tree and closed his eyes.

"I trust you are uninjured?" she asked sharply. *It would be nice of you to inquire the same of me.*

"Not a scratch." He cracked his eyes open and offered her a cocky grin. "Fortunately, when these savages come at us in reasonable numbers, they are no match for our muskets." He patted the gun resting upright against his shoulder. "I very much look forward to building our new fort and mounting our cannons at each corner. Only then will I be able to rest easy at night again."

His use of the word *savages* rankled. No one, in Agnes's view, was any more savage than the Archbishop of Whitgift who'd forced them to flee England for fear of their lives and set them on their current course. His violent arrests and interrogations had born an alarming resemblance to the Spanish Inquisition.

Most disturbing at the moment, however, was the fact

that Anthony still had not asked about her wellbeing following the attempted attack on her earlier. Did he not care she would most surely have died without Riapoke's intervention?

"I, too, will rest easier once we are safely ensconced in a more fortified location," Agnes muttered. "For a few moments this afternoon, I did not think I would survive."

"'Tis why I insisted you carry a gun." Anthony's tone grew stiff. "For the times when I am unable to come to your aid. Like today." He pushed away from the tree and rose to his full height to scowl over her. "Why didn't you use it, Agnes? You could have died."

So he *had* witnessed the attack on her! "There was no time. The warrior leaped on me too quickly. If one of our Native friends had not come to my aid—"

"All that matters is you and Jane survived. As I said before, Agnes. Providence was on our side."

So Anthony was going to ignore Riapoke's part in the matter altogether? Agnes was disappointed. Couldn't he spare a drop of gratitude to the man who'd saved the woman everyone presumed he was courting? Or at least for saving a friend, if that's all Agnes was to him?

She parted her lips, struggling to think of a way to tell Anthony that she and Riapoke were now courting, but he was already striding away. Their conversation had not gone the least bit the way she planned.

Agnes wanted to scream in frustration.

CHAPTER 17: JEALOUSIES

*T*he night dipped to unbearably cold temperatures while Agnes was pitching her tent. She could not wait to get beneath the canvas to escape the worst of the wind. A shadow fell over her while she worked. She rocked back on weary heels and grew instantly alert. It was Riapoke.

"Good evening." She rose unsteadily, exhausted both physically and emotionally.

He held out a cloak of thick, white fur. Bear fur, if she wasn't mistaken. On a person of her stature, it would hang nearly to the ground and provide the most luxurious barrier against the cold. "'Tis absolutely beautiful!" *And warm as a thousand blazes, no doubt.* What she would not give to wear something so glorious and cozy. She raised her eyes to his, sheer longing clogging her throat.

"For Ann-nes." He stepped behind her to drape the marvelous garment around her shoulders.

"Oh, Riapoke!" she gasped. *Another gift!* Her heart spun in chaotic wheels of joy, an emotion which was soon replaced with dismay as a new thought struck her. Did Riapoke have any idea how poor she was? How little she had to offer a man of his stature? As a war chief to the Roanoke and Croatoan tribes, he was something akin to a nobleman whereas she was common born and working class.

"You . . . do . . . not . . . like?"

"Oh, yes!" She exclaimed and hugged the ends of the precious garment tighter around her. "I love it!"

The tightness of his jaw relaxed, and the glint of pleasure infused his dark gaze.

Her heartbeat increased. It was a novel experience to bask beneath such guileless admiration. He made her feel desirable and utterly cherished, but she did not wish to take advantage of his generosity. Somehow he needed to be made to understand what desperate little she had to offer. There would be no reciprocal gifts and no dowry if he continued to pursue her.

She sought to explain. "'Tis the most wonderful gift anyone has ever given me. I only wish I had something to give you in return." Alas, she had nothing. *Other than a few spare outfits and my apothecary equipment.* "Plus, if you keep giving me gifts, people will talk." *Ugh! They were already talking. And pointing. And speculating.* "They will, er, think that you and I are . . ." She stopped, wondering if he understood a word she was saying.

Riapoke's expression did not change. When she fell silent, however, he held out his hand to her.

Unsure of his intent, she clasped it.

He enclosed her much smaller hand in both of his. "Let . . . them . . . talk." He bowed over her hand in the manner of an English gentleman.

Why, his response implied he understood every word she said! She wanted to melt straight to the ground at his saucy comeback. It was both humorous and wildly romantic. *Mercy!* She was close to swooning.

She placed her other hand atop his.

The harshness of his features softened. He stepped closer and bent his head. His lips touched hers, warm and reverent. Something powerful passed between them. Something that made her weak and strong at the same time. Something that made her long for things she'd all but stopped dreaming of ever finding in the harsh New World.

"Oh, Agnes!" The female voice jolted her from the blissful cocoon Riapoke had spun around her. It was Emme, flying in their direction.

"Pray forgive me for not helping put up the tent. I—" She skidded to a halt as she noted Riapoke's presence. Her eyes widened as they fell on their clasped hands "Oh," she murmured, backing away. "I, ah, did not mean to interrupt."

Agnes hastily disengaged her hands from Riapoke's. "Have you met?" Her head spun dizzily between the two of them. "This is my friend, Emme. Emme, this is Riapoke." *My new suitor.* Her face felt as hot as freshly stirred coals.

A smile spread across her wide features. "Ah, the one who saved you today. I am so grateful." She held out both hands to him. "Thank you for saving my friend. We are forever in your debt."

He briefly clasped her hands and bowed, but his smoldering gaze quickly returned to Agnes.

"Technically, Agnes is the one in your debt," she amended slyly. "According to our traditions, when a person saves your life, they belong to you 'til the end of their days or until the debt can be repaid."

The thought of belonging to a man like Riapoke was heady, indeed. He was so big and dangerous looking. So unlike the Englishmen of Agnes's acquaintance. Amazingly fast on his feet for a man his size. Skilled enough with his weapons to both take and spare lives. Wildly generous with his gifts and desperately tender with his kisses.

Agnes could hardly breathe beneath the warm possession glowing in his eyes.

Faith! How much of Emme's words did he understand?

She was dying to know if he believed she belonged to him.

---

*A*gnes kept the new fur cloak wrapped tightly around her beneath her blankets and slept better than she had since she'd departed England. She dreamt Riapoke was with her, holding her close and warming her with his enormous frame and gentle hands. Nuzzling her neck and whispering words to her in a language she could not understand. She had no trouble understanding the passion thickening his voice, however. She tipped her face up to his, wanting, seeking, claiming — as Jane insisted — was hers for the taking.

"Agnes?" Emme cried in alarm.

Agnes sat up with a yelp of surprise, face flaming and heart pounding as she faced her tent mate.

"Are you well, my friend?" Emme whispered in the dark.

Agnes gulped and nodded, pressing a hand to her rapidly rising and falling chest. "Just a dream, 'tis all." But her voice shook. She'd kissed two other men in her life and neither had stirred her this way. Neither had created such a sense of urgency as Riapoke had in her arms and in her dreams, such a wild longing for more, such a burning to discover and experience and live. *Heaven help me!*

She forced herself to lie down, but she was unable to fall asleep again.

Come morning, she met Riapoke's gaze across the camp as she and her companions tore down their tents. A knowing flame burned deep in his eyes. Her insides wrenched into a tight snarl of responding emotions. Oh, where was her practicality? Her composure? Her sense of reason? All of it seemed to evaporate when she was in Riapoke's presence. She no longer knew herself, what was up or down, what was left or right. She only knew she wanted to be with him. And what was a girl to do about such feelings out here on the open trail?

Were the feelings even real? Or were they a figment of her highly active imagination? Built on her intense desire to fall in love rather than on the cold reality that lay before them? Were her feelings merely some sort of emotional escape from the daily trauma they all suffered? What else could explain this inexplicable and sudden attraction to a man she'd just met?

She and Riapoke continued their dance of gazes for the next several days. He managed to find several opportunities to accost her, too, where they continued to speak haltingly to each other. They employed much sign language to communicate due to the enormous language barrier separating them. He impressed her as a man of few words, to begin with, so his efforts to get to know her better were that much more remarkable. Though she enjoyed every stolen moment with him, what was happening between them didn't seem to require many words. There was a special empathy and understanding that simply charged the air each time they were together.

He made an effort to sit beside her at meal times as often as possible, selecting the best of the rations and offering them silently to her. The colonists avoided her altogether when Riapoke was present, except for Emme. *Bless her!* Sometimes she joined Agnes and Riapoke for a meal when her beau, Mark Bennett, was on patrol. Though her shy and quiet personality added little to their already sparse conversations, Agnes very much appreciated her friend's support and acceptance. Despite the distance it created between her and the other English colonists, Agnes thoroughly enjoyed Riapoke's attentions. Being with him made her happier than she'd ever been before.

Her longing to get to know him better led her to teach him more English words, using much sign language to explain what they meant and thereby expand his limited vocabulary. He did the same with his native tongue, and she began to learn Powhatan. They passed many happy encounters practicing their newly learned phrases on each other. Meanwhile, her heart spun and flipped a thousand times each time their fingers, arms, or shoulders brushed.

One evening near nightfall, Anthony and Riapoke approached Agnes at the same time while she was raising her tent. At the sight of Anthony, Riapoke paused his advance, remaining in the tree line, arms crossed, watching them.

"You and that savage have been cozy for days," Anthony noted coolly. "I know you have the kindest heart in the world, Agnes, but people are starting to talk."

"That savage?" Her brows shot up. "If you are referring to the man who saved my life, he has a name. It's Riapoke."

"Of course he has a name. I fail to see your point."

"He is a good man, Anthony. Pray do not speak ill of him."

"Saving your life doesn't give him the right to come between us," Anthony growled.

"How is that possible?" Agnes raised her chin. "Are you saying we are no longer friends?"

"You know what I mean."

"Nay, Anthony, I do not," she admitted sadly. "There was a time I hoped we would become more." Faith, this conversation was turning out to be every bit as difficult as she imagined during the dozens of times she'd practiced it in her head. "I reckon it wasn't meant to be." There. She'd stated her mind at last. Jane would be proud.

His brows flew up. "On the contrary, I would argue that

what we have between us is *very* special. I care for you, Agnes."

Alas, you do not love me. She'd known it in her heart for some time, but his words confirmed it. She drew a deep breath, trying to choose her words carefully. "I care for you, too, Anthony. Very much." It was true. "We've been through so much together. I could not have made it this far without you, Rose, Manteo, and Jane. Any more than I would have survived the past few days without Riapoke." Faith! She wouldn't be standing in front of him, having this conversation if it weren't for the swift actions of her gallant rescuer.

CHAPTER 18: GOOD INTENTIONS

*A*nthony's curled lip indicated he wasn't ready to acknowledge Riapoke's contribution with any benevolence. He was silent for several moments, his expression growing colder by degrees. "I begin to worry you have forgotten our mission, Agnes," he said at last. "How we came here to colonize all lands not claimed by any Christian prince. To build the first permanent English settlement. To educate and convert the indigenous peoples."

"Indeed, I have not forgotten," she responded tartly. "We made our first convert when Chief Manteo declared his allegiance to both the Crown and our God upon his arrival. Afterwards, he was declared Lord of Roanoke and Dasmonquepeuc in the name of our Queen. I think we can both agree he has been our greatest ally ever since." Their only true ally, if they were being perfectly honest with each other.

"Aye, and he wasted no time helping himself to an English bride."

"Why, Anthony!" His sarcasm was shocking. All this time, she'd presumed he and Manteo were friends. "It was a most welcome surprise when he fell in love with our Rose and she with him. Their marriage formed a much needed alliance between our people."

"What about Chief Wanchese? I suppose you found his marriage to Jane another *much needed alliance?* I reckon he fills that role nice enough, if one overlooks his coarse manners and brutish ways. Oh, and the fact he's not once bothered to attend our devotionals. Don't you see what a downward spiral this path is taking us?"

"Nay, I do not." Agnes was incredulous at Anthony's narrow-minded view on the topic of their allies. It was a side of him she had not seen before and did not like. "We sailed to the New World to follow our convictions. Now that we are here, we can and should share our faith with others, but that is all. Afterwards, every man must follow his own convictions. To try and dictate otherwise would make us no better than the ones who sought our arrests back in England."

"I could not disagree more," Anthony cut in vehemently, swiping the air as if to brush away her words. "Manteo may be an exception because he attempts to honor our God and carry himself like a gentleman, but the rest of them are heathens, Agnes. Wanchese, Riapoke, the whole lot of them! They make no attempt to share our faith. This you cannot deny."

She plopped her hands on her hips. "Oh, but I do deny it. There is good in them, even if their customs are different from ours. Much good that you refuse to see." His callus dismissal of so many of her new friends infuriated her. "Do you really believe Jane would love Chief Wanchese to distraction and marry him if his soul was as dark as you claim?"

"We digress," he seethed between clenched teeth. "I am merely trying to point out the dangerous path you walk while allowing Riapoke to pursue you."

"How so?" she demanded.

145

Anthony jerked as if receiving a blow. He drew a heavy breath. "So you admit he is courting you?"

She lowered her arms to her sides. "That's what this whole conversation is really about, isn't it? Riapoke's interest in me."

"I though *I* was courting you."

"Are you?" she retorted, affronted by his attempt to make her feel like the guilty party in this matter. It was his lack of commitment to their relationship that had led to them going their separate ways. "'Tis news to me, as I cannot recall you once declaring your feelings on the matter."

He closed his eyes for an extended moment then reopened them. "I kissed you. Several times."

"So did the Viscount of Habbershire. A man who placed a ring on my hand and publicly announced his intentions to marry me, yet he never once spoke of love, either."

"Love?" Anthony's brows rose in surprise. "Why, good marriages are built on common," he paused, his gaze narrowing on her as if just then remembering she could boast neither wealth nor titles, "beliefs and interests. Many times they result in deep and abiding adoration. Not necessarily right away, but over time. You see? Love is not the only factor to consider in a marriage."

Agnes could not believe what she was hearing. She held common beliefs and interests with most of the colonists — both male and female, old and young. It was certainly not enough to base a marriage on. Without love, she could see no reason whatsoever to court a man.

When was Anthony finally going to accept the fact they'd been stripped of nearly everything the moment they reached the New World? His English title meant nothing here. They'd been entirely cut off from their families back home. He would never see his money and possessions again. All they had left was each other, yet he still wasn't willing to give her his heart.

"My parents married for love," Agnes declared softly. "They shared everything with each other and held nothing back — their faith, their hopes, their dreams. I cannot imagine settling for anything less."

"What are you saying, Agnes?" Anthony's features tightened.

"When I court and when I marry, it will be for love. Nothing less."

"I see." He looked troubled. "I know we were raised under a very different set of circumstances, you and I, but you've always carried yourself in such a manner that, well, I presumed it meant we share more of the same views on things."

"In what manner do I carry myself?" Agnes braced for another barrage of his lordly condescension. She could only blame herself for not seeing his shortcomings before now. Rose had tried to warn her many times that their differences would eventually come between them.

He waved a hand in impatience. "You speak and carry yourself like a lady, of course. One of culture and good breeding. That is all I meant."

"And I am no longer those things, in your eyes, because we do not share the same views on love and marriage?" She was aghast.

"Nay, I did not say that precisely."

Not precisely? She felt her face turn red. So she was less of a lady in his eyes, because she longed to be loved. What a ludicrous position to hold! She wanted to slap him.

Anthony cleared his throat. "I dare say, we will disagree on a good many points during our courtship."

She stared at him, aghast. He still anticipated a future for them together? It was unfathomable after the conversation they'd just shared, yet — she stared harder at him — it was true. He beheld her with a contented and satisfied air. *What a jumble!*

"But first," he continued. "We must establish our colony. At the moment, I am naught but a man with a few friends, small pile of travel bags, and a handful of coins in a bank back in London. I have much yet to accomplish before I can take on the responsibilities of a wife and any offspring that result from our happy union."

It was insult upon injury for him to presume she would continue to lap up whatever crumbs of hope he tossed in her direction. He had no interest in taking on a wife anytime soon. Possibly for years to come. Faith, she might be too old to bear children by the time the man made up his mind!

"If you are willing to wait, Agnes." His voice turned tender. "It is my dearest hope we will pursue the future I dream of. Together."

Agnes's jaw dropped at Anthony's odd and unexpected marriage proposal. Of sorts. She'd dreamed of hearing those words from him for so many months, but they'd come too late.

Nay, she could not give him the answer he wanted. Not this evening. Not ever. But the pleading in his gaze tore at her so much that she found herself mentally scrambling for a way to ease her coming rejection.

"I will consider your request." It was the best answer she could give him, and she only extended it out of respect for their past friendship, for the many life and death challenges they'd endured together. She would somehow come up with the right words to refuse his proposal on the morrow.

"Then I shall live in hope of an affirmative answer from you. Very soon."

Agnes's heart sank. *May the good Lord forgive me for extending the man false hope!* Jane sure wouldn't. She was going to shoot Agnes when she told her she had failed to end all romantic ties with Anthony tonight.

Too mentally and physically exhausted to continue their verbal sparring, she eyed him wearily, more than ready for him to take his leave. "'Tis been a long day for both of us," she said gently. "Goodnight, Anthony."

He nodded uncertainly and walked away, head lowered in thought. She watched him, furious with herself for not having the courage to speak more plainly. She was the world's worst cad for allowing things to drag along like this.

For so many months she had longed for him to declare his feelings for her. Well, this had certainly turned out to be one of those *be careful what you wish for* situations. She could see no graceful way out of it, either, not without hurting Anthony deeply. Even though she wasn't in love with him, she valued their friendship and deplored the thought of losing it, altogether. What a muddle!

Needing a moment to herself, she paced away from her tent, hands clasped tightly behind her back. Since the Native scouts were on patrol, she felt safe enough to stroll along the tree line.

"Ann-nes?"

Riapoke's low baritone startled her. "I— Oh!" She tried to offer him a smile, but she was unsure if she succeeded. He was such a kind man, such a good person; he deserved better than her company. Yet there she stood before him, a hopeless tangle of complicated emotions. Wildly attracted to him but not truly free to pursue those feelings. She blinked hard a few times, trying to stifle the rush of self-pitying tears that rose inside her. Alas, one traitorous droplet broke loose and streaked coldly down her face.

She raised her bruised gaze and heart to his, wishing their circumstances were different. Why couldn't they have met on a sunny day in June? During one of his tribe's famed celebration feasts, perhaps? She would have been in high spirits, wearing one of her best dresses, and...

She caught her breath as Riapoke beheld her with the same steady expression he always wore around her — tender and patient. Tonight it was full of understanding and empathy, as well. He removed his glove and reached out to brush her tear away with a callused thumb. His hand lingered on her face to tuck a loose strand of hair behind her ear. Then he adjusted her hood, pulling it more snugly over her head.

Her heart was too full for words, so she offered him a look of gratitude instead. The difference between the way he wooed her and the way Anthony had attempted to woo her were worlds apart. She'd spent the past several months trying to prove she was good enough for Anthony, whereas Riapoke had spent their much shorter time together looking out for her safety and trying to prove his worth to her.

The cold fingers of hurt gripping her heart slowly uncurled themselves. How could a woman fail to blossom beneath such pure intentions? It was such a welcome change in how any man had ever treated her. So unexpected, beautiful, and entirely wonderful.

She suddenly longed to throw herself into Riapoke's arms. She had no doubt he would welcome her there, hold her and cherish her, but she had no right to want such things. At least not yet. Not with Anthony's odd marriage proposal resting in the air between them. Anthony deserved a definitive answer before she allowed Riapoke to take his delightful courtship any further.

So she held back when Riapoke gazed deeply into her eyes, silently asking questions she could not answer tonight.

After several moments of silence, he released his hold on the ties of her hood and strode away.

It was if he understood she was not ready. She wanted to weep as his tall, broad shoulders disappeared in the night. Lord help her, she had bungled things with both men tonight. If she continued along this broken course, she would be a spinster on the proverbial shelf in no time.

CHAPTER 19: NEW WOUNDS

*A*gnes rose to another day of ever increasing cold and driving winds. It was late mid-November, but it felt more like December or January.

The scouts returned from their mid-morning patrol and declared they were less than twenty miles from their final destination. They would push to arrive there in time to pitch their tents before nightfall. The ranks of colonists broke into more chatter than usual. A few men danced jigs and women swung each other around and around in hugs. The lads skipped and scampered about. Even Valentine, the lads' mastiff, seemed to pick up on the excitement, offering a few excited yips and barks. All creatures both human and canine were summarily hushed by the Native scouts. Nevertheless, the sense of joviality stayed with them as they plodded forward.

Maybe the excitement in the air made them less vigilant than usual? They would question themselves for days afterward. All Agnes knew was no one saw the party of hostiles before they sprang on the caravan.

She did not recognize any of their faces, but she would be

willing to wager they were slavers from farther inland because of the captives they held chained and standing silently just inside the tree line.

The Englishmen fired their muskets while their Native comrades notched and let their arrows fly. In the end, their combined troops offered more resistance than their attackers expected, because they quickly fled with their original captives in tow. The Englishmen pursued them, shooting their muskets until they were out of sight.

In shock, the colonists reassembled themselves to assess their newest injuries. Most of the men waved away Agnes's assistance, wrapping their own scrapes and cuts with odd and end bits of cloth. The biggest hue and cry came from a huddle of Native women. Half a dozen hovered over a prostrate man. Agnes shuddered and forced her feet into motion, praying it wasn't Riapoke, Manteo, or Wanchese.

Jane stood as Agnes approached, waving her forward frantically. "Come quickly! Riapoke is hurt."

Dread sealed Agnes's throat, immobilizing her for a handful of seconds, but Jane's sharply repeated command jolted her back into motion.

"Hurry!" Jane ran forward to grab her arm and pull her to Riapoke's side.

Every step was filled with fear.

Frowning and muttering, the Native women reluctantly parted to allow Jane and Agnes access to their fallen war chief.

He lay silently on the ground, grim-faced and eyes glazed with pain. An arrow was lodged in his mid-section.

"Oh, dear God!" Agnes slid bonelessly to her knees. "Riapoke."

He blinked and affixed his gaze on her face, eyes sharpening to full awareness. "Ann-nes." He reached for her hand.

The relief and trust in his expression took her breath

away. She squeezed his fingers. "I am going to examine your wound and remove the arrow." *Please, God, do not let it be tipped with poison like the enemy's arrows so often are.* She tried to take heart in the fact Riapoke was still conscious, not writhing in the dance of death. It had to be a good sign. It had to be, or she was suddenly no longer certain she wanted to keep living.

Riapoke shivered as she lifted his tunic. The winds were picking up again.

"Bring me my aid bag," she shouted to no one in particular, "and build a fire, for Heaven's sake, lest he freeze while I remove the arrow."

To her enteral gratitude, Jane took charge and bade her maidens to speedily construct one of their marvelous teepees right atop them. She did not have to move Riapoke an inch. In a matter of minutes, a fire was blazing beside them, and Natives were gently shoving a roll of cloth beneath their beloved war counselor's head.

"Bless you." She nodded her thanks to each of them.

She reached for her scissors and cut straight through Riapoke's tunic to where the arrow was embedded. She peeled back the fabric. He was a beautiful creature. All coppery gold and corded with strength.

She was relieved to note there was not a great deal of blood oozing. By her best estimate, the arrow was sunk a good three or four inches. It was at an odd angle as if he had turned at the last second in the attempt to avoid its deadly strike. As a result, the arrow had caught the left side of his midriff. There was a chance it was nothing more than a flesh wound. Agnes's lips moved in a silent prayer that it had missed all vital organs.

Because it was not a through-and-through shot, she would have to cut out the arrowhead and stitch up the wound. One could not simply pull out an arrowhead backwards. The risk of an ensuing infection and fever were high.

"Set some water to boiling," Agnes beseeched, while uncapping her last small flask of wine. She tipped it against the edge of Riapoke's mouth. Without removing his gaze from her face, he drank and grimaced slightly. She bade him down most of the flask and prayed it would be enough.

Swabbing the site of the wound with a damp cloth, she produced a scalpel and one of her cylindrical biting sticks.

"*Tah.*" Riapoke pressed her hand against his lips in a gesture that could only be described as affectionate, then pushed the biting stick away.

Puzzled, she tried again to insert the stick in his mouth, demonstrating with her own teeth how he should bite down on it.

"*Tah!*" he repeated more firmly this time.

"It means no," Jane explained gently from the fire she manned. "Fear not. He will neither move nor cry out during the procedure."

"How can you be sure?" Agnes's voice trembled in agony.

"Because he is a warrior," Rose declared from the doorway, raising a lantern in one hand, "one who happens to trust you and your skills implicitly."

Agnes wanted to sob with relief at the sight of Rose's dear red head and slender frame that was swollen with her unborn babe.

Both Rose and Jane had assisted Agnes in the sick bay during their trans-Atlantic journey. It was a great comfort to have them both present now.

"He also bears the stripes of the Sun Dance on his back," Jane added. "I will tell you all about it. Later, of course. Suffice to say they further prove his bravery and resilience." She offered Agnes a cheeky grin. "No doubt you will have the opportunity to view his stripes for yourself some day soon."

"Jane!" Agnes gasped.

But her friend's sass had the affect of calming her enough to do what she needed to do. "Forgive me, my friend," she whispered to Riapoke as she prepared to make the incision.

"Ann-nes," he rasped again.

She winced as she broke the skin with her scalpel. She knew he had to be in horrible pain, but the complete trust in his gaze steadied her and gave her the strength to go on.

His breath shortened as she slid her narrow knife blade along the shaft of the arrow, pressing deeper in order to reach the tip of the arrow. Jane bent over Riapoke to swab the blood so Agnes could more easily continue to work. Rose kept the lantern suspended directly above her hands.

At one point Riapoke grunted softly and tensed his legs but not once did he try to move away from the scalpel. Mercy, but the arrowhead was embedded even farther than Agnes had first estimated, at least five inches. The man must have been afire with agony by the time she fully exposed the stony tip. Her own agony was at a screaming level.

She removed the arrow and poured the last few droplets of wine in the open wound.

Riapoke sucked in a breath but still did not move.

Jane continued to swab blood, while Agnes began the more laborious task of stitching. Fortunately, she was dealing with two perfectly straight flaps of skin, because it was mostly her own incision she was knitting together. It took no more than a handful of minutes.

"There." She raised anxious eyes to Riapoke's face, biting her lower lip.

He was gazing at her with awe and something more. "*Wironausqua crenepo*," he murmured, reaching for her hand and pressing it once more to his lips.

Agnes looked at Jane for help.

She glanced away and cleared her throat. "I'm not certain

of the exact translation, but I think he called you a queen among women, *his* queen."

"Oh," Agnes breathed. Her hands trembled as she covered his wound with a fresh white bandage.

He arched his back just enough to help her wind another strip of cloth around his abdomen to hold the bandage in place.

She clasped his hand afterward. "You are by far the bravest patient I have ever treated." She blinked back tears.

Several Natives lingered, but Rose and Jane said their goodbyes as soon as they perceived they were no longer needed. "I shall check on the two of you every hour," Jane promised.

Rose nodded vehemently. "Fetch me as well if you need anything."

Both women took turns bending to hug her.

"I do not know what the propriety is in this situation, but 'tis best I do not leave him tonight," Agnes confided to them worriedly. "If a fever sets in..." Her voice broke, and she dared not finish the sentence, not wanting to even contemplate such a thing.

"A pox on anyone who wants to carp about your treatment of an injured man," Jane declared scathingly. "He is fortunate to be alive. If he makes it through the night without a fever, you may consider him fully repaid for saving your own hide a few days ago."

Rose wrinkled her forehead. "No doubt you are worried the colonists will complain when you do not return to their side of camp." Her gaze narrowed fiercely. "Perhaps this is not the answer you seek, but I've long endured their criticism. It only matters if you let it." Indeed, she had been the first in their colony to marry a Native and now carried his child. Their union had made her the queen of her husband's tribe, but it had also made her a social outcast with the English.

Agnes's gaze returned to Riapoke's glazed and trusting one. "Very well. I shall stay." She owed him no less for saving her life. "I thank you for your council on the matter." She shot a grateful smile to her friends for their support of her decision and gently squeezed Riapoke's hand.

Shortly after the women left, Chief Manteo and Chief Wanchese paid a visit. They spoke in low tones to the man they knew as cousin and brother, respectively. Riapoke unabashedly refused to let go of her hand during the entire conversation.

Though both men subjected Agnes to varying degrees of curious scrutiny, making her blush, neither was hostile in expression or stance. For that she was grateful. As they left the teepee, they commanded the last of the lingering Natives to depart with them, leaving her alone with Riapoke.

She continued to hold his hand. As the day deepened into evening, she passed the time by talking, describing her parents and childhood and all the circumstances leading her here to him. She held nothing back, telling him both the good and the bad, the joyous and the heart-wrenching.

At one point, he laced his fingers through hers and shut his eyes, but she could tell he was still listening because his breathing did not deepen into slumber. It was the most wonderful feeling to be with him. To just be.

For the first time since leaving England, Agnes was at peace.

CHAPTER 20: THE KISS

*J*ane returned once an hour as promised until nightfall. She came bearing a food tray during the dinner hour. "The Roanokes and Croatoans absolutely refuse to continue our journey until the morrow. The English are furious, but the Natives will not budge. Riapoke is too important to them, and they fear moving him tonight. They have their scouts scouring every inch of the countryside for any sign of trouble. So far, it appears blessedly clear of marauders."

She took her leave, and Agnes proceeded to feed Riapoke. He kissed her hand after each bite.

She blushed and wondered how much the wine had to do with his incessant show of endearments.

Darkness fell, and her eyelids grew heavy. Riapoke, who was unbelievably still awake, tugged at her hand and motioned for her to lie down on the furs beside him. Since they had no audience, she was more than happy to comply. She pulled the fur blankets over them and rested her cheek on the outstretched arm of his uninjured side.

Agnes was a mass of tingling nerves at being so close to

him. Her heart raced, and her mouth grew dry. She was small compared to him, yet they seemed to fit perfectly. She rested a hand on his chest, a bold move for her. He covered it with his own, and it was the last thing she remembered.

Her dreams were anything but calm. In them, she was pressing closer to Riapoke, wanting more and craving more. Much more. His eyes opened and widened in surprise. Joy quickly overcame his surprise. He turned his head and captured her mouth.

The depth of emotion in his kiss shook her. His habitually stoic expression had given her no indication of the many layers of passion lying just beneath the surface. For a man who'd been shot only hours earlier, he was remarkably eager and astoundingly energetic.

When Riapoke deepened the kiss, she tasted restless desire and a need that matched her own.

Agnes cuddled closer, pressing her palm to his scarred cheek, heart thudding with wonder.

A moan roused her from her slumber. To her shock, she could still feel Riapoke's hot mouth on hers. It took her a moment to discern why. *Because we are actually kissing!*

With a cry of astonishment, she drew back.

He gazed at her in the dying firelight, eyes smoldering with promise. "Ann-nes. *Nouwmais*," he said huskily.

She did not know the meaning of the word but recognized it as an endearment. "Riapoke," she whispered, unable to form any other coherent words. She had lain beside him and kissed him like she had never kissed another man before. Like a lover.

It changed their relationship. Dramatically. According to English standards, she was thoroughly compromised and honor bound to marry him. She had no idea what the Native custom was in a situation like theirs. All she knew was, her reputation would be completely ruined in the eyes of her countrymen if anyone discovered what had just transpired between them.

Riapoke's eyes burned so brightly Agnes feared a fever was setting in, but his gaze was steady and his skin was a wonderfully even temperature when she pressed the back of her hand to his cheeks and forehead.

As far as his injury was concerned, he was fine. More than fine. The danger was past. She could safely leave him now and return to her own tent. Probably the wisest course of action before things waxed out of control between them.

"I must leave," she whispered, "but I will check on you first thing in the morning to change your bandage."

"*Nouwmais*," he said thickly and pulled her head down to his for another hot, branding kiss.

It was with great reluctance, she pulled back. "I must go, my love."

My love. Lord help her, she had just declared her love for him, and it was true. She was in love! The revelation shook and stunned her.

What was happening between her and Riapoke defied all logic. It was also happening much faster than she intended. She'd not yet broken things off with Anthony as she should have. Lord help her, but nothing was going as planned.

She desperately needed a few moments alone to collect her scattered emotions, to make sense of what was happening, to just breathe.

Agnes stirred the fire and added another log to keep it going. Then, with one last astounded look at Riapoke, she lifted the flap of his tent and carefully glanced in all directions. In the distance, she could see the silhouette of the English night watchmen with their muskets in hand as they pulled guard around the perimeter. No one else stirred. Even Valentine was asleep, curled next to Blade whose bedroll rested near the remains of a campfire.

She crept towards her tent and was nearly there when Margaret's voice stopped her.

"You've been with the one they call Riapoke, have you not? For hours." Her voice was an angry hiss, her pinched features as shriveled as an old crone in the moonlight.

Burn it all! Margaret was the last person on earth Agnes wanted to speak to at the moment. She slowly raised her gaze to the angry woman's face. Distaste churned her insides. "I've been sitting with him, yes. Watching for any sign of a fever. It is my hope he is past the danger point, but only time will tell." Agnes bit her lip. Her words sounded like nervous babbling, even to her own ears.

"Were you alone with him?"

"Only part of the time. Visitors came and went all evening."

"Were you alone with him just now?" Margaret's voice turned bitter. "Unchaperoned in the dead of night?"

"I do not care for where this conversation is headed," Agnes declared coldly. "I bid you goodnight."

"You *should* care," Margaret retorted, falling in step beside her.

Agnes stopped and placed her hands on her hips. "Why on earth, Margaret Lawrence, would you infer something so ill of me?"

"Because Lord Anthony Cage deserves better," she spat. "You are no better than Rose with the way she batted her lashes at every man who looked her way, from Reverend Cooper to Chief Manteo. According to rumor, she left a trail of broken hearts all the way from London to the New World."

"I cannot see how Rose's suitors have anything to do with me."

"I am trying to warn you." Margaret made a sound of frustration. "Do keep up. 'Tis foolish to risk your understanding with the good sheriff by so carelessly allowing that—that savage to follow you around like an adoring puppy. In case you've not heard, people are talking about the two of you."

So Anthony had said. Agnes sighed, not knowing how to respond.

"If you do not wish to have your name paired up with—"

"Not another word about Riapoke. Please." Agnes held up a hand. "A few days ago, he saved my life. Tonight, I was able to return the favor by tending his injuries. If anyone finds fault with that, then shame on them." *And shame on you.* Agnes reached for her tent flap.

"I find no fault with your doctoring skills." Margaret's tone was long-suffering, as if she was being forced to explain something complicated to a small child. "'Tis your ill judgment I worry about. To allow that savage to court you is foolhardy. You need to put an end to it before he ruins everything between you and Anthony, and that is all I have to say on the matter." She nudged Agnes aside none too gently and crawled in the tent ahead of her.

Agnes rolled her eyes, unsure if she'd ever met a more unpleasant person. Margaret was as sour as lemons. It was no wonder she possessed no beau of her own.

Agnes yanked open the tent flap and lowered herself on her bedroll. With nothing but the heat of four bodies to warm their tent, it was desperately cold. If it were not for Riapoke's gift of a fur cloak, she would surely have turned into an icicle.

Margaret's chattering teeth on the other side of Emme made Agnes feel guilty at her disgruntled feelings towards the woman. She could hardly blame Margaret for their collective misery. There was precious little in their situation to rejoice about. They were freezing, their food was running out, and they lived in constant fear of attack. Death loomed behind every shadow. At least Agnes's troubled pair of courtships offered some modicum of diversion from their plight.

Margaret had no such diversions.

Agnes really needed to make more of an effort to be nice to her. Maybe if she tried harder to befriend Margaret, the woman would be less inclined to spread gossip about her — the kind of gossip, most unfortunately, that could ruin her reputation with the colonists.

*A*gnes slept longer than she meant to and awoke to the bustle of breaking camp and hitting the road.

"Oh, no," she breathed. *Riapoke.* She needed to change his bandage. She hastily made some order out of her tangled hair and tried to smooth the wrinkles from her travel dress. It had been too cold to do anything but sleep fully clothed. Thankfully, her fur coat covered most of the wrinkles.

"I'll be back in a wink," she promised her tent mates. "I am off to check on my patient."

Margaret muttered something under her breath that Agnes did not fully understand, but she managed to catch the words, "no help with the tent as usual" and was relieved her grumbling was on a safer topic than the one they'd discussed the night before.

Aye, there was a chance Agnes would not return in time to help break down the tent, and who cared? It hardly required four grown women to accomplish such a simple task, and it would get their blood moving in the process. It wasn't as if Agnes was contributing nothing at all to their mission. Every time she tended the sick or injured, she was doing her part. With a self-righteous huff, she snatched up her aid bag and went in search of Riapoke.

CHAPTER 21: COLD SHOULDER

*R*iapoke was fully dressed and standing outside his tent, conferring with several other men in Chief Wanchese's council. He caught sight of Agnes and took his leave of them.

"Good morning," she greeted breathlessly, blushing at the way his features lit at her approach. "I need to change your bandage." She held up a roll of white cloth in case he did not understand.

"*Tah.*" He held up a hand. "It…is done."

She frowned. "Someone else changed your bandage?"

"*Cuppeh.*" He rolled up the lower part of his tunic to reveal a series of thick leather straps wrapped around him.

Since no blood or streaks of infection showed and he seemed blessedly free of fever, she could only nod. "Are you in any pain?" It troubled her to know he had several miles to march this morning, despite his injury.

Riapoke shrugged and reached for her hand.

Though she clasped it, she could feel the eyes of her fellow colonists on them and took a step back, unwittingly extending his arm from his body.

He winced as the movement no doubt pulled at his stitches.

"I must go." Regret thickened her voice. "But I will check on you again. Soon."

Confusion clouded his gaze for a moment and was gone. He bowed over her hand in the English manner and released her hand. His face was several degrees paler when he straightened.

Agnes was furious with herself for causing him more pain, both externally and internally. She should beg his forgiveness and give him more of her time and respect, but he was already striding away.

---

*A*gnes watched Riapoke discreetly as they began the final day of their long march inland. By the stiffness of his movements, she imagined he was in a great deal of pain. Despite her promise to check on him, she was too mortified by their encounter that morning to bring herself to approach him when they broke for an early lunch. She watched one of the elders light a pipe and pass it to him. He puffed on it awhile, ate his lunch rations, and puffed on it some more.

He swayed unsteadily when he stood to resume their march. Agnes covered her mouth with a hand until he righted himself and returned the pipe to the councilman. *Drat his pride!* The man should be riding on one of the wagons. She was going to tell him right away, and let the world think what they wanted about her interactions with him. But it was too late.

The Dares were calling for the colonists to resume their march. Dozens of other people filled the terrain between her and Riapoke, making her lose sight of him.

Within the next hour, the river they marched along widened into a V shape. They had arrived, at last, to their long-anticipated destination. Agnes gazed in curiosity and awe at the lush terrain of the delta where the Roanoke and Chowan rivers converged. Despite the lateness of the year, long green grasses swayed in the breezes along the banks.

The delta stretched before her eyes, rich and fertile, and delightfully unoccupied. Beyond it, the ground rose into a series of rolling hills. The lower grounds proved damp and spongy to the step, but the higher grounds the colonists excitedly deemed firm enough for building.

The Dares laid claim to the tallest hill inland on which to build the new English fort where they would mount the four cannons. Already, they were calling it Fort Chowan. This would place the English colonists on the southernmost section of their combined new settlement. Chief Manteo and his Croatoans chose the central hill to commence setting up their tents and longhouses. Chief Wanchese and his Roanoke tribe did the same on the next adjoining hill, placing them in the northernmost part of the settlement.

The tentative agreement was that the three groups would jointly inhabit the delta for the winter. Come spring, it was generally understood that the Roanokes would relocate to a more remote location. They did not care to live so close to the English for any longer length of time. Chief Manteo, however, indicated he would not mind continuing the alliance if the joint colonization efforts proved successful through the winter.

Agnes couldn't help wondering what Riapoke would choose to do. Would he move away with the Roanokes, come spring, or continue to serve as war chief to the Croatoans, alone? According to Jane, his services as a councilman had been shared between the two tribes for several years.

The Dares set the Englishmen to work digging an earthen

fort. Other men began the laborious process of hewing trees and cutting logs and planks with which to build cabins. The women went to work pitching tents and foraging for food.

When Agnes passed by a pair of Croatoan maidens foraging for fallen tree nuts, she overheard their furious muttering. She had no idea what they were saying, only that they were angry. When they looked up and saw her, they paused their work and glared. Then they yanked up their baskets and spun on their heels, leaving her alone.

What was all that about? She stared after them in surprise. Though she and her fellow Englishwomen foraged for hours, they came up with only a minimal supply of roots, dried berries, and nuts.

Agnes took a break from her work and ventured over to the Croatoan hill mid-afternoon to check on Rose in her tent. She discovered her protesting her husband's insistence that she lie down and rest.

"Chief Manteo is correct," Agnes announced from the doorway of their tent. "You should listen to him, my friend."

Manteo looked up with a relieved expression that turned wary at the sight of Agnes.

Rose scowled. "I am in the family way, which in no way makes me an invalid. There is much work to do, and none of it will get done with me lying here like some spoiled princess."

It was far from the truth, and they all knew it. The work would get done, thanks to the tireless efforts of the Roanoke maidens and braves.

"Nothing you accomplish will matter if something happens to you or your babe," Agnes returned evenly. "Fear not, Manteo. I will talk some sense into your lovely bride."

He searched her face for a moment. Looking satisfied, he nodded and left them together.

"You're a fine one to gang up on me." Rose turned away

from her, miffed, and snatched up a bit of mending. Shoving her needle in and out of the cloth, she muttered, "If I sit here stitching like a woman of leisure while the rest of the colony slaves away, they will lose respect for me. They will call me the weak Pale Face instead of the Princess of Croatoa. Not that you would understand." She shot Agnes a frustrated look. "You do not seem to care one whit what is said about *you*."

"Is that so, Madame Fussy Britches?" Agnes dropped to her knees beside her friend. "Explain yourself."

Rose's green eyes snapped with anger. "It hurts me to watch you toy with Riapoke's feelings the way you do. I thought you were better than that, Agnes."

"You think I'm toying with him?" she choked.

"You tell me." Rose's voice escalated to an angry pitch. "He is utterly besotted with you. 'Tis why he has spent the past several days courting you and giving you gifts. Everyone was exclaiming about how joyful you looked together. There was much speculation about a third match between the English and the Natives, before you suddenly turned a cold shoulder to him. They are greatly offended by what they perceive as a slight to one of their most beloved leaders. You must understand, he is like a lord to them. Like royalty."

Agnes turned red at her words. "It was never my intent to trifle with Riapoke's feelings. I care for him deeply."

"Then why—"

"Please let me explain!"

"I'm trying to!"

"I, er...Anthony finally proposed," Agnes blurted.

The sewing dropped unattended into Rose's lap. "When?"

"The night before Riapoke was shot. He says he is not ready to marry, that he wishes to get the colony planted and himself established before he takes on a wife, but he asked me to wait for him."

Rose's lip curled in disdain. "For how long?"

"As long as it takes, I suppose," she sighed.

"Do you love him enough to wait?"

"No, and there lies the problem. Out of respect for our longstanding friendship, I told Anthony I would consider his request instead of turning him down flat. I did not know what else to do. Alas, he deserves an answer before I can let anything come of Riapoke's courtship. Do you not agree?"

"Oh, Agnes!" Rose murmured. "I had no idea things had changed between you and Anthony."

"Dreadfully quick, and now I have no idea how to best end things between us. I fear losing his friendship forever. What should I do, my friend?"

"Do not wait," she instructed bluntly. "I know you care for Anthony, but waiting will not make the inevitable any easier. He wove his way into the affections of us all during our journey to the New World. He is a loyal friend, but I've long worried about whether he would make a good match for you."

"I know. You tried to warn me." Agnes blinked away the sting of tears. "I didn't want to listen before, but now I wish I had." She turned her blurry gaze to Rose. "Why, pray, were you so convinced Anthony and I would not suit?"

Rose sniffed. "He is too much of an English gentleman for your tastes. On the surface, it sounds like a compliment. Back in London, it *would* be a compliment. Here in the wilderness, though, not so much. Titles and positions, family names, and the accumulation of wealth? They still mean a great deal to him, even though they matter little on this side of the world. More importantly, they matter little to you."

"True." Agnes shook her head, offering her a sad smile, "yet he openly pursues both them and me. What am I to do?"

"You must follow your heart, of course. By now, you surely must realize the English may never succeed in establishing the colony they envisioned." Rose folded her hands in her lap. "With their dwindling numbers, I doubt they have enough people left to fill all the positions required to run such an organization."

"True. I will gladly settle for surviving the winter," Agnes confessed ruefully.

"Why settle?" Rose demanded sharply. "Why speak of settling when we can still establish something truly wonderful and worthwhile? A new kind of colony. A city built of both plank houses and Native longhouses. A city where two, three, or more languages are spoken. A city of many people from many cultures and many nations."

Agnes was surprised at the energy in her friend's voice, as well as the passion. Her words resonated deeply.

"You are right." Agnes spread her hands. "The colony you describe sounds like something worth fighting for." *Albeit a little too good to be true.* However, Rose's words gave Agnes hope. "If only our people would learn to work together, we could build such a place."

"Yes, we can." Rose's voice was firm and cool, as if discerning Agnes's doubts. "We will. Then what?" she persisted. "Will Anthony finally be ready to marry you? Or will he continue to pine and wait for a miniature England to resurface somewhere else on this side of the ocean?"

How cleverly her friend had steered the conversation back to the source of Agnes's greatest fears. "I do not know. Truly I do not. He was not specific enough on the details."

"There lies the problem with his proposal," she concluded with a triumphant gleam in her green eyes. "In the meantime, Riapoke is courting you with no such reservations. If you choose him, he will love and protect you until the end of his days. Starting here and now. Such is the way of our people," she declared proudly. "We all work hard and share alike in the fat times as well as the lean. Not so different than how it was for me growing up on a tenant farm."

Agnes bit her lip. "I did not mean to offend Riapoke with my exhibition of caution." She was growing more miserable by the second beneath Rose's gentle condemnation of her actions. "What can I do to fix things between us?"

"Go to him and make things right. Above all, you must be honest about your feelings for him. You are standing at a fork in the road, my friend. If you genuinely prefer to live the life of an Englishwoman, if you cannot give him any real hope of fully accepting him for who he is, if you are not capable of returning his affections, you must be honest about that, too. Either way, you must choose. If you remain divided inside your own heart for too long, you will lose everything."

Meaning I will lose both my current suitors.

"Thank you, Rose." Agnes drew a shuddering breath. "I will speak to Riapoke right away, though I will admit to being terrified about being so bold."

"Why?" Her brows flew up. "He is no monster."

Agnes let out a long sigh. "Even so, I find it hard to breathe in his presence, much less think. My composure disintegrates every time he looks my way. I think of him constantly and worry about his opinion every waking moment."

A trill of laughter escaped her. "You sound like a woman in love."

"Aye, Rose. Either I am going mad or what you say is true. Strange how such a thing can happen in such a short period of time. I do not think we've exchanged more than a few dozen different words though we are fast teaching each other new ones."

"Good heavens! You protest so much and so loudly I would know 'tis true even if you denied it." There was a teasing glint to her eyes.

"He and I are newly acquainted," Agnes insisted.

"True."

"So what is happening between us defies all logic. It—"

"Indeed, it does," she interrupted. "You need not try to convince me. Do not forget I was born to a poor tenant farmer in the Scottish Highlands, and now I am the Princess of Croatoa."

CHAPTER 22: IN LOVE

*A*gnes stumbled to her feet and clutched one of the tent poles as a wave of dizziness rocked her. "I did nothing to make this happen. Indeed, I was quite busy pursuing the heart of another."

Rose laughed. "That's the fascinating thing about falling in love. You don't get to choose. It chooses you."

"If I had a choice, I would have chosen to love Anthony." Agnes's voice trembled with guilt at the admission.

"I know, my dear," Rose acknowledged sadly. "You grew so close on the journey here from England. You endured so much together, and you share a depth of empathy and friendship some people never find in a lifetime."

"Yes, we do."

"But it is not the same as love."

"That's what Jane said," Agnes sighed. "Do you think I would have been able to fall in love with Anthony if Riapoke had not come along?"

"If I lived on what-ifs, my friend, I would not sleep another night." She sniffed. "Do not forget I, too, once fancied myself in love with a nobleman. The son of a duke, no less, but it wasn't meant to be. He was affianced to another since birth. With my lineage, I would have never stood a chance at becoming anything more than his mistress, a position he tried valiantly to convince me to take." Her eyes took on a faraway look. "He genuinely wanted me as his mistress, too. I never doubted it; but like you, I wanted something more. Something better. I wanted what God wanted for me." Her cat-like eyes grew damp. "I've learned to accept what was meant to be. To embrace, without question, what is." She rubbed a hand over the swell of her belly. "I could not be happier in doing so."

Agnes's conversation with Rose compelled her to seek out Riapoke. It was difficult to catch him alone. He alternated between meeting with the councilmen of both tribes, managing the patrols for their combined settlement, and helping to oversee the construction of the Roanoke community. Every time she attempted to approach him, she was waylaid by one colonist or another who needed something. Several times, Agnes was pulled away to treat injuries incurred during construction, but she continued to anxiously watch Riapoke's progress.

Unlike the English, neither the Croatians nor the Roanokes constructed their fortifications at the tops of their respective hills. They merely posted a pair of scouts at the pinnacle. Instead, they burrowed their structures into the sides of the hills, using sturdy trees and boulders as anchors. It was a clever move, considering their reed and sapling structures were covered with nothing more than bark mats and skins. Such items wouldn't hold as well against the buffeting winds compared to the brick and plank homes of the English. Agnes couldn't help admiring their strategy and wished the Dares would employ some of the same wisdom. Their masonry and woodwork would fare better beneath lesser winds, as well.

Agnes was unable to speak with Riapoke until nightfall. He was led into his tent between two braves, leaning heavily on their shoulders. Dropping everything, Agnes raced in his direction.

"I need to speak with him," she pleaded with the man who appeared to be guarding the entrance. "Please. He is ill."

"Ann-nes?" Riapoke's voice called weakly from the interior. He said something in Croatoan. The stoic-faced Native opened the tent flap and stepped aside to usher her through.

Another command from Riapoke sent the other two braves away. He settled himself heavily on a mat in front of his fire. "Come in." He indicated she was to sit beside him

Agnes slid to her knees before him, weak with relief at the sight of him and thrilled to be so close to him. For a moment she could think of nothing to say. Then her words tumbled one over the other. "Why did you work so hard today? With an injury like yours, you need rest. At least until your stitches have time to set."

The tightness around his eyes relaxed. "I must...help...my people."

"They need you to get well, Riapoke. Not burning with fever and—" She bit her lip with a sound of frustration, rising on her knees to gauge the temperature of his forehead and ears. Her heart pounded when her skin made contact with his. Their gaze locked for several breathless heartbeats.

"Ann-nes." He clasped her hands and drew them away from his face, but he did not let them go. "You...are... so...lovely."

"Oh, Riapoke!" She gently freed her hands from his. They needed to discuss a few important matters before things progressed any further between them. "I came to examine your wound, to change your bandage."

He reached for her hands again and stopped her examination. "I am...well. You?"

"I am sad. I never intended to disrespect or hurt you, Riapoke. It's just that one of our English colonists has asked me to marry him. Lord Anthony Cage. He is a good man, and I told him I would consider his request."

Surprise and pain leaped in his gaze. He dropped her hands.

"I need to tell him no before I am free to be with you." She motioned between them and shook her head, having no idea how much Riapoke understood of what she was saying.

His features settled into their usual stoic lines. "You do not...wish...to court a savage?"

"Oh, nay!" Her eyelashes swept her cheeks. "I think you are the kindest, bravest, and most amazing man I ever met!"

His hand tipped her face up to his. Hope crept back into his features.

"I sought you out on purpose to tell you I want to keep courting you. That I fully intend to break things off with Anthony. I," it was hard to breathe again, "I love you, Riapoke."

"Riapoke!" Chief Manteo entered the room in a rush. "Ah! I did not realize you were here, Agnes."

The joy in Riapoke's eyes was all she had come for. Her mission was complete.

Or not.

He did not immediately acknowledge Chief Manteo's intrusion. Instead, he cupped Agnes's face with both hands and leaned forward to brush his lips against hers.

"Nouwmais," he said huskily against her mouth.

"Pray pardon me," Chief Manteo interjected quietly, remaining in the room. Whatever he'd come for must be important.

Agnes and Riapoke drew away from each other dazedly.

"I was just leaving," she assured hastily. She squeezed Riapoke's hands and dropped her voice to a whisper. "Good day, my love." She dashed from his tent despite Manteo's efforts to call her back. Tears of happiness and anxiety threatened as she continued to run. It was time to tell Anthony the truth and put this burden behind them, once and for all.

She ran until she reached the construction site of the new English fort. It wasn't much to look at yet, only a few mounds of freshly dug earth. The most remarkable thing about it was the fair-skinned man standing at its center with his stark blonde hair blowing in the wind and the stunning Native woman standing beside him. His arm rested protectively on the small of her back, and her belly swelled with child.

Agnes gaped. "Christopher?" As sure as she was alive, it was their former vicar, Lord Christopher Cooper and Chief Wanchese's sister, Amitola.

He turned and smiled broadly in her direction.

"Agnes!" He held out his arms. "It is so good to see you alive and well, my friend." His voice was rich with affection.

She ran to embrace him. "You are returned to us. And Amitola." She spun to face the Roanoke princess. "You are beautiful and blooming." Agnes held both hands out to her.

Her dark fierce gaze sparkled with appreciation as she clasped Agnes's hands.

Agnes frowned up at Christopher. "Why are you here? I thought your plan was to keep her hidden until the babe is born."

Shouts sounded, and colonists quickly stopped their labors to gather around Christopher and Amitola.

"It was." He returned to Amitola's side and gazed down at her with admiration and concern. "However, we received word of an approaching war party and came to warn you."

Oh. Agnes took a step back to make way for Ananias who offered mugs of ale to their two guests. "Blade." He signaled one of the lads. "Pray fetch Chief Wanchese. His sister is arrived." To Christopher, he inquired, "Who is your informant, and what do they know of this war party?"

"'Tis a friend of Amitola's from a neighboring tribe. You are not familiar with them. It is one that is friendly to the Roanokes but not to the English. He says the people of Copper Mountain are assembling a war party. They come to reclaim her babe and exact their revenge on the English for taking her from them. They plan to strike before you can finish constructing your fort. Before winter hits."

While we are at our weakest. Agnes suddenly found it difficult to breathe.

It was devastating news. Until Christopher's arrival, their concerns had been focused on setting up camp, building the fort, erecting homes, and gathering food to survive the fast-approaching winter. As of yet, they'd had little time to plan for the next attack. Most were planning to spend the winter preparing for such an event, hoping the mountain people would settle deeper into their mountain for the season and hold off their next strike until spring.

Apparently, this wasn't the case.

"What about Virginia?" Eleanor Dare cried, flying up the hill. "Is there any news about the daughter they stole from me?"

Christopher's expression was wary. "Word has it they cherish the fair skinned infant like a goddess." He darted a knowing glance in Agnes's direction. She knew he meant the babe would bring a high price at the slave trading block in a few years, but it was kind of him to choose his words to inflict the least pain on Eleanor.

"My poor baby!" Eleanor exclaimed, dissolving into tears. "My poor, precious baby."

Christopher's voice was thick with sympathy. "At least you may take comfort in the fact she is unharmed. We have every reason to think they are taking the best of care of Virginia."

"Unharmed!" she gasped damply. "They tore a suckling babe from her mother's breasts. You have no idea how or what she suffers."

"Oh, Eleanor!" Agnes reached over to lay a comforting hand on her employer's arm, but she seemed not to notice. Her eyes glazed with grief.

Ananias gathered Eleanor in his arms with a sigh.

"Pray forgive my poor choice of words, madam. You are right, of course." Christopher bowed his apology. "My main purpose in coming here was to warn you about the coming strike."

"Thank you for your haste in coming, my lord." Ananias's handsome face had aged considerably since the capture of their newborn daughter. He held the weeping Eleanor against his chest and spoke over her hair. "What do you know of their numbers? Their weapons? How long until they arrive?"

"We know very little of their numbers and how many neighboring tribes may join them, only that they have not yet departed their mountain lair. It will take them several days to travel here, so we likely have upwards of a week to ready ourselves.

"We? Do you plan to stay, my lord?"

"Aye. Their scouts have pursued us without ceasing, forcing us to stay on the run. With winter coming and Amitola's condition advancing, 'tis time to choose a place for the birthing. What better place is there than this?" He held his arms wide to encompass the entire settlement. "Plus, you have Agnes." He spared her another one of his warm grins. "I can think of no better midwife when the times comes to deliver us a prince."

Chief Wanchese approached with his council. Jane was

among them, since she served as the Wise Woman of his tribe. Riapoke moved stiffly, a half step behind the others, face as stoic as ever, with the rest of the elders fanning out on either side of their party. Chief Manteo, Rose, and his advisers approached at a distance.

With a cry of happiness, Amitola flew down the hillside to greet her brother. He caught her in his embrace. Jane embraced her as well. Whatever Amitola said afterwards created a flurry of excitement among the councilmen. They pointed and talked soberly among themselves.

Ananias gently disengaged himself from his wife whose sobs were slowing. He nodded at Agnes, and she stepped forward to wrap her arms around Eleanor and lead her to her tent.

"There is another matter I wish to address with you." Christopher lowered his voice to confer with Ananias as Agnes and Eleanor walked away. She wondered if it had anything to do with the lovely Amitola. He was undeniably enamored with her and she with him. It was clear in the adoring cast to her features each time she gazed at him and the way he protectively hovered over her. An onlooker couldn't fail to miss their devotion to each other.

Agnes was envious of them. While leading Eleanor away, her gaze caught Riapoke's. She offered him a shy smile. He regarded her so soberly that she began to wonder if something was amiss. She glanced around the clearing and noted Anthony hurrying her way.

CHAPTER 23: MARGARET'S ACCUSATION

*T*he Croatoans and Roanokes called for a feast to celebrate the safe return of Christopher and Amitola, their princess. Wanchese and Manteo's braves produced three large bucks from their afternoon hunt, and dinner fires across their combined settlement were soon roasting generous portions of meat.

The Englishwomen added large pots of winter stew to the mix and a few loaves of bread from the scant remains of their grain supply.

Amitola moved from her brother's huddle of councilmen to sit beside Christopher in front of the roaring campfire. Margaret Lawrence's pinched features twisted first in pain, then in anger. Agnes recalled Rose mentioning something months ago about her bearing the torch for Christopher. If true, it would explain the myriad of emotions flitting across her face.

The poor woman. Her life seemed to be one ball of tightly wound misery.

Murmurs traveled around the fire as colonists acknowledged Amitola's actions and speculated on their meaning.

"He must mean to offer for her hand in marriage," Emme postulated dreamily. "Wouldn't it be lovely to celebrate another wedding soon?" She'd lost her extra pounds in recent months and looked like an entirely different person. Roses bloomed in her cheeks, as she darted a glance at the large and shy Mark Bennett. He was one of the hardest working and most loyal English colonists.

Agnes imagined it would not be long before he requested Emme's hand in marriage. Then they would celebrate yet another happy union. She dropped her eyes, glad for the joyful couples surrounding the campfire while inwardly envying them the simplicity of their happiness.

"'Tis not as if it was a love match," Margaret spat suddenly.

Agnes wasn't the only one to raise astonished eyes to stare at her.

"Why, with the way he was forced to travel with her and protect her these past several months, he has utterly and thoroughly compromised her. Maybe that was the plan all along. Force one of our finest men to marry and provide for her, now that she's in the family way."

A shocked silence greeted her outrageous claim.

"I think not!" Emme finally snorted. "One only has to look at them together to see no one is forcing them to enjoy one another's company."

Margaret's sharp intake of breath was the only indication of how painful Emme's observation must be to her.

"Oh, Margaret," Agnes declared softly. "I am sorry. I know how much it must cost you to see them together." She scooted closer to the distressed young woman, reminding herself of her vow to be kinder to her no matter how diffi-cult. She squeezed Margaret's too-thin shoulders in a brief hug.

She shook off Agnes's arm and rounded on her. "How dare you claim to understand! How dare you!"

Agnes drew back in consternation.

Margaret rocked back on her heels. "You are willing to risk the future you could have enjoyed with Lord Anthony Cage to cavort with one of them, yourself." She cast a dark glance in Riapoke's direction.

"Don't, Margaret," Agnes pleaded. "You are understandably hurt and upset, but nothing good can come of making such rash claims."

"Nothing good?" Her voice rose alarmingly. "I am merely trying to remind us of what is right and what is wrong. The good book says when a woman like yourself has been thoroughly compromised by another man...him," she pointed at Riapoke, "then you should marry."

Every muscle in Agnes's body clenched in alarm. "Why, Margaret? Why are you doing this?"

Her smile turned ugly and she lowered her voice so only Agnes could hear her next words. "I see no reason for you to keep one of our most eligible gentlemen dangling when your interests clearly lie elsewhere. You might as well give the rest of us ladies a shot at him."

Agnes drew back in horror. Margaret actually thought she stood a hair's chance of capturing the affections of Lord Anthony Cage? She would have pitied the miserable woman if she wasn't so busy being angry at her for creating such a scene.

Eleanor hurried over to the women. "Shush, Margaret! There is nothing you have to say that could not have been said to me in private."

"Pshaw! What does it matter, after all?" Margaret rolled her eyes, clearly beyond caring. "I am weary to death of all the lies and duplicity surrounding us."

"What does it matter, you ask!" Eleanor retorted. "Everything we do can affect our alliance with the Natives. I would remind you how desperate our situation would be without their aid. Not another outburst of any sort from you. If you have something to say, you will say it to me first. Are we clear?"

Margaret raised her chin stubbornly. "You will not listen. Nobody ever listens to me."

"My lands, Margaret!" Impatience infused Eleanor's voice. "Do you have any basis whatsoever for your claims?"

"Aye. Agnes tended Riapoke most of the night in his tent after he was shot."

"So?"

"Alone, madam." Margaret shot Agnes a satisfied smile and crossed her arms.

Eleanor waved her hand. "Visitors were coming and going the entire time. Agnes treated the injuries of many in the sick bay. You did not demand she marry any of the sailors. What is different about Riapoke?"

"She was alone with him when she let herself out of his tent in the wee hours of the morn. Right after I overheard them exchanging endearments and kisses."

Agnes's breath came out in a slow release of pent up air. Margaret had spied on them in the most despicable manner possible!

Eleanor made a sound of disgust. "What an imagination you have! You try my patience to no end. Agnes will deny the claim, and you will apologize to her at once." She shot Agnes an exasperated look.

Agnes's lips parted and clamped shut. She had no easy answer to give them. This was not how she imagined sharing her feelings for Riapoke with her friends.

A pained silence stretched.

"Agnes?" Eleanor's voice grew tight. "Did you or did you not kiss Riapoke?"

"I, ah, yes. Yes, I did."

Her mouth fell open and her already pale cheeks paled further.

"May I speak with you alone?" She glared a threat in Margaret's direction, lest she dare try to follow.

Eleanor was so staggered by Agnes's revelation that she had to assist her employer to her feet. They strolled away, arm in arm, from the campfire.

"Tell me why, my friend." She sounded tired and strained.

"I care for him." It was easier to say it aloud now that the secret was out of the bag.

"Oh, Agnes! Are you quite certain of your feelings? I was aware Riapoke was courting you, but I had no idea things had progressed this far between you."

Agnes grimaced. "I stopped him when he kissed me and left his tent immediately, because Anthony had just proposed the night before. It all happened so fast and didn't seem right under the circumstances. I—"

"Anthony has finally declared himself? Dear heavens!" Eleanor stopped abruptly to face her. "Talk to me, Agnes. Tell me everything!"

Agnes shrugged. *In for a ha-pence.* "He said he is not ready to marry but wishes for me to wait for him. I told him I would consider his request out of respect for our friendship, but I should not have. Not when Riapoke is the one who holds my heart."

"Oh, dear! How can you be so sure?" Eleanor exclaimed, looking aghast. "You and Riapoke are barely acquainted, and he speaks so little English."

"I am sure of my feelings for him, Eleanor. I know it makes little sense, but I have rarely been so sure of anything in all my life."

Twin spots of red appeared in her cheeks. "Then I am inclined to agree with Margaret, as much as I deplore the hateful manner in which she went about it." Her sigh was as much a sob as a sigh. "We must consider our next move carefully, my friend. Riapoke is a war chief. He is like royalty to his people. His affections for you mean more than your happiness, in the fact that your marriage would form another powerful alliance for our colony."

It was a stark reminder of how the English had started off as enemies with his brother's tribe, the Roanokes. When the colonists first arrived to Roanoke Island, Wanchese's warriors had slain George Howell, one of their Assistants, in retaliation to a previous group of Englishmen slaying their chief. It had taken months of negotiations plus a marriage between Jane and their chief to repair the damage. Even now, it was only partially repaired.

"What do you intend to do?" Agnes inquired shakily. So much for her hope of tying up loose ends with Anthony before plunging full speed ahead into her courtship with Riapoke.

"Since you admit you care for him, I will bring the matter to our church elders before Margaret causes any more trouble. I imagine they will approach Chief Wanchese with an offer of marriage between you and his brother. Do you have any last requests to make beforehand?"

Last requests! Did she mean to sound so dooms-day-ish? It was a marriage they were discussing, not an execution. Agnes suddenly wished she had her mother to confide in. Mother would have understood what to say in a situation like this, how to provide the exact sort of council her daughter so desperately needed. Eleanor had served as a friend and confidante during the last several months, but it wasn't the same.

"Nay," Agnes whispered. She had no last requests.

*A*s it turned out, the church elders leaped at the prospect of forming another alliance with the Natives. Thus, it was not the marriage of Christopher and Amitola arranged over the feast but rather Agnes's to Riapoke.

Oddly enough, Riapoke, himself, was not present for the announcement. Fearful that his injury was the reason for his absence, Agnes took her leave of the festivities at first opportunity to seek his whereabouts.

She paced the outskirts of the new settlement, ducking between partially constructed cottages and hoping to slip away unnoticed. Alas, Anthony found her in the darkness.

"What is this I hear about a marriage agreement between you and Riapoke? I thought…good God!" He shook his head, taking in her expression.

"I said I would consider your proposal, and I did," Agnes assured softly. "Thank you for honoring me with your request, but my answer is no. I will always treasure our friendship, but we are not suited for marriage."

"Why not?" he demanded. She could tell he was hurt and angry and hated that their relationship had come to such a painful point.

It made each word rising in her throat burn like fire, but he deserved to hear the unfettered truth. It would be better for both of them in the long run. "You and I care for each other deeply, but we do not love each other."

An oath escaped beneath his breath. "We've had this discussion. Love comes in time, Agnes. We have plenty enough affection and regard between us to build a marriage on."

Maybe it is enough for you, but not for me.

"Nay, Anthony, it is not enough." Her heart clenched with sadness. "Please do not make this any harder than it is. 'Tis my biggest hope we will remain friends. There are too few of us left. We need to stick together no matter what happens."

"Stick together! How can we stick together when I am losing you, altogether, Agnes? This matter with the Croatoans came about so quickly, I feel as if I am missing something. Please assure me you are not being forced to marry against your will."

Ah. He must not yet have heard Margaret's role in the swift arrangement of Agnes's marriage contract to Riapoke. She might as well be the one to break the news to him.

She drew a deep breath. "Earlier today, Margaret brought to Eleanor's attention that my recent interactions with Riapoke have compromised me."

"She is mad!" he exclaimed furiously. "All you did was treat the man's wounds. I will put a stop to this insanity at once."

"Nay! Pray do not interfere," Agnes pleaded. "Let the matter be handled by the elders."

"You ask me to stand by and do nothing while the end result may very well be your marriage to that sav—"

"Don't say it," she cried. "Please, let's not say anything else to each other we might both live to regret."

"I regret nothing!" He paced the ground in front of her like a wild stallion ready to bolt.

She could see he was quickly moving beyond reason and struggled to think of something calming to say. Alas, she could think of nothing that would not further incense him.

"Why?" He rounded on her abruptly. "Just tell me why! None of this makes any sense. Did something else happen you are not divulging?" His tone turned coldly dangerous. "If he laid a hand on you, so help me God—"

"He is a good man, Anthony, and you know it. He has done nothing I have not allowed him to do." *There. Let him ponder that.*

He studied her in fury for several moments longer. "Fine," he said at last. "I will get to the bottom of this mess, with or without your help. Mark my words, if that heathen has done one thing to hurt you, he is a dead man."

Agnes watched Anthony stride away, thoroughly incinerated by his high-handedness. How dare he declare himself lord and commander over matters concerning her own heart! She should have turned him down flat the moment he first uttered his halfhearted proposal. She no longer believed he ever genuinely wanted her for his wife. He simply wasn't ready to give up the possibility in the face of his dwindling marital options. He was a selfish boor who cared little about her personal happiness. This whole tempest was about his pride and nothing more. She should have listened to Rose and Jane. They'd figured out his true intentions long before she had.

So help her, if he lifted one finger against Riapoke— *Well, it won't be the first time I've killed a man, either.*

Great merciful God! The ugly direction of Agnes's thoughts shook her back to reality. No one was killing anybody on her behalf. Not tonight or any other night. She needed to find Riapoke with haste and warn him.

My poor, dear Riapoke! Assuming he'd even been notified of their pending marriage, she could only imagine what he must think of the English colonists right now with their crazy notions of propriety. Would he even understand their snippety accusation that he'd compromised her? He'd done nothing but save her life during a brutal ambush and shower his affections on her afterwards. A more blameless and worthy creature she'd never met.

The whole world was turning upside down. She would be a very lucky girl, indeed, if he still wanted to marry her after her countrymen made such a ruckus over nothing.

CHAPTER 24: THE PROPOSAL

Several paces from the perimeter of the new English colony, Riapoke's voice jolted Agnes from her agonized thoughts.

"Ann-nes."

She whirled to face him, anxiously searching his face in the moonlight. Had he been informed about their pending nuptials yet? It was difficult to read him.

His arms were crossed in front of his chest. A full moon kept vigil overhead, and the wide delta spread beyond his broad shoulders.

"I am s-so sorry, Riapoke," she stammered, reaching out to touch his forearm. "So sorry to draw you into this mess."

"Sorry?" His expression turned cautious, though he covered her hand with his. "You do not...wish...to marry me?"

He knew! Thank God he knew.

"Yes, of course I wish to marry you! Believe me. I—" She pressed a hand to her chest, trying to catch her breath. She needed to stop babbling. With his fragile command of the English language, Riapoke was only picking up bits and pieces of her conversation. She was confusing him. "Do *you* wish to marry me, Riapoke?"

"Yes, Ann-nes." The proof was in his honest gaze. "You do not…seem…happy."

"I am." *I am overcome. I can hardly breath.* "I am honored." And lightheaded and fearful on his behalf. Anthony was out there somewhere with revenge in his heart.

Riapoke cocked his head and beheld her with concern. "Are you…well?"

She summoned her courage. "There is something you need to know about—"

Before she could finish her sentence, the furious conversation of two men floated their way. It was Anthony speaking to Ananias. "She was merely doing her job," he seethed. "'Tis not her fault if he attacked her. She cannot be forced to marry him."

Riapoke's expression darkened at the hateful accusation. Faith, but he understood more than she'd been giving him credit for.

She gripped his arm with both hands. "That is what I was trying to tell you. I spoke to Anthony tonight. I told him I would never marry him, that he and I are not suited, but he wouldn't listen. He is trying to stop my marriage to you."

"He cannot."

Relief flooded her at Riapoke's adamant response. "I am glad," she cried softly. "Very, very glad."

His arms came around her. He clasped her against him, pulling her to her tiptoes to claim her mouth.

The movement surely pained him, since her much smaller frame dangled against his injured torso. She wrapped her arms around his neck, attempting to ease the pressure of her body weight away from the site of his wound. Then all rational thoughts flew from her head.

Riapoke's kiss was not gentle and searching like before.

This time it was a wild plundering. A staking of his claim on her.

Mindless joy battered her senses among a myriad of other sensations. She could only cling to him and ride the storm he unleashed.

"You are...mine, Ann-nes," he said roughly, setting her back on her feet at last.

His. "Yes." Dazed, she nodded and raised tentative fingers to her lips. "I am yours, Riapoke, and you are mine."

He pressed her head against his chest, one large hand in her hair, and kissed her forehead. "My warriors...will keep you...safe." He uttered a short, guttural command in his native tongue. Then he departed and left her standing alone the moonlight.

Nay, not alone. Three of his braves surrounded her.

Eleanor and Ananias found her there.

"Agnes." Eleanor reached out to touch her cheek, glancing worriedly at Riapoke's men. "What are they doing here with you?"

Agnes offered a damp laugh, since she was ridiculously close to shedding happy tears. "Watching over me. Riapoke ordered them to do so."

"I presume this means the two of you have taken the opportunity to discuss your coming nuptials."

"Aye." Agnes gulped. She still couldn't believe it was happening. The dampness in her eyes made Eleanor's features blur.

"Oh, my friend! I hardly know what to say."

Ananias raked a hand through his beard. "He is a good man."

"Yes, he is." Agnes offered them a wobbly smile. "One of the best."

Eleanor clasped her shoulders and shook her lightly. "Listen well. I know their ways are different from ours. The

Native men do not smile or speak much, but it was clear to me during our private meeting with Chief Wanchese and his council tonight that Riapoke cares a great deal for you."

A fresh burst of warmth flooded Agnes's heart at the knowledge that Riapoke had openly welcomed the marriage offer from her countrymen. Oh, how she adored him!

She gave a shaky chuckle. "That is good, since we are to be married." She and Eleanor embraced, and she found myself laughing and crying on her employer's shoulder.

"I will admit I did not see this one coming," Eleanor sighed regretfully. "Apparently, I did not see a lot of things coming."

It was Agnes's turn to offer comfort. She hugged Eleanor tighter.

"I will miss you," her employer bemoaned. She would not be Agnes's employer for much longer.

"I will not be far away," Agnes reminded. *Only two hills over.*

"It won't be the same, my friend." Eleanor's voice caught. "It won't ever be the same again. You will move to live with the Roanokes, and I will remain here."

It was true.

She would remain without her kidnapped daughter in a dwindling settlement of English colonists — one that sheltered bitter and disillusioned settlers like Margaret who was in no way capable of providing the friendship and support Agnes and Eleanor had given each other the past several months.

Agnes's heart went out to her. They stood there, clinging to each other, while Ananias waited patiently beside them, shifting from one foot to the other. Agnes's Roanoke guards silently patrolled the area around them.

"We were all prepared for Anthony to declare himself," Eleanor murmured against her shoulder. "Indeed, I do not understand why he diddled around so carelessly with you. All this might have been prevented, otherwise."

"Maybe it is because he does not love me." Agnes drew away from her gently. "We adore each other and will always be friends, I think, after his initial upset dies down. Way down deep, I think we both knew we were not meant to marry. Rose knew it, too. She tried to caution me several times."

Eleanor made a scoffing sound. "Rose has maintained a suspicion of all titled gentleman after the one who broke her heart back in London."

"Not quite all." Agnes smiled. "She married a chief, you know."

Ananias broke his silence. "Agnes, we pray you find all the happiness you deserve in your marriage to Riapoke."

"Now, An," his wife chided. "Do not jump ahead to congratulations and well wishes just yet. Allow me a little longer to bemoan the loss of yet another Englishwoman. The Native men are snapping them up right and left. Who will remain for our own men to marry?"

He chuckled. "Not all of the Englishmen require a match, my love. A good many of them possess wives back home whom they hope to be reunited with soon."

His words ended their brief moment of jocularity. Aye, so many of the colonists had wives. Wives they'd lost contact with. Wives they might never see again.

"They are in God's hands," Eleanor whispered. "As you will be when we deliver you to Riapoke." She enclosed Agnes in another hug.

Agnes shivered. They would deliver her soon into the arms of a husband she had just met. A man who spoke limited English yet who inspired feelings in her she'd previously only dreamed of. She would have preferred a longer courtship. Time to get to know him better first, but apparently fate had other things in mind.

---

*O*nce their engagement was announced, Riapoke seemed to withdraw entirely from the English settlement. Agnes watched him from a distance, but the only times he approached her were when she ventured outside the perimeter of the palisade wall the colonists were constructing. She presumed he was doing all he could to avoid a confrontation with Anthony, yet she missed his adoring looks and gifts.

Their wedding date was set a week away, mainly because they were so busy setting up camp and preparing for battle. Each day dragged past like an eternity.

The Native scouts continued their patrols and spoke with their contacts from neighboring tribes, but no one could ferret out more details concerning the coming strike.

It took a full three days of back breaking digging for the earthen walls of the English fort to take shape. The small canons they'd traveled with were mounted at the four corners. Next, the colonists put their biggest efforts into raising log cabins. It would take weeks to manufacture new bricks, so they were not hopeful of adding any masonry before spring unless winter delayed its arrival.

Despite Agnes's approaching wedding to Riapoke, the Roanoke braves and maidens acted less friendly towards her than ever. The women continued to stare at her and whisper behind their hands, and all too few approached her with medicinal requests. Their lack of acceptance of her apothecary and nursing skills troubled her greatly. It was all she had to offer them, or at least the best she had to offer. She was otherwise a poor cook and a poor tailor and couldn't hunt well enough to keep a babe alive.

Anthony continued to hound her with unwanted attention and concerns. If anything, the man paid her more attention now that she was engaged to another man than he had before. Two evenings prior to her wedding, he dogged her down to the delta while she was foraging for food. "If you change your mind about going through with this disastrous marriage, just say the word. I will argue your case before the elders," he offered.

"I have not changed my mind, Anthony."

"If he hurts you in any way." His voice turned rough. "As I've said before, I swear I'll—"

"Ann-nes, come."

Her heart leaped at Riapoke's voice. She whirled to find him staring hard at Anthony. Three armed braves hovered near their war counselor, hands resting suggestively on an impressive array of hatches and knives hanging from their waists.

With a muttered expletive, Anthony stormed away.

"Riapoke." She pressed a hand to her chest. "How good to see you, my lord."

The hard lines around his eyes became more pronounced. "Not lord. Riapoke." He held out a hand. "Come."

She took it, mystified, as he led her to his tent and held aside the opening flap. Heart thudding nearly from her chest, Agnes stepped inside ahead of him. His trio of braves remained outside. For this, she was grateful. It had been too long since they'd enjoyed any time alone.

He drew her closer to the fire crackling in the center of his tent. There he unbuttoned and removed her coat, stepping away from her briefly to hang it on a hook fastened to one of his sturdy tent poles. He returned to the fire and held his arms out to her. She gladly walked into them and pressed

.

her face to his chest to soak in the scent and feel and strength of him.

"I have missed you," she confided softly.

"Good." He stroked a hand through her hair and bent his head to press a kiss to my collarbone. She trembled at the intimate gesture.

He raised his head and captured her lips. The tenderness of his kiss made her weak all over. Afterwards, he simply held her for a while. "I am...building...a longhouse." His deep baritone voice resounded deliciously against her temple, stirring the ringlets of hair resting there.

"That's so wonderful!" She couldn't contain a squeal of excitement. She gripped his upper arms and drew back a few inches to gaze up at him. "Our very own home. Thank you, Riapoke." It was almost too good to be true.

To her disappointment, he lowered his arms. He reached inside one of his cross body pouches and produced a pair of copper bracelets. He clasped one to each arm, right atop the sleeves of her workaday gown. Next he withdrew a trio of necklaces from his pouch and draped them over her head. They were not copper like his other gifts. Rather they were made from hundreds of tiny, delicate shells.

"Thank you." She longed to give him something in return. Alas, she had traveled with nothing more than a few blankets and gowns. What if he thought her un-generous? Her cheeks burned. Maybe she should speak to Eleanor. Surely she and Ananias could provide something for Agnes to present to her groom as a wedding gift.

Riapoke said nothing, only watching her in the stoic manner she was growing accustomed to. She wished she could discern his thoughts.

"I will treasure your gifts. Always." She curtsied deeply to him.

Was that a softening of his expression? She held her breath, hoping he would say something.

When he remained silent, she bit back a sigh and searched for something to keep their conversation going. "Pray assure me your wound continues to heal." She ever so gently splayed a hand over his injury.

He captured her hand and lifted it to his lips. "I am...well."

"Are you in any pain?"

"*Tah.*"

She smiled. "I am glad you are healing so quickly. Very glad."

He pressed her hand to his heart, but Anthony's voice outside the tent had both their heads spinning towards the closed tent flap.

"He took her inside," Anthony accused. "Does he not understand he must wait until their wedding night to bed her?"

Riapoke's expression tightened with anger. He lowered her hand and quickly reached for her coat. He tugged it around her shoulders and helped her button it.

"Come," he whispered and led her out the back of his tent through another opening she didn't know existed until now. One of his braves was waiting to lead her away.

She turned and reached for Riapoke one last time. "Please be careful."

He kissed her again. "Do...not...worry."

She caught her lower lip between her teeth. Didn't he know that worrying was all she could do these days? She turned away from him with great reluctance and allowed his brave to lead her away within the deepening shadows.

CHAPTER 25: UNCERTAIN LOYALTIES

The Englishmen took turns with the Croatoan and Roanoke warriors on their patrols around the combined settlement. It was a three-day rotation. On their off-duty days, the men hunted and fished from dawn until dusk. However, the Natives harvested far more from their hunting and fishing efforts than did the English.

At first there was much grumbling among the Natives at how little the colonists contributed to the food rations. However, the Englishmen proved more skilled at construction, and no wonder. They were highly skilled carpenters, brick masons, coopers, blacksmiths, and ship builders. In comparison, the Native women erected temporary nomadic structures — little more than tents — albeit the braves pitched in to help raise a few larger, sturdier longhouses.

The Dares intervened in the squabble with their impeccable diplomatic skills and negotiated a deal where the Englishmen would build the chiefs of each tribe a two-story plank home in exchange for teaching their men how to hunt on the delta terrain. They also promised to show them how to construct the unique fishing weirs Chief Manteo's people were so famous for. A fresh crop of herring would migrate through the river basin come spring, and it would take their combined efforts to maximize the harvest.

All negotiations aside, the English continued to hunt when it was their turn, though their results remained dismal. Armed with their muskets, they returned with small game such as rabbits and foxes, while men like Riapoke and his hunters brought down bucks, a black bear, and an ambitiously hungry bobcat who'd been stalking the bear. Agnes's heart swelled with pride over her soon-to-be-husband's hunting prowess. The meat they brought home would be enough to feed their people for weeks.

Preparing for the winter so late in the year was a massive undertaking. The colonists worked without ceasing to hew logs and sand down planks, chop and stack firewood, and cure meat. Agnes fished out splinters aplenty and patched up enough cuts and scrapes to help the colonists maintain their relentless pace.

Beneath the strict oversight of Jane, who'd been taught by Nadie the Wise before she passed, the Englishwomen learned how to turn skins and furs into clothing and blankets. They worked from the wee hours of morning until sundown. They were a small but hardworking group — Eleanor, Margaret, Emme, Helen, a diminutive Oriental woman named Mrs. Thomas Colman who insisted on being called Mrs. Thomas, and Agnes. Unfortunately, working in such close proximity with women she knew so well left her open to endless questions about her coming nuptials to Riapoke.

"What is this I hear about your marriage being nothing more than a political alliance?" Jane declared the afternoon before her wedding. It was one of those rare occasions where she and Agnes were working alone together. "A marriage in name only will not get a babe in your belly."

Agnes's lips parted in surprise. The fact that her pending

marriage was a sham was news, indeed, to her. She hardly knew how to respond.

"The Roanokes are furious at the notion you do not truly wish to marry Riapoke." Jane's oval features were in full-blown storm mode.

Agnes stared at her, aghast. "Who would spread such a tale?"

She rolled her eyes. "Who do you think?"

"Margaret and Anthony come to mind. She is a venomous snake, and he is playing the part of a thwarted lover."

"You are correct. They are very much responsible for spreading the tale that you and Riapoke are being forced into an unwanted marriage."

"That makes little sense," Agnes protested, pushing back her hood to meet Jane's gaze. "Anthony followed me to Riapoke's tent the night he gave me these bracelets and neck-laces. Here. I can show you." She unbuttoned her coat and slid it from her shoulders to display the jewelry.

"You mean to say, he caught you in Riapoke's tent?"

"Not exactly," she admitted. "He thought he saw me entering the tent, but he definitely did not witness me leaving it. It was dark. Riapoke spirited me out a back exit, and one of his braves escorted me to the edge of our English village."

"What a harebrained thing to do!" Jane snorted. "He is Chief Wanchese's brother. He can do as he pleases and that includes openly spending time with you."

Agnes twisted her hands together. "Twice Anthony has threatened to do Riapoke harm if he lays a hand on me."

"Huh! I'd like to see him try. Riapoke's warriors would cut him down to size before he has the chance to draw his weapon."

"His behavior is understandable, I suppose." Agnes continued to twist her hands. "He is angry, hurt, and jealous and wants more than anything to prevent our union. However, I do not understand why Margaret continues to vent her poison all over me. I thought she was heart-broken over Christopher's interest in Amitola. Why she is trying to interfere in Riapoke's courting is beyond me."

Jane's lip curled. "There are some people in the world so miserable, they cannot stand seeing anyone else happy. As for Anthony? If he truly cares for you, then he is a fool for waiting so long to declare himself."

Agnes stabbed a stick into the ground, digging furiously along a root she hoped to harvest for tea making. "He does not love me, Jane. He doesn't even fancy the notion of being in love. My theory is both he and Margaret are simply terrified at the dwindling number of eligible Englishmen and women to court. I suspect Anthony kept me dangling as long as he could in case no one better came along. Margaret, well, she's so unpleasant that—" Agnes bit her lip, feeling guilty at all the unflattering images and words flooding her mind.

"She'd be lucky to have a blind, deaf, and dumb man court her," Jane supplied.

They chuckled at the miserable young woman's expense and continued working.

"What should I do, Jane?" Agnes kept her face averted, blushing furiously. "Despite all the forces working against us, I have done my best to share with Riapoke what is on my heart, to convince him I do indeed wish to marry him. But I worry he doesn't understand much of what I say."

"What you say matters little." Her tone was emphatic. "You do not need words to show a man you care. One of the Croatoan squaws does plenty of simpering at him. Methinks he is well aware of *her* interest."

Agnes straightened her spine. "But he is engaged to me!"

"True, but it is a longtime tradition of the highest ranking Roanokes and Croatoans to take on multiple wives and concubines. I think the risk is greater, in your case, where rumors claim your union will be a political alliance, only."

Jane rounded the wide, knobby knees of a cypress and planted a hard stare on her. "Riapoke didn't become a war chief by being anything less than a mighty warrior. Men and women alike admire him. The only reason he stayed single for this long was because he was grieving for the wife and son he lost . During an English raid on his people, mind you. An awful event that of lot of Natives have yet to forgive. It is my opinion you'd best claim your husband in every way before another comes along and snatches him from beneath your nose. And after laying claim to Riapoke, you must lay claim to his people. Prove yourself. Win their hearts. Earn their trust and loyalty. In this country, you cannot afford to stand by idly. You must take, take, take what is yours, Agnes."

Her words inspired a whole new way of thinking. All Agnes's life, she'd been the underdog, the untitled, the dowerless, the impoverished. She'd been taught to curtsy, bow, fawn, and grovel before those who outranked her. Before those who held the wealth and the power. Both Lord Brandbury and Anthony had contributed to her feelings of inadequacy. Lord Brandbury had never let her forget how he was covering the costs of her aunt and uncle's excesses. He had always made sure she felt beholden to him. Then Anthony had reminded her again and again how important family, position, and legacy were — three things she possessed in precious little quantities.

The idea that she could take control of her own destiny was a new concept, one she wasn't entirely comfortable with. It would require her to risk everything, including her feelings and her pride. It would require her to stretch beyond the ladylike decorum she'd always prided herself in. To give up some of her soft-spoken reserve. Her ironclad control.

To be bold and brash. To take.

CHAPTER 26: THE WEDDING

*A*gnes's wedding day dawned clear and cold. She had to rub her hands together briskly to warm them enough to do the buttons of her dress and coat. The colonists were too busy preparing for the coming raid to worry about non-essential details, so there was no decorating to do and no fineries to don. She pried open the tiny heart-shaped locket around her neck and gazed with brimming eyes at her parents. "This is my big day, Mum. Father. I wish you were here to see it." She closed the locket before she started to weep. Best not to arrive at her own wedding with swollen eyes.

Eleanor bustled into her tent without announcing her arrival. She took one look at Agnes's face and gathered her in a tight embrace. "There, lass. This is no time for you to be alone. The construction is not yet finished on my home, but there is plenty more room there than here to get you ready."

It was plain and humble according to London standards, but the Dares' four-room cabin, complete with a fireplace, was a luxury in the wilderness. It was built on a bed of river rock and a thick layer of creosote to discourage rot. When complete, it would contain a second story with two more rooms. The walls would be chinked and sealed and the thatched roof reinforced once the river rushes draped atop it finished drying.

Depending on how many cabins were complete before winter, the Dares planned to take in boarders. They feared the tents would not be near enough protection during the most severe snowstorms. Then again, the colonists' existence was not about luxury or privacy but about survival. Amenities and creature comforts would come later. Much later.

Rose was waiting for them in the front drawing room before a roaring fire. She handed Agnes a deerskin bundle tied with dried grasses. Two pinecones were tucked in the bow.

"For me?" Agnes cradled the bundle in her arms. It was heavier than it looked. "'Tis almost too pretty to open."

She smiled. "Manteo and I thought we would go for the practical instead of the frivolous, but I couldn't resist adding a bit of festiveness to the package."

It turned out to be a pair of new clay pots, one resting inside the other with an extra sheet of deerskin between them to keep them from scratching each another. An intricate pattern of eagle wings and triangles was etched on the outer rim of each pot.

"Oh, Rose," Agnes murmured.

"They are fireproof," she declared excitedly. "I made them myself."

Agnes possessed so few belongings. To think these were hers to keep, made by one of her dearest friends in the world, meant she would treasure them always. "I thank you. What an amazing skill to have! Where did you learn it?"

"From my people," she said proudly. "I would be glad to show you how, when you have the time."

"Indeed, yes. Thank you!" Agnes set them down and

threw her arms around Rose, but she gently set Agnes away after a few moments. "Come. We haven't much time to dress you in the Roanoke and Croatoan manner, so we must begin at once." She rapidly unbuttoned Agnes's coat.

"But—" Agnes watched, perplexed, as she tossed it aside, then just as quickly rid her of her tattered work gown. If it weren't for the fire, Agnes would have frozen to death.

"Here. Put these on." Eleanor produced a set of deerskin leggings, beautifully stitched with bright colored threads down the legs and along the hem. Again, the pattern was eagle wings and triangles. Over Agnes's shift, the two women drew a knee-length tunic of the same material and pattern. Then they produced a set of fringed moccasins.

Agnes surveyed herself with mixed feelings. It certainly wasn't a form-fitting gown suited for a London ball, but it was far nicer and far warmer than her patched wool dress.

When Rose started tugging Agnes's hair down, she gave a yelp of protest. "It took me more than half an hour to pin up my hair."

Rose clucked beneath her breath. "Pity, since we are taking it down."

"Why? What are you doing?"

"Turning you into a proper maiden. Riapoke will be delighted by your efforts to please him. Trust me on this."

At the mention of Riapoke, Agnes ceased her struggles. Faith, but Rose was married to a tribal chief. She must know a thing or two about the ways of the indigenous people.

Agnes cringed when Rose produced a pair of scissors. "Ugh! Will you shave me like a sheep?"

"Hardly," she chuckled and combed a thin fringe of hair over Agnes's eyes. She cut the hair straight across until the raw ends brushed the tops of her eyebrows. "There. These are called bangs. Instead of tying your hair up each night to curl around your face the next day, you can fluff these each morning and voila! They will form a flattering frame to your face."

Instead of pinning up the length of Agnes's hair, she parted it down the middle and plaited it into two, thick braids that hung over her shoulders. Then Rose painstakingly pinned bits and pieces of dried roses and vines behind an ear.

"Well done!" Eleanor clapped her hands. "Agnes, you are a rare beauty to begin with, but Rose has outdone herself." She ran to fetch a small mirror from the trestle table beside her bed. "See for yourself."

Agnes did not recognize herself. Everything she wore was assembled in the wilderness without the aid of fabric, spindles, or looms; yet it was surprisingly beautiful in a foreign and exotic sort of way.

At the sound of drums in the distance, Eleanor disappeared and reappeared with Harvye in her arms and Ananias at her side. Her eyes glinted with unshed tears. "It is time." Agnes's wedding would begin in minutes.

"Oh, wait! I almost forgot." Rose dug in her knapsack and produced what appeared to be a long, sharp piece of charcoal. "Close your eyes. I need to add one last finishing touch." She outlined Agnes's eyes with it and pressed the mirror into her hands once more.

Again, the change was shocking. The kohl color of the charcoal accentuated Agnes's blue eyes, drawing attention to them and making them pop from her face. "Are you certain it is not too much?" she whispered.

"Oh, darling, 'tis no more overdone than the powdered faces of the ladies in London with their paint-reddened lips and cheeks and their beauty patches. You look stunning, my friend." Rose draped the coat from Riapoke around Agnes's shoulders once more and secured it with a brooch borrowed from Eleanor.

Ananias spared Agnes an admiring glance and held out his arm. "I am the lucky man who will give away the bride." He winked. "Eleanor's orders, of course." Then he added more seriously, "'Tis my honor." As he ushered her out the door, he confided in low tones, "In the event you miss a few faces in the crowd, our men are pulling patrol around the perimeter. Blade, his pa, and a few others are out scouting."

Outside the cabin, they were met with a flurry of festivities in a plateau halfway down the hill from the fort. Native musicians pounded their snare drums and shook tiny bells. A pair of singers took up a singsong tune in a minor key. Agnes did not understand the words, but she found the muted notes of their song soothing to her tightly wound nerves. Thomas Ellis from one of the church vestries back in England produced a lute and plucked at the strings in harmony with the singers. At the edge of the plateau overlooking the valley, Christopher Cooper and Powaw, the elder Croatoan priest, stood beneath an archway woven of vines.

During their trans-Atlantic journey, Christopher had served as one of their reverends and was expected to be named head pastor upon his arrival to the New World. A lot had happened since then, including the necessity of him leaving the English settlement. He'd chosen to go on the road to protect Amitola and her unborn babe, the offspring of the late Copper Mountain king. Alas, Amitola's short-lived marriage to him made her child the prince of the mountain people, and they were determined to recapture him.

Riapoke strode up the hill to stand beneath the archway, facing Agnes. Wanchese and his council gathered on one side, and Chief Manteo and his council gathered on the other side. To Agnes's surprise, Riapoke was dressed like an English gentleman in a dark brown suit and a pair of gleaming boots. An ornate leather cape swung around his shoulders, and an ornamental sword rested against his thigh.

Agnes's friends were right. He was apparently trying as hard to please her as she was trying to please him.

He was so handsome it took her breath away. When her steps faltered, Ananias's hand tightened on her arm. Riapoke's gaze smoldered over Agnes, searing her from head to toe. His admiration and approval gave her the confidence to step away from Ananias and take her place at his side.

Take, take, take what is yours! Jane's words revolved in Agnes's mind as Riapoke took her hand and placed it on his arm. She slid her hand down his arm, to entwine her fingers in his, and placed her other hand atop his forearm.

She was rewarded with the tightening of his fingers around hers.

The music dimmed, and Powaw commenced the ceremony in a singsong voice that shook with age. Agnes's breathing turned shallow. Their wedding had begun. If only her parents could see her now. Deep down, she was confident they would approve of Riapoke.

When Powaw finished his speech, Christopher opened his Bible and read through the wedding scriptures. "'Whoso findeth a wife findeth a good thing, and obtaineth favour of the Lord.'" He thumbed through the pages and continued to read, "'Therefore shall a man leave his father and his mother, and shall cleave unto his wife: and they shall be one flesh.'" He droned through the ancient passages, but Agnes could hardly focus on what he said. She was too busy absorbing every sound, every movement, every nuance in the stance of the man who was about to become her husband. The eagerness in him, the suppressed energy.

"'What therefore God hath joined together, let not man put asunder.'" He bent his head to offer up a blessing, then opened his eyes and addressed Riapoke directly. "I pronounce you man and wife. You may kiss the bride."

Riapoke turned to Agnes, a question in his gaze. *Take,*

take, take. She stood on her toes, hands on his shoulders, tipping her face up to his.

He crushed his mouth to hers amidst the whooping of several braves and the faint clapping of colonists. Her heart raced and her knees turned weak when he deepened the kiss. She liked how he had no English scruples against claiming her openly as his. Maybe a few more of his people would finally believe their marriage was a real one.

The singers and musicians resumed their song before he lifted his head. When he finally ended his kiss, his dark gaze caressed her, exultant and possessive. They might as well have been alone for how little attention he gave their guests.

"Ann-nes." He cupped her cheek with one large hand.

She reached behind her neck with shaking hands to undo the clasp of her silver pendent necklace that contained the portraits of her parents. Passed down to her by her Mum when she was a small girl, it was the only thing she owned worth giving away. She lowered the hand Riapoke was using to caress her cheek and pressed the precious piece of jewelry into it.

"For Riapoke. My husband."

He gazed at it for a moment in stunned silence. Then he swept her into his arms. At what cost to his healing midriff, she did not know. She wrapped her arms around his neck and pressed her flaming cheek against his, thoroughly satisfied with his response to her gift. Gone was the stoic set to his features. In its place was impassioned determination.

A cry sounded. At first Agnes thought it was part of the Native's chanting. When it was followed by a volley of arrows, she realized they were again under attack.

CHAPTER 27: THE ATTACK

*A*gnes recognized the Mountain warriors by the copper dripping from nearly every part of their bodies. Copper breastplates protected their chests, and their arms and legs were fitted with sheets of body armor that made her think of Roman gladiators. Even the arrows thudding down around the colonists were crafted of the metal — including the one that plunged through Powaw's priestly garments as he stood beneath the ceremonial trellis, arms raised in supplication, lips moving in prayer.

Riapoke bent forward to shield Agnes with his body and dashed with her to the nearest wigwam. The room appeared to be a meeting room with a fire pit in the center. It was surrounded by boulders. For seating, perhaps?

Or not. Her new husband shoved aside one of the heavy boulders. Beneath it, a cavern yawned. "Get in!" he commanded harshly.

Wordlessly, she let herself down into the hold, and he pushed the boulder back into place, shutting her in.

She expected utter blackness. Instead, six Native women and four Native children stared back at her from a cavern that could easily hold twenty or more people comfortably. It was lit by a single torch ensconced against the wall.

"Ah, hello," Agnes whispered, raising her hand to them. She did not smile, since it was a somber situation with an ambush playing itself out over their heads.

The women stared back, eyes dark with suspicion. One gathered a suckling babe closer and edged away from her.

Mystified, Agnes took a step farther into the room.

"Tah!" the eldest woman spat at a whisper. By the furious waving of her hands, Agnes could only deduce she was bidding her to come no closer.

She slid to the floor where she stood and rested her head against the wall, feeling utterly helpless. Her new husband of a scant few minutes was above ground fighting for his life and the lives of everyone in their settlement, and here she was down below being treated as if *she* was the enemy. She wanted to ask why, to demand answers, but the women probably couldn't understand. Besides, making too much noise would defeat the purpose of hiding.

Instead, she clasped her hands beneath her chin, squeezing her eyes closed, and sent up unceasing prayers for their loved ones who were engaged in battle.

It might have been minutes. It might have been hours. Either way, the passage of time in the dim cavern surrounded by silent, hostile women felt like eons.

They collectively froze when the boulder sealing them inside scraped as if someone was dragging it. Each of the women crouched as if prepared for a fight. They shoved their children behind them, and knives appeared in their hands. Agnes rolled away from her position directly beneath the boulder and pressed farther into the shadows since she had no weapon. Daylight poured down from the opening, and a dark face popped into view. It was Amonsoquath, Chief Wanchese's nephew.

Following a sharp exclamation from the eldest woman, the collection of knives disappeared and the women relaxed their fighting stances. Amonsoquath reached a coppery hand down to draw the first woman up. Agnes could only presume the ambush was over and their people had prevailed, but at what cost?

Please, God, let Riapoke be safe. Agnes waited until the other women and children scrambled from the cavern. Only then did she reach for Amonsoquath's assistance for herself. She was their war chief's wife now. Surely it was her place to look after them.

He hesitated before taking her hand. His dark gaze raked over her as if taking her measure. She shivered at the suspicion she saw there. *What is going on?*

Then he reached for her. She clasped his arm with both hands, eyes never leaving his, while he raised her into the wigwam. She wondered if he would speak to her. As the chief's nephew, he probably knew a few bits and phrases of English. At least she hoped.

"How many are hurt?" She dared not ask how many were dead. Her heart was not ready to hear about any more losses.

"*Caumear.*" Amonsoquath led her outside. She had to shield her eyes from the sudden blast of sun.

Colonists and Natives were working together to drag and discard copper-covered bodies to a pile at the edge of camp. More Natives were standing vigil around the growing pile. Their task seemed to be to divest the corpses of their copper before throwing them atop a burning pyre.

A single Copper Mountain attacker was bound to a tree squirming and arching beneath his bonds. His eyes bulged in terror. Agnes wondered if he was their only prisoner or if there were more.

"Agnes!" Rose ran up to her and grabbed her upper arms,

scanning her face. "You are the last one to be accounted for. Where have you been?"

"In a cave beneath the ground."

She looked perplexed. "The other women did not mention you."

"They acted is if I was made of poison." She frowned. "What is going on? Why are your people so angry with me?"

"Our people, Agnes. You are married to Riapoke. They are your people now."

"Why do they hate me so much?"

"Caumear-ah!" Amonsoquath's voice was more urgent.

Rose fell in step beside them as he led Agnes to the priest's tent.

"The colonists were on patrol during your wedding," Rose explained in a loud whisper. "They failed to detect the approach of the Mountain People. The Croatoans and Roanokes blame the English for the attack. Most unfortunately, many of them include you, me, and Jane in that blame."

"How many did we lose?" Agnes asked, dread pounding through her chest.

"None yet, but Powaw was hit, and it doesn't look good for him."

"He's alive," she breathed, greatly relieved to hear it. So long as he still breathed, there was hope she could save him. Agnes knew little about the Croatoan priest, only that he and Riapoke conversed often and seemed closely acquainted.

"Aye, he still lives, but barely," Rose confirmed. "The reason we did not suffer more casualties was because the mountain people were so weighed down with copper they could not move as quickly as our warriors. Plus, the sun glinted off their breast plates, making them easy targets."

"They are fools!" Agnes snapped.

"Aye, to the tune of eleven dead and one captured.

Manteo suspects they were sent to test our strength. He says a much larger war party will follow."

Lord, have mercy! Agnes shuddered.

Jane met them at the door of the tent with Agnes's aid bag.

Agnes grabbed the bag and ducked inside, fearing what she would see.

Powaw reclined on a bedroll beside the fire, shivering. The copper arrow in his chest could not have pierced his heart, or he would already be dead. Riapoke crouched beside him, speaking softly in their native tongue.

Powaw touched her husband's forehead with a gnarled hand and spoke something in a singsong chant. There was something so poignant, so final about the gesture that it filled Agnes with unspeakable sadness.

She waited until he was finished speaking before creeping silently forward to stand beside her husband. Only when he glanced up to acknowledge her did she drop to her knees beside him. She rested her hands on his shoulders. "You are well, my husband?"

"*Cuppeh,*" he answered. He removed Agnes's hands from his shoulders and turned her to face the injured councilman. "Can…you…help?"

She took in the gray pallor of the man's features, the glistening sweat on his temples, and her heart sank. "I will do my best." She could make no promises.

She opened her bag and laid out her tools. "We need to remove the arrow as quickly as possible. I'll need hot water."

Riapoke gave a sharp command to the brave standing next to the door of the tent. The young warrior pounded a fist over his chest and ducked through the exit.

Just as Rose had done for Agnes during Riapoke's surgery, he held a candle over her hands to make it easier to work.

When his brave returned with a hollowed-out log filled

with steaming water, Jane was right behind him. "How can I help?"

"Swab, my friend." Agnes handed her a length of muslin and cut away Powaw's tunic. They cleaned the site of the wound then Agnes commenced the procedure. The arrow was embedded perpendicular to the skin, and it was deep. Alas, the incision would have to go as far as the arrowhead.

Powaw waved away both the wine and the biting stick. Riapoke offered him a pipe instead, which the man swiftly accepted and puffed on readily. Agnes fought a wave of light-headedness as she inhaled the strong woodsy scent of the smoke.

"Take shallow breaths," Jane cautioned. "There's something mighty strong in their tobacco. Always makes the elders a bit woozy when they use it. Like they've had too much wine."

Agnes batted away a swirl of it with her hand and averted her face as much as possible from the fresh smoke rings. She bent over Powaw and lanced one side of the arrow wound then probed deeper with her scalpel.

To her surprise, Powaw did not even flinch. Glancing at his face, Agnes was sickened by the glazed cast to his eyes and the peaceful expression settling across his features. *Oh, nay! I am losing him. Please God, help me save him.*

As soon as she nudged the arrowhead with her scalpel, she began the slow and precarious process of pulling it free.

When at last Agnes held the offending weapon in her bloodstained hands, Jane pressed her swab firmly against the opening of the wound.

Powaw's chest seized. He coughed and made a choking sound, eyes rolling back in his head. Despite Jane's effort to apply pressure, more blood belched from the wound and spread beneath her fingers.

Agonized, Agnes and Jane stared at each other. There was nothing more they could do for him.

Powaw shuddered once more. Then his body stilled for the last time. He was gone.

Agnes glanced over her shoulder at Riapoke and shook her head. Tears burned her eyes. She had failed him and his people.

All the emotion seemed to drain from his face. His features turned stony, and he settled noiselessly on the ground beside his departed friend.

He spoke something softly to no one in particular.

"He asks us to leave him so he can mourn in private," Jane whispered.

Agnes did not blame her husband for sending them away. They represented everything he hated, everything he had lost from past to present. Agnes's heart ached for him, but there was no way to make it right. The Englishmen on patrol had failed to detect the approach of their enemies, and Agnes had failed to save their councilman from his deadly wounds. Her hope faltered. If Riapoke did not find it in his heart to forgive her, their short-lived marriage was over.

Medical bag in hand, Agnes stumbled from Riapoke's tent into the sunlight. Unsure what else she was expected to do, she wandered to the edge of the Croatoan camp. As Riapoke's new wife, she was displaced from her own people, but she was not wanted by his. The maidens had made that abundantly clear. And now her own husband was sending her from his tent. She had to no place left to go.

"Where are you, God?" Agnes rested her hand against a bald cypress. "You promised never to leave us, but we seem to have lost You somewhere between England and here. Where, oh, where, did we go wrong?"

CHAPTER 28: WAR COUNCIL

*A*monsoquath came to collect Agnes when dusk fell. He led her to a nearly frozen spring at the base of the hill and helped wash the blood from her hands and clothing. She barely registered his presence. She no longer cared about anything. Her heart and brain were numb.

"*Caumear.*" His expression was drawn, but his voice was gentle. He led her to Riapoke's tent, where a fire burned. Her few belongings were present — Rose and Manteo's gift of clay pots, a change of buckskin clothing, and a pair of moccasins.

She sat on a raised platform draped in bear furs and stared at the fire for hours, but Riapoke did not return home. The fire finally sputtered out. She curled on her side and pulled the furs over her, not caring how cold the air was.

When morning broke, her new husband was still gone. Agnes straightened her hair and clothing, took care of her basic necessities, and went in search of him.

Rose met her at the main campfire.

"Where is he? My husband?"

"See that tent ahead of us where all the smoke is coming from?"

Agnes hadn't considered it before, but now that Rose pointed it out, an unusual amount of smoke billowed from the holes in its ceiling. Steam, too.

"It is called a sweat lodge. Our people go there to meditate." She handed Agnes a small clay pot with something steaming in it. "It is tea, but be careful. It's scalding."

Agnes cupped the bowl between both hands and blew on it before taking a tentative sip. It tasted of roots and berries and did wonders to warm her insides.

"The counsel interrogated our captive, who was more than happy to talk after sitting a few minutes on a pile of fire ants. He warned that another war party is headed our way. The first group was merely sent to gather intelligence about our numbers and resources."

Things were exactly as Chief Manteo had postulated.

"What will we do?"

She shrugged. "We are at war. We've been expecting it. The elders have convened to their sweat tent to seek divine guidance for our next course of action. The coming war is not the only thing I fear, though." She made an impatient sound. "Drink, my friend. You've hardly touched your tea."

The tea was delicious. Agnes shivered and sipped it slowly. "What else do you fear?"

"There is talk of the Roanokes and Croatoans pulling away from the colonial settlement and starting over somewhere else."

Agnes lowered her bowl. "They wish to abandon the English, altogether?"

"Aye. The Natives bear a list of grievances against our countrymen a mile long. We've shot at them by accident, sickened them with our diseases, and made mistake after mistake in battle. Can you blame them?"

"Nay, not when you put it that way. But we both know the Dares and the rest of the colonists meant no ill to their neighbors. They were simply unprepared for this." Agnes waved her hands to encompass the English section of their combined settlement. "The ambushes, kidnappings, and constant fear that put the English on the run. Faith! They're not soldiers, Rose. They came to the New World to explore and draw maps, to raise crops and build ships, to start schools and churches, to weave and to carve — not to fight."

Rose nodded. "Indeed, my husband is working hard to convince them of our need to stick together, but it is becoming more and more difficult to do so." A smile lit her face as she pointed. "Speaking of husbands, there they are, dearest."

The councilmen filed from the sweat lodge, stoic of face and reddened by the heat. One of the elders stumbled. Rose hurried to her husband's side, snatching up a fresh bowl of tea on her way. More women converged on the other councilmen.

Stomach churning with anxiety, Agnes forced her feet to move. She refilled her bowl of tea from the pitcher hanging over the fire and approached her husband. He was conferring with another elder and did not look up. She was half a dozen paces away when a pair of young maidens stepped in front of her. They draped blankets around the two men's shoulders and offered them steaming beverages, which the men gratefully accepted. Agnes bit her lip and paused. It would be foolish to offer her husband a second bowl of tea.

She stood her ground in growing anger, as one of the young women remained at Riapoke's side, fussing over him far longer than Agnes deemed necessary. She was beautiful in a foreign way with her high cheekbones, energetic movements, and sun-kissed complexion. She was several inches taller than Agnes, too, with a willowy frame encased in a short tunic and pair of much tighter breeches than the ones she'd been given to wear to her wedding. It was as if the woman had nearly outgrown them. The result was the show-casing of her curvy frame in a way that left little to the imagination. *What a strumpet!*

While Agnes was trying to determine the most ladylike way to divert her husband's attentions from the young woman, someone bumped into her roughly from behind, making her stumble forward. The bowl slipped from her hands. The clay dish shattered on impact with the hard packed earth, and tea splattered in all directions.

She was unable to regain her equilibrium and fell to her knees. Her hands landed in the middle of the shards. One of them sliced her palm. *So much for a graceful approach.* She glanced over her shoulder in time to see one of the women from the cavern ducking behind a tent. Had she pushed Agnes on purpose? Her face burned in mortification at being made to look so clumsy in front of her husband. Knowing she would be criticized over the needless waste of a dish, she scrambled to pick up the broken pieces.

While she worked, Agnes darted a glance at Riapoke. He was finally looking at her, his expression unreadable. The young maiden continued to hover, making occasional adjustments to the blanket around his shoulders.

She raised her chin beneath his perusal. *A fine time to notice your own wife after she's been made to look the fool!* She finished picking up the pieces, rose, and turned on her heel. *Go ahead. Let your people mock me. 'Tis only one more miserable detail to add to my already miserable existence.* Like kicking a dog when he was down.

She pulled deep within her exemplary upbringing to maintain her composure and forced herself to walk at a normal pace to Riapoke's tent. His people could shame her. They could conspire together to make her look her worst.

Apparently, they could also injure her. Her throbbing palm was proof of it. But they could only steal her dignity if she let them.

Once inside his wigwam, she blew on the dying embers and coaxed the fire back to life. By the light of the fire, she determined the cut on her hand was more serious than she originally thought. It needed stitches. With a sigh, she rinsed away the dirt using water from one of the rain basket run-offs on the floor and poured a few precious drops of wine into the wound to ward off infection. Fortunately, the wound was on her left hand. She was right-handed.

She threaded a needle and bit down on one of the pain sticks. Let everyone else play the part of hero. She was grateful to have something to gnash her teeth into when she pierced her hand with the needle.

A rustling just outside the tent gave her pause. When the sound did not repeat itself, she resumed stitching. She neatly tied the knot at the end and cut the thread. Only then did she take a full breath, wildly grateful the worst part was over. She dabbed away the remaining drops of blood and wrapped her hand in thick gauze. It would continue to ooze through the night, and she did not wish to stain her clothing.

She set away her medical supplies and reached beneath her sleeping platform for the beautiful new clay pots from Rose. If her husband ever decided to return home, she would have a stew pot simmering. Her hands connected with nothing but air. Biting her lip against the pain, Agnes dropped to her knees to peer beneath the platform. The pots were missing.

She heard the rustling sound again. It was followed by a scraping sound, then the pounding of feet. Someone was running away.

Agnes shoved aside the curtain between the two rooms but could discern nothing amiss. Shaking her head, she proceeded to search the longhouse, growing more frantic by the minute. She rummaged through baskets and tools, wondering if someone had moved her clay pots. Perhaps the stranger she'd heard skulking in the back room had. Her search proved fruitless. The pots were gone.

She sank on the bed and dropped her face in her hands. *Nay! I will not cry over a set of missing pots.* There were far more important things to concern herself with. Preparations for Powaw's funeral. The coming war. The potential abandonment of her English friends. Her endless prayers for the safety of her parents. Reminding herself of all the greater matters at stake turned out to be a useless exercise. The disappearance of her two cooking pots was apparently her breaking point.

Agnes wept. Silently, of course. She refused to give her tormentors outside the longhouse the satisfaction of hearing her accept defeat.

Her husband did not bother returning home the second night of their marriage, and her spirits plummeted to a new low. She began to doubt the wisdom of marrying Riapoke. She did not doubt her feelings for him or the magic in his kisses, only the wisdom of fancying she could marry a Native war chief and dance away with him into the sunset. She'd not counted on the emotional tide of his people turning entirely against the English. She had not counted on being viewed as their enemy. It was a battle she hadn't seen coming and one she didn't know how to fight.

Rose came to fetch her at daybreak. "The council has voted to send a small party of warriors to intercept the next flood of Mountain People headed our way."

Agnes leaped from her sleeping platform and folded her blankets. "We will ambush the ambushers, eh?"

"Aye, to prevent another attack on our camp, as well as to avenge Powaw. Riapoke is to lead them."

Dread settled in Agnes's belly. He was still healing from his last battle wound. "When do they leave?" She hurriedly finger combed her hair to undo yesterday's braids, so she could re-plait it.

"Nay, Agnes. There's no time to primp. Your husband will depart any moment. If you want to bid him farewell, you must go now."

Agnes gaped at her for a moment, knowing how sleep rumpled she must look with her waist length hair flowing over her shoulders and chest. It appeared Rose was serious. *Ah, very well.* She yanked on her fur coat and moccasins and followed her friend into the frigid morning breezes.

The warriors were applying mud to their faces. *Only a dozen?* Surely they were sending more. Agnes glanced around the settlement at the other men, but no others joined their ranks. The men traveled light. Only their weapons and water packs were strapped to their sides plus a series of cross body pouches, which she hoped contained plenty of dried meat rations. She recognized Amonsoquath but none of the others.

Rose named them for her in undertones. "Those two are brothers, Kemi and Kitchi. Then—"

"Who is she?" Agnes interrupted. The young woman who'd flirted with her husband the day before was at his side again, chattering animatedly as he swung his quiver of arrows across his back and strapped it in place.

She held his quiver up while he adjusted the straps.

"Her name is Poca." Rose sounded disapproving. "She is a good worker, but..." Her voice dwindled.

I see. It looked like it was time for her and Poca to establish a few boundaries between them. Agnes's anger simmered, but she forced her voice to remain calm. "How do I say *thank you* in Croatoan?"

"*Kenah.* Why?"

"I need to thank someone for her continuous but entirely unnecessary tending to my husband's needs," Agnes said through gritted teeth as she glided towards Riapoke.

Bestowing what she hoped was a gracious smile on the young woman, she spoke in her most dismissive tone, "*Kenah, Poca.*"

The maiden's eyes widened in surprise at hearing Agnes speak her language. Agnes wedged herself between Poca and Riapoke, earning a huff of shocked disapproval from her. The maiden could no longer reach him without bodily shoving Agnes out of the way. Her gut told her the ill-mannered chit would not dare do such a thing to the man's wife in his presence. Or so she hoped.

Heart pounding in trepidation, Agnes pretended to completely ignore Poca. She kept her hand on Riapoke's quiver until he finished securing it.

With a sharp sound of fury, the woman spun away from them. Agnes watched from the corners of her eyes but did not spare the maiden a full glance. She stepped around her husband's large frame to face him.

"Ann-nes." His hard features softened, and his hands settled on her waist.

The tired lines around his eyes made her wonder if he'd slept at all since Powaw's death. Between grieving and attending war party meetings, he had to be exhausted. Her heart melted for him. "Riapoke." She stepped closer.

With a grunt of surprise, he lifted the injured hand she placed on his chest. "You…are…hurt."

As if he hadn't witnessed the whole humiliating event last night. She rolled her eyes as he began to untie the gauze. She grimaced at the dried and caked blood. She hadn't had the time yet this morning to change her dressing.

He froze at the sight of the stitches, realization dawning that she had tended the wound herself. "Ann-nes," he said regretfully and briefly closed his eyes. He opened one of the many pouches at his side and dabbed a dark, pasty substance over the stitches. Then he wound a fresh strip of deerskin over them and tied it in place more snugly than she'd been able to do on her own.

"*Kenah*," she said softly and cupped his cheeks when he lowered his head over hers. "Rose told me to bid you farewell, but I will not. I've said farewell to enough of the people I love. All I want is for you to come home safely and be my husband. No matter how far you travel and how long you must stay, know this. I am yours, and you are mine."

Riapoke's gaze flared with passion. "*Nouwmais*," he said thickly, cupping a hand behind her head and claiming her lips. Her knees buckled, which must have thrown him off balance, because they tumbled together to the ground. Somehow he landed beneath her. Instead of pulling her to her feet, however, he cradled her against his large body and slanted his mouth over hers.

The many pouches slung across his chest and secured to his waist dug into her belly and chest, but Agnes did not care. All that mattered was for him to understand she wanted to be his wife in every sense of the word when he returned from battle.

His lips traveled hotly across her cheeks and temples, settling at last in her hair. "Mine," he rasped and rolled with her, still kissing her as if his life depended on it. He sprang to a crouch and pulled her to her feet. All the while, his dark gaze drank in her well-kissed lips and disheveled state.

"I...will...come back," he promised in the halting guttural tones she adored. He struck his fist across his chest and returned to the dozen men he'd assembled.

Giving a sharp order, he took off at a jog. His warriors followed. None of them looked back.

CHAPTER 29: OUTSIDER

*F*ortunately, Chief Manteo and Rose remained at camp one hill over. Otherwise, Agnes would have felt completely isolated from the rest of the settlement. When she visited the Croatoans, they were worshipful of their red-haired princess but showed little interest in adopting a second Englishwoman into their midst.

It was worse on the hill where Agnes now lived with the Roanokes. They made no effort to include her in their conversations or activities, not even their tasks.

The Roanokes and Croatoans, alike, had all but cut off communications with the English on the southernmost hill, sending out their own patrols and only rotating shifts between the two tribes. It mattered not that the English continued to send out patrols every third day. They were summarily ignored by the Natives. Chief Manteo increased his efforts to restore relations. He still held meetings with the Dares, Anthony, and Christopher but it was more symbolic than effective.

Agnes watched from a distance as her English friends finished building Fort Chowan. When it was finished, they put up the final stretch of palisade to enclose the structure. Next, they worked as quickly as they could to raise more log cabins around the perimeter of the fort. Construction commenced on an outer palisade wall to enclose the homes.

Despite the hostile attitude of the Roanokes towards the new wife of their war chief, she chose to spend most of her time with them. It was only right, since this was her new home. Besides, the English were not as adept at hunting as the Natives, so staying away from them amounted to one less mouth for them to feed.

With her pots stolen, Agnes could not cook her own stew to contribute to the tribe, so she set to work foraging for winter berries, roots, and nuts and offering her finds to those who owned stew pots. She received many reluctant huffs and snorts for her efforts, but the women always accepted her gifts. She considered it progress that they didn't spit in her face or toss them at her feet. Fortunately, food was too precious a commodity to turn down.

Poca and another young handmaiden, whose name Agnes learned was Kaliska, mocked her at every opportunity. "Pale Face," Poca spat each time Agnes passed by them. Those were the only English words she seemed to know. Agnes supposed she could be grateful for the maiden's limited vocabulary. She listened very closely to the Roanokes in order to learn as many of their words as possible. She also watched their gestures and studied their habits.

There was not much she could do to win over Poca, because the maiden wanted the one thing Agnes had no intention of sharing with anyone — her husband. So Agnes latched on to the eldest woman in the tribe, instead. She remembered her from being sealed in the underground chamber together. Her name was Winona.

The elder woman pretty much ignored Agnes, but she did not chase her away when she followed her around. From

Winona, Agnes learned she did not need wheat to make flour. She ground many of the nuts and seeds Agnes gathered and used the pasty substance the same as wheat flour. Excited at the discovery, Agnes fetched her mortar and pestle and mimicked the woman's moves. She also observed Winona boiling roots like potatoes and eating them in a similar manner. Other roots she dried and ground into flour. During Agnes's brief visits to Fort Chowan, she shared both tricks with her English friends, most of whom were accustomed to purchasing these items from a shop, not creating them from scratch.

"I need to make more clay pots," Agnes informed Rose a few days later. She was fast running out of makeshift cloth pouches to store all the flour she'd made. Riapoke owned few dishes of his own, since cooking was generally considered by his people to be women's work.

"Certainly. We'll need to harvest a good amount of clay. Meet me at the edge of the Chowan River in about an hour."

The river's edge stretched for miles, and Agnes did not immediately see Rose when she arrived. She bided her time by digging up roots in the tree line while keeping an eye out for her friend.

Once her pouch was full to bursting with roots, she stood to stretch her back and absorb the beauty of the forest. She rubbed her gloved hands together to warm them and breathed in the cool, earthy scents of the morning. The centuries-old cypresses surrounding her were lovely. Back in the lumber-starved landscapes of England where the human population was growing quicker than the plant population, it was difficult to find a tree so tall and mature these days. Even more beautiful than the cypresses were the endless acres of tupelos growing straight up though the marshy delta. Many grew so closely together as to form triangular caverns at their bases. Some of these caverns were large enough to stand inside. Unable to resist exploring, Agnes climbed a short knoll to firmer ground and stepped inside one of the tented stands of trees.

She stood amazed, gazing up at the pointed ceiling composed of gnarled tree roots, until a rustling sound had her spinning around. The thud of a hard object against the back of her head sent her to her hands and knees. *Heavens! Did one of the branches collapse?* Maybe she should have been more careful before plunging into the forest alone. When the second hit came, Agnes perceived the thud to be too precise to be an accident. She tried to twist around to catch a glimpse of her attacker, but a third hit sent her world spiraling into blackness.

Agnes awoke to a dark and smoky room of pain.

"Agnes? Thank God! You're awake at last."

Agnes could hear Rose but could not see her. *Why can't I open my blasted eyes?* "I can't see you." Fear trembled in her chest.

"Quit struggling, darling. I'm trying to tend to your poor face, but your eyes are swollen shut. I don't reckon it will do any good to ask what happened?"

"Someone hit me from behind."

"They did more than that, my friend." Rose draped something across Agnes's eyes that felt warm and sticky. "I'm trying to determine if your nose is broken."

So I was beaten by my attacker. At least it was only a beating. If her attacker had wanted her dead, she would be dead. What was this, then? A punishment? A warning? Agnes's thoughts immediately flew to Poca and her friend, Kaliska. Did they hate their war chief's wife enough to beat her to a pulp? *Aye, more than likely.* She would have to be more careful in the future, more diligent. No more wandering around alone, not even in their own camp, which was a dead shame. The area within their border patrol should have been safe and probably was for everyone but her. It was a depressing thought.

"Are there any protruding bone fragments?" Agnes asked calmly.

"Nay," Rose sighed.

Good. "Is it listing to one side or the other?"

"Nay."

"Any unusually large bumps?"

"Aye. Your whole face is swollen. I can only presume you've a nose hidden in there somewhere. Oh, Agnes! I cannot imagine who would do such a thing. Within the perimeter of our own camp, too. 'Tis unheard of."

"At least they let me live," Agnes mumbled. Her mind was swarming with thoughts. The Roanokes had not let George Howe live when he'd wandered off alone during the first few days of their arrival to the New World. They'd learned later he'd been killed to avenge Pemisapan, the chief who had perished at the hands of the previous shipload of English explorers.

"I am grateful you are alive, but whoever did this to you attacked the wife of our war chief." Rose's voice was grave. "Manteo is inquiring into the matter. Whoever is responsible for your wounds will be severely punished."

"It will only make matters worse, and you know it," Agnes grumbled. "The Natives are simply angry about my failure to save Powaw's life."

"The arrow you pulled from him was poisoned. There was naught you could do to save him."

"Aye, but it is hard to see reason when you're looking for someone to blame, and the English are a convenient target. Our men failed to prevent the attack of the Mountain People, which led to Powaw's injuries."

"Are you listening to yourself?" Rose cried. "I would argue the Mountain People are one hundred percent to blame for the attack. I know the Englishmen on patrol failed to pick up their trail, but they are not soldiers. They are ship builders, blacksmiths, and construction workers. Men trained to run the daily affairs of a town or parish, not to wage war. By all that is holy, it is past time the Natives stop blaming the English for not being Natives and for the English to stop blaming the Natives for not being English. I told my husband the same this morning. If we do not start working together and sharing our respective skills, we shall perish together and rightly so."

"Here, here!" Agnes smiled or at least attempted to, despite the pain in her cracked lips. To hear their former ship clerk speak so passionately was a treat. When she and Rose first met, Rose was silent as a ghost and kept to herself in the ship's hull, taking inventories every waking moment. She had blindly signed up for the risky colonial venture to outrun a broken heart and had nearly died in the process — multiple times. It was a delight to hear her exhibit the sturdy spine she'd developed during their overseas journey.

"Hush." Rose applied something oily to Agnes's lips. A minty scent filled the air. "Until this matter is resolved, Manteo and Wanchese have assigned two braves to keep watch over you day and night. Their names are Chogan and Mantunaaga, one brave from each tribe your husband serves. They are in their teens but are skilled hunters and trackers already. I do not know Mantunaaga personally, but I adore Chogan. He's the son of one of the warriors on the road with Riapoke. Mantunaaga is a Roanoke scout. He will mainly rotate to give Chogan enough time to sleep, but Chogan will spend every waking moment with you."

"Oh, nay," Agnes groaned. "I can only imagine how they must feel to be stuck playing nanny. Probably strangle me in the night and be done with it."

"Then you know nothing about our people, Agnes. Both

men volunteered for the task. Chogan worships your husband and considers it an honor to serve you in his absence."

"Oh." *Seriously?*

"There will be no more stealing from you, either," Rose added severely. "When were you going to admit the loss of my wedding gifts was the real reason you needed to make more pots?"

Agnes sniffed and discovered sniffing hurt as much as smiling. "Tattling will get me no closer to winning the hearts of our people. We are so different from them, Rose. They think we are weak, and maybe we are in the physical sense. We've not spent our lives outdoors living like nomads as they have. However, we have other strengths to offer. Masonry and construction skills, furniture making, the art of weaving, sewing and embroidery, and medicinal skills. We've coopers and carvers, cutlers and blacksmiths. If only they'd give us a chance, we could improve their existence immensely. I—"

"There you go again, thinking like an Englishwoman," Rose interrupted in a tone of reprimand. "The Natives survived for generations without us and therefore put little value in our skills. Do not stand by and wait for opportunities to show off your English skills. We must give of ourselves freely every day, without any expectation of personal gain. Only then will we begin to break down the barriers of distrust and hate that lie between us."

Rose was right. Agnes nodded, another movement that hurt unbelievably. "How did you get to be so wise, my friend?"

"Seeing your broken face," she retorted with a hitch in her voice. "I vow this is the last straw, Agnes. The very last straw. I am done dancing around the issue. As soon as I finish tending you, I am calling our women together for a special meeting, and I am going to share what is on my heart with every one of them."

Agnes could tell by her tone her friend was deadly serious. Rose went so far as to make Agnes sit outside while she made her speech in halting Powhata. Though Agnes could neither see a thing nor understand most of what Rose said, she was proud of Rose for the sentiment behind the gesture. At the end of her speech, it seemed she was chastising the women for their treatment of Riapoke in their abuse of his wife. Agnes could feel her cheeks burning with embarrassment and was greatly relieved when Rose led her back inside her tent.

Rose and Winona took turns tending Agnes most of the next day and a half until the swelling went down enough for her to crack open her eyelids. Agnes was alone when she could finally see again. She immediately marched outside in search of Rose with the warrior, Chogan, silently stalking her heels.

Rose was busy mending a pair of deerskin leggings. She eyed Agnes with concern. "How are you, my friend?"

"I believe we were interrupted in our plans for making pots."

She laughed aloud. "Ready to go to work already, are you? At least we will have Chogan's help this time." She handed him a large pot to carry. He silently accepted it from her.

They dug a good twenty pounds or more of clay from the walls of the river. It was a thick, plasticky substance that could be bent and coiled without cracking. They returned to camp, and Rose transferred it to a large hollowed out log outside her tent. She added a few cups of finely crushed shells to the mixture. With a broom-sized pestle, she demonstrated how to knead out the air bubbles. They took turns with this task. When the mixture was kneaded to her satisfaction, Rose showed Agnes how to form her first bowl. A hollowed out hole in the ground served as the mold to shape the vessel.

"If you want to etch a design in the sides, you must do so before it dries." Rose provided an array of sharp-edged rock and bone tools for decorating the pots. With respect to time, Agnes kept her designs simple. She scraped a border of ivy and rosebuds around the rim of one. Around the rim of another, she etched a series of spread eagle wings, the symbol of the Croatoan tribe. Around a third pot, she engraved a trail of bear claws like the ones so many of the Roanoke warriors boasted on their bodies. Her hands were steady from years of medical work, and she was able to wield the tools with skill. She was immensely satisfied with the results.

Rose smiled widely as she turned one of the pots for a better view. "You are quite the artist, my friend."

They made five new bowls from the amount of clay they'd gathered. Then they placed them in a shallow fiery pit to harden them. When the bowls were finished, Rose insisted Agnes keep all five of them. "As a newlywed, you need them more than I do." It was kind of her not to point out Agnes had brought next to nothing into her marriage.

Rose helped her stack the pots with a layer of deer cloth between each one to keep them from scraping together. Chogan helped Agnes carry them to the tent she shared with Riapoke. Despite Chogan and Mantunaaga taking turns standing guard, she was taking no chances this time. She spent the next hour hollowing out an enormous hole in the ground. She secured four out of five of the new dishes inside and placed a wide, flat rock atop them. Then she piled baskets and tools atop the rock.

She lifted the fifth pot, which she thought turned out the finest, and hurried with it in her arms to seek out Winona.

She grunted in disdain at Agnes's approach.

She held out the pot to the elder woman and carefully

enunciated the words she'd practiced with Rose. *"Paatch-ah, Winona. Netab." A gift for Winona. My friend.*

Winona stiffened, and her grimace deepened. At first she refused to look at Agnes, but she must have caught a glimpse of the pot out of the corner of her eye. In a stiff-jointed manner, she shifted sideways to stare at it.

"Paatch-ah, Winona?" Her voice rose in a question as she examined the pot more closely. She ran a callused finger over the delicate etching of ivy and rosebuds. Her finger rested on one of the buds for a moment. Then she raised her head and pierced Agnes with a dark look. She abruptly snatched the pot from her hands and continued to examine it, murmuring over the design.

Pleased at Winona's response, Agnes went back to work. She pulled out her pouch of freshly ground nut flour and proceeded to mix a pasty dough for bread, helping herself to one of the duck eggs she'd helped gather and a bit of bear fat from the first hunt. Following Winona's example from the day before, Agnes wrapped the dough in damp leaves and bark and placed it in a pit of ashes to bake.

An agonized wail from a young girl gave her pause. A taller girl was swinging her round and round within a circle of children. When the taller girl set her down, the younger one clutched one of her arms and continued to wail, louder than before. The arm appeared immobile.

Perceiving the limb was dislocated, Agnes stood. A woman brushed past to examine the arm, bending and moving it to test it for a break. Agnes cringed as the child cried harder, her voice taking on a wild edge.

Unable to stand by and watch the child's misery, Agnes dashed to the small group. "Please." She signed to the woman. "Let me help."

At first the maiden ignored her, turning the child to face in another direction so a different woman could examine her. When none of their efforts proved helpful and the child remained inconsolable, Winona stomped over to the group. A few sharp words in her guttural voice had the other women stepping aside.

Winona motioned Agnes forward. Agnes signed for her to place her arms tightly around the child. Winona complied with a heavy scowl marring her features. Agnes plucked a small branch from a nearby tree and quickly broke it to form a makeshift biting stick. Placing it between the child's teeth, she positioned herself on the child's injured side and raised the useless arm. Without giving her a chance to figure out her intentions, Agnes yanked quickly and firmly, wrenching the arm straight out from her body.

The biting stick fell from her lips as she uttered another piercing wail. The arm snapped back in its socket, and she abruptly fell silent. She stood there panting and staring at Agnes, wide-eyed with surprise and fear. Perceiving she could use her arm again, she wiggled it experimentally.

Due to her resemblance to the child, a woman Agnes presumed was either the mother or an older sister approached her. "*Kenah,*" she said gruffly.

"You are welcome." Agnes smiled at her and repeated it in her native tongue. "*Chamah.*"

Fixing the child's dislocated shoulder improved Agnes's relationship with Winona. It also caused the children to flock around her, which was a pleasant change. They might be small, but they were fabulous company and Agnes was too lonely to be picky. She knitted shirts for their cornhusk dolls and braided a rope, which she then taught them how to jump like an English child. The tallest girl proved to be the most skilled at jumping. Her lithe, graceful frame lasted ten minutes or more during one of Agnes's observations.

After the shoulder incident, the women in general seemed less chilly to her, allowing her to more freely observe them at work. Several took the time to painstakingly instruct her on how to make use of each part of the animals their men hunted, including the parts Agnes was accustomed to throwing away.

They cured, dried, and stored meat. From the hides, they prepared clothing and blankets. From the bones, they crafted tools and instruments. From the sinew, they pulled apart thin strands to use for cordage. The innards they fed to the dogs. All in all, Agnes was amazed by the Natives' lack of waste and made a mental note to share her new skills with her English friends at the next opportunity.

Despite Agnes's progress with the rest of the women, Poca and Kaliska continued to keep their distance. Since she was fairly certain these two women were responsible for her attack, Agnes knew better than to let down her guard. She continually watched her back when she was awake. Chogan and Mantunaaga kept vigil while she slept.

She didn't dare visit Fort Chowan for the next couple of weeks for fear of what her countrymen might do if they found out about the assault on her.

CHAPTER 30: UNBORN BABE

*R*ose declared Agnes's face was much improved, just in time for one of Chief Manteo's joint council meetings. Ananias, Christopher, and Anthony arrived to represent the English. Agnes was sitting outside her wigwam, crushing nuts into flour, when they arrived. Anthony strode in her direction the moment he caught sight of her. He took one look at the residual bruising on her face and stiffened in alarm.

"What happened to you?" he demanded.

"A good morning to you as well, my friend." she answered evenly, squinting up at him through the morning sun.

He glared at the tall man standing beside the entrance of her tent. "Still guarding you every moment, eh? It's like you're a prisoner here."

Agnes smiled up at her protector. "This is Chogan. He looks after me."

"Not well enough, apparently. What happened to your face?"

"I fell in the forest. So clumsy of me." Agnes bent her head and continued crushing nuts with her mortar. With a little luck, Anthony would soon rejoin the councilmen and leave her be.

He crouched beside her, forearms resting on his knees. "You are the most graceful and least clumsy of all my female acquaintances on two continents."

"Thank you, my lord." She chuckled in appreciation, unable to be anything but flattered by his compliment. When she glanced up again, he was smiling.

Oh, how wonderful it was to behold a friendly face, especially one as handsome as his! She drank in the welcome sight of his aristocratic nose and features, his well-clipped hair and sideburns, and his short van-dyke beard. For a brief moment, she allowed herself to wander through the forbidden territory of what might have been between them. She winced when those thoughts brought a quick stab of sadness and forced them aside. She was married to another man. A man darker, taller, and more dangerous looking. A man with the ability to kiss away all coherent thoughts. A man who loved her in ways Anthony never would.

He made a sound of frustration. "Do not start my-lording me again after all this time, Agnes. I cannot bear it."

Her heart warmed at his words. He sounded as if he missed her. She had missed him, too. She'd missed their friendship, stimulating conversations, and humor that frequently erupted from them. Agnes still harbored hopes that their friendship would survive her marriage.

"I was only teasing you." She laid down her tools and crossed her arms. "Trying to distract you from your needless worries about me."

"Teasing, eh? While you're at it, you should concoct a more convincing story about your face."

He wanted a better story, eh? She grinned at him. "You think my face looks bad? You should see the creature who caused it. Oh, wait! You cannot." She struck her hand against her forehead as if just remembering something. "His insides are turning over my fire and his fur warms my bed at night."

Anthony gave a bark of laughter. "You went hunting? No wonder you did not wish to confess what you'd done. Someone should throttle you for the risks you took."

She expelled a breath of relief at the knowledge he seemed to believe her second fabrication better than the first.

His expression turned serious. "Do not let them change you too much, Agnes. You are more nurse than huntress. I would prefer you focus more of your time on healing than slaughtering. Let your husband do the—" He broke off, shamefaced, as he remembered her husband was off fighting to protect them all.

A shadow fell over Agnes.

"A good morning to you, Agnes," Christopher greeted her cheerfully. He slapped Anthony on the shoulder. "The meeting is beginning, my friend. Your presence is needed."

As Anthony and Christopher strolled away, heads bent in conversation, Agnes caught Poca and Kaliska staring hard at her.

She waved to them and received the expected lack of response. With a sigh, she returned to her flour grinding.

Another shadow fell across her.

"Chogan?" She glanced up at Chogan, but he remained at his post, staring straight ahead. The shadow was Christopher's. He had returned.

He squatted down beside her. "You were wise to hide your recent beating from Anthony."

She dropped her eyes. "If you found out the truth so easily, it is only a matter of time before he does."

"Not necessarily. I have channels of communication he is not privy to."

Was he referring to his romantic entanglement with

Amitola? Agnes studied him, but his expression gave nothing away.

"He is still too upset by your marriage to Riapoke to listen to reason on the topic. We must keep it from him as long as we can. Lord only knows what mischief he will stir when he learns the truth." Christopher dropped his voice another notch. "Is it true you cannot identify your assailant, or are you protecting someone?"

"Nay, it is true." She shaded her eyes with a hand to ward off the glare of the sun. "I was hit from behind at the river's edge. I saw nothing."

"Amitola and I have our suspicions about who is behind this."

So the chief's sister *was* his source of information. She knew it!

"As do I, but I am unsure what to do about it. Tell me, Christopher," Agnes rushed on before he could quiz her further. "Before the Dares approached Chief Manteo with their proposal to marry me to Riapoke, were there any other negotiations for his hand in marriage?"

He shook his head, looking puzzled. "None that I am aware of."

"What about the Croatoan maidens? Were any of them vying for his hand?"

He cleared his throat. "The council does not typically involve itself in arranging marriages within their own tribe. They are more concerned with arranging marriages *between* tribes."

"You did not answer my question."

He looked embarrassed. "By thunder, you know how to put a man on the spot. Your husband is a brawny man. No doubt there were Croatoan maids a-plenty interested in warming his bed, if that is what you mean, but we stray from the topic."

"Nay, we do not." She pointed at her face. "It is my belief that this was done by a woman who has feelings for my husband. Think about it, Christopher. The only point in such a beating would be to scare or punish me. You and I both know if she wanted me dead, I would be dead."

"You may be right." He sounded wary. "What do you plan to do about it?"

"Nothing." At his incredulous expression, she held up a hand. "Believe me, I have given it much thought, and I am convinced no good can come of retaliating. Someone was able to expend their ire on me without any permanent damage. I think this is best handled by turning the cheek, so to speak. My hope is her own guilt and remorse will be punishment enough."

"Such a kind soul you are, Agnes! I hardly know what to say."

"Good. It means you have no reason to question my judgment in this matter. Maybe you will discuss my wishes with Chief Manteo and put an end to his investigation into the matter, hmm?"

"I will consider what you ask." He walked away, a troubled expression marring his handsome features.

It was several more days before the bruising faded entirely from Agnes's face. She was grateful her husband did not have the misfortune to see her like this. By the time he returned home, she would be as good as new.

When Riapoke's two-week absence faded into three weeks, her anxiety grew. *Please God, bring him home to me. Safely.*

Winona fetched her in the middle of the following night. Mantunaaga, who was giving Chogan a break, muttered something but allowed Winona to lead Agnes from her tent. He remained close behind them and insisted on remaining at her side when they reached their destination, despite Winona's protests.

She led them inside a tent where a near-naked woman in the throes of giving birth rested weakly against the bare knees of two other women. Chogan muttered an apology and hurriedly returned outside. To Agnes's chagrin, the two women holding up the soon-to-be mother were Poca and Kaliska. Their expressions tightened as Agnes approached them.

Winona said something sharply, and their features turned to bitter acceptance of her presence. To Agnes, Winona confided, "Baby…not…come."

Agnes frowned, cupping the mother's face in her hands to stare directly in her eyes. Her face was cool and clammy. Two fingers on her wrist revealed a weaker than desired pulse.

"I am Agnes." She pointed to her chest and repeated her name. "What is your name?" She pointed to the young mother.

"Sooleawa," she murmured, head sagging.

Agnes stepped back. "Water for Sooleawa," she instructed Winona, making the motion of drinking. She gestured at Poca and gave a sharp command that sent the younger woman running.

With Winona's help, Agnes gently lowered her patient to a bedroll beside the fire where she could more thoroughly examine her. A quick peek revealed Sooleawa was fully dilated, but there was no sign of the babe's head. *The babe isn't turned*. Agnes's resolve trembled. She's been trained by one of the women at her parish back home in the birthing process. But she'd only observed the more experienced midwife turning a babe in the womb. She'd never attempted such a thing on her own, and the thought terrified her. Way too many women died during childbirth.

And if Sooleawa didn't survive the turning, would the Roanokes blame Agnes for her death, too? Another glance at the woman's pale and drawn features had her mentally berating herself. *How dare I entertain thoughts of death while there is still life pulsing through her veins?* This woman needed Agnes's help, come what may.

Once her mind was made up, her thoughts returned to their normally focused channels. She had a baby to turn. It was going to be a difficult task but not an impossible one. There was no time to waste.

Poca arrived with a skin of berry flavored water. Agnes tipped it against Sooleawa's mouth. The young woman sipped at it, but her movements were weak. Agnes insisted she drink more before removing the skin.

Next, Agnes positioned herself behind the mother's head and dug her fingers gently into her belly and sides until she found the baby's head. Aye, it was just as she suspected. The poor mite was stretched sideways across Sooleawa's swollen middle.

The mother grunted in pain, causing her comrades to cast half-fearful, half-angry glances at Agnes. She continued to palpitate the area around the unborn child's head, hoping to agitate him enough to stimulate movement — preferably to flip him in the correct direction.

Breathing constant prayers, Agnes coaxed the baby until she felt it begin to move. Sooleawa groaned loudly and her arms began to shake, eliciting a few angry words from their listeners.

Agnes smiled encouragement. "The babe is moving." It was actually working! She could barely contain her excitement.

The mother continued to gasp through the pain as Agnes guided the babe's head downward.

Winona shouted something and pointed. The elder

woman's gaze was so frenzied, Agnes perceived the babe's head had appeared at long last.

Thank the good Lord! Tears of relief prickled the backs of her eyelids, though their work was far from done. "Help me." She made the motion of standing their patient up once more.

Without hesitation, Poca and Kaliska tugged Sooleawa upright to rest on their thighs.

Agnes slid to her knees in front of young mother. "Now push!" she cried, clapping her hands and imitating the movement of bearing down. "Push!" *Please push, before your baby decides to turn again.*

Sooleawa revived and summoned what energy she had left. Though dazed and trembling, she pushed. Her eyes fastened themselves on Agnes, and she blindly responded to her repeated commands and hand signals.

"Yes! *Cuppeh!* Push!"

The babe's head popped out, and Winona shouted with glee. Together, she and Agnes gently tugged first one shoulder free then the other. The babe slithered easily into their eager hands.

He was a fine squalling son, plump and robust of lungs, punching the air with energy.

The new mother gave a faint sob. Sweat and tears streaked her face.

Winona took charge of the babe, swabbing him down and wrapping him snugly in a blanket.

Agnes helped Sooleawa lie down again and massaged her belly until the birthing was complete. *Good. Everything is as it should be.* Another examination confirmed the maiden would require a few stitches, so Agnes cleaned her and bade her drink more water. The new mother guzzled it this time.

"Sucki," she pleaded and held out her arms for the babe. "She pronounced the name with a long drawn-out "oo" sound, as in Soo-kee.

"Sucki." Winona rocked the bundle in her arms, crooning the name.

Only when Sooleawa was expertly suckling her child did Agnes collect Mantunaaga and make her departure. He had switched out guard duty with Chogan during the delivery. Agnes ducked her head through the door flap of the birthing tent one last time to motion to Winona to keep Sooleawa drinking. She nodded her understanding, satisfaction and approval gleaming in her dark eyes.

An answering pride glowed in Agnes's chest. She had done her job well tonight. Surely, even Poka and Kaliska could not come up with any criticisms of her work.

The next morning, she awoke to discover her stolen pots resting outside her tent. Since Chogan was back on duty and the closest person in proximity, she launched herself at him and gave him a hug.

He patted her back awkwardly, understanding in his dark gaze. Did he know who had taken the pots or who had returned them? When he did not speak, she shrugged and gratefully took the recovered pots inside her tent. It didn't matter who had taken them, only that they'd been returned. She tucked them carefully away in her hidden storage compartment.

The sound of vomiting outside captured her attention. *What?* Agnes flew to the door flap and thrust it open. Poca stumbled from her tent, clutching her belly. She jogged in the direction of the river.

"Medicine...woman." Winona ambled her way. "*Caumear-ah.*" She bade Agnes follow her in the direction Poca had taken. Ever Agnes's faithful shadow, Chogan wordlessly followed them.

Medicine Woman. Agnes liked her new title. It was far more respectable than *Pale Face.* It was a strange feeling, though, to be called on to help a woman who treated her like an enemy. Despite her constant antagonizing, Agnes hoped nothing serious was wrong with her. Life was precious, and they could not afford to lose one more person. Everyone's contribution was desperately needed for the greater chance of their collective survival.

Perhaps Poca had eaten something that did not settle well on her stomach?

They found her kneeling on the bank of the river, not far from where Agnes had been assaulted. The coincidence was unnerving. Agnes found herself glancing over her shoulder despite Chogan's presence.

Winona approached Poca and spoke softly in her ear. The younger woman mumbled something in return, and Winona raised her head to meet Agnes's gaze. "She is… with…child." She pressed a hand to Poca's flat belly. "Two moons."

Two moons? Agnes knew that meant two months, since the Natives liked to measure time by the cycle of the moon. It also meant Poca had been pregnant when Riapoke and his war party departed camp.

"Who is the father?" A penetrating coldness not born of the winter temperatures seeped through Agnes's limbs.

Winona bent to speak with the young woman again. Between gags, Poca answered.

"He is gone…to war." Winona searched Agnes's face.

"I see." Icy tentacles surrounded her heart and squeezed. Nevertheless, she squatted beside Poca.

The young maiden shot a sly look at Agnes and touched her belly. "Baby."

"Aye, baby. Congratulations." Fear gripped Agnes as she considered the possibility that Poca might be bearing Riapoke's child. The maiden had spent so much time with him in the days leading up to his departure, and her affections were clearly engaged. Not to mention, tribal chiefs and their top councilmen often took on extra wives and concubines.

Winona and Agnes stayed with Poca until her dry heaving subsided and she was able to drink a few sips of berry-flavored water.

"*T*his is outrageous!" Rose stormed around the wide, domed lodge she shared with Manteo. "As if beating your face to a pulp was not bad enough. She keeps her silence on the name of the father only to cause you more grief. I don't believe for one moment the babe is Riapoke's, but I do believe she wishes for others to speculate exactly that. The hussy!"

"It makes sense that the babe could be his," Agnes countered quietly. "It would explain why she hates me so much."

"Bah! The fact you are English is reason enough for her to hate."

"Or maybe it is because he married me. What if she aspires to become his wife, as well?"

"Well, that is too bad, because Riapoke chose you."

"Technically, the council arranged our marriage," Agnes reminded dryly.

"Ha! He chose you long before the council arranged anything, and you know it!"

"Even so," Agnes persisted. "She may still live in the hope of becoming his second wife."

"Not a chance," Rose assured matter-of-factly. "According to Manteo, Riapoke made no effort to take on more than one wife during his first marriage, and he is well aware how the English look upon such practices now that he is married to you."

"Unless something were to happen to me," Agnes

suggested slowly. "In that case, the position of first wife would become open again."

Rose whirled so quickly she had to press a hand to her blooming belly to dispel a cramp. "Nay, Agnes. Not another blooming word in that direction. Riapoke loves you and only you."

Agnes nodded, but doubt crept from the shadows. She could remind herself as often as she wanted that she was Riapoke's only wife, but it did not dispel the gossip about their marriage, the curious glances, or Poca's gleeful, mean-spirited attitude. If she wanted Agnes to suffer, she was succeeding.

There was only one thing left for Agnes to do — to prove to their tribe she was suited to be Riapoke's wife. As the wife of their war chief, they would expect her to be proficient in the ways of both the English and the Roanokes. She would also need to prove to them her skills were up to the task of serving as their Medicine Woman. And when her husband returned, she alone would fulfill his most intimate needs and desires. She would give him no reason to take another wife, not even one who might already be pregnant with his babe.

It was a bitter pill for Agnes to tend Poca every few days the way she had tended Rose. She tried to swallow her anger and misgivings as she mixed herbal potions to strengthen the young mother and keep her as healthy as possible during her pregnancy. She resisted the temptation to add ingredients that would cause all sorts of discomforts from itching to belching to excessive bloating and flatulating. It was tempting. Oh, it was tempting! But she refused to stoop to such a low level.

She threw herself harder than ever into her work. She learned everything she could from Winona, Rose, Jane, and Sooleawa. She botched as many projects as she succeeded in, but she slowly gained the respect of her tribe.

Chogan even taught her how to shoot a bow and arrow. During late evening hours around the campfire, he helped her craft a bow to suit her much smaller arm span. When they were finished, a few passers-by scoffed at its size.

However, when Agnes used the small bow to down her first fox with it, their mutters turned to nods of approval.

CHAPTER 31: A MATTER OF FAITH

A

*R*iapoke's absence extended to a fourth week, and Agnes grew more anxious for his safety with every passing moment. The rampant rumors that Poca was bearing his child did not help. The rumors crackled into hellfire when they reached the ears of her English friends.

Anthony's response was so explosive, the Dares called an emergency meeting with Chief Manteo. They beseeched him to deny the claim. Alas with Poca maintaining her stubborn silence and Riapoke continuing to be absent, Manteo could not satisfy them with a definitive answer.

Under constant pressure from the Dares, Manteo reluctantly sent Agnes to Fort Chowan for a dinner visit to discuss their concerns. She was accompanied by Chogan and Mantunaaga, for which she was wildly grateful. She'd grown so accustomed to traveling with her protectors, she would have felt less safe without them, even in the presence of her own countrymen.

To show her loyalty to her husband and his tribe, she wore the soft deerskin wedding garments given to her by Rose. She also came bearing a gift, one of the newest pots she'd made and etched with the rose and eagle design. Alas, it did not look so nice next to Eleanor's silver and china as it did inside the Roanoke settlement at their much humbler gatherings. However, Eleanor exclaimed over it with genuine excitement.

"You made this from river clay, you say? You must show me how. The scant resources we brought with us from England will not last us forever."

Eleanor gathered a platter of meat and breads from a trestle table beside the hearth. "It is so good to see you again, Agnes. We've missed you. It's not the same with you over there and us over here." She blinked through the mist of tears.

Ananias sat at the head of the table with Anthony on one side and his wife on the other. Christopher and Amitola sat on the other side of Eleanor. Agnes was placed beside Anthony, which made her mildly uncomfortable considering his feelings for her.

"I am sorry for the strained relations between our people." Agnes accepted the serving of meat Eleanor forked on her plate, glancing over her shoulder at her two faithful over-seers. She lifted her plate to Chogan. "Are you hungry, my friend?"

He and Mantunaaga shook their heads simultaneously.

"Forgive my manners." Ananias rose and pulled out two more chairs at the end of the table for Agnes's guards.

Again, they shook their heads.

Eleanor sighed and leaned on the table with both elbows, hands clasped beneath her chin. "The reason we invited you is to see for ourselves that you are well."

Agnes nodded and smiled. "Indeed I am, thank you."

Eleanor cast a sideways glance at her two guards. "I trust you are not making that claim under duress."

"Good gracious, no!" Agnes offered a lighthearted chuckle

she hoped would dispel any doubts, but the tension in the room rose a few degrees despite her efforts.

Eleanor sighed again. "We were distraught to hear of the attack on you within the boundaries of your own camp."

Oh, dear! Did you really have to bring that up?

Christopher's fork remained suspended in the air on the way to his mouth, as he awaited Anthony's response. Anthony's expression registered shock and horror.

The color drained from his face. He carefully laid down his utensils. "What attack, and why am I just now hearing about it?"

"It was nothing more than a female spat." Agnes shifted uncomfortably in her chair. "As you can see, I am wonderfully recovered."

"And what exactly did you need to recover from?"

Christopher cleared his throat. "Amitola did a little investigating. She has reason to believe a pair of maidens named Poca and Kaliska are responsible for the incident."

Agnes's smile froze. She finished chewing her bite of meat with difficulty. "What proof do you have?"

Amitola studied Agnes, her face void of expression. "I assure you they will be punished." Her cold, unforgiving expression indicated the punishment would be severe.

"Nay, please! Poca is pregnant." *Possibly with my husband's child.* Agnes pushed back her plate. "I came into the Roanoke tribe as a foreigner and a stranger right after one of their councilmen died. They already blamed the English for the attack. I was simply a convenient target. We can debate the merits of their actions all day and all night long, but it will not change how hurt, scared, and angry they were when Powaw died. It's understandable that—"

"Understandable?" Anthony sputtered, turning in his chair to face her. "I think not! The councilman's death was

255

not your fault. I cannot believe how easily you try to excuse such violence."

"They did not permanently mark me," Agnes protested. "It was no accident, methinks. Very likely they spared me out of regard for my husband."

Amitola's gaze glinted with approval at her words.

Anthony's handsome mouth twisted bitterly. Agnes suspected it was because he didn't care for the reminder that she was married. "If regard for your husband resulted in such brutality against you, by all that is holy, Agnes! What have we done in allowing you to marrying him?"

Mercy! The man had a dreadful habit of twisting a person's words.

"As I have already stated," Amitola broke in coolly. "The women will be punished."

"Nay!" Agnes cried. "As Medicine Woman of the Roanokes and the wife of their war chief, I denounce any and all punishments on my behalf."

A stunned silence followed her grand pronouncement.

Eleanor finally bestirred herself to whisper, "They have named you their Medicine Woman? Truly, Agnes?"

In a manner of speaking. It was only a matter of time before it became official. In the meantime, it appeared as if her new unofficial title carried no small amount of weight with the Dares. Agnes intended to press it to her advantage. "I will handle Poca in my own time and in my own way," she declared firmly. "Already our relationship is improving."

"How?" Anthony demanded.

"I believe she is the one who returned a set of pots to me this morning I previously believed were stolen. They were undamaged. It happened right after I delivered the breech babe of her friend Sooleawa. I think, at least I hope, my midwifery skills gave her a reason to think less ill of me as an Englishwoman."

"She beat you and she stole from you," Anthony reminded tersely. "The Good Book itself tells us the 'laws are for the lawless.' As Amitola rightfully stated, she should be punished."

Agnes raised her chin. "The same book also calls for turning the cheek. If there was ever a time for turning the cheek, this is one of them. I would rather win the hearts of my people by choosing to show mercy than to lose their hearts forever by exacting punishment over an incident that straddles so many grey areas."

Amitola, who at first had looked puzzled by the exchange, nodded her approval. Admiration flitted across her fine-boned features.

Agnes's English friends, however, regarded her in disapproving silence.

Agnes shook her head in disbelief at them. "Pray recall we've the safety of an unborn child at stake here. That should count for something."

Eleanor rubbed her eyes. "Aye, that brings up a whole new problem, my dear, considering the unborn babe's father is in question."

Agnes gritted her teeth. "That is nothing but rumor and does not bear repeating."

"Oh, my sweet friend, but it does." Eleanor pressed her hands together and tapped them against her lips. "I understand how painful the topic must be for you, but you need to prepare yourself in the event the rumor turns out to be true."

"It is *not* true," Agnes snapped.

"We pray it is not," Ananias assured with a slight shake of his head at his wife. "Eleanor is simply trying to emphasize the fact you will *always* be welcome here among us. No matter what."

"Are you suggesting I leave my husband?" Agnes rose and

pushed back her chair in alarm. She was quite finished listening to such nonsense.

"Nay! Here me out, Agnes." Eleanor stood and faced her from across the table. "We mean only to inform you that leaving your husband is allowed by Roanoke law if he proves to be unfaithful."

Good heavens! Poca had been impregnated before she and Riapoke started courting. Even if he turned out to be responsible for the deed, how were his actions any different than the philandering of so many highborn Englishmen? The double standard of her countrymen sickened her. She could not recall anyone standing up to demand English lasses annul their weddings to titled men back home who'd fathered bastard children.

Agnes nodded her dismissal to her friends and reached for her coat. "I thank you for dinner, but I've no plans to divorce my husband." Certainly not over an alleged infraction from which he'd been given no chance to defend himself. *Faith, he was at battle defending all of them right now!*

"Of course not, darling." Eleanor followed her to the front door. "We just wanted to read you your options. To let you know you are still loved her at Fort Chowan, and you will always have a place among us if you need somewhere to go."

Not all the English colonists loved her. Agnes was fairly certain Margaret Lawrence despised her. "I thank you," she said again, but she was starting to feel detached from them. It was an unexpected emotion, but it felt right. Despite all the obstacles she'd overcome in the last few weeks to reach this juncture, she was beginning to feel more Roanoke than English. "Now, if you don't mind, it is late and I must be going. I have several patients to tend in the morning."

Eleanor hugged her fiercely. "I know relations are strained between our people, but please don't let it come between you and me. I have finally come to terms with the fact you live two hills over, but I cannot bear the thought of losing you as my friend. Not ever!"

Agnes was trying not to let their present circumstances come between them, but it was hard. "I will host our next visit, hopefully in our longhouse if it is finished in time." She infused false cheer into her voice. "I have much to show you about all the things I've learned. Wait 'til you see the arrow I made."

Eleanor's eyes widened. "Do tell all."

"I will." Agnes kissed her check. "When you next visit me, my friend."

Chogan and Mantunaaga hovered on either side of her as she exited the Dares' cabin.

Anthony followed her and her guards down the hill. "May we have a moment of privacy?" he begged with a frustrated glance at her two companions.

She continued walking. "I am afraid not."

"Aren't you at liberty to dismiss them?"

Agnes doubted it, but she had no desire to, at any rate. She slowed her pace. "I am listening. What is it you wish to discuss with me?"

"I want to beg your forgiveness."

It certainly wasn't what she expected him to say. Agnes studied Anthony's side profile, wondering at his latest game.

He scrubbed a hand over his short, clipped beard. "It was my own blasted pride that put you in this mess. My unwillingness to declare my feelings for you in the midst of so much war and strife. I realize my mistake now and want you to know that I still care for you. More than ever. One word from you, and I will drop everything to come extract you from this deplorable situation. That is all." He swept off his top hat and stepped directly in her path to bow low before her. The gesture forced her to halt, at last.

It was a sly move, one that both flattered and made her

suspicious. She hid a smile at his antics so as not to encourage him further. "Thank you for your concerns, Anthony, no matter how misplaced they may be. I will always treasure our friendship." She made an effort to step around him.

"Wait," he pleaded, reaching for her arm.

Chogan stepped between them, forcing Anthony to drop his hold on her. "Medicine…Woman…must go."

"Chogan is right," Agnes agreed hastily. "It is good to see you again, my friend. Farewell for now." She fluttered a hand at Anthony, and her two protectors hustled her down the hill. They returned her to the Roanoke camp in short order.

The encounter left her shaken, however. She didn't want to contemplate what might have happened if she'd not traveled with protection. *Poor Anthony.* She hated being the source of his grief, yet she could not allow him to behave in such a manner now that she was married. He needed to accept the fact her affairs were no longer his concern.

She shuddered over the Dares' offer to accept her back into the fold at Fort Chowan. *Faith, that is exactly what Poca wants.* If Agnes willingly left Riapoke, it would make things that much easier for her to stake her claim on him when he returned.

---

*T*he Roanoke camp was in an uproar when Agnes and her guards stepped through its protective palisade. Their raiding party was returned from the Mountain People. Or rather, nine of the warriors were returned. They had both good and bad news to share. The dozen Roanoke and Croatoan warriors had intercepted the second war party and dismantled their ranks, sending them on the run. However, a third even larger war party was already on its way.

Would the nightmare never end?

Riapoke, Amonsoquath, and another warrior named Tikoosoo had broken away from the group to head off the third war party, or at least run interference in their advance. It was nothing short of a suicide mission. Riapoke had sent the remaining nine warriors home to prepare the settlement for the coming attack.

The news that her husband was still alive when he was last seen made Agnes sag against Chogan. Until his men delivered his lifeless frame to her, she would live in hope of his safe return. Poca, however, fell into a fit of weeping. She was inconsolable, regardless of Kaliska's ministrations, so much so that Agnes feared for her babe. She bade Kaliska to escort her friend to her tent and to keep her drinking water.

Poca's behavior only strengthened Agnes's fears she might be carrying Riapoke's child. She must truly love him. Why else would she become so distraught over his wellbeing?

Both Jane and Rose were quick to console Agnes. "I know this isn't the news we were hoping for, my friend, but you must keep faith," Rose pleaded. "Riapoke is one of the strongest and bravest men I know. He is cunning and resourceful on the battlefield, which is how he earned his position as Manteo's war chief."

"And Wanchese's war chief," Jane reminded dryly.

It did not make him immune to deadly arrows, though, or the slash of hatchets and knives. Agnes had firsthand experience patching up his battle wounds. However, she saw no reason to remind Rose and Jane of these things when they were simply trying to be encouraging. Every maiden and brave in both tribes were anxious to receive news of Riapoke, Amonsoquath, and Tikooso's whereabouts.

Chief Wanchese sent a runner to the Dares, warning them of the Copper Mountain war party heading their way. He called for an emergency meeting to plan their settlement's combined course of action.

While the war council met, a handful of Englishmen remained in the fort to load the canons. They had a limited amount of gun powder remaining after all the skirmishes they'd engaged in thus far, so it was vitally important to make each remaining blast count.

At the end of the war council meeting, the Englishmen filed into their fort and placed themselves at even intervals along both their outer and inner palisades, muskets loaded and pointed. *Sweet mercy!* They were so orderly and predictable, Agnes feared for their safety for that reason, alone.

The Croatoan and Roanoke warriors did not line up in even intervals. Instead, they blended into the environment like chameleons. They stuffed twigs and dried grasses in their hair and smeared mud on their faces. Unlike the navy tunics and white shirts the English wore, their deerskin clothing was much harder to detect with the naked eye. They secreted themselves behind boulders and logs and disappeared high in the branches of trees. Some of them hid their women and children in the trees with them. Other women and children were led to the cavern beneath the earth.

Anxious to be among the first to catch a glimpse of her husband when he returned, Agnes clutched at Chogan when he started to lead her to the subterranean cavern. "Let me go with you," she pleaded, raising her bow and clutch of arrows.

Chogan and Mantunaaga exchanged worried glances.

"Please, let me fight for Riapoke." According to Riapoke's warriors, the war party heading their way was about three hundred warriors in strength. The combined strength of their three camps were less than two hundred, and that included women and children. They were sadly outnumbered. Fair fight or not, Agnes preferred to fight alongside her people, not cower in some cave.

When Mantunaaga shrugged, Chogan reluctantly led her to a massive fir tree at the edge of camp. Together they collected loose twigs and stuffed them in their hair and clothing. It was a terribly scratchy form of camouflage that instantly made Agnes itch, but it helped her blend into the landscape. Chogan smeared a black and brown paste across her face and hands then boosted her up a tree trunk. He climbed up behind her.

They maintained their vigil for the rest of the afternoon, taking only short breaks to unthaw by the main campfire, snatch a few bites to fill their bellies, and occasionally answer the call of nature.

At best, they estimated their enemies were still a few hours away. At worse, they could arrive any moment.

CHAPTER 32: WAR

*T*he distant cry of an eagle from a Croatoan scout was their signal that the Copper Mountain war party had been sighted. Less than a minute later, Agnes could detect the sounds of their approach. Faint at first, the horrifying howls and screeches of their attackers were all too familiar and grew louder as they neared the fort. She briefly closed her eyes, recalling the images of those who'd ambushed the colonists the moment they'd set foot on the mainland. She'd lost two thirds of her countrymen that day to death and captivity.

The unearthly sounds of their enemies had simply inspired fear at the time. Today, however, they inspired resolve. The surviving colonists and their Native allies would take a stand on these hills at this river delta. This time, they were prepared for an attack. Though greatly outnumbered, this time they stood a chance at holding their ground.

Like a beacon on the highest hill of their combined settlement, Fort Chowan, with its corner towers and mounted cannons, attracted the first raid. Copper-clad warriors swarmed like angry insects up all sides of the hill. There were far too many of them to count.

Agnes held her breath, gripping her bow so tightly it was a wonder it didn't snap in two. More enemy warriors poured into the valley at the base of the hill and began their ascent, far too rapidly for her comfort. *What were the English waiting for? Sweet mercy!* If they didn't fire soon, the hill would be lost and every English man, woman, and child on it.

In perfect cadence, the canons fired their first shots, belching fire and recoiling atop their earth-packed platforms. The explosion shook the ground and echoed off the surrounding hills like claps of thunder. Flames streaked down the hillside, scattering the Copper Mountain warriors like toy soldiers. Their war whoops dissolved into screams of terror.

When the smoke dissipated, the human carnage was horrifying. Enemy warriors were scattered everywhere, and the ground was drenched in crimson.

Agnes covered her nose and mouth with an arm to muffle her cry of horror. Four gaping holes of death now punctuated the approaching legions of warriors. As if frozen in time, the advance party paused their advance. Their war cries stilled in their mouths as they tried to make sense of what had just happened. A chief in full coppery headdress stalked up to his man of council, pointing at the iron beasts which had caused such devastation.

Agnes wondered if he was Askook, Chief Wanchese's traitorous cousin, son of the late Mountain king. She craned for a better look at the chief, trying to recall the details of Jane's description of him, but Chogan grabbed her arm and pulled her back into the safety of the tree limbs.

The enemy chief gave a mighty cry and pointed at the canons. Dozens of the remaining enemy warriors raised their bows. *Faith, how quickly he had figured out where to concentrate his resources.* Agnes whispered a hasty prayer. "You've brought us this far, Lord God. All our hope is in you."

Chogan clamped a hand over her mouth.

She knew the Englishmen behind the cannons were working frantically to reload and fire off a second round, but another swarm of warriors covered the hill before they could ignite the shot. The Englishmen secreted behind the palisade walls fired their muskets, in the attempt to slow their advance. The air was awash with the clash of weapons and the screams of the fighting and the wounded.

Agnes feared the soldiers manning the cannons had been injured or worse. Muskets continued to pop and smoke every few feet along the fort's palisade walls. The English were putting up a valiant fight to give their cannoneers time to regroup and reload.

The second round of shots fired, and the hill itself seemed to erupt. The blasts scored their way down the hillside in a hideous trail of fire. This time, the explosions reduced the number of enemy soldiers to half of what they'd begun with, maybe less. It was enough to send the rest of them swirling into terrified chaos. Some tried to retreat and ended up impeding the advance of their comrades. Their chief was nowhere to be seen.

It was upon this carnage, the Roanokes and Croatoans descended from the trees and crept up from the valley. Careful to stay out of range of the cannons, the tribesmen converged on the Copper Mountain people, firing arrows with each step.

Stray pockets of frantic enemy warriors attempted to scatter to the surrounding hills, but those still hiding in the trees picked them off one by one. It was a deadly trap the Copper Mountain people had pridefully marched into, likely assuming they were safe with their superior numbers.

As the last of them fell or scattered, the Roanoke and Croatoan scouts followed to finish them off. Almost almost felt sorry for the Copper Mountain people. Almost but not quite. They still held an untold number of English colonists captive inside their mountain home, forcing them to mine copper day and night. From what Chief Wanchese and Christopher had been able to gather on their various trips to Copper Mountain, the mines were worked by one hundred percent slave labor. For years, the Copper Mountain chief had been paying rogue warriors to capture small pockets of people from every surrounding tribe in the region. Rumor had it, they kept the number captured from each tribe small so that it wasn't worth the while of the affected tribes to go to war to retrieve them.

Their mistake, as luck would have it, had been in the taking of the Roanoke princess, Amitola. It was a bold and calculated move, born of pride and the false sense of infalli-bility. Askook, son of the Mountain king, had come to live with his cousin, Chief Wanchese, a few months ago. He'd stirred up dissension at every opportunity. Amitola had gone missing during his stay and ended up on Copper Mountain. It was too much to be a coincidence. Alas, she had not served in the copper mines. Rather, she'd been forced to marry the Copper Mountain king. By the time Christopher had poisoned the lecher and rescued her, she was carrying his child.

Askook had taken his father's place, vowing revenge on the English and Roanokes alike for their interference in his plans. He'd not been prepared for the Croatoan and Roanoke show of solidarity with the English.

If by some miracle, he had survived today's failed attack, he would not soon forget it.

*R*oanokes, Croatoans, and the English worked in shifts through the night, snatching only a few hours of sleep where they could. Their main goal was to gather and burn the slain as quickly as possible before the scent attracted wild animals. The large fires did their part to hold the unwelcome creatures as bay, but whole packs of wolves gathered at a distance. Their howls punctured the heavens for hours. No doubt they could smell the scent of carnage from the battleground on the wings of the night breezes.

Agnes could not sleep, so she lay in the darkness with her eyes wide open. *Why, oh, why, didn't Riapoke and his remaining two warriors return now that the battle was over?* She tried not to entertain the most obvious answer — that they weren't coming back.

The Roanoke Medicine Man, Winona, and Agnes treated and patched their wounded warriors. They'd suffered no deaths in the latest attack, thanks to the English cannons, but they'd suffered countless injuries.

By the light of dawn, they assessed the damage to their homes and palisades and pronounced most of them salvageable. Fort Chowan had taken the worst brunt of the attack. The lower palisade was lying in shambles and several homes were burned to the ground by the fiery arrows. So focused had the Copper Mountain warriors been on breaching the fort, however, the Native camps were left largely intact.

"At last the Roanokes and Croatoans can see what use the English are to them," Rose confided in Agnes soberly. "Without those manning the cannons and muskets, the Copper Mountain raid might have had a very different ending."

Agnes nodded but could not work up a smile. For her, there was nothing to celebrate if her husband did not return.

She had lost too much during the past year of her life. The idea of losing her new husband before they enjoyed any real chance at happiness together was utterly depressing.

The members of their combined settlement worked three days straight to help repair the lower English palisade.

Anthony maneuvered himself to work by Agnes's side most of the time. "Any word from your husband?" he inquired.

She shook her head, not wanting to discuss how long Riapoke had been absent or her growing fears about his safety. She pounded a nail in a fence slat so fiercely that it embedded in a single whack.

"If anything has happened to him, know this, my friend." Anthony placed his hand over hers and gave it a squeeze. "I will always be here for you."

A few months ago, Agnes would have swooned at his touch, but he no longer had that affect on her. His friendship, no matter now much it meant to her, was not enough. It was never going to be enough. A sob wrenched itself from her throat. Horrified, she covered her mouth and turned away.

Anthony prevented her from leaving by tightening his hold on her hand. "I will take care of you 'til the end of my days. I promise, Agnes. No more doubts. No more delays. I've learned life is too short, our chance at happiness too fleeting."

She gritted her teeth and swallowed hard to muffle her sobs. When she could find her voice again, she said with as much energy as she could muster, "He will come home."

Taken aback at her words, Anthony scanned her face. Sadness deepened the lines of exhaustion around his eyes. "You truly want him to come home to you?"

"Aye." Agnes hated hurting him this way, but they were past the point of pretenses.

He released her hand, his brown eyes clouded with shock

and pain. "Pray forgive me for making a fool of myself," he muttered. "All this time, I presumed you'd been forced to marry against your will. I never dreamt you actually had feelings for the man."

"I love my husband, Anthony." There was something wildly liberating about admitting the truth at last. "There is no shame in that."

Confusion flashed in his eyes. "How is that possible? You barely know each other."

It was interesting how that fact didn't bother her in the least anymore. She loved her husband well enough to marry him, and that was that.

Fortunately, Anthony didn't seem to expect an answer. He strode farther down the fence line and began swinging his hammer with the energy of ten men.

Margaret Lawrence interrupted them midday, bearing a tray of rations. She batted her lashes at Anthony and offered it to him first. "We finally showed those savages who is superior on the battlefield, eh, my lord? Agnes," she added stiffly.

"Aye." Agnes forced a smile. "Working together, the Roanokes, Croatoans, and English achieved a resounding victory." It was the exact sort of progress Rose and her diplomatic husband had been working towards for months.

Anthony waved away the food. "Let Agnes eat. I am not hungry."

Margaret huffed out an angry breath. "Well, I never!" She offered the plate to him again. "You must keep up your strength, my lord. For all our sakes." She batted her lashes again.

"You are right," he conceded. With a mocking grin, he swept up two pieces of the dried meat from her tray. "You heard the woman, Agnes. She commanded us to eat."

He did not allow her to resume work until she'd choked down an entire piece.

Margaret's gaze darted between them in consternation. If she'd hoped to gain a few moments alone with Anthony, she was sorely disappointed.

CHAPTER 33: THE MISSING

*D*espite how much Agnes grieved for her missing husband and how much their tribe grieved for all three of the missing warriors, they did not have the luxury of allowing their mourning to halt their construction projects or war planning. Their survival depended on keeping vigil around the clock, gathering as much food as they could hunt and scavenge, and digging into their respective hills to fortify themselves against future raids. To presume they were finished fighting would be naive. The Copper Mountain people might be beat back for now, but they would return — for revenge and for their unborn prince Amitola carried in her womb.

The Roanoke braves and maidens completed the new longhouse Riapoke had ordered for his new bride. Chogan and Mantunaaga helped her move in.

Shortly afterwards, Anthony began a new regiment of checking on Agnes's wellbeing daily. She tried to discourage him from doing so, but he persisted in injecting himself into her personal affairs. He ignored her guards each time he visited, staring through Chogan and Mantunaaga as if they didn't exist. This made it difficult for Agnes to muster any gratitude she might have otherwise harbored at his stubborn show of concern on her behalf.

Instead of working at Fort Chowan until sundown like the other Englishmen, Anthony fell into the habit of spending his evenings in Agnes's presence. He generally arrived after the dinner hour and began his visit by meticulously checking her newly constructed longhouse for weaknesses. He puttered through it, making odd and end patches and additions that he swore were improvements. She privately complained to anyone who would listen — Eleanor, Rose, Jane, and Winona — but none of them possessed any solid ideas as to how to rid her of her growing Anthony problem.

"Be patient with him," Eleanor admonished. "He still cares for you deeply and is trying to come to grips with losing you."

"Would you like me to gut him and hide the body?" Jane inquired, tapping her blade against her palm.

Rose merely shook her head, and Winona grumbled beneath her breath but refused to offer any sage words. Thus, Anthony became a permanent fixture once more in Agnes's life.

"It's been over a month, Agnes," he announced one evening as they warmed themselves in front of the dinner fire outside her longhouse. "I understand you are grieving, but nearly everyone else agrees the missing Roanoke warriors aren't going to return. We appreciate their sacrifice, but they're gone, my love. Don't you think it's time to count our losses?"

His love? Not in this life or the next! Agnes set aside her dinner ration of dried meat and stared at him in anger. She wasn't very hungry to begin with, but his words quenched what little appetite she had. "How can you say such a thing about men who've risked so much for us all? They deserve better. I'm not ready to bury and forget them. Not yet."

"How long will you wait?" He bent his head to peer more closely at her.

She tasted bitterness. *Strange how Anthony had asked her to wait indefinitely to marry him — maybe years — and now he was anxious for her to dissolve her marriage with Riapoke who'd only been missing a month.* "I don't know, my friend." She used the endearment in the attempt to calm him, since she could see he was working himself into a lather. "All I know is I'm far from convinced my husband is dead. There's no body, no proof whatsoever of his demise. I would much rather send out another search party than plan a funeral."

"We cannot spare the men, and you know it. Besides, where would we send them?" he demanded.

She uttered a long-suffering sigh at his single-mindedness in making her a widow. "We'd start at their last known location, of course. Northwest along the river channel. Last we heard, they were trying to head off the third wave attack."

"Then Riapoke and his men failed in their mission. We were the ones who fought off the third wave."

Or maybe they'd been captured, injured, or worse while trying. Agnes wanted to scream in frustration. She'd gone over the possibilities of every scenario a thousand times in her head. If she did not get some answers soon, she might truly go mad.

"Eat, Agnes." Anthony's voice gentled. "You need to keep up your strength."

She took another bite of dried meat but had trouble chewing it. It was growing more difficult to go through the motions of daily living. It seemed wrong to pretend things were normal while Riapoke might be out there injured. Or captured. A fresh wave of dread filled Agnes's belly. Logic told her that if the Copper Mountain people had slaughtered their men, they would have made a brutal display of it. They'd been ruling the region by terror for decades. They would have left their rotting corpses for them to be found as a warning.

Nay, it was far more likely her husband and his comrades had been captured. They would be tortured and interrogated until they broke and—

"Please, Agnes?"

Jolted from her horrified train of thought, Agnes glanced up at Anthony's worried features.

What?

"You need to eat more. Your husband would tell you the same thing if he was here."

She stiffened. It was the first time Anthony had ever mentioned Riapoke in anything but derision. Her instincts told her not to trust his intentions; he was simply trying a new tactic in order to bend her to his will.

"He would want what is best for you," Anthony pressed more softly. "To keep living and not mourn forever."

I knew it! He was notching up his arguments as to why she should bury her husband and move on with her life. Well, unless someone produced a body, she would continue to hope.

"I'm tired. I'll be heading inside for the night." Agnes rose without waiting for his response. It was better for both of them that she end their conversation before she said or did something she would regret.

"'Til tomorrow then, love." Anthony rose and bowed to her.

Or you could skip a day and give me a break from your constant hounding. Agnes nodded stiffly and spun on her heels to enter her lodge. Chogan followed and she motioned for him to sit. He refused as usual, taking his position by the door to keep vigil through the night.

She fell to her knees to stir the coals of her dying fire, knowing she would not be able to sleep. How could she sleep in the home her husband had built for them when he was not here to share its warmth and safety? In her heart, she was certain something bad had happened to him. The same sort of dread had gripped her when she'd watched their enemies row away with the kidnapped baby Virginia and the battered, unconscious Jane. The same sort of dread had lodged itself in her stomach when the English colonists had been sold as slaves on the Great Trading Path. And in each instance, her dread had been accompanied by the same overwhelming sense of helplessness and defeat she felt now. It was no true victory to those who'd escaped with their own lives intact when it came at such a steep a cost.

Agnes poked more viciously at the coals, enough to make the sparks fly in the air. Chogan tensed in alarm from his position at the door. She met his inquisitive gaze with fierce intent. A plan was forming in her mind.

He took a step in her direction. "Ann-nes?"

She was tired of accepting what fate dealt. Fate was too fickle a mistress to trust with her peace of mind, much less her happiness. So what if the Natives had already sent multiple search parties and returned with no news? There was no law that said she couldn't launch a search of her own. She was a woman caught between two worlds — the old and the new — and mistress of neither. She could do as she pleased. It was a liberating thought, the closest she'd come to experiencing a moment of inner peace since her husband's disappearance.

She stood and faced Chogan. Her mind was made up. She was going after her husband, all the way to Copper Mountain, if that's what it took. She was going to get him back or die trying.

Agnes slapped her fist to her chest in the greeting of

warriors. "We are going to find Riapoke." She signed to Chogan to ensure he understood her. She knew she succeeded when his gaze lit. "We will leave at first light. Find Mantunaaga and gather whatever supplies you can."

He straightened to his full height and pounded his fist to his chest. Then he departed the longhouse.

A new energy filled Agnes, one born of hope. She rummaged with frenzy through her sparse belongings, donning extra layers of clothing and strapping on several cross body pouches. In the pouches, she stuffed small tools, bandages, and medicines. She wished to be prepared for whatever state in which she found her husband and his comrades.

"Medicine Woman."

Startled, Agnes spun around. It was Winona. She hadn't heard her enter. "Good evening, my friend. How can I help you?"

She nodded at Agnes. "You leave us?"

The pain in her dark eyes tugged at Agnes's heartstrings. She shook her head vehemently. "Never! I am leaving at first light to search for Riapoke. I will come back."

Her features cleared and settled into their habitual stoicism. "I go with you."

"Nay, it's too risky. You must stay and care for our maidens."

Her lip curled, and her chin came up. "I go."

Agnes knew from experience there was no changing her mind once it was made up.

She sighed. "Very well, but do not tell anyone else." She signed to her that she should keep silent and move in absolute stealth.

Winona nodded and disappeared from the room, as silently as she'd entered it.

My rescue mission is growing. She could use the help, so it was hard to complain. Hands on her hips, Agnes surveyed her small collection of travel supplies. It was essential that she travel light to keep up her speed. There would be no bedrolls or creature comforts. They would make do with whatever they found on the road.

"Hello in there!" a familiar voice called from outside the door of her longhouse.

Eleanor! Agnes's excitement slipped a few notches. What could she possibly want at this late hour? If she'd come to beg her assistance for someone sick or injured, it could take hours. Hours Agnes did not have to spare tonight.

"Come in," she called cautiously. Alas, there was no time to change her clothing or hide the fact she was packing for a trip.

Eleanor pushed her hood down and instantly deduced something was amiss. "Where are you going, my friend?" Her gaze scanned the room anxiously. "And where is your guard?"

"Answering the call of nature." Agnes gave a vague wave of her hand. "He will return shortly."

"You're a bad liar," Eleanor accused. "Chogan would never leave you for something so trivial. That is the reason you have two guards, my friend. To switch out for breaks and the like. Maybe we should start this conversation over. Where are you going?"

Agnes glared at her former employer, fists on her hips. "You're as bad as Anthony! Neither of you seem to understand I am married now. I do not answer to either of you, anymore. My business is my own."

Eleanor's chin stubbornly came up. "I know this is hard for you to accept, my friend, but you are married to a man who is gone. He is not coming back."

"Is that so?" Agnes returned testily.

"Nay, love, he is not. I know what you are going through. I've suffered the same loss."

"Nay, you've not suffered the same loss," Agnes snapped. "Your child lives, yet you do nothing to get her back. Instead, you've found some sort of twisted solace in walking around like a woman already dead on the inside."

"Why, Agnes!" Eleanor stumbled back a step. "I've never known you to be so cruel."

"And I've never known you to be such a coward! Look at you!" she seethed. "Grieving and unable to go on. Pretending for the sakes of others that everything is alright when it's not. Do not tell me you don't see your child's face every waking moment and dream about her every time you close your eyes. That, my good woman, is the way I suffer day and night for the one I have lost."

Eleanor paled in the firelight and pressed a hand to her chest. "Please, Agnes. Stop this mad talk. I cannot bear it."

"You cannot bear your loss, you mean. But my words make you feel something again, do they not? Anger and frustration. The desire for justice."

"Yes, but—"

"Isn't it a relief to want to scream and cry again and shake your fist at the moon? Instead of walking around like a block of ice?"

"My screaming and crying will do no good. Nor will yours. Lord know I've done enough of it." Eleanor's voice shook. "You are distraught, Agnes, and that is the very thing I came to discuss with you."

Agne bent to gather the dinner rations she'd barely touched for days. They were hidden in a clay pot beneath her sleeping platform. She tucked the strips of dried meat inside one of her pouches. It was at least five days worth of sustenance, maybe more, if she continued to eat sparingly on the road.

She straightened and spun around to face her friend again. "I know what you came to discuss. Anthony has made it abundantly clear he is tired of waiting for my husband to return. He's been making noises about getting me officially declared a widow."

Eleanor dropped her gaze. "Oh, my love. You do not understand a great number of things. Your marriage was never consummated, so if Riapoke does not return soon, we will have no choice but to request an annulment on your behalf."

An annulment. Her words staggered Agnes, in the fact that the English did not even intend to treat her with the dignity of a widow. They wanted to erase her marriage to Riapoke as if it had never happened.

An ugly cry of pain wrenched itself from deep within her. "Leave me," she ground out between clenched teeth. "Unlike you, I intend to keep living. Go be dead somewhere else."

"Why, Agnes! How can you be so heartless? So ungrateful for all I've done for you?" Eleanor choked on a sob.

"Ungrateful?" Agnes raged. "You've let a man I do not love talk you into destroying my marriage, that's what!"

"Anthony cares for you. You know that," she protested. "He hates to see you suffer like this and would do anything to fix it."

"He can't fix anything. Don't you understand?" Agnes cried. "Nobody can." Nothing but the return of her husband would mend her shattered heart.

"Maybe if you gave him half the chance?" Eleanor prodded softly. "He blames himself for every ounce of your current suffering. If only he'd declared his love for you sooner."

"Aha! But he didn't, did he?" Agnes snarled. "Mayhap because he does not love me. Nay!" She held up a hand. "He cares for me as a friend, true, but not in the way you are talking about." Some of the anger seeped out of her. "It is not his fault, Eleanor. One cannot force such feelings no matter how hard they try. Therefore, he may as well forgive himself and be done with it. I've already forgiven him."

"He still wants to marry you, Agnes."

"And I want this foolish war to be ended and food aplenty to fill our baskets to overflowing. We can't always have what we want."

Chogan and Mantunaaga slipped inside the lodge and positioned themselves on either side of the door. Both were dressed for the road and for battle. Their gazes darted between Agnes and Eleanor, registering surprise.

Eleanor cast an accusing look at her. "You *are* leaving! Do not try to deny it again."

At Agnes's silence, she stomped her foot. The old starchy Eleanor was returning to her voice and stance. "You'd best start talking, my friend. I mean to get to the bottom of this, else you're not going anywhere."

Agnes removed a coil of rope from the wall and tossed it to Chogan. She signed to him. *Tie her up.*

His eyes widened. She repeated the command and did not remove her hard stare from him until he started moving.

"Well, I never!" Eleanor gasped as he pressed her to her knees before the fire.

Agnes drew a deep breath. "You'd best stay quiet and listen to me, else I will gag you next."

This elicited another surprised gasp. To her credit, Eleanor remained silent as Agnes began to explain.

"You want the truth? I'm launching a search party for my husband. Unlike you, I cannot go on in the face of my loss. I cannot stand by in silence while my marriage is annulled and then callously marry another. To me, that is not what it means to keep living. Maybe you're content to move on with your life, because you have the satisfaction of knowing your daughter still lives, albeit in captivity. I have no such satisfaction, but I intend to work until I get it. We leave at first light, and there is nothing you or anyone else can do to stop me."

Chogan tied Eleanor's hands and feet, then stood beside her with his hand on his knife.

"I can see that now," she quavered. "I am sorry I did not see it before." She hung her head. "Where will you go?"

"All the way to Copper Mountain, if need be."

"'Tis a dangerous plan, my friend."

"I am well aware of the risks, and my husband is worth every one of them."

Her soft sobs filled the longhouse.

Agnes knelt beside her and gathered her in her embrace. "I will not ask your forgiveness, because I am not sorry for what I am about to do. If I don't make it back, please know I died trying to rescue our loved ones, both yours and mine. You will live in the comfort of knowing that my very last hope and prayer was to be reunited with my husband and to see you reunited with your daughter."

She raised her head. "Nay, I am the one who is sorry. You're strong. Much stronger than I." She sniffed and seemed to be trying to collect herself. "You've the fitting spirit for the wife of a war chief. I am proud, so proud of you, Agnes. He would be, too, if he could see you now."

Agnes smiled at her reference to Riapoke. It was nice hearing one of her English friends speak kindly about him, for once. A little belated, perhaps, but she was glad to hear it anyway.

Eleanor struggled to stand and failed, bumping her forehead smartly against Agnes's.

Agnes chuckled and rubbed her head as she stood. "All I ask is that you keep quiet until we are safely on the road. Then you can shout the foolishness of my mission to the winds."

"Or," her former employer countered. The old spark that

was once Eleanor fired her gaze. "You can untie me and allow me to join your cause."

"What?" It was Agnes's turn to gasp. "You would go with us?"

She shrugged as best as a woman can shrug with her arms tied behind her back. "As you so eloquently pointed out, I haven't really been living since Virginia was taken from me. Your courage has inspired me to hope again. In truth? There's nothing more I'd rather do than accompany you. If you refuse, I might very well attempt to come after you. Alone."

Now *that* was a foolish mission. She wouldn't survive more than a few days on her own in the wilderness. Surely she knew that. Agnes treated her to a hard stare. Her eyes twinkled back. Aye, she did know.

"Are you threatening me, Madam Dare?" Agnes couldn't suppress a grin.

"I believe I am, Madame Medicine Woman. Yes. Yes, I am." She grinned back.

Agnes motioned to the puzzled Chogan to untie her. He complied and helped her stand. The two women embraced again. Then Agnes turned and signed to Chogan and Mantunaaga that Eleanor would be accompanying them. Chogan spoke something low to Mantunaaga, who took off again.

Agnes resumed her preparations beneath Chogan's watchful eyes and Eleanor's long list of whispered questions and suggestions. A female clearing her voice behind them had them both straightening and spinning around.

Jane stood in the doorway, arms crossed like a Roanoke. Her face was painted in a ferocious manner that made no sense to Agnes, and an endless supply of weapons were strapped to nearly every spare inch of her gloriously tall person. "I don't suppose you intended to leave camp without saying goodbye?" she grumbled, "because that would be excessively rude."

Agnes chuckled guiltily. "Who says I am going anywhere?"

She gave a low sharp whistle, and Mantunaaga re-entered the longhouse. Winona, Kaliska, and three other Roanoke maidens whose names Agnes did not recall filed in silently behind him. "He did. I cannot believe you meant to leave without me. I know the way far better than you."

"Oh, Jane! I don't know what to say." Of course, she knew the way. She'd been sold as a concubine to the king of Copper Mountain, rescued by Chief Wanchese who was now her husband, and had returned with him afterwards to rescue a small group of colonists from the copper mines. Cecil Prat, Edward Powell, a teenage lad named Will Withers, young Robert Ellis, and their dearly departed friend, George Howe. *May he rest in peace!*

"Then say nothing." Jane gestured swiftly to the three additional Roanoke women. "My maidens are Bly, Dioni, and Chitsa. Chitsa is James's wife, if you recall."

Agnes smiled. Of course she recalled them. James and William were the two scraggly, middle-aged ex-convicts who'd attached themselves to Jane on the ship ride over from England. They'd been imprisoned with her on Copper Mountain, rescued at the same time, and had refused to leave her side when she married Chief Wanchese. Her faithful hounds, both had become permanent fixtures in the Roanoke tribe.

Her maidens swiftly outfitted Eleanor with a change of Native clothing, far more appropriate for travel in the wilderness than her English gown and stockings.

"There are ten of us in all." Agnes threw a sideways glance at Jane. "I never intended to take so many. A group our size is far more likely to be missed, you know."

"I'm counting on it." She gave a satisfied nod as her

maidens finished braiding and tucking Eleanor's hair beneath her cap.

"You are?" Agnes's eyebrows rose.

She snorted. "What? You think ten people is enough to storm an entire mountain?"

Actually, Agnes had pictured herself going alone with only Chogan and Mantunaaga at her side, and she didn't have much of a plan. She'd intended to come up with one along the way. "I haven't thought that far ahead," she admitted sheepishly.

Jane clucked her tongue. "You brave but foolish woman! Fortunately, you have me."

"Yes," Agnes murmured, dazed at the fortunate turn of events.

"When our people come after us, pray they have the sense to bring a cannon or two," she muttered as she fastened the final skin of water to her side.

The cannons! All Agnes had in mind was a rescue mission, whereas it sounded as if Jane was planning a war.

CHAPTER 34: RESCUE OPERATION

*J*ane saw no sense in waiting until first light to depart. "Best to get on the road right away before anyone else finds out what we're up to and tries to stop us."

She had a point. In less than an hour, their search and rescue party had grown from three individuals to ten.

She directed them to exit the longhouse in staggered groups of two. Agnes and Chogan exited first. They slipped from the back of her lodge into the night. It was unlikely anyone would question her these days. She'd gained the respect of her maidens, and their tribe was accustomed to seeing her move about in either Chogan or Mantunaaga's company. Plus, they sidled through the rear gate of camp as if attending the call of nature.

A few campfires were still burning outside, but the crowds were dwindling in lieu of their bedrolls and sleeping platforms. By Agnes's best estimate, it was somewhere upwards of ten o'clock.

She resisted the urge to pause at the gate of their protective palisade and look back, not wanting to arouse the suspicions of the gate guards. However, she suffered a few twinges of heartache as she left her new home behind — the home Riapoke had built for her. *May the good Lord allow us to complete our mission and return here safely. Together.*

The village lay nearly silent in the moonlight, a hill dotted with tents and lodges, fortified by nothing more than the brave scouts ever on patrol and their collective will to survive. By morning, the tents and lodges would be glistening with November frost. Agnes prayed she would live to see the village and its inhabitants again. Somewhere, in her struggle to become one of them, they had grown precious to her.

She and Chogan plunged into the frigid forest and followed the line of the river to the agreed-upon rendezvous point. It was the location Riapoke, Amonsoquath, and Tikoosoo were last seen — high on the bluffs overlooking the delta where the Chowan and Roanoke Rivers converged. That is where they would have climbed to catch a glimpse of the approaching third wave of enemy warriors. That is where they would have taken their stand and sent their fiery arrows plunging in the midst of the advancing army.

A glint of something shiny hanging from a deadened tree branch caught Agnes's eye in the moonlight. Whatever it was, it was half concealed in an abandoned birds nest. She moved to stand beneath the object for a better look, and her insides trembled. It was her silver necklace and locket bearing the portraits of her parents. Riapoke would have never willingly parted with it; and if anyone had stolen it from him, they would not likely have left it behind. He must have deliberately planted it as a message to her, should she come looking for him.

She inwardly pummeled herself for not having the

courage to launch her own search party sooner. The Roanoke and Croatoan scouts had searched the ground for clues countless times, scouring for footprints and trampled underbrush. Apparently, they'd not spent much time looking up.

"Help me." She motioned for Chogan to hoist her into the tree. He complied, and she edged her way along the branch bearing the abandoned nest until her gloved hand closed around the locket.

"What in tarnation are you doing up there?" Jane called. When Agnes glanced down, Chitsa, Bly, Dioni, and Jane were assembled below. Mantunaaga and Eleanor materialized behind them. They only needed Kaliska and Winona to arrive before they departed for Copper Mountain.

She scooted back down the tree and leaped from the final branch. Chogan's hands closed around her waist and gentled the fall. "Thank you, my friend." She struck her fist to her chest, and he returned the salute.

"I was retrieving this." She unsnapped the locket and noted its contents in dismay. A copper coin was wedged between the portraits. She turned to Jane. "I believe this erases any doubts about where my husband and his warriors were taken." She tipped the open locket in Jane's direction so her friend could see for herself.

"Aye, it also means they were taken alive," she confirmed gravely. "Let me wedge the coin into the base of this tree as a message to those who will follow behind us. It will help Wanchese convince the others what needs to be done."

Winona and Kaliska slipped noiselessly into view.

Dioni held the coin against the tree while Jane hammered it in with the handle of her blade. Then Jane led them into the woods.

Agnes was grateful for her assistance. Jane was an excellent tracker, huntress, and warrior. Their chances of surviving the elements without getting lost were much higher with her running point.

However, her presence didn't make the winds less icy or keep the first snow from blanketing the world before dawn broke. Lord help them, but they were cold. They were growing tired, too. However, they had no choice but to press on. Movement was the only thing that kept them from turning to icicles.

When Dioni's teeth started to chatter, Jane increased their pace. "Come on," she urged. "It'll get our blood pumping harder."

They jogged in the direction of Copper Mountain, keeping within hearing distance of the rushing river current. It served as their compass. They also stayed within the tree line. It didn't protect them entirely from the winds, but it helped break the brunt of them.

A light snow drifted lazily down to rest on their noses and eyelashes. Thank God, it wasn't enough to stick to the ground. Otherwise, it would have outlined their footprints. Agnes silently prayed it would cease falling soon before it started to accumulate. It was critical that they move undetected by any hostiles who might be out on patrol.

They stopped every two hours to sip at their water skins and answer the call of nature. Otherwise, they maintained they steady pace. As they ran, it occurred to Agnes how much stronger her body was after months in the wilderness. Back in London, she never would have contemplated making a journey like this, not with her breath-constricting corsets, high-heeled dance slippers, skirts, and petticoats best designed for promenades in the park. And certainly not on foot.

Her deerskin leggings, tunic, and cloak were much lighter

in weight that her debutante wardrobe had been, snugger and more practical for ease of movement. She was proud that she, Jane, and Eleanor had no trouble keeping pace with their Native comrades. Pale Faces they might be, but their bodies were every bit as strong and fit.

They slept in shifts midday in a cavern, keeping two on guard at all times. They resumed their journey at the brink of nightfall. It took the better part of two days to bring them to the outskirts of their destination. Copper Mountain towered before them at dusk on the second day. Its very presence was menacing. The lack of movement on the mountain was a reminder of how secluded its inhabitants were within the low-lying cloud cover. Though its rocky walls went straight up, giving the mountain the appearance of being barren and impassable, they knew nothing was further from the truth. The mountain was very much inhabited by their enemies and their platoons of copper mining slaves, many of whom were English friends and loved ones.

It was quickly discovered all previously known entrances had been sealed or barricaded shut. They would have to find the newest entrances and force their way in.

"Remember, they use guard dogs. Lots of them." Jane passed around a foul-smelling substance and bade everyone in their party to lather it on. "This will mask our scent."

And keep us on the verge of gagging. Ugh! Agnes could barely fill her lungs after applying the dreadful stuff to her skin and clothing. For the first time in two days, she was grateful for the icy breezes swirling around them. They helped to clear her nostrils. Otherwise, she would have found it difficult to breathe at all.

"You'll get used to it," Jane assured with a wink.

Agnes highly doubted it, but there was no point in arguing the matter. It was essential that they scout the perimeter of the mountain undetected, so hiding their scent from the droves of guard dogs was not optional. Once night fell, they split into two groups and circled the base of the mountain in opposite directions, performing their first search for the mine entrances.

They passed the one Jane had used to rescue four colonists a few months earlier. It was now sealed shut with a pile of boulders, most of them bigger than Agnes's arm span. Short of a miracle, they would be unable to move them. She wondered how the Mountain people had managed to plant them there. Craning her neck to peer up the side of the mountain, she found her answer. The moonlight illuminated a large indention in the mountainside, which meant the pile of boulders below was the result of a rockslide. Whether natural or man-made, her conclusion remained the same: They would have to find another way into the mine.

An hour later, they reconvened on the opposite side of the mountain. In the distance, they could hear dogs barking. It was time for the next Copper Mountain canine patrol. Using hand signals, Jane led them away from the mountain at a jog. They waited until they were a good half mile from the mountain before they dared to speak again.

They clustered in a small clearing beneath a copse of naked trees. There was just enough moonlight filtering through their gnarled branches for Agnes to shake her head at the others and be seen. "We found no way in. What next?"

Eleanor splayed her upturned hands. "Well, none of us expected this to be easy. We must keep looking."

Jane and Agnes exchanged glances. "The caves," they declared in unison.

"What caves?" Eleanor asked curiously.

"They're all over the place. As many constructed ones as natural ones." Jane rummaged for a stick and scored the ground with it. "According to Cecil Prat, the mine shafts join a series of tunnels leading away from the mountain. When he was imprisoned, the main tunnels extended from the base of the mountain to here, here, and here." She stabbed her rough drawing in three places with her stick. "The sealed entrance rests above this one." Her drawing resembled a round wheel with three spokes extending from nearly equal distances. "The inhabitants of Copper Mountain come and go from them to hunt slaves, conduct business on the Great Trading Path, run security patrols, and fight an occasional skirmish. Cecil claimed his captors were paranoid about security. They were forever building new tunnels and sealing old ones to disorient the prisoners and remove all hope of escape."

Winona and Kaliska observed Jane's sketch and chattered softly in their native tongue. Chogan bent over to point something out to them on the ground.

Jane grunted in disdain as she marked another spot on her map with the stick. "Cecil said this area was used as a set of interrogation and torture chambers. Even the smallest acts of defiance were dealt with swiftly and without mercy."

"Barbaric and despicable!" Eleanor waved her hand beneath her nose. Agnes did not think she was fanning away their foul scent so much as trying to rid herself of the horrible mental pictures of the plight of the imprisoned colonists. "Mayhap we can find a way to use their paranoia against them."

Agnes smiled at her. "I love the way your mind thinks." She'd walked around like a beaten dog far too long. It was good to have the old Eleanor back, the one with wisdom, courage, and spunk.

Winona pointed and asked a question about Jane's drawing.

Jane answered, then lifted her head from her digging. "Thanks to their paranoia, Copper Mountain rests atop a veritable maze of tunnels. We should be able to dig or blast our way in from nearly any vantage point."

She made it sound easy, if one didn't count the hours of backbreaking work ahead of us. "What I wouldn't give for a pile of good English shovels," Agnes sighed.

"Would you settle for a few English canons?"

CHAPTER 35: CHRISTOPHER'S RETURN

"*W*ell, now. What have we here?"

Their group spun in unison, weapons drawn, at the sound of Christopher Cooper's voice.

"What took you so long?" Jane shouldered her rifle, as they gathered in a semi-circle around him.

Agnes feared their countrymen would be furious when they discovered so many women missing, but his cocky grin said otherwise.

He waved a taunting finger beneath first Agnes, then Jane's noses. "You left on awfully short notice, minxes."

Jane sniffed. "We gave you all that you needed to know to find us."

"Aye, thank God you had the sense to pin that copper coin to the tree. Otherwise," he shook his head in admonition, "well, we wouldn't have otherwise traveled with the cannons, that's for sure."

"Thank God you had the sense to bring the cannons." Jane mimicked his chiding tone perfectly. "How many of our men did you manage to press into service?"

His features tightened, as if bracing himself for a reaction from them. "All of them," he said in carefully modulated tones.

Along with the rest of their small rescue party, Agnes could only gape at him for several seconds.

"All of them?" she repeated cautiously. "Then who is guarding Fort Chowan?" It was foolhardy in the extreme to leave their women and children so exposed. The Copper Mountain people might be beaten back for a time, but there were plenty of other hostile neighbors to worry about.

He steepled his hands below his chin. "When the colonists realized you and Eleanor had gone in search of your husband and her child, they were put to shame. Not one of them was willing to stay behind. They are on their way to join your cause — every man, woman, and child. They bring with them all our food stores, all our weapons, and the last of our ammunition."

The English had utterly abandoned their fort? Agnes could not have been more shocked. Or humbled. It took her several moments to absorb the enormity of their sacrifice. They were coming to take their last stand beside her and her small collection of maidens. In the next few days, they were going to face their biggest enemy one last time, and they were either going to live together or die together.

Ananias stepped from the trees. "If this is to be our final battle on this God-forsaken continent, then I say let us fight it together." He hurried to his wife's side and hooked an arm around her shoulders to pull her close. "We should have done this months ago, love. I'm sorry it took me so long to realize this was the right thing to do."

She hugged him back. "We weren't ready then." She lifted her head to meet the gazes of everyone in our group. "We are now."

Several heads nodded in agreement.

Agnes blinked back tears. It was an enormous change of

heart and direction, but it felt right. Though her voice shook, she had a few things to say, as well. "We've been living in fear too long. Always bracing for the next attack. Well, no more. This time, we're taking the fight to them."

"Hear, hear!" Christopher crowed softly.

She offered him a shaky smile. "No more waiting for England to rescue us. We're going to save ourselves. No more standing by meekly while our friends are rounded up like cattle and forced into slavery. It's time to take back who is ours and what is ours."

A muffled cheer rose at her words. Amitola emerged from the shadowy tree line and joined Christopher, pressing her very pregnant body against his. She ran her hands over his chest as if trying to assure herself he was well.

"My husband, I am here to help."

Husband! Her words created no small stir among her listeners. *But of course!* All their talk of negotiating a marriage contract was a delightful sham, nothing more than a gesture to appease those who still clung to Old World pomp and circumstance. The two of them hadn't waited for the blessing of her tribe or the English council. They'd gone ahead and gotten married on their own. Lord only knew how long they'd been together as man and wife. Agnes wanted to laugh in glee at their total disregard for tradition. It was refreshing to witness people unafraid to live life to its fullest without apology.

Beaming in pride, Christopher laid a possessive hand on his wife's waist and bent to whisper something to her. He kissed the tip of her ear, then straightened and held up his hand. He sought Agnes out again with his striking silvery gaze. "I'm not nearly finished, so hear me out, Mrs. Riapoke."

Mrs. Riapoke. She immediately adored the English-sounding version of her married name.

"When the Roanokes heard of your somewhat wild-haired but courageous attempt to send a search party after their beloved war chief on the brink of wintertide, well...let me just say this. They, too, gave one hundred percent of their support to your cause. They will arrive shortly with all their canoes, all their weapons, and all their food stores. Like the English, they bring every man, woman, and child."

At a shiver of movement in the trees, he gave a wry chuckle. "I'll let Chief Wanchese give his own accounting as to how the Roanoke council came to this decision on such short notice."

Moments later, Jane gave a short cry of surprise when her husband materialized and swept her from her feet to deliver a rough and very thorough kiss. It was no small feat given her above average height, but he was a tall man and more than capable of managing his strong-willed wife.

Her face was as red as a sunrise when he set her down, though in the moonlight, it merely looked a few shades darker. "I missed you, too," she muttered and yanked his head down for another kiss.

Agnes could have swooned with envy. They were so happy together. A more perfect match she'd never witnessed. Both were excellent trackers and hunters, wildly independent, and afraid of nothing. Jane's blunt way of speaking and Wanchese's devil-may-care attitude were a little much for some of the other English colonists, but she loved them dearly for the spark and vigor in which they approached each day. She wouldn't change one thing about them if she could.

"There now!" After Wanchese relinquished her lips, it didn't take Jane long to throw herself back into the task at hand. "Seeing as how we're all in agreement about what needs to happen next..." With her stick, she mapped out a series of patrols for us.

Most of the group seemed approving of Jane's plan.

Kaliska was the only one not paying attention. She scrutinized Amitola as if she was pondering something of critical importance. Agnes wondered what was on her mind, and wished she could understand what she was saying when she finally broke her silence. She jogged to Amitola's side and carried on a heated conversation with lots of gesturing, but Agnes's grasp of the Powhatan language wasn't strong enough to keep up. She appeared to be trying to convince Amitola of something, and Amitola appeared to be disagreeing wholeheartedly.

As she studied the two women, it occurred to Agnes that Kaliska's resemblance to Amitola was striking. She hadn't given it much thought before. Though they belonged to different tribes, they were similar in height and build. Aside from Amitola's pregnancy, they looked enough alike to be related. Were they?

Jane must have been eavesdropping. "It could work," she announced grimly when the two women paused their arguing.

"Tah!" Amitola responded tartly. "She would die."

Kaliska chattered again in Powhatan, voice rising as she made her point. She glanced pleadingly first in Winona's direction, then in Agnes's. "It…is…best," she protested.

The winds picked up. "Translation please." Eleanor rubbed her hands together and danced in place to keep warm.

Jane's tone was harsh, her expression tight. "Fine, but this is not the time to think like missish debutante's on their way to a ball. This is war, my friends." She tapped the stick she held against her leg. "Kaliska has an excellent plan to get one of us inside. She wishes to pose as Amitola. If the mountain people are convinced they snagged the mother of their unborn prince, they will whisk her into the presence of their council with haste."

"They will be angry," Amitola fumed.

"Aye, and when they discover her ruse, they will interrogate her. With any luck at all, they will place her with the other prisoners."

Like Riapoke, Amonsoquath, and Tikoosoo. It was risky, but it might be their only chance of getting a message to the captives. The only way of mobilizing them for the next part of their plan.

Amitola's lips parted in anger. "They will torture her!"

"I...strong!" Kaliska announced proudly, swelling her thin chest.

"Indeed, you are," Jane assured firmly. "She can carry word to any prisoners she comes in contact with and prepare them to fight back when the time comes."

Or Kaliska might die in vain at the hands of a bitter, vengeful enemy. Agnes silently prayed this would not be the case, but the fact remained; the Copper Mountain people were still reeling from the heavy losses sustained in their attack of Fort Chowan. Given the chance to make someone in their tribe pay? *Lord have mercy...*

"It's too risky, Jane!" Agnes implored when her jaw remained set. Amitola was right. Kaliska could hardly hope to survive such an ordeal. "This isn't even her fight." *It is mine and Eleanor's.*

"She feels differently. Riapoke is her war chief, and Amitola is her cousin. This isn't just the fight of a few. Remember who's down in the copper mines? It's our fight. We're all in this together."

So the two women were cousins. The bond of family was strong. "Even so, it's far too risky to send her in alone." Agnes clasped her hands in front of her. "I will accompany her."

"Of what value would your presence add?" Jane exploded. "They would detect your English heritage before you stepped within ten yards of their council."

Agnes raised her chin. "If I may remind you, Kaliska is one of our tribeswomen. I'll not let her go in alone, so there is no point in trying to dissuade me. Maybe you can create a disguise that would allow me to pose as her attending maiden." She tapped her foot thoughtfully, warming to the merits of the plan. "Once they figure out I am English, what is the worse they will do, eh?"

Jane's lip curled into a full-blown snarl. "If they allow you to live, they will slap you in irons and toss you in the copper mines, never again to see the light of day."

"My thoughts exactly." Agnes offered her a saucy grin. "Then we will have a spy in the interrogation chambers as well as one in the mines. Once underground, I can mobilize the prisoners for an uprising of Armageddon proportions. Fear not, my friend. I fully intend to see the light of day again, and it will be your job to ensure that I do, General Jane."

Eleanor gave a tremulous laugh. "You'll do nothing of the sort, my friend. We both know Anthony would never allow it, and that is that."

"Then he cannot be informed of our plans until I am on the inside."

"But—"

Agnes pounded her gloved fists together. "We do not have the numbers to defeat the Copper Mountain people without using every resource available, every ounce of cunning. Even with their recent losses in battle, they outnumber us ten to one. It is imperative we mobilize their prisoners against them."

"It sounds like a good plan, but so many things could go wrong," Eleanor moaned. "As the governor's daughter, I-I cannot condone such a sacrifice. I will not. There must be a better way."

"There's not," Jane cut in icily. "Much as I despise Agnes's plan, she has the right of it. It's all or nothing, folks."

Jane was correct. They had very few options at their disposal and none of them good. Agnes cleared her throat. "How badly do you want to see your daughter again, Eleanor?"

"With every bone in my body. But the risk!" she wailed.

"Is one I'm willing to take. My husband is worth it. I do not wish to go one more day without knowing his fate."

She wrung her hands. "If we were to let you perform such a mad task — and I am not yet giving my approval, mind you — what can we do on the outside to help you and Kaliska on the inside? To increase your chances of survival?"

Agnes could almost hear the fishhook sink in to Eleanor's jaw. It was only a matter of reeling her in before she was fully on board with their mission. She shot a furtive glance in Kaliska's direction, and her heartbeat stuttered. Aye, the Roanoke maiden understood the risks. Her expression was one of grim anticipation. Agnes was overwhelmingly grateful she had chosen to keep silent about Kaliska's part in her beating a few weeks earlier. If she'd received the punishment Amitola had assured was forthcoming — banishment was a common sentence handed out to Native women for more severe infractions — she might not be here to help them now. As Mum used to say, *doing what is right always pays better in the long run.*

Mum had been willing to risk never seeing her only daughter again in the hopes of sending her to a safer place. It was ironic for Agnes to find herself in a similar situation on the other side of the world — risking it all for those she'd come to love so dearly. Mum had raised her to be strong and resilient, and she was more grateful than ever for her upbringing.

Jane yanked down Agnes's fur hood, drawing her attention back to the present. She uncoiled Agnes's long braid. "Are you certain about this, my friend?"

Agnes lifted her chin. "Wouldn't you do it for your husband?"

"You know I would." She whipped out her blade and sliced off the length of Agnes's hair.

Agnes tried not to flinch and didn't quite succeed. It would take years to grow it back.

"There," Jane noted in satisfaction. "What is left will be much easier to dye."

Eleanor whimpered in alarm. "Oh, Jane! Oh, Agnes!"

Agnes sighed. "'Tis only hair. It will grow back. For our plan to work, we need to convince them I'm a Roanoke maiden long enough for me to get inside their mountain village."

"God have mercy on us all," Eleanor whispered and fell silent. Her lips continued to tremble in silent prayer.

CHAPTER 36: IN FOR A PENNY

*W*inona worked quickly to help Kaliska appear pregnant. They traded her tunic for a larger one and stuffed the front of it with dried grass. Amitola was due any day now. The Copper Mountain people would know that.

Jane and her maidens took charge of Agnes's disguise, which required dying her hair and darkening her skin. Neither were easy tasks. With respect to time, they opted to smear a tar-like substance in her hair. It felt like cool, gooey slime and smelled so awful Agnes didn't dare inquire about its ingredients. To turn her skin darker, they rubbed what seemed like a gallon of mud on her face, neck, hands, and wrists.

"I've not yet decided if you're the world's biggest fool or the bravest." Jane dabbed mud on Agnes's closed eyelids and carefully rubbed it in.

"A brave fool." Agnes's lips stretched into a grin. "I can own up to that."

Jane pinched her earlobe. "You twist my words, wench."

There was little point in covering the rest of her body in

mud. Like Kaliska, Agnes only needed to gain entrance to the mountain. Once inside, the plan was to be taken prisoner as quickly as possible. She could only pray Kaliska would be sent to the interrogation chambers, while she, herself, would be sent to the copper mines. If they failed to mobilize the other prisoners, their sacrifice would be for nothing.

A muffled hubbub of voices in the distance made Agnes freeze. Anthony had arrived and was arguing with someone.

"Come!" Agnes beckoned sharply to Kaliska. "We must go." If they weren't on their way to the mountain before Anthony arrived, he would surely put a stop to their plans.

She nodded and exchanged a final speaking glance with Winona. The elder woman's finely honed features mirrored Kaliska's grim acceptance and a flash of pain that was all her own. Agnes's intuitions told her that the older woman feared for their safety, but she couldn't afford to dwell on misgivings. She needed to maintain her resolve.

When Winona nodded her farewell, Agnes gave her the salute of a warrior. At her gesture, Winona straightened her sagging shoulders and pounded her fist to her heart. Agnes held her gaze a moment longer, silently willing her to be strong in their absence.

"Where is she?" Anthony's voice sounded closer.

Kaliska and Agnes crept silently away from the group and plunged into the shadowy forests. They jogged to put distance between them and their comrades. As they ran, Agnes pondered the best way to gain entrance to the mountain, since they'd been unsuccessful in locating any doors or tunnels thus far.

They were halfway to the mountain, when the faint barking of dogs met their ears. Agnes tensed and laid a hand on Kaliska's arm to slow their gait. They were unarmed and could not easily put down the dogs. Running away would only alert them to their presence, possibly putting the rest of their people in danger. Why couldn't they have encountered the blasted dogs closer to their destination?

Kaliska dove in a shallow ravine and threw handfuls of dirt over her person. Agnes followed and mimicked her actions. The dogs barked and snuffled their way past their hiding place at little more than ten paces away. Agnes wilted against the ground, chest heaving in relief. Not so with Kaliska. She was already back on her feet.

They straightened their disguises the best they could in the dark and resumed their jog. The barking of the dogs never faded, not even when the two women drew in sight of the mountain. It was almost as if they were following them.

Rough hands grabbed Agnes from behind and threw her to the ground. From the scuffling and grunting sounds, she perceived Kaliska was struggling with their captors, as well.

Agnes's heart pounded with dread and anticipation. *Well, this is it.* This was their one chance to get inside the mountain if their captors let them live that long.

"Amitola!" Her name was spat in anger and disgust.

Good. Our disguises are working so far.

She shot a retort to them in her native tongue. The only word Agnes understood was *English.* Bless her for remembering their plan while the heat of their circumstances mounted to the boiling point.

Their hands were tied and blindfolds placed over their eyes. They were half-prodded, half-dragged through the woods. To Agnes's alarm, they seemed to be heading farther away from the mountain instead of closer.

Did they mean to execute them, then? *Please, God, no!*

She didn't know how long they marched. With so much fear sickening her gut, every passing minute felt like an hour. She attempted to count their paces and keep track of the number of turns, but her efforts proved futile. It merely felt like they were traveling in circles. She stumbled and fell more times than she could count.

After awhile, Agnes realized she could no longer hear Kaliska's quiet expulsions of air each time she was yanked back to her feet.

Had they been separated? What was happening to them? Agnes's fears nearly brought her to the brink of swooning. She crumpled to her knees, barely conscious, and no amount of cuffing and prodding could draw her back to her feet.

She was furious with herself for dissolving so completely, but no amount of inner berating restored her ability to stand. It was as if her legs were made of liquid the way they sank to the cold, hard ground.

A cuff to her right ear made everything go black.

---

*A*gnes awoke to the uncomfortable sensation of being stretched. Blinking, she realized her blindfold was gone. A dying fire dimly illuminated her surroundings. She was in a small, circular room with rocky walls. Her arms were bound and secured to a copper ring embedded in the wall above her head. An assortment of copper knives and spears half-immersed in the red-hot coals in the center of the room filled her with horror. Their various hooks and prongs were covered in blood, and the room smelled of burnt flesh. *Mercy! Where am I?*

Her head pounded so hard she could barely move it without seeing stars. She managed to twist it just enough to one side to discern there were prisoners lining the walls, bound in the same manner as she was. One of them was Kaliska. She appeared oblivious to her surroundings, head lolling to one side and eyes closed. Her face was a maze of cuts, and it was swollen nearly beyond recognition. Agnes's heart ached for the poor maiden's suffering. At least she'd escaped it a few blessed minutes. But nay, the faint trembling of her eyelids indicated she was only feigning unconsciousness.

Be strong, young warrior. Be strong.

Agnes twisted harder to take in more of the room. From the mangled appearance of the other prisoners — all of them male besides her and Kaliska — this had to be the horrific interrogation chamber Cecil Prat had warned them about. Alas, Agnes had not made it to the copper mines as she'd hoped. It was a troubling setback, indeed. If she couldn't get word to the prisoners below ground, her plan for their escape was doomed.

"Ann-nes?" Her name was spoken so softly she wondered if she dreamt it.

It was Riapoke!

Ignoring the pain caused by the movement, she twisted her head frantically to determine the whereabouts of her husband's voice.

He was bound to the wall across from her, no more than a few paces away. He wasn't looking in her direction, though. Quite the contrary. His chin was resting on his chest, and his eyes were closed. Amonsoquath was bound on his left, and Tikoosoo on his right. Amonsoquath appeared unconscious but not Tikoosoo. He was worriedly eyeing Kaliska.

Agnes drank in the sight of her husband, cringing at the scars crisscrossing his chest and torso. Some of them were scabbed. Others oozed fresh blood. *Mercy!* The bear claws tattooed to his upper arms were flayed to pieces. She longed for her medicinal supplies to nurse his wounds.

"I knew you were alive." She couldn't keep the sob from her voice and didn't care. It was important to her that he understood she had come looking for him on purpose. Unwanted tears streaked her cheeks, probably turning the brown paint to mud. Following his lead, she carefully lowered her head. "Our people are gathering outside the mountain. They plan to blast their way in with cannons, so we must be ready to escape when—"

Two men with cudgels in hand burst into the room. They circled the prisoners, shouting words she could not understand, pounding already-crumpled bodies without an ounce of compassion.

Kaliska muttered something feverishly. Her voice was so weak, Agnes could make out nothing she said other than the word *English.*

One of their captors raised his cudgel again. *Oh, God! Nay!* He brought it crashing down against her ribs. A breathy exhale escaped her. Then her chin dipped to her chest, and she stopped moving altogether. Agnes watched anxiously for her lungs to expand with air again. *Breathe, sister, breathe!* But they didn't. It was over for her.

Rest in peace, dear maiden. Your fight is over.

Agnes fought to get her emotions under control, enough to mimic her fellow prisoners who were pretending unconsciousness, but it was no use. She couldn't stop weeping. Her sobs came out in enormous damp gasps.

What a weakling! She was ashamed at her utter lack of composure. Kaliska had been much braver, right to the very end.

It broke Agnes's heart that they had failed in their mission, that their deaths would be for nothing. *May God have mercy on all the innocent men, women, and children awaiting us outside!* The poor souls were still blindly assembling themselves for the next phase of a coordinated attack, one that would never come. Jane had been right. Agnes was a fool — the world's worst fool — and all her friends and countrymen would pay for it.

She didn't cringe or writhe when the men with cudgels

approached her. Her tears stopped, and she was able to breathe again. *It is over.* An unaccountable calmness settled on her head and shoulders and worked its way down her arms and legs. Her worst fears were realized. Now that the dread she'd lived with for so long was coming to an end, she welcomed it.

One of her captors gave a sharp exclamation. He swiped a filthy thumb across Agnes's face and stared at it in wonder. She attempted to spit in his direction but failed. Her mouth was too dry to produce any moisture.

The other man grabbed her tunic and ripped it open. Both of them pointed and jabbered excitedly. The first one produced a double-edged copper blade and raised it over her.

"Heathen swine!" she hissed, though it was difficult to form the words with her swollen tongue.

Instead of striking the fatal blow she anticipated, he sliced the ropes above her head. Her hands fell lifelessly to her sides. There was not enough blood left in them to feel anything more than a tingling numbness.

"Ireh!" He sheathed his knife and prodded her with his cudgel. She perceived he wanted her to move towards the doorway.

Her fear returned tenfold. She didn't want to know what was on the other side of the door. Apparently, instead of a quick death, they had something else in mind for her. It couldn't be good. Mental images of every savage form of public execution filled her mind.

More subterranean dimness met her on the other side of the door. A flame flickered from a single torch mounted crudely to a rock wall. It illuminated a long, narrow passage. Multi-colored metallic veins splintered their way along its rocky surface.

Agnes dazedly perceived she had made it to the copper

mines after all! She was led with much shoving and cursing deeper beneath the ground, until she could hear the sound of tools striking against rock. The only other sounds were the occasional slapping of leather against skin followed by cries of pain.

They walked until the narrow passage fanned out to a much wider cavern. Once inside, the stench of unwashed bodies was nearly unbearable. Agnes gagged as she absorbed the sights and sounds of her new surroundings. Like the tunnel, this room was lit by torches. Across the floor stretched at least a dozen bodies with ill-kempt bandages wrapping their various wounds.

She was shoved to her knees before a shriveled old crone with matted hair that hung across her face. Then her captors exited the chamber, leaving her alone with the woman. The crone reached for her roughly and proceeded to examine her. She poked and prodded until Agnes groaned from the number of scrapes and bruises she discovered.

At one point, she inhaled sharply and rose to her feet. She stomped to the wall, stepping over the bodies in her way, and snatched up the nearest torch. She carried it back to Agnes and thrust it so close to her face she feared it would melt her skin clean off.

"It is you! Agnes Wood, in the flesh," the woman grated in a voice as dry as sand. "I thought I must be dreaming. More's the pity."

Joyce Archard? Agnes squinted at her, recognizing her voice but unable to match it to her gaunt figure. Aye, the woman was taller than she first estimated due to her stooped posture, but that was her only familiar feature. Gone was her ample girth, richly adorned gowns, and haughty tilt to her head. In her place was a broken and bitter shell of a woman.

"Yes, and I've come to rescue you." Agnes attempted to straighten her spine. "You and all the others down here."

Joyce Archard gave a dry snuffle of derision and reached for Agnes's shoulders. She was stronger than she looked, because she managed to shake her until her ribs rattled. "You've died and gone to hell, lass. The sooner you realize that, the better for us all."

"Lord, have mercy! Stop," Agnes groaned. Her shaking revived every ache in her body.

"He's dead, too, lass. No use calling on God anymore."

"Why, Joyce!" Agnes gasped. "'Tis not so, and I'll prove it to you."

She snorted again. "Get some rest, lass. You're lucky they think you're injured worse than you are. Otherwise, they'd have put you right to work in the mines."

"Nay, I'm not ready to sleep. We've much to discuss."

"Lie down!" she snapped, stomping back to the wall to return the torch to its holder.

Though the ground was rough and rocky, Agnes was happy to comply. "I will rest, if you will hear me out," she pressed with a sense of urgency like she'd never known before. "We've nearly two hundred friends and allies camped above ground who are about to blast their way in."

She squatted beside Agnes and pressed the back of her hand to her forehead. "No fever," she muttered. "They must have whacked you on the head, then."

"No cracks. My head is fine," Agnes assured cheerfully. "Eleanor Dare is out there, Joyce. Plus Ananias, Anthony, Margaret, Emme, Mark, Christopher, and Jane. Two of our allies are with us, too. The Roanoke and Croatoan tribes."

"Huh!" She shook her head. "Now I know for certain your head is cracked. The Roanokes are the spawn of the devil. Once upon a time, I fancied they were our worst enemies. Alas, I've since learned there are more dreadful creatures than them scuttling around these tunnels."

Agnes did not doubt her claim, but she could not afford

to dwell on the woman's personal fears and misery at the moment. There was too much at stake.

"The Roanokes no longer hate us. At least not as much as they did." Agnes mustered up a chuckle, trying to lighten the air in the room. "At the risk of further convincing you of my cracked-headedness, I am happy to report that our Jane went and married their chief. Chief Wanchese is a besotted fool over her, too, which has turned him into an ally." *Of sorts.*

Joyce Archard shook her head again, but a dazed sheen had crept across her tired eyes. "Is that so, Agnes? Is all that you say really true?"

"Aye, God still lives, my friend."

She looked too dry and dusty to muster up tears, but a light mist dampened her gaze. "Either that or I'm seeing and hearing things that aren't real." She slapped at her cheeks, as if trying to awaken herself.

"Joyce, you know I've never been anything but honest with you, right down to deploring your silly superstitions about witches back on the ship."

A faint smile tugged at her dry, cracked lips. "I'm not so sure that I wasn't right after all, lass. She made off with that heathen husband of hers and escaped this hell the rest of us had to endure, didn't she?"

"Not exactly." Agnes's patience was starting to wear thin with Joyce's knack for clinging to the negative. That was something that hadn't changed about her. "She is here to help. She, her husband, and their entire tribe. She's in the family way, Joyce, yet she risked everything to be here."

"Iffen you expect me to believe that—"

Agnes stopped her with an upraised hand, unable to listen to any more of her crabbing. "Here me well, Joyce. You must share everything I told you with the other prisoners. As discreetly as possible, of course, so as not to arouse the suspicions of our captors. You need to prepare them for our escape."

She bent to tend to one of the horrifically gaunt creatures on the floor. It was hard to believe the man was still alive. His clothes were in such tatters, she could make out nearly every protruding bone in his body. It was a gruesome sight.

She straightened and shook a dirt-encrusted finger at Agnes. "I see no point in giving them false hope, lass. There's no way out of here 'cept dying."

"Not so, if the good Lord wills it." Agnes sat up on a burst of anger. Kaliska had died helping her get inside Copper Mountain, and there were many others prepared to risk their lives in the coming hours to attempt this massive rescue. A little gratitude for their sacrifices would have been nice.

As Agnes studied Joyce, however, her anger faded. It wasn't her fault that her circumstances had snuffed out her hope. She'd been sold as a slave, plunged into a life of darkness, and nearly starved to death, poor soul.

Agnes mentally scrambled to say anything that might generate a spark of hope in her. "Our English friends brought four cannons with them. Four, Joyce! They're going to surround this hellish place and blast their way in. That's when we'll make our run to freedom."

She jolted in alarm. "Then they'll be risking lots of innocent lives. The mountain men are nearly always off fighting. It's mostly their womenfolk and children living on the mountain. That includes Virginia Dare, in case you haven't heard."

"Virginia!" Agnes leaped at the sound of the babe's name. "Is she well?"

Joyce grimaced. "I hear different things. Some say she's worshipped like a goddess. Some say she's to be traded for prisoners of war before the year is through. Others claim she'll be sold like the rest of us for a steep price when she's older."

The babe was alive and well for now. That was all that mattered. Agnes smiled at Joyce, though she doubted the woman could see her smile in the dim cavern. "Our cannons aren't going to be used to burn down the mountain. They're going to be used to blast open the tunnels and help us escape. This is really happening, my friend. We're going to get you out of here."

Joyce sighed a dusty relent. "If I promise to spread your crazy tale, will you try to get some sleep, lass?"

"I'll do more than try." Agnes's frenzied burst of energy was ebbing. She collapsed on the floor and stretched out, wincing with every movement. "Don't you forget what you promised. This may be our only chance in this lifetime to escape this place."

"Mercy me," Joyce muttered and moved unsteadily in the direction of the door. Her feet shuffled against the rocky terrain as if they almost were too heavy to lift.

CHAPTER 37: SIEGE

Jane

"Do you think they made it in, Jane?" Eleanor asked for the dozenth time.

Ananias muttered an answer, but Jane couldn't make out his words.

She tapped the ground with her boot. She was lying in the prone, helping to form the protective perimeter around their growing number of new arrivals. She respected how anxious Eleanor was, but she was losing patience with the woman's prattling. Asking questions no one had the answers to didn't help them prepare for what was coming next — war.

Winona squatted down next to Jane and spoke slowly in her Powhatan dialect. "The last of your people and mine have arrived. I can brief them and have them ready to depart within the hour. Chief Wanchese and Chief Manteo say we are to do whatever you tell us."

Aye, miracle of miracles! The Natives were letting her lead this raid, something the English would have never permitted a woman to do. Her husband had no such qualms.

He knew she was an excellent tracker, had a strong command of all the languages represented, and was one of the few who'd survived a stint on Copper Mountain. He also knew she liked being in charge.

Truth be told, she was happier than a hog in waller to be in charge of this particular raid. By now, Agnes and Kaliska should have succeeded in gaining entrance to Copper Mountain. At least, she hoped with all her might that was the case, since their scouts could find no trace of them.

Not particularly a religious creature, Jane gave in to one of her rare penchants for prayer. *Please, God, keep them safe.*

From this point on, Agnes would be counting on her to think how she thought and anticipate what needed to be done following her and Kaliska's efforts to mobilize the prisoners. Lord only knew what physical and mental condition the slaves were in. It was a gamble, for sure. However, they were going to need to help in their own escape once the English cannons opened fire.

Jane rose from her firing position and motioned Winona to follow her. They assembled their two chiefs and councilmen, along with their English counterparts. Representing the English were Eleanor and Ananias Dare, Anthony Cage, and Christopher Cooper. Jane did not relish the thought of dealing with Anthony's lordly temperament tonight, but avoiding him simply wasn't possible.

The moment he caught sight of her, he erupted. "How could you allow Agnes to do such a thing? I thought the two of you were friends!" He tossed his top hat on a tree stump and dragged both hands through his hair. "I shall go mad if anything happens to her." He took a threatening step in Janes direction. "And then I shall—"

She ignored his threat and resisted the urge to roll her eyes. However, she did make sure he caught sight of her fingering one of the knives sheathed at her waist. "If you wish to keep all your pretty appendages, my friend, you'll do everything in your power to help us bring her back safely."

He balled his hands at his sides. "How do we know she's still alive?"

They didn't. Since he already knew the answer to his foolish question, she didn't bother answering it. Ignoring him, she faced the chiefs and their councilmen, first addressing them in their native tongue, then interpreting it in English for her countrymen.

"Agnes and Kaliska's continued absence means the mountain people have taken them as prisoners. It also means the mountain people are on high alert. They will increase the frequency and scope of their dog patrols. They will want to determine if our women acted alone or as part of something bigger."

She received several affirmative nods. "Kaliska and Agnes's brave actions are, indeed, part of something bigger. Much bigger." Both women were doing their part to mobilize the captives to help in this raid. "Copper Mountain has grown rich and powerful on the backs of slaves. Not only do we plan to free those slaves, we will strike a decisive blow against their defenses that will cripple them for years to come."

A low rumble of assent sounded in her ears.

"We can use the return of their captives to forge new alliances with tribes across the region."

Jane sketched out the details of her plan on the ground. Several councilmen stepped closer to examine her drawing. She marked the tunnel sites they would blast open with the cannons and the position where each group would position themselves for the coming rescue operation.

"I like your plan." Excitement snapped in Christopher's silver gaze. Anthony continued to look distressed, but Ananias was full of questions. "Pray do not take offense, my friend, but 'tis like listening to a fairy tale. How can we hope to prevail against such solid fortifications?"

You can't see it, because you haven't the heart or mind of a warrior. Like your wife, you've been rotting in grief instead of fighting to rescue your kidnapped babe. "My husband once gained entrance to the mountain and rescued five colonists, myself included." Jane beamed in pride at him. His dark eyes gleamed back, scorching with passion and possessiveness. "One man created enough havoc and confusion to escape their clutches without a single scrape."

She allowed her gaze to settle on each attending listener. "One man. This time we have two brave maidens on the inside and an entire army on the outside. Scouts, bowmen, gunmen, and cannoneers. We possess the cunning of the eagle and the fierceness of the bear."

At her words, the native councilmen struck their fists to their hearts.

"Agnes may be on the mountain, but she is *not* a warrior," Anthony muttered bitterly.

Again, Jane did not grace his grumbling with a response. She resisted the urge to slap him. Agnes possessed the spirit of the bravest warrior Jane had ever known. She packed more cunning and resourcefulness in her tiny frame than most men four times her size. Aye, but she was well matched with Riapoke. She hoped they would be reunited soon and enjoy all the happiness they'd been cheated out of thus far.

Winona signed to her that the cannons had arrived. That was the last thing they'd been waiting for. They were ready to commence with the next part of their plan.

"Scouts on the perimeter!" Jane ordered crisply. "Bowmen on the flanks. Gunmen and cannoneers to the front and center." She set Blade and his father over the English scouts and her husband over the Native ones. He was the best tracker she knew.

Manteo took charge of the bowmen, and Anthony grudgingly took charge of the gunmen. A nod from her had Ananias scurrying to help him. She wasn't convinced Anthony was in the correct frame of mind to lead a successful charge alone. Plus, it put Ananias in the position to coordinate between the gunmen and cannoneers led by Mark Bennett, Emme's beau.

Winona checked the maidens and their supplies. They were strapped with knives, axes, medicine and bandages, and as many blankets and spare pieces of clothing as they could carry. Eleanor distributed handguns, more medicinal supplies, and more blankets to Margaret and Emme. Helen Pierce would stay behind with Christopher and a small group of native guards to work in shifts. They would hunt game and watch over the pregnant Rose and Amitola as well as the children. They were secreted in the same springs where she and Chief Wanchese had enjoyed their brief honeymoon. Her memories of that stolen hour still had the power to make her blush.

"We will eliminate every patrol in our path, both hounds and handlers," Jane continued to instruct those overseeing key positions. "Can't afford to have them sound any alarms. When we reach the mountain, we will take our places. Then we will blast the cannons to open the gates of hell, and prepare ourselves for whatever comes next." It was her last verbal directive. Her next hand signal propelled everyone into motion. There would be little chatter from here on, except from the runners who would move up and down the lines to keep communication open.

She liked how they'd managed to time their assault in the dead of night. The mountain people might consider themselves on high alert, but she could count on the fact that a good number of them were sleeping, whereas her people were not. They were wide awake, marching on Copper

Mountain, and preparing for battle with vengeance in their hearts. That gave her side the advantage.

Hold on a little longer, my friend. We are on our way. She would not consider their mission a success until she laid eyes on Agnes's china doll face again. She did not have as high of hopes for Kaliska's wellbeing. The mountain people were still smarting from the poor outcome of their latest assault against the colonists. They would be pawing at the ground for someone to blame, and "Amitola" was the perfect target. Nay, it wasn't likely Kaliska was long for this world.

I did not know you well, brave maiden, but I will never forget your sacrifice.

They were less than a hundred paces from the mountain when two dog patrols erupted seemingly from nowhere, barking and snapping. One patrol burst from the underbrush outside their left flank of bowmen. The other came from inside the gunmen's unit. Jane made a mental note of where she first caught sight of the dogs. Their sudden appearances bore investigating.

The bowmen swiftly and silently put an end to a dozen or so hounds and their two handlers. The English weren't so fortunate. Jane had instructed them not to fire their guns at the dogs, because it would alert the mountain people to their presence.

Thus, the Englishmen were left fighting off the dogs' attack with the butts of their rifles. The bowmen from the right flank descended to offer their aid, and the second pack of dogs was rapidly laid to rest long with two more handlers. Unfortunately, one of the Englishmen was bitten several times before the last dog shivered into silence.

He lay gasping on the ground with his hands clutching a torn and bloody pants leg. "I can no longer walk. Shoot me," he begged. There was a wild light in his eyes. Jane suspected he was in too much pain to know what he was saying.

She signaled to Margaret and Emme to treat and bind his wounds and make him as comfortable as possible. He was their first casualty, and there would likely be more. Alas, they couldn't spare the time or the men to send him back to the underground springs. He would have to suffer in silence until the first band of rescued prisoners was ready to retreat.

A careful examination of the terrain where the dog patrols had originated proved fruitful. At long last, they uncovered two tunnel entrances to the mine shafts. The doors were so cleverly concealed, they might never have located them in the dead of night without the unwitting help of the dogs.

The colonists dug four small mounds of dirt and mounted the cannons atop them, facing downward. That way, two muzzles were pointed directly at the tunnel entrances and two muzzles were pointed across the tops of the tunnel passages. The plan was to score the surface of the ground deep enough to raise the roofs of as many tunnels as possible. If Kaliska and Agnes had succeeded in their mission, prisoners would pour out of them to escape.

The scouts continued to patrol. The gunmen formed a perfect semi-circle around the side of the mountain and took a knee. The bowmen assembled themselves behind the gunmen. *Blast the Englishmen's need for straight lines and rows! They looked more like toy soldiers than men.* A few of them took a cue from the Natives and secreted themselves in the trees. Lord willing and they survived this mess, she intended to address the issue of battle strategies with the Dares and Anthony.

Jane sent a runner to the cannoneers to give them the countdown warning. She waited a full minute to ensure her message was delivered before lighting her torch. She held it high enough for the cannoneers to see, then extinguished it. It was their signal to fire in unison.

The cannons belched fire and roared out their shots, shaking the earth beneath their feet. Clouds of sparks scattered the terrain, catching flame in the underbrush. Smoke and dirt swirled through the air and slowly settled. Jane waited tensely, hoping with every ounce of energy in her.

Please, God.

By the light of the moon, she could see the hoped-for jagged and gaping holes take shape as the smoke cleared.

Thank you! Thank you, Lord! Thank you!

The explosions exposed a formerly hidden maze of tunnels. Jane watched with bated breath. After a few heartbeats, bodies started pouring from them. They hardly looked human with their too-thin bodies covered in rags. Many of them had chains clasping their ankles, restricting their gait, but they hobbled in the direction of the braves and Englishmen as fast as they could muster. She counted eight figures, then twelve, then twenty before she lost count. A few who were free of the ankle bonds took off on their own through the woods. Knowing they would not survive long in the biting cold, Jane signaled a pair of scouts to follow and round them up. The rest of the escaped copper slaves huddled in groups for warmth.

The braves sent their axes flying to break apart the chains. The ankle clamps would have to be removed later, but at least the men and women could stretch their legs to a full stride now. Maidens and colonists rushed forward to cover them in blankets and offer spare items of clothing. It was not nearly enough, so Winona directed them to huddle closer to share body heat and the scarce supplies. It didn't take her long to organize and send the first group back to the underground springs to be cleaned, fed, and warmed before proper fires.

"Thirty-seven," Winona reported back to Jane, wide-eyed with concern. Jane knew she was pondering how they were going to feed so many more mouths. It was a problem Jane would worry about another day. She directed Winona to have them eat the fresh meat their warriors hunted first and to open the precious food stores only as a last resort.

A dozen possibilities spun crazily through her mind. Maybe the survivors' loved ones would pay their rescuers in food for their safe return. It was an idea they would have to pursue later. If Providence was on their side, they would find a way. It was as simple as that.

Jane directed the scouts, bowmen, and gunmen to maintain their vigil while the cannoneers re-calibrated and reloaded. The second round of shot scored more ground and revealed more tunnels, from which more bodies poured. Though crusted with filth, many of them appeared fair skinned beneath the light of the full moon.

Awestruck, the English men and women surveyed them in silence, at first, then with murmurings of joy as they began to recognize the decimated faces and bodies of missing friends and loved ones.

Tears flowed and embraces were exchanged, but they did not have the luxury of celebrating yet. Winona handed out the rest of the blankets and rapidly organized their ranks for departure.

She was shocked to see the stooped figure of what used to be the taller and much wider Joyce Archard. She limped Jane's way. "Agnes Wood, bless her soul, told us you were coming."

"Where is she?" Jane demanded anxiously.

Her dim gaze grew misty. "She refused to come with us. Some nonsense about not leaving her husband behind, which makes no sense." She pointed. "Aye, Lord Anthony is right over there."

At her words, Jane tried to bustle her to the innermost

circle of survivors in the hopes of avoiding another confrontation with Anthony. She was not so fortunate.

He questioned every colonist, quickly learned Agnes remained in the mines, and lunged in Jane's direction. "We must send in a rescue party. Now, Jane! There's no time to waste."

She hardened her heart against the frantic tenor of his voice. This was war. She had to think with her head, not her emotions. "You know we cannot, my friend."

Denying his request was one of the most difficult things she'd ever done in her life, but they could not afford to send anyone below ground. Not at the moment. Their best course of action was to maintain their siege on the mines and exercise patience. Hopefully, it would buy Agnes the time she needed to locate Riapoke. She would never forgive Jane if Jane did otherwise.

"You're signing her death warrant!" Anthony spluttered. His hand flew to his pistol. Two of her braves swiftly knocked him to his knees before her and twisted his arms behind his back.

"Not another word," she said coldly. "This was her choice. We will honor it."

Horror twisted his features as he perceived himself powerless to exert his will in the matter. Jane pitied the agony he was surely suffering as he imagined every possible outcome of Agnes's actions. Until now, she had doubted his regard for her friend, but no longer. He was genuinely out of his mind with worry on her behalf. What a pickle!

Alas, Jane had the safety of more than two hundred men, women, and children depending on her decisions tonight. She could not afford to have one man's impetuous nature put them at a greater risk.

Anger chased away her pity. Anthony had spent years serving as an enforcer of the law. How dare he — of all people — openly defy her orders? Men had been executed on the battlefield for lesser sins. She suspected the main reason he was having difficulty accepting her authority was because she was a woman, which was a sorry excuse for insubordination.

She silently debated her next course of action, knowing dozens of pairs of eyes were on them.

As it turned out, Anthony had plenty of fight left in him, despite his lack of mobility. He spat on the ground at her feet. "Her blood will stain your black soul for eternity." His normally handsome features were so distorted with rage she hardly recognized him.

Her braves sprang into movement at his impudence. She raised her hand to indicate they should spare his life but did nothing to stop their punishing blows. They swiftly silenced his foolish raging and dragged him to the rear of their assembly.

It was a much more sober and wary group of Englishmen who loaded the third round of cannon shot. Blade, her favorite teen runner, refused to meet her eyes. Then again, no one else questioned her authority after that.

CHAPTER 38: TRAPPED

Agnes - ten minutes earlier

An explosion shook the ground above Agnes, bringing her short nap to an end. The ceiling disintegrated in a cloud of flying rocks and dirt. She squeezed herself in a ball and curled her arms protectively around her head, flinching when several heavy shards struck her back and buttocks.

The debris settled, half-burying her. Digging and choking, she slowly clawed her way free. The torches were doused, but a full moon glowed through an enormous jagged hole in the ceiling.

The ringing in her ears subsided, and the screams and shouts of her fellow prisoners wafted over her.

"This way!" Joyce Archard shouted, beckoning frenziedly. She stood atop a pile of dirt and rock in the far corner of what used to be the sick bay. She was no more than an arm's span from the exit hole. The occupants of the room were working with her to boost themselves to freedom. Their efforts were hampered by the chains clamped to their ankles, but their stubborn persistence was rewarded. One body at a time, they boosted each other from their subterranean hell.

Agnes craned her neck to peer through the door leading from the room. *Miracle of miracles!* The blast had knocked the bolts loose. Knowing Joyce wouldn't understand what she was about to do, Agnes did not stop to explain her next course of action. Instead, she dashed to the door and tugged with all her might to pry it open. Stones littered the floor, but she managed to drag it open wide enough to fit her narrow frame through it.

"What are you doing?" Joyce cried. Excitement and impatience vibrated her tall frame. "Hurry! We must escape before the guards catch up to us."

Assuming they were still alive and not buried in the ruble.

"Go on, my friend." With one hand on the door leading deeper into the mineshaft, Agnes summoned what she hoped was an assuring smile. "Get them to safety. I'll be back as soon as I fetch my husband." *Along with Amonsoquath and Tikoosoo.* There was no way she was leaving without them, come what may.

"Agnes, no!"

Ignoring Joyce Archards's protest, Agnes squeezed through the doorway. Hopefully, Riapoke would be in the condition to push it open wider on their return trip. Thankfully, she'd not been blindfolded on her trek from the interrogation chamber to the sick bay, so she was confident she could retrace her steps.

Pandemonium met her on the other side of the door. She dodged slaves as they shouted to one another and fled through the nearest openings. Several grabbed her arms and tried to propel her to freedom, but she wrested herself from their well-meaning grasp and pressed deeper into the tunnel.

It might be her only chance to save Riapoke, so she had to try. So far she hadn't sighted a single guard, but she knew her good fortune wouldn't last forever. The mountain people would regroup and quell the rebellion at first opportunity, and they would show no mercy to any slaves they caught trying to escape.

She slowed her pace as she drew within sight of the interrogation chamber door. *Alas, my good fortune is at an end.* It was blocked by two sturdy guards with faces painted in ominous black and red stripes. Both wielded wooden cudgels. Smoke seeped through the crack beneath the door.

So much smoke! It was as if the room was on fire! Why weren't the guards doing anything to douse it? Cold fingers clenched Agnes's heart as she considered the possibilities. Instead of saving the prisoners for future interrogations, had the guards been ordered to exterminate them? Was it some sort of barbaric measure to ensure the poor creatures within had no chance to escape during today's melee?

Her stomach heaved. She pressed as tightly to the wall as possible, praying to avoid detection. She needed to create a distraction to draw away the guards long enough to slip inside the interrogation room. It seemed like an impossible task, considering her weakened physical state and lack of resources. There was no way she could hope to outmaneuver two such brawny men on her own.

Please, God. A little more help.

A second explosion tore through the rocky ceiling. She dropped to the floor again and huddled while the aftershocks reverberated through the maze of tunnels. When the debris settled, the two men and the door they'd been guarding were missing. In its place was a gaping hole leading to the interrogation chamber.

Fear gripped her at the sight. Clouds of smoke puffed from the room, making it impossible to see more than a few feet in front of her.

Waving her hands and coughing, she climbed over

sharp-edged boulders and piles of debris to reach the room. The hot, sooty smoke made her eyes water. It was so thick it hurt to breathe. She shielded her face with a raised elbow and pressed forward. It was like stepping into a steaming cauldron. She ventured a few steps inside the doorway and scanned the room. The walls were still lined with captives. A few were motionless, but most were coughing uncontrollably and yanking at their chains. Riapoke was one of them.

Abandoning all caution, she bent and snatched up a palm-sized rock and ran screaming for her husband.

His eyes widened in shock at the sight of her. His shock quickly faded to horror. With the fury of a thousand demons, she beat her stone against the copper chains binding his wrists and ankles.

"Tah, Ann-nes! Go!" he shouted.

She could no longer breathe well enough to respond. The ebbing oxygen in the room was making her dizzy. She choked and gagged, but she had come too far and risked too much to give up this close to her goal. There was absolutely no way she was leaving without her husband.

The stone in her hand shattered against Riapoke's bonds. She dropped to her knees and scrambled blindly along the ground in search of another. Her fingers came in contact with something narrow and metallic. It was blisteringly hot, but she wasn't in the position to be picky. She lifted it with both hands and swung. This time, the chain holding Riapoke's left wrist broke loose.

He swiftly snatched the length of metal from her and smashed himself free. He continued to swing the poker, releasing Amonsoquath, Tikoosoo, and two other men from their bonds. The two strangers immediately fled the inferno. Not so with Tikoosoo and Amonsoquath. Tikoosoo seemed to be having difficulty putting his weight on his left foot.

Riapoke's shouting urged him on, however, and he hobbled out the door, clutching the wall for support.

Amonsoquath sagged against Riapoke, unable to walk on his own.

The flames were so close they were blistering Agnes's exposed skin. It was time to leave, lest they perish.

She and Riapoke lifted Amonsoquath between them and dragged him through the doorway. Smoke and tiny pieces of burning ash filtered down on them, singing their clothing and skin.

Please, God. We're almost there.

Slaves congregated beneath the opening in the ceiling outside the interrogation chamber, boosting each other up as quickly as they could. Agnes and Riapoke pressed into their midst and were lifted to the cold world above.

Tikoosoo was waiting for them at the surface, helping to pull Amonsoquath to freedom.

At first, the frigid wind served as a soothing balm to their singed and smarting skin. All too soon, however, it enveloped them in its icy fingers, making them shiver and their teeth chatter.

"Agnes!" an anxious female voice called. It sounded like Jane, but she was too woozy from smoke and exhaustion to respond. She tottered on her feet, fighting to keep her eyelids open. Riapoke caught her. He plodded forward in a stooped position with Amonsoquath cradled in one arm and her in the other.

Poca came shrieking in their direction to throw herself at Tikoosoo. From the way she was clinging to him, Agnes deduced the truth at long last. Tikoosoo was the father of Poca's child, not Riapoke.

More hands reached for them, and Riapoke relinquished Amonsoquath to them. He refused to let go of Agnes, however. They were propelled away from the mountain.

Blankets were pressed around their shoulders, and they were nudged into a tight huddle with a dozen or so others. Their extremities were still cold, but the wall of bodies provided a haven from the worst bite of the winds.

"Ann-nes," a familiar baritone crooned in her ear. "My Ann-nes."

Agnes sank into the haven of her husband's embrace. The scent of smoke and the wail of winds faded.

*S*he awoke to a much lighter waft of smoke and the sounds of gently rushing water. The air was toasty warm. Agnes cracked her eyelids open and stretched in appreciation, then moaned from the pain her movements caused.

"Ann-nes?"

Riapoke's concerned face swam into view above her. He smelled clean and his hair glistened with dampness. She reached up to cup his cheek. "My husband."

"*Nouwmais.*" He bent to rest his forehead against hers. Cool droplets of water plopped from the ends of his hair to her nose and cheeks.

She chuckled and slid her arms around his middle. When her fingertips came into contact with nothing but warm flesh, she blushed to realize he was missing his shirt.

He brushed his lips over hers. For a moment, she was lost beneath the spell of his taste and scent. Then she realized he was the only one who'd had the opportunity to bathe.

Self-conscious about her icky appearance, she reached ruefully for her hair. Aye, the dye was still intact, and her short locks were pointing in all directions. She must look and smell like a monster.

Her husband's amber eyes took on a wicked glint, as if

discerning her thoughts and finding them humorous. He dragged a hand through the short, sticky strands to cup the back of her head, angling it to take possession of her mouth once more.

Unable to resist him, she sighed and kissed him back, twining her arms around his sinewy shoulders. He was hers at long last — all hers — but her womanly sensitivities demanded to be clean again before she could fully enjoy being with him.

She broke off the kiss. "Where did you bathe?" Her voice came out as a husky whisper from her smoke-battered lungs and throat.

He reared back and pulled her to a sitting position.

She gazed around them and discovered they were inside a cozy cavern with a low ceiling. A small fire burned to one side, and *glory be!* A stream ran through the center of the room and disappeared in the distant shadows. Agnes was close enough to trail her fingers in the water and discovered it was warm. An underground spring in a secluded hide-away? *Am I dreaming?*

She cast a look of pure delight at Riapoke.

His expression softened in understanding, and he nudged a clay pot of soap leaves in her direction. Then he swiftly removed his leggings and leaped in the spring, feet first, splashing her thoroughly on his way in. When he stood, the water rose to his chest.

She worriedly scanned his injuries. Someone had done a thorough job of stitching several cuts on his chest and arms. Though the skin was pink and puckered around the seams, there were no streaks of infection. Nevertheless, he had to be in an indecent amount of pain.

He held out his arms to her, clearly uninterested in convalescing.

Agnes needed no more urging. She quickly peeled away

her hunting gear, grabbed two fistfuls of the soap leaves, and leaped in after him.

He caught her, and she tumbled breathlessly against him, careful to avoid grazing his stitches. A minty-scented substance was smeared lightly over them. Gratitude flooded her at the care in which his wounds had been tended. She didn't recognize the paste. Perhaps it was a concoction of one of the medicine men?

Riapoke tipped her chin up, loving her with his eyes for several heartbeats. He gently pried open her hands and removed the leaves, crushing them to a lather between his palms. He plunged both hands in her hair, massaging her scalp and loosening the dreadful dye.

Agnes ducked beneath the water to rinse, scrubbing furiously at the mud on her face while she was at it. When she surfaced, Riapoke was lathering more soap. This time, he slicked it down her shoulders and arms.

His scarred and callused fingers cherished every inch of her, soothing away all the aches, bruises, fears, and horrors of the past couple of days.

Her breath clogged in her throat. She'd never dreamed something as mundane as bathing could be transformed into something so enchanting. She ducked under the water to rinse again, and Riapoke dove in after her. He melded his mouth to hers, kissing her under water. They surfaced, dripping and clinging to each other.

"My Ann-nes."

Capturing her gaze with his dark, impassioned one, he drew her closer.

"I am yours, Riapoke, and you are mine."

Before she finished declaring her heart to him, he was already kissing her again. It was heaven to be in his arms. She'd never dreamt a man so big could be so gentle or so tender. In addition, he was uncommonly brave, noble of heart, and very much in love with her. There was no more holding anything back. It was her greatest joy and honor to give herself completely to him.

They climbed from the stream and stretched out beside the fire to dry. They lay facing each other.

Riapoke brushed a damp strand of hair from her cheek, wearing a a wondrously dazed look. "You came...for me."

"Of course I did!" She traced a finger along the outline of his jaw. "You are mine."

He captured her hand and kissed it, regarding her intently. "You could...have died."

A slow sigh escaped her. It was a miracle both of them lived. Providence had been on their side. "I prayed the good Lord would give me the strength to do what needed to be done, because I had no wish to live without you." That was the simple truth.

"*Kenah,* Ann-nes." It touched her to accept his humble thanks, though the fact he lived was the only thanks she truly needed.

Happy tears stung her eyes. "I love you so much, Riapoke."

He reached for her, and she sank into his love and strength once more.

It was a silly thing to worry about, considering all they'd been through, but Agnes was greatly relieved to discover her husband's passion was utterly unaffected by her shorn tresses or the bruises staining her pale limbs. He kissed every inch of her — cherishing, worshipping, and adoring his new wife.

CHAPTER 39: FAMILIAR FACES

he Copper Mountain people held out a full two weeks against their cannon fire. The Roanoke, Croatoans, and Englishmen blockaded every tunnel entrance they could locate and blasted the tops from countless mine shafts, setting free nigh on seventy slaves. Once the maze of tunnels was exposed, they directed the cannons at the mountain, itself, tearing gaping holes in its sides and causing dozens of rockslides. On the eve of the fourteenth day, the Copper Mountain war council sent an emissary to meet with Jane.

They were ready to negotiate.

The Roanoke and Croatoan warriors erected a large tent about a mile from the mountain to host the meeting. The wounded and the children remained in the caves, but most of their people remained armed and on guard in strategic positions around the site of the meeting. The scouts patrolled a much wider perimeter. Their experience with the Copper Mountain tribe had taught them to handle their enemies with the same caution one might give a venomous cobra. They were taking no chances.

They'd long suspected Askook, Chief Wanchese's traitorous cousin, was now serving as chief of the Copper Mountain tribe. Still it made Agnes shiver to see his hateful face again as he strode into view. He kept them waiting a full hour past the appointed time. It was nearly dusk when he appeared with twelve councilmen — twice the number of tribe members they'd agreed upon. They were heavily armed, too, with hatchets, knives, and bows. It was a useless and unnecessary show of force, however. Should a fight break out, they would be no match for the legion of gunmen and bowmen outside the tent or the solders inside bearing muskets.

Askook wore his favored ominous black and white paint. It traversed his face in even lines, making his hateful dark eyes appear to be peering between the slats of a fence. Malice oozed from him like sweat and made the clearing around the tent seem darker than the coming night.

Riapoke's beloved, scarred face and the countenances of the rest of the councilmen might as well have been carved from stone as they observed Askook's cocky approach. They stood in a semi-circle outside the meeting tent. Jane, on the other hand, was visibly incensed by his antics. She stood a few steps in front of the men, arms akimbo and boots firmly planted on the ground.

She was armed with a punishing list of demands for Chief Askook. Agnes imagined his tardiness and disrespect for the terms of their agreement only made her list grow longer.

She was right.

Jane and the other members of their war council walked away from the treaty table with a month's supply of corn and dried meat plus all the remaining Croatoan, Roanoke, and English prisoners. Before allowing Askook and his men to leave, Jane had the newly released prisoners questioned to ensure there were no other captives being held back.

There were very few dry eyes among the English colonists as the rest of their formerly imprisoned friends and loved ones were led in chains to the clearing. It tore at Agnes's heart to see they'd been forced to march an entire mile in the painful restraints. Askook's sneer indicated their final minutes of shame and discomfort had been at his command.

Jane wisely held on to her temper. Like Agnes and the rest of the colonists, she was well versed on the topic of Native justice. It was largely built on the eye-for-an-eye and tooth-for-a-tooth mentality. Or life-for-a-life mentality, in their case. Though the colonists and their allies had suffered much at the hands of the Copper Mountain tribe, they'd delivered a brutal comeback — twice. Since the Copper Mountain people were willing to meet and discuss peace, albeit grudgingly, no good would come from publicly shaming Askook any further in front of his council.

Agnes stood next to Eleanor as the last of the English prisoners were released. "My daughter!" she cried frantically. "I don't see her. Do you?"

"Not yet," Agnes breathed. They stood arm in arm, waiting.

Cold dread settled in the pit of Agnes's stomach. Surely Chief Askook was not foolish enough to harm the babe or refuse to return her, after all that had transpired. Though she knew he was capable of such cruelty, a dastardly move like that could easily be construed as an act of war. How could he hope to walk away from the peace talks with his life intact if he did not return every last English colonist as promised?

A lone figure materialized in the tree line. She drew closer, holding a bundle in her arms. It was a young, grave-eyed maiden, drenched in copper ornaments. Ananias Dare met her at a run and snatched the bundle from her. He slowly turned to meet his wife's gaze and nodded, his features alight with victory.

"It's Virginia. She's safe now." Agnes squeezed Eleanor's hand. "The good Lord saw fit to give us both the greatest desires of our heart."

Eleanor stumbled against Agnes, as if her legs would no longer hold her. Agnes wrapped her arms around her former employer, while her shoulders shook with silent sobs.

"It was all because of your bravery," she choked. "Yours and Rose's and Jane's. To my everlasting shame, I had given up hope, but not the three of you. Nay, not you."

"There now," Agnes soothed, giving her a gentle nudge in the direction of her husband. "It's time to welcome your daughter back."

Ananias held out the precious bundle to his wife. His rugged features were twisted with emotion, and he appeared to be fighting tears.

Agnes peeked down at the infant. She was heavily swaddled against the cold, and she was fast sleep. As far as Agnes could see, she was unharmed. A perfect little cherubim with long, glossy lashes resting against pink cheeks.

"Oh, oh, oh!" Eleanor swiftly reached for her daughter and clutched her against her chest. Her eyes poured with grateful tears.

To witness their reunion was one of the most satisfying moments of Agnes's existence. As if sensing the momentous event taking place, Virginia stirred from her slumber and blinked up at her mother. She neither reached for her nor shied away from her touch when Eleanor touched a featherlight fingertip to her plump cheeks.

She was an utterly silent babe and seemed to absorb the world around her with her enormous sad, blue eyes. She jolted at every noise and scanned her surroundings as if she was looking for something or someone, but she never cried or made any other sounds.

All the changes she'd endured in her short life had to be shocking to her senses. Had she grown attached to her captors? Was she missing them? If she was, only time would heal those wounds.

For now, it was enough that her life had been spared and she was safely returned to her family.

---

*W*ith the addition of so many newly freed slaves, the group returning to Fort Chowan was much larger that the original group that had set out for Copper Mountain. They were also carrying a month's worth of provisions from the mountain people as spoils of war. It was a slow journey due to the fragile condition of several rescued slaves. Some of them had been missing from their families for years. During those endless days beneath the earth, they'd not once seen the sun nor breathed fresh air. Nor had they been fed and hydrated properly. Their bones had grown brittle, and their papery skin was crisscrossed with scars from the lash and cudgel.

They loaded the weakest ones on the canoes by day and carried them to makeshift tent shelters at night. Agnes made her rounds each evening, examining and treating their various conditions. By now, they were running vastly short of medical supplies, but she washed and stitched wounds and created temporary bandages with whatever materials she could muster. She also ensured her patients were eating and drinking their rations.

They were able to deliver more than twenty of their charges to their original tribes on their way to Fort Chowan. As Jane had hoped, several tribes were happy to show their appreciation with gifts of food. One tribe went so far as to throw them a celebratory feast and insist they spend the night to partake of it.

The feast made the trip easier on the convalescents who were able to eat, bathe, and rest before striking out on the trail again. The other benefit to their various stops was the vital groundwork laid for future alliances. As it turned out, much misinformation had been spread about the colonists and their Native allies, which they quickly put to rest.

Over campfires, the tribes they met shared horrifying stories about English monsters eating Native children in the night. They also fearfully recounted varying versions of the Copper Mountain attack on Fort Chowan. They spoke of mighty fire-breathing dragons circling the fort that burned everyone in sight to a crisp. To counter these fables, the Roanoke and Croatoan councilmen led their hosts to the wagons bearing the cannons. Many peace treaties sprang from these first-hand inspections of artillery. Very few tribes wished to be at odds with the owners of the iron dragons. Three combined settlements were enough to present formidable numbers, and their weaponry was undeniably superior. Not to mention, they'd just finished defeating the feared Copper Mountain tribe.

Nearly thirty English colonists in all were released from the copper mines. Another twenty or so Natives chose to remain with them. Accustomed to years of hard labor, they turned out to be a welcome addition to our hunting and food foraging expeditions.

When at last they reached the river delta, Agnes and her comrades were amazed and grateful to find their vacant English cottages and Native longhouses still standing. Even their tools and fire pits were still intact beneath a fresh fall of snow. Footprints walked in and out of doorways, proving they'd had visitors in their absence, but very few items were missing — a clay pot here, a pipe there. The intruders had most likely been looking for food or weaponry, but they'd taken all of those things on the warpath to Copper Mountain.

"We did it, Agnes!" Eleanor beamed down at baby Virginia, who slurped goat's milk noisily from a silver cup. "I will admit I did not think we would prevail against Copper Mountain. The night you gave me that tongue-lashing about how I was acting like someone already dead," she shook her head, still smiling, "well, you were right, my friend. About everything. It's good to be alive again."

"Yes, it is." Agnes stirred the coals of her cooking fire. They were reclining on thick reed mats scattered on the floor of her longhouse. "I know this is not the kind of life we pictured when we boarded our ships and left England." *Gracious, but that felt like years ago — make that lifetimes ago — even though only seven months had elapsed.* Agnes laid down her stirring spoon and spread her arms. "But we have everything we need here. Shelter. Food. Friends. Fertile land to farm come spring. Plenty of game to hunt. A growing list of allies."

"'Tis hard to argue your logic." Eleanor gave a contented sigh. "Some of the English will not agree with you, though. La, but a group of them is already making noises about returning to Roanoke Island come spring."

"What!" It was the first she'd heard of such nonsense. "After all we've endured together? Who would be foolish enough to strike out on their own again?"

"Ha!" she shot back. "I think you can guess who."

Oh, nay! Agnes's heart sank. "Please assure me 'tis not Anthony." But of course it was. He was still smarting from her rejection of his marriage proposal. No doubt his confrontation with Jane had severely damaged his pride, as well.

"Aye. The one and only dashing sheriff in our ranks.," she murmured sadly.

"Have Ananias talk some sense into him," Agnes pleaded. She and Anthony had their differences, but she did not wish him any ill.

"Believe me, he's tried." Eleanor wiped away the milk droplets on her daughter's chin. "You know how stubborn Anthony can be."

"Who is going with him?"

"A small group of noblemen and women. I fear they've long had their fill of the wilderness. They plan to intercept the supply ships my father will send our way come spring and beg a ride back to England."

"What if Master White is not successful in sending supplies? Or what if his ships get separated like they did on the way over?" Agnes bit her lower lip. "It was a miracle the crew of the Roebuck found us at all. Why tempt fate again?"

So many things could go wrong. Plus there would be those who would do everything in their power to ensure Master White did not return to the colony. Those who conspired to steal their land rights would not have been happy about his return to the Queen's courts — the same rogue investors who'd plotted against them and had done everything in their power to ensure the colony failed. As far as the world was concerned, they'd succeeded, too. Soon the land rights in question would expire and be granted by the Queen to another group of investors.

Eleanor sighed. "Christopher is meeting with Anthony as we speak. He intends to remind him that he and his followers will be exposed and poorly armed once separated from us. What with so many hostile tribes surrounding Roanoke…"

Her voice trailed away as Riapoke ducked his tall frame through the entryway.

"My lord." She inclined her head with respect.

He raised his hand to return her greeting and traversed the room to Agnes. She jumped to her feet and gladly launched herself into his arms. Ever since his rescue, she'd thrown propriety to the wind where he was concerned. Let the English and Natives, alike, say or think what they wished about her lack of decorum. So long as she lived, she did not ever again want Riapoke or his people to have any reason to doubt her affections or her loyalty to him.

He splayed one large hand against her lower back, drawing her closer. "My Ann-nes." He'd been hunting all morning. His harshly sculpted cheeks were flushed with cold, and he smelled of the earth and sun.

She cupped his cheeks with both hands to warm them. They gazed at each other for several timeless moments. "How was your hunt, my love?"

His amber gaze softened as he drank her in. "Six deer. Three fox." He still spoke haltingly, but his command of the English language was improving. They two of them spoke a mixture of English and Powhatan and still signed with their hands on occasion. They had no difficulty communicating.

"That is good news indeed!" Agnes stretched on her tiptoes to celebrate his success with what she intended as a playful kiss.

He captured her lips, however, in a fiercely tender kiss that lasted a while.

Eleanor made a few rustling noises as she bundled her babe and slipped as quietly as possible from their longhouse.

EPILOGUE: CITY ON A HILL

*A*fter storming Copper Mountain, all talk of Chief Wanchese and the Roanoke tribe's defection from the alliance with the colonists was abandoned. He was finally convinced they were stronger together than apart. To Agnes's dismay, the only person who was still bent on leaving the fold was Lord Anthony Cage — and his tight circle of noble friends, of course. They backed his every move, right down to his insistence that they *would* still build the City of Raleigh. They called Fort Chowan a temporary "stopover," and refused to accept a "cheap substitute" for the original plan to build the first permanent English settlement in the New World.

Anthony no longer spoke to Agnes, avoided eye contact, and avoiding being alone in her presence. It made her sad. She'd tried so hard to maintain their friendship these past several months and had sorely failed. After all they'd been through together, it hurt that he couldn't bring himself to even acknowledge her these days. She only got to see him from a distance during large gatherings. Every time she caught sight of his tall, handsome figure, she prayed he would change his mind about leaving their eclectic colony come spring.

Their growing colony was a mix of tribes, languages, and cultures with three distinct communities surrounding three distinct hills in the river delta. They clearly had their differences, but their combined assault on Copper Mountain had proven they could turn those differences into strengths. If the Roanokes, Croatoans, and English colonists continued to work together in this manner, they would do more than have each others' backs during the next raid. They would do more than survive the winter.

For the first time since her arrival to the New World, Agnes began to believe she and her comrades had a real chance of making a better life for themselves here in the wilderness. Maybe this new and dangerous world would never resemble the streets of London, but there were a good many things about London she didn't miss — the overcrowded cities, the stench and refuse lining the streets, the widespread poverty. She would choose the wide open spaces, unsullied air, and clear skies of the New World any day.

This was her home now. Agnes gazed around the Roanoke settlement with pride. They were nearly finished rebuilding, and they were making considerable progress in bridging their many differences with the English colonists two hills over. It started with a few small gestures that turned into much bigger ones.

As promised, the braves taught the colonists how to build fishing weirs. In return, the colonists shared the fundamentals of English construction and masonry. Before January came to a frosty close, sturdy plank cottages dotted all three hills of their combined settlement. The Natives also taught the English how to live off the land and only take what was needed. How to preserve and conserve the wild and natural beauty surrounding them.

Between snowstorms, everyone pitched in to extend the palisades and reinforce the earthen fortifications of Fort Chowan. They also hunted and foraged for food daily. It was a winter of hard, unceasing work except for the colonists' weekly devotions on the Sabbath.

At first, the maidens and braves muttered disdainfully over how the English halted their labors on Sundays to honor their God. Soon, however, they began trickling to the services and devotions in pairs and threes. What started out as curious gawking eventually turned into regular attendance and genuine participation in the devotions. Several members of the Roanoke tribe began to refer to the Lord as the God of Agnes or the God-who-tears-down-mountains. Their display of reverence moved her greatly.

Most of the colonists were of the Protestant persuasion, but Rose remained a staunch Catholic. She continued to pray in the privacy of her longhouse with her rosary beads in hand. Agnes noted several of the maidens in her inner circle making the sign of the cross during their larger gathering.

Faith is a beautiful thing!

At sundown one Sabbath in February, Jane plopped herself down next to Agnes at their community campfire. The braves were scurrying around camp, readying themselves for the next hunt on the morrow. They usually departed at first light. Agnes was surprised Jane wasn't in the middle of their planning and scurrying. Most days, she chose to go hunting with the men instead of working with Winona and the other women.

"Just look at them." Jane rubbed her hands together in satisfaction. "Our people. Finally making a half-arsed effort to get along. I thought we'd never live to see this day." She reached beneath her tunic with a grimace and loosened the ties holding up her leggings.

"Why, Jane!" Agnes sat up straighter. "Are you feeling

346

well?" She was acting like someone with the start of a stomach ache.

Jane made another face. "My clothing has grown snug, is all."

Agnes clapped a hand over her mouth to muffle a squeal of sheer delight. "Does that mean—"

"Of course it does!" Jane slung her dark braid over her shoulder. "I'm with child, and Wanchese hasn't stopped crowing about it all morning."

Agnes burst out laughing. "That's what you get for making him such a happy man."

Jane snorted. "You'd think we're the first couple to ever produce a babe the way he's strutting around."

"It's your first," Agnes reminded. *A happy and momentous occasion I hope Riapoke and I will enjoy soon.* "Let the man crow."

A grin split her friend's tanned and freckled features. She spent most of her time outdoors, even in the winter. "At any rate, I figured I'd hunt you down for some peace and quiet until he winds down."

Rose moved unsteadily in their direction. She'd been increasing nigh on six months now. Thin and pale to begin with, she certainly hadn't gained much weight. Chief Manteo hardly let her out of his sight these days, which meant he was sauntering somewhere around the Roanoke settlement, himself — probably enjoying a bit of Chief Wanchese's crowing.

"La, but I'm exhausted," she moaned. She was tucked snugly inside a bear fur coat and hood. As she eased herself down on the other side of Agnes, a few tendrils of red hair escaped her hood and hugged her cheeks like wispy flames.

"Then rest," Agnes urged. She stood to ladle some hot water she'd been heating into a pair of carved mugs for her friends. Dropping in a pinch of herbs and roots to steep, she served them with a courtly flourish.

"You angel!" Rose cupped the mug with gloved hands. The spicy tendrils of steam curled around her nose. "Dare I ask what magic you've concocted for us this time?"

Agnes scanned her pale features, wondering if a little game would take her friend's mind off her exhaustion. "I'll give you three guesses."

She arched a brow and adopted a mocking expression. "Rainbows mixed with pixie dust?"

"Nice try. Next guess."

"Snake eyes and frog warts," Jane suggested.

The three of them dissolved in a round of snickering, making Riapoke glance their way from the opposite side of the community fire. He was supposed to be engaged in an informal weekly debriefing session with the leadership at Fort Chowan. However, he seemed more interested in ogling his wife.

The Dares and Christopher Cooper were in attendance. Christopher, interestingly enough, had officially been anointed as pastor, at long last. Chief Manteo and Chief Wanchese strode over to join the meeting. Both men sat, legs crossed beneath them, half-facing Rose, Jane, and Agnes. Though they spoke and signed with their hands to the Dares and Christopher, Agnes's instincts told her their attention was focused every bit as much on their wives as Riapoke's was.

"Closer." Agnes's laughter slowed on a dreamy sigh as she drank in her husband's dark hair and broad shoulders. Good gracious, but he was a stunning creature! The bear claw scars on one cheek only enhanced his wickedly good looks. "But nay, my loves. No snake parts or frog bits in today's soup." It was a broth of wild chicken and her secret mix of herbs and spices.

Riapoke captured her gaze with his beautiful amber eyes. For a few moments, her conversation with her friends muted.

Rose reached for her hand and squeezed it.

Agnes shot her a startled glance, wondering what was amiss.

"Say what you want, sweet friend, but I think I was right about the rainbows and pixie dust. Just look at you." She waved at them, smiling. "Look at all three of us. We're living our dreams. It was a long, hard fight to get here, but I would do it all over again to be where we are now. Wouldn't you?"

For a moment, mist clouded Agnes's vision. She nodded and squeezed Rose's hand back. It felt alarmingly delicate beneath her sturdy glove, but she'd learned her friend was tougher than she looked. Much tougher. Indeed, each of them had discovered their own brand of strength in this New World through the many hardships they'd suffered. Rose was right, though. They'd also stumbled across a bit of magic in the wilderness.

Agnes nodded fervently. She would endure every drop of misery in her life a thousand times over to lay claim once more to the love and happiness she'd found with Riapoke.

She pressed her lips to two fingertips and blew a kiss in his direction.

To her surprise, he broke his rigid posture to swipe the air with one hand, as if he was catching her kiss. He pressed his hand first to his mouth, then to his heart.

A deliciously lightheaded sensation assailed her. Good gracious! She loved him more than life itself.

"Ahem!" Jane's fist tapped her shoulder in a light punch. "We're trying to have a ladies' moment here. You can bed your man later."

Her words elicited another snort of laughter, which more

or less ruined Agnes's attempt to glare and fake a shoulder injury from Jane's tap.

"I'll admit, nothing turned out the way I imagined when I first signed up for this venture." Agnes shook her head and took a sip of her broth.

"Aye, this settlement is a far cry from the mini-London we were expecting to build." Rose didn't sound too disappointed at the failed colonial venture, however. Agnes understood her sentiments. The three of them had not abandoned lives in London they had any wish to return to.

"The sabotage and betrayal wasn't easy at the time, but we're in a better place for it." Jane blew on her broth and took a larger gulp. "All in all, I've no regrets."

"Nor I," Agnes agreed emphatically.

"Nor I," Rose echoed softly.

Agnes waved her arms to include the three hills and surrounding farmlands that comprised their combined settlement. "We're like the proverbial city on the hill. Our resources might be spread thin right now, but that won't stop us. A little salt goes a long way, and so can we."

"We're more like a city on three hills," Jane pointed out.

Rose raised her mug. "Three hills are better than one. From them, we will spread the light of our faith, our love for our neighbors and each other, and our hope for peace."

Peace. "Hear, hear!" Agnes raised her mug, and Jane did the same. They clinked them together.

"Ann-nes?"

Her husband's voice settled over her like a warm, toasty cloak.

Jane reached for Agnes's mug. "Go. You cooked. I'll clean up."

"Thank you." Agnes swiveled to face her husband. His hand was outstretched. She threaded her fingers through his to pull herself to her feet. The second she was standing upright, he swept her into his arms.

"My Ann-nes," he whispered.

His adoring gaze made her insides tremble all the way to her toes. He could inspire so many emotions in her with a single look. In his presence, she never had to doubt how much she was wanted, needed, cherished, and loved.

Heedless of their companions, she cradled his face in her hands. She'd almost lost him to the terrors of Copper Mountain. Whatever time they had left together — may it be long! — she intended to treasure. She traced the scars on his cheek, the old ones and the new, and stretched on her tiptoes to brush her lips against his smooth jaw line. Despite the biting temperatures, his skin warmed beneath her touch.

His chest rose and fell sharply. "I...love...you." If the age-old words in his halting guttural baritone hadn't been her undoing, the searing kiss that followed would have.

"I love you, too." So much that her heart almost couldn't contain it. Happy tears stung her eyelids. "Take me home, Riapoke." The word *home* slipped out as naturally as breathing.

His land had become her land, his people her people; but it was more than that. Every moment she and Riapoke spent together, she was home. He was her anchor on choppy seas. Her safe haven when she needed a place to rest. Her best friend. Her perfect match.

"Home," he repeated. Arms tightening around her, he sealed the promise with another kiss.

Agnes certainly wasn't the first person to travel across the world in search of a place to belong. She was just one of the fortunate ones who'd found it.

<<<< THE END >>>>

Turn the page for an excerpt from
HIGHER TIDES
Book FOUR in the Lost Colony Series

NOTE FROM JO:

To be honest, I intended for this series to be a trilogy. However, I've had so many wonderful requests from readers who wanted to hear Lord Anthony Cage's story, that I couldn't resist giving you what you asked for.

***Higher Tides** is the direct result of your letters and emails. I hope you're happy with the grand finale to this series!*

Much love,

Jo

SNEAK PREVIEW: HIGHER TIDES

*S*urviving our dangerous trek through the wilderness was never my primary goal. Surviving only means you get to live another day. That is all. I want more than that — much more.

I want to build an English city and walk on cobbled streets. I want to look out the window of my mansion on a hill and see the smoke curling from the chimneys of shops, inns, and taverns below me. I want to see a church with a bell tower and a schoolhouse full of mathematicians, budding astronomers and deep thinkers. I want to see a theater where the actors breathe life into the scripts of up and coming literary geniuses like William Shakespeare and Oliver Thorne. I want music and poetry in my life again, dancing and high society, intellectual conversations and political intrigue.

I want it all.

Most unfortunately, my ambitions seem to have cast me as a villain in the eyes of the woman I love.

—*Lord Anthony Cage*

HIGHER TIDES
Book FOUR in the Lost Colony Series
Available now on Amazon!

ertha Langston dragged her spoon around her
soup bowl, trying to block out the cheerful prattle
of her lunch companions. *Dear heavens!* If she heard another

word about dresses, sashes, proper manners, or courting, she was going to scream.

She'd traveled all the way to Bent, Colorado, to marry and be done with it, for lands sakes — not endlessly discuss and debate the horrid but necessary institution of marriage. It wasn't her fault that Miss Redburn, the matchmaker she'd been corresponding with for months, had passed of pneumonia right before her arrival into town. It wasn't her fault that the woman hadn't left her nephew, Chance, any clue as to whom her ten latest brides were to marry. His new wife, Violet, had proven rather skilled at helping unravel that mystery in recent weeks. Together, the two of them had succeeded in finding matches for seven of the young brides-to-be so far, including Violet's own marriage to the new matchmaker, himself.

However, they'd utterly and miserably failed to find the perfect match for her thus far. Again, not her fault.

"Bert?" Violet Redburn delicately cleared her throat. "Bert Langston?"

"Yes?" The fact she'd convinced the members of their household to use the shortened version of her name was her one small victory. She swallowed her irritation and raised her gaze from the diced vegetables floating around her bowl to meet her benefactor's mildly censorious brown eyes.

"I know the last few weeks have been difficult for you. For all of us."

Though the former school teacher's words were kind, Bert shrugged, sensing another scolding was forthcoming. She wasn't wrong.

"Please be assured that Chance and I," Violet reached across the corner of the table to clasp her new husband's callused hand and treat him to one of her sunny, slightly crooked smiles, "are doing everything possible to find you a match. What we need from you is a little more...enthusiasm with the process."

Bert resisted the urge to roll her eyes. She'd attempted to rub elbows with every dusty cowboy and townsman they'd nudged in her direction, hadn't she? Surely, Violet and Chance weren't blaming her for their own bumbling attempts at matchmaking or their frustrating lack of interest in any of the things that made her happy. Her inventions, for instance. Right now, she was tinkering on a new design for a hot-air balloon, yet the Redburns had not scraped up a single prospective beau for her who possessed the faintest interest in air travel. Quite the contrary. They'd stared at her like she was some monstrous oddity every time her conversation strayed from light, meaningless chitchat.

"I'm trying," she muttered, at a loss for anything else to say. The truth was she had no idea how to attract the attentions of a gentleman. The other truth was she didn't much care. She was far more interested in her inventions than the prospect of settling down and starting a family with some dusty cowpoke she barely knew.

"I know you are, dear," Violet soothed. "What we're asking is for you to try harder."

An awkward silence settled across the dining room. The two other brides, Abigail Bowen and Jasmine Hammond, ceased their cheerful discussion about the dresses they were wearing to the upcoming town picnic. Well, technically, Jasmine was doing all the talking and Abigail was doing all the listening. Both of them beheld Violet with expressions of open-mouthed fascination.

Just what I needed! Bert curled her upper lip. *An audience to witness my nonstop humiliation.* Her mind raced across her dismal prospects. She didn't possess the funds to purchase a train ticket home to Boston. And what a disappointment that would be to her impoverished family if she did! They could barely keep enough food on the table for her four younger siblings. They desperately needed her to find a match and make her way in the world. Which left her in Bent, Colorado at the mercy of Chance and Violet Redburn. For now, at least…

"Well." Chance broke the silence at last. He stood and stooped over his wife to brush a kiss against the top of her head. "It sounds as if you ladies have this matter well enough in hand. If you'll please excuse me." His longish blonde hair tumbled rakishly across his brow, half-hiding his green eyes, but not enough to hide the wink he shot in Bert's direction. "I've business to attend to with a horse dealer."

"Darling!" Violet protested. "I didn't think he was arriving for another few hours."

"True." Chance affectionately tucked a loose strand of hair behind her ear. "But first, there's paperwork to prepare and other, er, matters that need my attention."

Bert hid a grin behind her hand. *Lucky man!* She recognized an escape attempt when she saw one. Unlike her fellow brides, she'd approved of him from the start. They were kindred spirits. He was plain spoken and honest, two traits she understood and respected, and he was no more interested in being a matchmaker than she was in being matched. He meant well, of course. He'd proven again and again that he possessed a kind heart where the young women in his care were concerned. She could work with that.

"Ah, Mr. Redburn?" Her words made him pause in his rapid retreat from the room. "Before you leave, I've been meaning to ask if I could set up shop in a corner of one of the barns out back. Maybe, the older one you don't use for much besides storage?" She tried to keep her voice nonchalant but couldn't quite snuff out the pleading note. She was growing desperate. There just *had* to be some place on his and Violet's sprawling estate where it was quiet enough to hear her own thoughts, where she could dream and sketch her ideas, where she could house her growing supply of tools and materials for her inventing projects.

Out of the corner of her eye, Bert saw Violet give Chance a slight shake of her head, but he was no longer looking at her. He was observing Bert with sly consideration. "I might could find a bit of space for you to tinker with your gadgets."

At his wife's gasp, he held up one tanned finger. "That is," he warned with a twinkle in his eyes, "if you will agree to attend the town picnic and dance this evening with Rafe Adams."

Jasmine tittered and clapped a hand over her mouth to muffle the sound, looking a tad guilty. She allowed her sable hair to fall forward to hide her face.

"Surely, you're jesting." Bert made no attempt to hide her dismay. "Rafe isn't the least interested in courting me, and everyone in town besides you knows it." Nor was she the least interested in courting him. He seemed like a decent bloke, but he bored her senseless.

"I think Rafe is rather afraid of her, sir." Abigail's voice was kind but firm.

Bert glanced up, amazed to hear the young bride-to-be string so many words together at once. Abigail had entered their lives a complete introvert. Braving the perils of match-making together, however, had made her comfortable enough around Bert and the other brides to end her silence. "He's one of those gentle souls, whereas Bert is, well...Bert." Her expression was infused with her own unique brand of sweetness and understanding that took the sting out of her observation.

Violet nodded vehemently. "I think Abigail has a point, dear."

"Nonsense!" Chance clapped his Stetson on his head. "Rafe's a carpenter, and Bert's an inventor. I say they're plenty compatible. All they need is a little more time in the pen together."

Bert snorted out a laugh at his constant inability to view matching brides and grooms any differently than he viewed cattle and horse breeding. "It's a deal, sir. If you give me a bit of space to work out back, I promise to dance with Rafe this evening until he's dizzy." An easy promise to keep, since she was a horrible dancer. He'd probably take home a few bruised toes, as well. She stood and sauntered towards Chance, holding out her hand.

"I don't know about this," Violet sighed.

"It's a deal." Chance Redburn clasped her hand in his large paw and winked again. "So long as you keep your end of the bargain, I reckon I can have a stall cleaned out for you by nightfall."

"You can count on it, sir!" She shook his hand heartily, wanting to break into a joyful jig right there in the corner of the dining room.

"I know I can, lass." He reached out to tug the thick braid of dark hair that had come uncoiled from atop her head and now hung over her shoulder. "You might want to let one of the other girls help you polish yourself up a bit before the dance."

"I will, sir. I'm much obliged, sir." She took no offense at his jibe at her lack of hairdressing abilities. Jasmine would enjoy fussing over her. All she'd have to do is bite her tongue and endure it.

Violet rose and spun after her husband in a swirl of blue and white checkered skirts. "Wait for me, love. I'll walk with you." There was no mistaking the agitation in her voice.

Bert slowly turned back to the table with the intention of retrieving her plate and carrying it to the kitchen to be washed. She stopped short at the sight of Jasmine and Abigail standing shoulder-to-shoulder, facing her with determined expressions.

Jasmine reached out to jiggle the same braid Chance had tugged on. "I believe you agreed to submit yourself to our stylish ministrations." She was the only other bridal candidate as short as Bert, which Bert appreciated. She was tired of craning her neck up at the others.

"Right now?" She shot a distressed look over her shoulder, but the Redburns had already disappeared.

"Yes, now," Jasmine retorted. "It's only a few hours before the dance, and you're a full day's work." She slowly circled Bert, tweaking at her skirts and bending down to dust something off her hem. "It's a good thing there are two of us to take you on. Abigail has just agreed to help me."

Without taking their eyes off Bert, the two women shook hands like a pair of soldiers sealing a pact.

I'm outnumbered. This is so unfair! "What about Beans?" she blurted in desperation. Their grizzled old cook's real name was Clarence McGruder, but he preferred to be called Beans. "We have to stay and clean up first. You know how cantankerous he can be about leaving the dining room a mess."

For an answer, Jasmine clapped her hands smartly three times. To Bert's surprise, Mrs. Long, one of the widows from the Ladies Auxiliary, sailed into the room. She began to gather their empty plates and silverware along with their discarded linen napkins.

She treated Bert to a hard-nosed look over her spectacles as she worked. "Well, what are you waiting for, girls? Run along now." Not a single gray hair was out of place in her severe up-do, and her white blouse and navy skirts were starched to perfection.

So very outnumbered! How did this happen? Shaking her head, Bert grudgingly followed Jasmine and Abigail into the hall and up the stairs to their rooms. "Beans will have a fit," she threatened. "You know he hates it when anyone invades his kitchen, especially Widow Long." The two of them seemed to butt heads on a regular basis about how the kitchen should be run.

Jasmine sniffed and waved an unconcerned hand. "Their ongoing tiff is no concern of ours. Though I'll admit I quite enjoy how many rounds of kitchen duty it's gotten us out of."

"You're shameless!" Bert hissed, slowing her pace as Jasmine flung open Bert's bedroom door.

"You're a fine one to talk," Abigail admonished gently. She gave Bert's shoulders a nudge from behind to speed up her entry into her room. "Yes, indeed, we found that pair of trousers you hid under your mattress." She shut the door smartly behind her and stood there with her arms folded like a general around one of the books she was forever clutching. "What do you have to say for yourself?"

Bert's chin came up. "Yes, they are mine. I happen to think riding sidesaddle is foolish; my way is much safer. I only hid them because I knew the two of you would act like complete nincompoops if you found out about them." She glared defiantly at her fellow brides.

Jasmine looked up from rummaging in their shared dresser. "However did you acquire them, Bertie?" She sounded more amused than scandalized.

"Beans," Bert admitted. "I patched up a few pairs for him, and he agreed to let me keep one as payment."

Abigail smiled and lowered her arms. "It's no wonder you're always so concerned about staying on his good side. It appears you have a little bartering business going on behind our backs, don't you?" She caught the brush Jasmine sailed her direction with one hand, tossed her book on the bed, and started to unbraid Bert's hair.

It was true. Bert guiltily kept her silence. In exchange for her skill in repairing his various tools and appliances, Beans had proven himself a master in helping her acquire things. He'd supplied her with a great number of cast-off items, like the hammer with the broken handle she'd replaced.

To her intense misery, Jasmine and Abigail spent the rest of the afternoon redressing and primping her for their outing.

"There you are!" Jasmine finally announced in satisfaction. "A right and proper Miss Bertha Langston, for once." She spun Bert around on their dresser stool to face the vanity mirror.

She gave a yelp of alarm at the stylish stranger staring back at her. She'd allowed her thoughts to wander while the young women had worked, so she'd entirely missed the fact they'd left her hair down.

It spilled in dark auburn waves down her shoulders, providing a shocking contrast to the all-white dress and jacket they'd bade her step into. A matching, gauzy white hat perched atop her head, lending her an air of sass.

"What you do you think?" Jasmine gave a small bounce in her dress shoes. Somehow she and Abigail had managed to dress and prepare for the party themselves while fussing over Bert. She wore a pale pink gown with petticoats that puffed down from her slender waist like a pink cloud.

"I...I don't know what to say." Bert was amazed at the transformation. Gone was her faded poplin dress and mussed braids. Jasmine was right. She looked like a real lady now.

"We'll settle for a thank you when that beau of yours stutters out an offer for your hand this evening," Abigail assured. Her dress was a riot of sky blue ruffles and lace. She smoothed a hand over Bert's hair, tucking in a stray lock. "Rafe is going to be stunned when he sees you."

*T*hen again, Rafe always looked a bit dazed and disconcerted.

When he arrived at the front door to escort her to the town square, he stood riveted. "M-Miss B-Bert. Y-you l-l-look s-so p-p-pretty."

Bert tried to console herself with the fact that at least he didn't appear afraid of her this evening like he normally did.

"Thank you, Rafe." She forced a smile. "You don't look so bad yourself." Not that his looks had ever been a problem. She simply wasn't interested in him as a potential husband.

He grinned and crooked an arm at her. "M-may I?"

She took his arm without comment and allowed him to escort her down Main Street. She recognized the two gentlemen escorting Jasmine and Abigail but couldn't remember their names. A widow from the Ladies Auxiliary wordlessly joined them at the bottom of the church stairs as they strolled past. Her dark hair was piled so high that Bert wondered if it was giving her a headache. She also wondered how the woman managed to keep it from tumbling down. *Extra pins? Hidden globs of glue?* Annabelle Bradshaw was a fashionably dressed woman in her late thirties, if a body didn't object to the fact her entire wardrobe seemed to consist of solid black. She was the youngest of the widows, still in mourning, and the most recent addition to their ranks.

"A good afternoon to you, Mrs. Bradshaw." Jasmine trilled and fluttered her hand in a wave.

"If you say so, my dear," the woman returned in a soft, weary voice that indicated she was having trouble finding anything good about it. "Are you on your way to the picnic?"

"We are, ma'am. And you?" Abigail inquired politely.

Bert gritted her teeth at the question. *Of course, we're heading to the picnic! But you already knew that, didn't you?*

Chance Redburn was forever enlisting the aid of the widows in town to help him chaperone his young brides-to-be. She doubted their encounter was an accident.

Mrs. Bradshaw raised and lowered delicate shoulders. "I am, unless there is anything else more exciting going on in town today. I do so love the opera," she sighed.

Bert snorted. An opera, indeed! There were no operas in Bent, Colorado, but she opted to let someone else break the news to the uppity little woman from Atlanta.

A small crowd was gathered at the town square when they arrived. Temporary tables had been raised to hold the mountains of sandwiches prepared by the Ladies Auxiliary. Plus, there were trays of diced fruits, vegetables, and cheeses arranged amidst tall pitchers of lemonade and tea dripping with condensation.

The dance was already in full swing with a good dozen or more couples twirling their way around the wide gazebo that marked town square. A quartet of violin players provided an upbeat backdrop of music. No doubt the lovely instruments were from Joseph Penella's shop, since he was one of the musicians up there spinning the lively tune. He was Myrakle's husband, the second bride in their group to find her perfect match.

"C-c-come on B-Bert." Rafe swung her gallantly into the dance. "L-let's dance."

Frowning in concentration, Bert kept her word to Chance Redburn and did her best to follow her partner's lead. *Try harder. I will try harder.*

To his credit, Rafe did his best to avoid her awkward attempts to bob and sway to the music. He hopped nimbly out of her way at least three times, narrowly missing having his toes crushed by her black, lace-up boots. His luck ran out near the end of the dance when he tried to twirl her.

"Oh-h-h-h-h," Bert moaned as she lost her balance. She

flapped her arms wildly in the attempt to reach him and regain her footing. Despite her efforts, she pitched head-first toward the ground.

"B-Bert! Rafe cried.

They ended up sprawled on the ground beside each other. He pressed a palm to his temple while she stared in horror at the grass stains on her ivory skirts.

"Pray forgive me!" they cried in unison.

For a moment, Bert was too shocked and embarrassed to move. A quick glance around her proved Widow Bradshaw had not missed her unladylike display. *Drat!* She would report the incident to Chance and Violet Redburn, and they might finally wash their hands of her. At best, Chance would withhold carving out a space for her in his barns to work on her inventions. At worst, they would turn her out of their home on her ears.

She wondered idly if their tumble to the ground could have been avoided if she'd been wearing her trousers. She stared at Rafe in remorse. He was a true gentleman to try to take the blame for their failed attempts at dancing, but they both knew it was her fault.

He scrambled to his feet, still clutching his head. "How about I g-go fetch us s-s-some lemonade?"

"I would be so grateful." Bert shot him a rueful look without really seeing him. Her hearing was fast tuning in to a conversation taking place a few strides away from them.

She narrowed her gaze at the group of fashionably dressed gentlemen. One very tanned, very tall cowboy was gesturing with both his hands. "I'm telling you, the horseless carriage is only the beginning, my friends. Air travel will be the next breakthrough in public transportation. Mark my words!"

Air travel! Bert couldn't agree with the man more. She yanked her soiled skirts aside to avoid tripping on them as she curled her body forward to her feet. Now *that* was a conversation worth having! Trying to keep her steps measured and ladylike, she resisted the urge to gallop in his direction.

The tall blonde cowboy spared her an admiring glance as she approached. He was dressed in a black suit, starched white dress shirt, and a silver bolo.

"I couldn't help overhearing your commentary on air travel," she blurted by way of an introduction. "And I agree wholeheartedly."

The man tipped his Stetson back to assess her with clear, slate-colored eyes. "Well, I can't rightly argue with that, seeing as I just stated the same thing, Miss ah…"

"Bertha Langston," she supplied tartly. "But most folks just call me Bert." She stuck out a hand, anxious to complete their introductions and get on with the topic of air travel.

The other men in his party stared at her with growing interest.

"Kane Jameson." The man treated her to a gallant bow. "At your service, Madame Bert." He angled his chin at the man standing nearest him. There was a strong resemblance between them, though Kane was built a bit more on the rangy side. "And this tiresome chap is my older brother, Griffin."

"Griff," the man corrected, thrusting a hand in her direction. He was an inch or two shorter than his younger brother and a bit thicker in the chest. "We run the Black Barrel Inn down the street."

"By night, at least," Kane added. "We run cattle most days at the ranch while our sister, Paisley, holds down the front desk."

Bert frowned at the brothers and their three companions who'd yet to make their introductions, immensely disappointed to hear no connection whatsoever between their current vocations and their marvelous opinions about air travel. "Have any of you flown before? A glider, perhaps, or a hot-air balloon? Anything at all?"

At her terse line of questioning, two of the men mumbled something about needing to be excused and made a beeline for the food tables.

"I have." The third man leaned closer to shake her hand. "Matthew Crutchfield. I believe you've already met my sister, Annabelle Bradshaw?"

No small amount of guilt stabbed her at the mention of her chaperone's name. *Good gracious!* She hadn't given the woman a single thought since her arrival to the picnic. Glancing covertly across the town square at the many people reclining and eating on bright-colored blankets, she failed to catch a glimpse of the oh-so-proper Mrs. Bradshaw. It was probably for the best, considering the current state of her gown.

Bert glanced down at her wrinkled and grass-stained skirts and grimaced. When she raised her head, Kane was studying her with amusement.

"What about you, Miss Langston? Have you ever flown?"

"Bert," she corrected abruptly. All thoughts of the missing Mrs. Bradshaw flew from her head. *Not unless you count my one disastrous attempt at tower jumping from the roof of our apartment in Boston.* Her chin came up. "I'm in the process of designing my own hot-air balloon." *There!* Let the cocky cowboy chew on that.

"Are you, now?" He exchanged a curiously gleeful glance with his brother.

She tossed her head. "Yes. The Redburns have allowed me to set up shop in one of their barns."

"The Redburns?" Griff exclaimed, blinking thoughtfully. "I reckon that would make you one of their—"

"Friends," she snapped.

I hope you enjoyed this excerpt from
THE BRIDE HERDER:
Herd the Heavens
This story is available in ebook, paperback, and Kindle Unlimited on Amazon!

Much love,
Jo

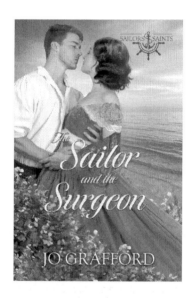

1887, Pacific coast of Mexico

A hoarse, male cough made Margery Fields sit straight up on her cot. As her father's apprentice, she'd spent the last ten of her nineteen years helping him tend the sick and the injured aboard the Black Shark. Naturally, she'd learned to sleep lightly and rise to her duties at a moment's notice. It was a fortunate trait to possess while serving their heartless Capitan, the most notorious pirate in the Pacific.

The cough repeated itself. This time it crackled deep in the man's chest.

"Father!" Margery's bare feet hit the rough plank flooring of the cramped living quarters she shared with her father — Doc Fields, the ship's surgeon. She leaned across the narrow expanse separating her cot from his and bent over him to touch the back of her hand to his forehead. It felt like a thousand flames were heating it. *Mercy!* He was burning with fever.

She swiftly lit a candle and rummaged through his beloved medicine chest. It was a mahogany cabinet about two feet tall with a pair of doors in front. He'd spent years collecting the treasures it held, and she was blessed to have trained first-hand on the use of each item. There were forceps, probes, cauterizing irons, and stitching needles. There were also grippers for extracting teeth, sponges and soft rags for cleaning and bandaging wounds, and a mortar and pestle for grinding and mixing medicines and potions. Unfortunately, none of these items would help reduce a fever.

Her fingers slid over the collection of bottles containing her father's prized collection of herbs and potions. She had to squint to read them in the shadows. "Please, God," she breathed, holding the candle closer. Her gaze ran over the labels: Rosemary, clover, mint, sage, juniper, hollyhock, and angelica. *No, no, no, no, no, no, and no. Ah. There it is.* She snatched up the bottle of castor oil and reached for a medicine cup.

"Stuff a cold, starve a fever," she chanted softly in what she hoped was a cheerful voice. She poured a generous dose of oil into the cup. "Open wide, my dear." She cradled her father's burning head in one strong hand and lifted until his lips brushed the cup.

He shook his prematurely gray head and sucked in a breath, which most unfortunately elicited another heavy round of coughing. He sat up, wheezing and crackling for several heart-wrenching moments into his hands. When he paused, he swiped angrily in the air at her. "Begone!" he rasped. "Else you'll catch whatever ails me."

"But—"

"I said go, Marg!" he grated harshly and fell into another fit of coughing. "Ye've not made it this far by being a fool." He hunched his wiry, too-thin shoulders forward for yet another alarming bout of choking and wheezing. "Take the medicine chest and stay in the sick bay. I'll send Fix-It to fetch you when it's safe to return."

With a snarl of irritation at his stubbornness, Margery shoved the cup of castor oil in his scarred hands. "Drink it." She'd have Fix-It John bring him more later if he stopped by the sick bay, which he often did. Usually it was to deliver their rations, since it was difficult for them to break away from the sick bay on busier days.

Her heartbeat quickened at the thought of seeing the brawny carpenter again. He'd started off as an apprentice when he was pressed into service as a lad and had proved himself so handy that he'd quickly earned the nickname of Fix-It John, although many sailors dropped the John and merely called him Fix-It. At age twenty, he now performed nearly all the ship's repairs though the corrupt and cranky head carpenter, Peg-leg Patch, tended to take credit for everything he did. Margery knew better, though. John was the kindest, most decent, and hardest working person she knew…and the handsomest. He was also the only other person besides her father on the ship's crew whom she could trust. She wished with all her heart she could be as honest with him as he was with her...about everything — especially about the fact she was actually a woman.

"Bah!" With another fierce gesture for her to depart, Doc Fields turned up the cup and downed its contents. "I can look after myself. Been looking after the both of us for as many years as ye've been alive."

A normal woman would have blinked back the sting of tears at his reference to everything they'd suffered together, but not Margery. She'd long since learned to control her emotions and facial expressions. Her safety had depended on it ever since her father had been pressed into service with a nine-year-old "son" in tow.

She never laughed or smiled — not that she had any cause for mirth while living on a pirate ship — and was generally accepted as Doc Fields' silent assistant. On the few occasions when she was required to speak, she employed a gruff, affected voice to mask her feminine alto.

Accustomed to gritting her teeth and enduring her frustrations in silence, she merely ducked her head to roll a change of clothing and a few necessities in a blanket. She didn't require much to survive, because she kept her hair short and stuffed inside a cap. The rest of her female curves she kept hidden beneath a pair of her father's breeches and a white sailor's tunic made of cotton sacks. Fortunately, she was a petite creature to begin with.

With one last worried glance at her father, she snatched up his medicine chest and exited the room.

Two things were immediately apparent to her in the dim and dank passageway in the bow of the ship. The few sailors scurrying about were in desperate need of baths, and the floor was pitching and rolling beneath her feet. They must be entering choppy waters. Several times, she had to lean a shoulder against the wall to catch her balance because her hands were too full to hold on.

She had to stow her rolled blanket and personal supplies in a corner before climbing the ladder through the hatch leading to the next level. She hurried with the medicine chest to the sick bay, lashed it to the wall with a cord, then dashed back downstairs to retrieve her bedroll. To her relief, it remained where she left it. To her chagrin, one of the coal boys was standing over it with a sly expression on his features. It was Sharpie, her least favorite coal boy due to his foul mouth and equally foul temperament. He darted a look around the empty hall and reached for her bedroll.

God, give me strength. She jogged in his direction, reached around him, and neatly scooped it up before his filthy hands could claim it.

He whirled on her with a growling sound, fists balled.

"It's for the sick bay," she explained gruffly, clutching the bundle to her chest.

"Huh!" he snorted. "Why should I believe you?"

"I'm to deliver it to Doc Fields." She lied, backing towards the ladder stairs and bracing herself for the blows that were sure to follow.

To the rough and tumble crew on the Black Shark, she was Doc Fields' wraithlike son, Marg, the lad with the strange name who spent most of his days below deck tending the sick and injured. She applied poultices and wrapped their wounds with quiet efficiency, always keeping their visits to the sick bay as brief as possible. The older sailors otherwise ignored her during their infrequent encounters above deck. The younger ones were a different story entirely. They seemed to take great satisfaction in calling her names and mocking her tiny size. Sharpie was their ringleader.

"Maybe I want to be the one to deliver it to Doc Fields."

He shoved her towards the ladder so hard, her head snapped back and collided with one of the iron rungs.

For a moment, it hurt so badly she couldn't breathe. She also couldn't see for the stars dancing across her vision. On sheer instinct, she twisted her lithe body around and blindly started to climb the stairs. Halfway up the ladder, Sharpie's hand closed around her ankle, stopping her progress.

"You didn't answer me, boy." He yanked cruelly on her foot, nearly pulling her loose.

Margery's vision slowly cleared, but it clouded again with terror. She couldn't afford a bout of fisticuffs. It wasn't simply the fear of sustaining injuries, although she certainly dreaded that; it was mostly the fear of having her gender discovered.

A shadowy faced loomed over the hatch opening above her head. "What's taking so long, Marg?" a man barked. "You shoulda been in the sick bay already with that load."

The sound of Fix-It John's voice made Margery's insides go weak with relief. Not only was he the kindest person on her very short list of acquaintances, apparently, he was to serve as her angle of mercy this morning as well.

When Sharpie didn't immediately release her foot, John dipped his head closer to the hatch opening. "Is that you, Sharp? You'd best scuttle along before the bo'sun discovers you don't have enough work to keep ya busy." The threat in his tone was real.

With a muttered curse, the bully released her foot and shuffled on down the dim corridor.

Margery scrambled as fast as she could up the ladder, ignoring the hand John held out to her. "I thank you," she mumbled, pushing past him. It wouldn't do her any good for someone to witness him coddling her.

Once upon a time, he'd been as rail-thin and wraithlike as she was due to years of not having enough to eat. She recalled all the times he'd been pummeled and his food rations confiscated by the inner circles of rogues and bullies who terrorized their ship.

But no longer. John had grown into a tanned and broad-shouldered sailor with arms corded with muscle. No one fought him for his food rations anymore.

All the time he'd been filling out and growing bigger, she'd remained the same size she was at age fifteen. Unlike the coal boys, though, John didn't seem to hold her tiny size against her. Quite the contrary. If anything, he'd become more watchful and protective of her, a state of affairs she wasn't certain was a good thing or a bad thing.

To her consternation, he followed her inside the sick bay and quietly shut the door behind them. The first shoots of morning sun were creeping through the portholes lining the east wall, so it wasn't necessary to light a lantern.

The small room was exactly as she'd left it the night before. Approximately twelve feet long and eight feet wide, it boasted a work counter against the far wall with a row of storage cabinets tucked beneath it. She'd lashed the medicine chest to the left side of the counter. On either side of her, a cot for treating patients was tucked against the wall, leaving a narrow walkway between them.

She tossed her bedroll on the cot to her right and slowly pivoted to face him. "What brings you to the sick bay this morning?" she inquired politely.

He was regarding her with such an intense look of concern in his coffee bean eyes that it made her catch her breath. "Why are you alone? Where is Doc Fields?"

She shrugged and glanced away, avoiding the temptation to stare at his wind-tousled dark hair and the way his faded shirtsleeves were rolled up his tanned forearms. "He's feeling poorly." Her eyes settled on the only adornment on the wall, a hand-carved crucifix that had been in her father's possession as long as she could remember. It was less than a foot tall and half as wide.

"Poorly enough to remain in bed?" he asked sharply.

She met his gaze once more, steeling herself against the alarm and sympathy she read there. "He has a cough and a fever that I treated with castor oil. Perhaps you might deliver his next dose come noon?" It wasn't safe for her to roam the halls alone.

"Of course." He ran a calloused hand over his stubbled chin and cast a speaking look at her rolled blanket. "I reckon he insisted you stay here until the fever breaks?"

"Yes. You'll keep this between us?" she inquired anxiously. She had no desire to describe her father's dubious health to the Capitan. The crew had a high mortality rate, as it was; she did not wish to find out what he might do to an ailing surgeon and his fragile "son."

"It saddens me that you feel the need to ask," he replied bluntly. He gestured at her head. "How is your noggin?" he added in a gentler tone. "I saw what Sharpie did to you, lad."

At his reference to her as a lad, her heart sank. Was it all she would ever be to him? The short, pale boy who worked in the sick bay?

She reached up to gingerly finger the knot rising on the back of her head. It hurt like the dickens, though she kept her expression bland. "I am well, thank you."

In that same moment, an enormous wave crashed against the portholes, viciously rocking the boat.

Margery lost her balance, collapsed on the nearest cot, and bumped her head smartly against the wall.

Again.

"Ouch!" she yelped, feeling the blood leave her face. John's anxious features wavered in and out of focus for several seconds.

"Marg!" He took a seat beside her. "Hold still." He gently

probed her scalp and located the knot. "You're hurt," he accused, frowning with concern. "You might have a concussion."

"I can treat it," she informed him stiffly. "I've all the training I need."

Another swell of water rocked the ship, this time more fiercely than before.

They pitched towards the wall, but he used his large body to absorb the brunt of the impact. Unfortunately, the power of the swell pressed her flush against his chest.

Though she always wore loose clothing, she generally kept her distance from people so they had no opportunity to discern her true shape.

She could see the moment the truth dawned on John.

He blinked once, twice, and slowly untwined his arms from her waist. "Marg?" he asked quietly. A look of shock spread across his tanned features. He shot to his feet. "Well, blow me down! How could I have been so blind?"

"You know," she stated dully, wondering what he would do with the knowledge. Life as she knew it was over, not that she had much of a life to begin with.

"I do now." He clapped a hand to his forehead. "I'm such a fool. The truth has been bopping me in the nose for years. Your size, your voice... I just never considered the possibility that—"

"What will you do now that you know?" she inquired sharply.

His eyed darkened with determination, and his jaw clenched. "Fear not, lass. I will protect you with my life."

Her eyes widened at the fierceness of his tone. "I can take care of myself."

Her lie settled between them like a jarring bell. They both knew it wasn't true, but he was too much of a gentleman to contradict her.

"I'll keep an eye on the doc, too, while he's ill," he assured in a tight voice. "It's the least I can do for all the times he's sewn and bandaged me back together."

Margery swallowed hard at the memory of the many floggings he'd endured as a lad and none of them deserved. He'd been blamed again and again for the mistakes of others and taken their punishments without complaint. Beneath his shirt, his back was a crisscross of scars.

"I don't know how to thank you," she whispered, fearing it was only a matter of time now before her secret spread across the ship.

"What is your name?" he whispered back. "Your real name, lass?"

"Margery." She removed her cap and allowed her longish locks to tumble against her neck. On a whim, she'd grown her hair out a few inches over the past several weeks, craving some reminder of her real identity. It was still short, but not as closely shorn as usual.

He shook his head, the dazed look returning to his eyes. "I don't know how I could have missed it." He gave a snort of self-disgust. "You're like a tiny woodland fairy."

Her heart skipped a few beats at the knowledge that she reminded the handsomest man on the ship of a delicate, mystical creature. She could tell the magnitude of his discovery was still sinking in. "You mustn't treat me any differently," she warned. "Not even when we're alone." Sailors were forever bursting through the door of the sick bay. Pirates weren't inclined to knock or demonstrate any other civilized manners.

"Impossible!" he scoffed, with such an admiring look on his face that she felt a surge of heat rise to her cheeks. "But I promise to be cautious."

She resisted the urge to cover her burning face with her hands. *Mercy!* Was this what it felt like to blush? In that moment, she felt entirely female and utterly vulnerable, which would never do. If he refused to employ good sense where she was concerned, she'd have to employ enough good sense for both of them.

"You'll *not* treat me differently," she returned tartly. "Else I'll dose you with a powder that will give you such a heavy rash, you'll not be able to sit for a week."

To her astonishment, he burst out laughing. It was such a foreign sound, all she could do was gape. She couldn't remember the last time she'd heard anyone laugh. It gave her the sudden urge to chuckle herself.

"John!" she admonished in a loud hiss with a worried glance at the closed door.

"Margery!" he retorted softly, removing his cap and sweeping her a gallant bow. "Fuss at me all you wish, lass. Ye've given me a new reason to live." His dark eyes shone with determination. "And hope."

Hope? She shook her head in puzzlement, not knowing what else to say.

"Yesterday was an especially wearisome day," he admitted, though he didn't elaborate. "So I asked the good Lord for a sign. Anything to prove He hasn't forgotten about us out here on the open seas." His smile broadened. "I never dreamt He'd deliver such a miraculous sign."

The handsome carpenter thought her lovely *and* miraculous? Margery lost all power of speech as he clapped his cap back on his head and reached for the door handle.

"A good morning to you, Miss Margery Fields." His faint British accent turned her given name into something warm and wonderful in the midst of so much loneliness and despair. "I'll return shortly with your rations."

I hope you enjoyed this excerpt from
SAILOR AND SAINTS SERIES:

The Sailor and the Surgeon

This story is available in ebook, paperback, and Kindle Unlimited on Amazon!

Much love,
Jo

ALSO BY JO GRAFFORD

Mail Order Brides Rescue Series

written exclusively by Jo Grafford

Hot-Tempered Hannah

Cold-Feet Callie

Fiery Felicity

Misunderstood Meg

Dare-Devil Daisy

Outrageous Olivia

Jinglebell Jane

Absentminded Amelia

Bookish Belinda — *coming March!*

Once Upon a Church House Series

written exclusively by Jo Grafford

Abigail

Rachel — *coming March!*

The Lawkeepers

A Multi-Author Series

Lawfully Ours

Lawfully Loyal

Lawfully Witnessed

Lawfully Brave

Lawfully Courageous

_____

Disaster City Search and Rescue
A Multi-Author Series
The Rebound Rescue
The Plus One Rescue — *coming April!*
The Blind Date Rescue — *coming July!*
The Fake Bride Rescue — *coming September!*

_____

Playing For Keeps
A Multi-Author Series
Going All In — *coming June!*

_____

Billionaire's Birthday Club
A Multi-Author Series
The Birthday Date — *coming June!*

_____

The Pinkerton Matchmaker
A Multi-Author Series
An Agent for Bernadette
An Agent for Lorelai — *coming April!*
An Agent for Jolene — *coming May!*
An Agent for Madeleine — *coming July!*

Lost Colony Series

written exclusively by Jo Grafford

Breaking Ties

Trail of Crosses

Into the Mainland

Higher Tides (Series Finale)

Black Tie Billionaires

written exclusively by Jo Grafford

Her Billionaire Boss

Her Billionaire Bodyguard

Her Billionaire Secret Admirer — *coming soon!*

Ornamental Match Maker Series

A Mini-Series by Jo Grafford

within a Multi-Author Series

Angel Cookie Christmas

Star Studded Christmas

Stolen Heart Valentine

Miracle for Christmas in July

Home For Christmas

Whispers In Wyoming

A Multi-Author Series

His Wish, Her Command

His Heart, Her Love

Other Christmas Books

Angel Creek Christmas Brides: Elizabeth

Angel Creek Christmas Brides: Grace — *coming November!*

Holliday Islands Resort: The Dashing Groom

Other Multi-Author Series Titles

Silverpines Series —Wanted: Bounty Hunter

Silverpines Companion Tale —The Bounty Hunter's Sister

The Bride Herder — Herd the Heavens

The Belles of Wyoming — Wild Rose Summer

Brides of Pelican Rapids — Rebecca's Dream

Sailors and Saints — The Sailor and the Surgeon

Widows, Brides & Secret Babies — Mail Order Mallory

READ MORE JO

I write — *a lot!* — and I'm currently writing these series:

Disaster City Search & Rescue Series — A city where officers, firefighters, military, and medics train and work alongside each other with the dogs they love, to do the most dangerous job of all — help lost and injured victims find their way home

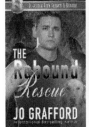 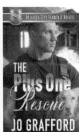  

Mail Order Brides Rescue Series — a mad dash of gallant rescuers, racing against time to snatch all the mail order brides from the jaws of mayhem on their journey West

Billionaire's Birthday Club — What can you buy a man who already has everything?

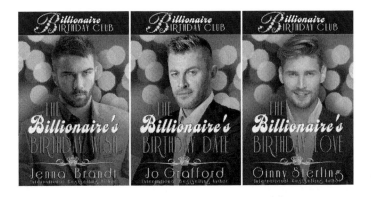

Once Upon A Church House Series — Be careful what you ask for, because the good Lord's in the business of answering prayers!

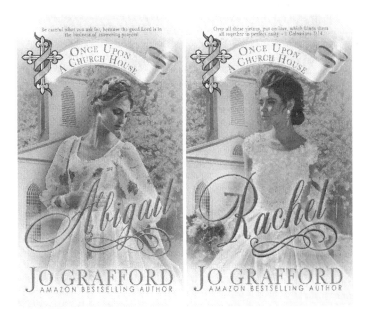

I will continue to release 2-3 new titles every month! You can find out more about each series by visiting and following me at:

1.) Amazon Author Page:
amazon.com/author/jografford

2.) Bookbub:
https://www.bookbub.com/authors/jo-grafford

3.) Cuppa Jo Readers Group :
https://www.facebook.com/groups/CuppaJoReaders

4.) Heroes and Hunks Readers Group:
https://www.facebook.com/groups/HeroesandHunks/

5.) New Release Newsletter Sign-Up:
https://www.JoGrafford.com

Happy reading! — Jo

amazon.com/authors/jo-grafford
bookbub.com/authors/jo-grafford
facebook.com/jografford
twitter.com/jografford
instagram.com/jografford
pinterest.com/jografford

CAST OF CHARACTERS

Agnes Wood - an apothecary apprentice who lives in the English countryside and works at her father's parish, main character in Book Three of the Lost Colony Series, INTO THE MAINLAND

Abbott Wood - vicar of Worcestershire, Agnes's father

Hester Ravenspire - Agnes's aunt who lives in London, comes from old family money, owns Ravenspire Keep

Hilbert Brandbury, Viscount of Habbershire - the man Aunt Hester wants Agnes to marry

Holly - Agnes's maid and dear friend

Skip - hackney driver, Holly's beau

Archbishop Whitgift - English archbishop in 1587; authorized a massive roundup of arrests and interrogations of

Separatists (non supporters of the Church of England) that some felt rivaled the Spanish Inquisition

ROANOKE TRIBE

Riapoke *(pronounced REE-a-poke)* - newly appointed war chief of the the Croatoan tribe, elder half-brother of Chief Wanchese of the Roanokes, cousin to Chief Wanchese of the Croatoans

Amitola - Chief Wanchese's sister, daughter of the late Nadie the Wise

Amonsoquath - strong warrior and trusted friend of Chief Wanchese, primarily serves the Roanoke tribe, brother of Askook

Powaw - temple priest

Winona - senior tribeswoman who grudgingly mentors Agnes

Bly, Dyoni, and Chitsa - Jane's faithful tribeswomen

Chogan - the main bodyguard assigned to Agnes

Mantunaaga - another one of the bodyguards assigned to Agnes

Poca - tribeswoman hostile to Agnes

Kaliska - Poca's spiteful best friend

Tikoosoo - Croatoan warrior

Sooleawa - pregnant maiden having trouble delivering a breech baby

Sucki *(pronounced SOO-kee)* - Sooleawa's infant son

MARRIAGE ALLIANCES BETWEEN THE NATIVE AMERICANS AND THE ENGLISH

Rose, Princess of Croatoa - main character in Book One of the Lost Colony Series, BREAKING TIES; married to Chief Manteo of the Croatoan tribe

Chief Manteo - Chief of the Croatoans, strong ally to the English colonists, married to Rose

Jane Mannering - a tall, tanned, chestnut-haired amazon of a woman; huntress, tracker, and main character in Book Two of the Lost Colony Series, TRAIL OF CROSSES; married to Chief Wanchese, Wise Woman of the Roanoke tribe

Chief Wanchese - Chief of the fearsome Roanoke tribe, a grudging ally of the English; married to Jane, the new Roanoke Wise Woman; cousin to Chief Manteo of the Croatoan tribe

ENGLISH WOMEN

Eleanor Dare - daughter of the absent Governor White; wife of the interim leader of the scattered English colonists, Ananias Dare; mother of the kidnapped baby Virginia

Helen Pierce - kindhearted widow and mentor to the younger women

Emme Merrimoth - friendly colonist who is sweet on farmer Mark Bennet

Margaret Lawrence - not-so-friendly colonist who is sweet on Reverend Christopher Cooper and wildly jealous of Rose, Jane, and Agnes.

Joyce Archard - noblewoman who was widowed during the ambush; served as a slave on Copper Mountain until she was rescued by the surviving English colonists

Virginia Dare - infant daughter of the Dares, kidnapped by the Copper Mountain tribe during an ambush

ENGLISHMEN

Ex-con James Hynde - flirtatious jack-of-all-trades; Jane's adoring and faithful follower and self-appointed guardian

Ex-con William Clement - balding, faithful sidekick to James; equally loyal to Jane

Blade Prat - son of Assistant Cecil Prat, the cutler; separated from his father during the ambush on the English

Anthony Cage - charming aristocratic explorer, trades in his badge as Sheriff of Huntington to become a colonist on the Roanoke venture

Reverend Christopher Cooper - white-blonde demigod of a vicar whose loyalties are divided between the English Crown, the Roanoke Colonists, and the missing Roanoke tribal princess, Amitola

Mark Bennet - giant of a man, humble farmer, Emme Merrimoth's beau

Thomas Harris - retired professor and fellow of Corpus Christi College at Cambridge, skilled cartographer, employed by Anthony Cage

Thomas Ellis - pious former member of the St. Petrock parish vestry, grieving father of the missing young Robert Ellis

Robert Ellis - son of Thomas Ellis, missing since the ambush on the English

Edward Powell - surviving husband of Winnifred who died in the ambush, missing since the ambush on the English

Will Withers - orphaned teen of a missing English soldier, missing since the ambush on the English

Harvye - the orphaned son of the Harvyes who died in the ambush against the English, infant nursed by Eleanor Dare, has no first name

SURVIVING MEMBERS OF THE ENGLISH GOVERNING BOARD

Assistant Ananias Dare - husband of Governor White's daughter, Eleanor

Demoted/Reverend Christopher Cooper - expected to be named lead pastor over the new City of Raleigh church until his role as a double agent puts his loyalties under scrutiny; serves as self-appointed bodyguard on-the-run to Chief Wanchese's pregnant sister, Amitola

Assistant Cecil Prat - culter by trade, excellent hunter and woodsman, father of Blade

Anthony Cage - former Sheriff of Huntington, not an official Assistant but is regarded by the English colonists as an unofficial leader in the absence of so many of the original Assistants

COMPLETE LIST OF THE LOST COLONISTS

(Not all names are depicted in The Lost Colony Series. Name spellings and precise list of names may vary in historical records.)

MEN

John White, Governor
Roger Bailie, Assistant
Ananias Dare, Assistant
Christopher Cooper, Assistant
Thomas Stevens, Assistant
John Sampson, Assistant

Dyonis Harvie, Assistant
Roger Prat, Assistant
George Howe, Assistant

Morris Allen
Arnold Archard
Richard Arthur
Mark Bennet
William Berde
Henry Berrye
Richard Berrye
Michael Bishop
John Borden
John Bridger
John Bright
John Brooke
Henry Browne
William Browne
John Burden
Thomas Butler
Anthony Cage
John Chapman
John Cheven
William Clement
Thomas Colman
John Cotsmur
Richard Darige
Henry Dorrell
William Dutton
John Earnest
Thomas Ellis
Edmond English
John Farre
Charles Florrie

John Gibbes
Thomas Gramme
Thomas Harris
Thomas Harris
John Hemmington
Thomas Hewet
James Hynde
Henry Johnson
Nicholas Johnson
Griffen Jones
John Jones
Richard Kemme
James Lasie
Peter Little
Robert Little
William Lucas
George Martyn
Michael Myllet
Henry Mylton
Humfrey Newton
William Nicholes
Hugh Pattenson
Henry Payne
Edward Powell
Henry Rufoote
Thomas Scot
Richard Shaberdge
Thomas Smith
William Sole
John Spendlove
John Starte
Thomas Stevens
John Stilman
Martyn Sutton

Richard Taverner
Clement Tayler
Hugh Tayler
Richard Tomkins
Thomas Topan
John Tydway
Ambrose Viccars
Thomas Warner
William Waters
Cutbert White
Richard Wildye
Robert Wilkinson
William Willes
Lewes Wotton
John Wright
Brian Wyles
John Wyles

WOMEN

Joyce Archard
Alis Chapman
------ Colman
Eleanor Dare
Elizabeth Glane
Margery Harvye
Jane Jones
Margaret Lawrence
Jane Mannering
Emme Merrimoth
Rose Payne
Jane Pierce
Winnifred Powell
Audrey Tappan
Elizabeth Viccars

Joan Warren
Agnes Wood

CHILDREN
Thomas Archard
Robert Ellis
George Howe, Jr.
Thomas Humfrey
John Prat
John Sampson
Thomas Smart
Ambrose Viccars
William Wythers

BORN IN VIRGINIA
Virginia Dare
Baby Harvye

Made in the USA
Monee, IL
07 August 2021